'Rachel! ⬛⬛⬛⬛⬛⬛⬛ried easily to ⬛⬛⬛⬛⬛⬛⬛ was a mere tw⬛⬛⬛⬛⬛⬛⬛ had been thinking recently,' he continued, 'how nice it would be to see more of you.'

'I can see almost all of you at present, and it is a deal too much! What are you doing? Where are your clothes? Go away and get dressed at once!'

But far from retreating modestly behind his curtain of willow, Cory appeared to be intending to approach her directly, sauntering up the bank for all the world as though he were entering a London drawing room rather than strolling naked through the Suffolk countryside.

Rachel gave him a severe look. 'You may be my friend, but I am a young lady of unimpeachable reputation and I do not intend to compromise that through being seen in conversation with a rake wrapped in a blanket!'

Cory's shoulders shook slightly. 'A rake wrapped in a blanket! You make me sound like some sort of delicate gardening tool.'

'Go away, please, Cory,' she said. 'You are improper.'

Cory laughed. 'I am. But you have always known that and you still like me.'

Dear Reader

It is 1803, and along the coast of Suffolk the threat of French invasion is at its highest. Smugglers, pirates, treasure-seekers and spies are all drawn to the quiet Midwinter villages, where the comfortable surface of village life conceals treason and danger as well as romance and excitement...

This is the world that I have inhabited for the last year whilst I wrote the *Bluestocking Brides* trilogy. It has been a wonderful experience. I have always loved the county of Suffolk for its remoteness, the peace of the woods, the wind in the reeds at the water's edge and the sunset over the sea. It is one of the most atmospheric and inspiring places for a storyteller.

About a year ago I was reading a book about 'The Great Terror', the years between 1801 and 1805, when Britain was permanently on the alert against the threat of Napoleonic invasion. It made me wonder what life would have been like in the coastal villages of Britain, where there was always the chance that the business of everyday living would conceal something more dangerous. I thought about a group of gentlemen dedicated to hunting down a spy—gentlemen for whom romance was no part of the plan, but who found that the ladies of Midwinter were more than a match for them! And so the idea of the *Bluestocking Brides* trilogy was born...

I hope that you enjoy these stories of love and romance in the Midwinter villages! It has been a real pleasure to write this trilogy.

Nicola

THE NOTORIOUS LORD

Nicola Cornick

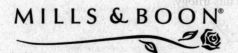

MILLS & BOON®

First published in Great Britain 2004
Harlequin Mills & Boon Limited,
Eton House, 18-24 Paradise Road, Richmond, Surrey TW9 1SR

© Nicola Cornick 2004

ISBN 0 263 83972 9

Set in Times Roman 10½ on 11¼ pt.
04-0804-93702

Printed and bound in Spain
by Litografia Rosés S.A., Barcelona

*To my editor, Kimberley Young,
with very many thanks for her unfailing support and
enthusiasm for my writing.*

Nicola Cornick became fascinated by history when she was a child, and spent hours poring over historical novels and watching costume drama. She still does! She has worked in a variety of jobs, from serving refreshments on a steam train to arranging university graduation ceremonies. When she is not writing she enjoys walking in the English countryside, taking her husband, dog and even her cats with her. Nicola loves to hear from readers and can be contacted by e-mail at ncornick@madasafish.com and via her website at www.nicolacornick.co.uk

Recent titles by the same author:

A COMPANION OF QUALITY*
THE RAKE'S BRIDE
   (short story in *Regency Brides*)
AN UNLIKELY SUITOR*
THE EARL'S PRIZE
THE CHAPERON BRIDE
WAYWARD WIDOW
THE PENNILESS BRIDE

**The Steepwood Scandal* series

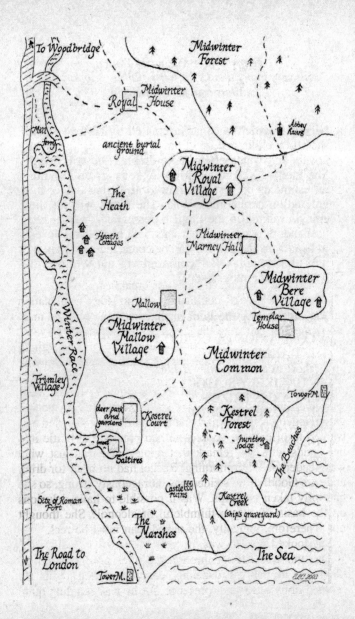

Chapter One

June 1803

She had taken too much cider for breakfast.

Miss Rachel Odell could think of no other explanation for the sudden and wholly unexpected sight of a naked man, who emerged from the thicket of willows some fifty yards down the riverbank and started to stroll towards her with all the aplomb of a gentleman entering a dowager's drawing room.

Rachel blinked, stared, and looked down at the earthenware flask in her hand. She had known that drinking alcohol was dangerous, particularly at breakfast, but she had not wanted to offend the cook, who had pressed the bottle into her hands with the remark that apple juice was just what was needed on a hot morning. Rachel had no head for drink and Mrs Goodfellow's cider was outrageously strong, so she had only taken two sips. Was it possible to have delusions on the basis of only a thimbleful of alcohol? She thought not. Therefore, logically, the naked man must be real.

She looked up. He was.

The sun was cutting through the trees now and fell on his body in bars of dazzling, dancing golden light. He seemed oblivious to her presence, for he was standing quite still, his head tilted towards the sky as though he were drinking in the morning air. He was tall and perfectly proportioned and he moved with unhurried precision and grace. The bright white sunlight slid over his body and sparkled on the tiny droplets of water that were cascading from his naked skin. He put his hands up to his head and smoothed the tawny hair back so that it was as sleek and wet as an otter's pelt. Then he stretched. To Rachel's eyes he looked like a pagan god who had sprung directly out of the earth.

As the daughter of the most renowned antiquaries in the country, Rachel knew all about the worship of pagan gods. Her parents had dug up relics of many cultures from Egypt to the Rhine, and from Greece to Alexandria. Rachel had learned about Greek mythology and Roman deities in her earliest youth, but she had never seen a man who resembled these creatures of legend. Never before now.

For one long, riveting moment she stared at him—at the powerful set of his shoulders, at his broad chest tapering to a hard, flat stomach, at the sheen of his brown skin and the elemental strength and intensity of him. Suddenly the worship of pagan deities did not seem as far-fetched as Rachel had always imagined it. Her mouth went dry, her heart started to race and she felt a prickly sort of heat break out over her entire body.

She had not seen any man in the nude before. She had seen statues, drawings, frescoes and paintings as a result of the highly unorthodox classical education bestowed on her by her parents, but she had never seen the real thing. Until now, Tuesday the twelfth of June at eight of the clock, when she was in her twenty second year and had not been expecting anything more exciting than a Tufted Duck to emerge from the waters of the Winter Race.

The book Rachel had been reading slid from her hand and fell against the earthenware flask of cider with a tiny clink. In the quiet air the sound was enough to carry. Rachel saw the man go still, like an animal sensing danger. He turned his head and looked directly towards her. Rachel's heart skipped several beats. The excited feeling in the pit of her stomach faded. Now that she could see his face clearly, she recognised him at once as Cory Newlyn, a childhood friend of hers and colleague of her parents. She was embarrassed that she had not realised his identity sooner, and felt a curious mix of awareness and familiarity. She had not recognised him because she had been concentrating, most improperly, on other parts of his anatomy rather than his face. And she had enjoyed the view. Now, however, she felt differently. He was an old friend, after all, and one did not ogle old friends in such a manner. It was over a year since she had seen Cory, and she had not anticipated coming across him here, but he was not the sort of man that one forgot. And she was never, ever going to forget him in future, not after this experience.

Rachel found her voice. 'Cory Newlyn! What on *earth* are you doing?'

Her words came out like the screech of a fishwife on the wharves at Deptford. She saw Cory jump, his eyes widening with surprise. He grabbed at a large lily leaf from a nearby pool and held it strategically in front of him as he came towards her along the bank. As an item of clothing it left a great deal to be desired and Rachel kept her gaze riveted on his face, avoiding a shocking compulsion to focus elsewhere.

'Rachel! How delightful to find you here.' Cory's voice carried easily to her, for by now he was a mere twenty yards away. 'I had been thinking recently,' he continued, 'how nice it would be to see more of you.'

'I can see almost all of you at present,' Rachel said, shielding her eyes with her hand, 'and it is a deal too much! What are you doing? Where are your clothes? Go away and get dressed at once!'

Somewhat belatedly, she grabbed her straw bonnet from the rug beside her, and pulled it down low over her eyes so that the rim obscured her view. Then, realising that she could not see anything at all, she peered underneath it in order to check what was happening. The scene was not reassuring. Far from retreating modestly behind his curtain of willow, Cory appeared to be intending to approach her directly, sauntering up the bank for all the world as though he were entering a London drawing room rather than strolling naked through the Suffolk countryside.

'Stop!' Rachel shrieked. 'I thought I told you to go away?'

Cory stopped. He was now no more than ten feet away from Rachel and, seated as she was on the ground, his knees and thighs were level with her line of sight. His body was firm, muscular and tanned, which she would have expected had she ever considered it. Cory worked outdoors a great deal and much of that labour was physically demanding. It was no wonder that his body was in such fine shape.

Rachel reminded herself that it was not appropriate for her to dwell on the physical attributes of her parents' colleagues. This had not been a problem for her before. Most of them would look ancient and flabby without their clothes, which was not a description that could be applied to Lord Newlyn...

Rachel tried to wrench her mind on to other topics, but found that she did not seem able to drag her gaze from the dusting of tiny golden hairs across Cory's thighs. The more she thought about the impropriety of what she was doing, the more flustered she became. She felt hot and feverish. She turned her head and stared fixedly at the trunk of a large poplar tree some twenty feet away, forcing her agitated mind to concentrate on botany rather than anatomy. Was it a white poplar or a grey poplar? She must remember to look it up in her reference books when she returned home. The leaves were very pretty and white underneath... She was starting to get a pain in her neck from the effort of keeping her head turned away from Cory. She could see absolutely nothing at all but her other senses—and her imagination—more than made up for the deficit. She could feel the sun beating down on the top of her head where it penetrated the leaves of the pine canopy above her. She could smell the resinous scent of the pine needles as they warmed up. She could visualise Cory, tall, powerful, virile—and naked, her memory reminded her unnecessarily—standing right next to her.

'Why are you still standing there?' she asked. 'I do not wish to speak with you at present, not whilst you are quite unclothed.'

'You noticed, then,' Cory said. He sounded amused.

'Of course I noticed!' Rachel retorted. 'I would have to be quite unobservant *not* to have noticed! What are you doing here, Cory?'

'Pray do not persist in addressing me if you wish me to leave, Rachel,' Cory said reasonably. 'I cannot preserve both propriety and courtesy at the same time.'

'I would far rather that you preserve both your modesty and mine for the time being,' Rachel said. 'Where are your clothes?'

She heard Cory sigh. 'I left them further up the bank and swam downriver,' he said. 'I felt inclined to take a dip and was not expecting to meet anyone so early in the morning. I was hoping that you might lend me your rug,' he added, shifting slightly beside her and increasing Rachel's discomfort by several notches. 'If you would be kind enough to help me cover my embarrassment…'

Rachel gave a little exasperated squeak and pulled the rug out forcibly from underneath her, thrusting it in his direction. 'Take it! Quick! Begone!'

'Thank you,' Cory said politely. She could hear the amusement in his voice. 'Please do not wave your hands about like that, Rae, or you may grab hold of more than you bargained for.'

Rachel could take no more. She scrambled to her feet, intent only on putting some distance between them. Inevi-

tably she collided at once with Cory's lean, hard body. Her
flailing hand touched his skin; touched some unidentified
part of him that was warm and very slightly damp from the
river water. She felt the soft abrasion of fine hair against
her skin and almost fainted.

'It's all right,' Cory said reassuringly. 'That was only
my—'

'Cory! No! I do *not* want to know!' Rachel's voice was
in danger of failing her. 'I realise that we are old friends,'
she added shakily, 'but there are some things that one simply does not wish to share…'

Cory laughed. Rachel could sense movement as he
grasped the rug and started to wrap it about himself. A flash
of tartan colour caught the corner of her eye and she forced
herself ruthlessly to look the other way.

'I am almost ready,' Cory murmured.

Rachel turned towards him in relief. She was too quick.
She caught a glimpse of the curve of his buttocks and gave
a weak gasp.

'But not quite,' Cory finished.

'Oh, this is dreadful!' Rachel tried to move away, but
found her knees so shaky that all she succeeded in doing
was tripping over her picnic basket. Cory caught her arm
and steadied her.

'Careful,' he said, a laugh breaking through his words,
'you are like to do one of us an injury if you continue like
this.'

'I would manage so much better if you were just to go
away,' Rachel snapped, thoroughly flustered. 'Surely you do
not need to make such a meal of this!'

'You would manage better if you took off that ridiculous
hat and looked about you,' Cory said.

'Thank you, but I have already seen quite enough!' Rachel took a careful step away from him and pushed the brim
of her hat up. When she peeped out she was relieved to see
that Cory had tied the blanket about his waist like a kilt. It

sat low on his hips and left what seemed like an inordinate amount of him uncovered, but it was a great improvement on before. Even so, there was something disturbing about him. With his clothes on, Cory possessed a masculine vitality and attraction that Rachel, old friend that she was, could recognise without difficulty. Seeing him in a minimum of clothing was a jolt to the senses of the most fundamental sort.

Rachel realised that she was still staring, cleared her throat and looked up at his face, catching a look of vivid amusement there. Cory's face was barely less disturbing than the rest of him, for he was quite devastatingly attractive, with silver grey eyes and a very wicked smile. There were those who said that Cory Newlyn was not in any way conventionally handsome. His nose and much else had been broken once on an expedition when a fall of rocks had almost killed him and he had a thin scar like a sabre cut down one cheek. His face was too lean to be classically good looking. Yet none of these things mattered. He had character—and it showed. It also made women throw themselves at him with tedious regularity.

Embarrassed to be caught looking at him, Rachel averted her gaze. 'Thank goodness that it is a large rug,' she said.

'I am flattered that you think I require something large to do the job properly,' Cory said, the smile still in his eyes.

Rachel blushed. She had forgotten Cory's propensity to shock by word as well as deed. He understood the requirements of polite society perfectly well. It was merely that sometimes he chose not to heed them.

'Go away, please, Cory,' she said. 'You are improper.'

Cory laughed. 'I am. But you have always known that and you still like me.'

Rachel gave him a severe look. 'You may be my friend, but I am a young lady of unimpeachable reputation and I do not intend to compromise that through being seen in conversation with a rake wrapped in a blanket!'

Cory's shoulders shook slightly. 'A rake wrapped in a blanket! You make me sound like some sort of delicate gardening tool.'

Rachel looked down her nose at him. She felt a deal more confident now that something relatively substantial was between her and Cory's nakedness.

'There is very little of delicacy about you, Cory,' she said.

Cory shrugged. 'Perhaps not,' he said. 'I am sorry if I disturbed you, Rae. I can see that you are still looking very flustered.'

Rachel knew that she was and it did not make her any less self-conscious that he was drawing attention to it.

'Of course I am flustered,' she said. 'I never expected to see you naked, Cory. Such things do not generally occur between childhood friends.'

'No, indeed,' Cory said. 'You must excuse me, Rae. I had no wish to shock you.'

'To think that I came down here for some peace,' Rachel said, shaking her head. 'You know how difficult it can be to find any solitude once an excavation starts. Mama and Papa have been busy digging all hours of the day for the last two weeks.' She laid a hand lightly on Cory's arm. It was a part of him that she felt relatively secure in touching. 'What are you doing in Suffolk?' she asked. 'I did not expect you to be joining us because I thought you were still in Cornwall.'

'I came up to London last month,' Cory said. 'Your parents wrote to my club, inviting me to join them on the excavation here.' He cocked an enquiring eyebrow. 'They did not tell you?'

Rachel sighed. 'I dare say they intended to,' she said. 'You know how Mama forgets things.'

Cory went down on one knee to rummage in the picnic basket. He looked up, a piece of bread and cheese in his hand. 'You do not mind?'

'That you are here or that you are stealing my breakfast?'

Rachel laughed. 'I do not mind in either case, Cory. Although I would counsel you to wear more clothes in future if you are intent on staying. It is not the done thing to walk around nude in England, at least not in public. I realise that you have been abroad for so long that you may have forgotten our conventions.'

'I never was governed by them in the first place,' Cory said. He stretched lazily. The blanket slipped lower. Rachel took a hasty step up the bank.

'Go,' she said, 'before you catch a chill or that rug falls off and takes the last of my composure with it. We may talk when you have your clothes on again.'

Cory smiled. 'I never thought to hear that phrase from you, Rae.'

'Well, no doubt I am not the first to say it to you,' Rachel said, repressing a rueful smile. She knew all about Cory's reputation.

Cory started to retreat down the bank, one hand raised in conciliation. 'I am going now. I apologise if I upset you, Rae.'

'I was not particularly discomfited,' Rachel said untruthfully, smoothing her skirts, 'but it was a slight shock.'

Cory bent and retrieved another piece of bread and ham from Rachel's upturned breakfast basket. He sank his teeth into the thick slice and nodded slowly. 'Delicious. Just what I need after an early morning swim.'

He gave a negligent wave of his hand and walked away.

'Mind the rose bushes at the top of the bank,' Rachel called suddenly. 'The thorns are sharp—' She winced as she heard a crashing sound and a muffled expletive. 'Oh, too late.'

She sank down on to the sandy bank and rested her back against the nearest pine tree, closing her eyes and tilting her head back against the trunk. The sunlight pricked her eyelids. She gave a huge sigh and, once she was convinced that Cory had genuinely gone, she allowed her body to relax.

She had not been expecting to see him on this excavation in Suffolk. Her mother had completely neglected to tell her that he would be coming to visit, but then that was no great surprise since Lady Odell had no memory for anything other than her antiquities. She might be able to list the rulers of Rome in chronological order, she might be the acknowledged expert on dating the Egyptian tombs, but when it came to simple social matters she was completely hopeless.

The last time that Rachel had heard news of Cory was six months previously. He had written from his home in Cornwall to say that he was returned from an expedition in Patagonia and was suffering from malaria. Rachel had sent him a tincture that she had made herself, for she had developed quite an array of medicines to cope with the more arcane of her parents' ailments. Cory had sent a note of thanks and a big bouquet of roses, and Rachel had smiled to receive them for it had been a thoughtful gesture. She had then become preoccupied with the move to Suffolk, and had forgotten about Cory Newlyn until the moment she had seen him emerge from the river.

For the previous seventeen years Cory had been a feature in her life, but one that came and went like a fitful comet. He was an explorer and collector with a legendary reputation. According to folklore, Cory had wrestled with crocodiles, battled for his life against poisonous snakes, explored the wastes of impassable deserts and discovered fantastical treasures. Rachel knew that a great deal of this was nonsense. As an antiquarian, Cory spent much of his time excavating tombs that were full of nothing but bits of bones. She doubted very much that the ladies of the London *ton,* whose eyes sparkled with delight whenever Cory's name was so much as mentioned, would think him quite so dashing if they had seen him up to his knees in mud in a howling gale in the Orkneys. One thing she was obliged to recognise, however, was that Cory was very good at what he did. He was skilful, knowledgeable and a talented antiquarian with an almost uncanny knack for finding interesting artefacts. Plenty of men travelled the world buying up antiquities these days, but Cory was special. He was no armchair antiquary. He wanted to be in on the hunt.

Rachel sighed. No doubt that was why Cory was here in Midwinter Royal. He knew her parents were digging the famous Anglo-Saxon burial ground and he wanted to be part of the excavation. It would have been useful if Lady Odell had remembered to tell her. But then, Rachel thought, she would still have been quite unprepared for the sight that had met her eyes that morning. Nothing could prepare one for the sight of Lord Newlyn in a state of undress. It had been a very disturbing experience. Just thinking about it now caused the little shivers to run all the way along her skin, leaving her breathless and distinctly unsettled.

Without the rug to protect her, the ground felt cold and a little damp. It was early and the dew was still on the grass. Rachel got to her feet, dusted her skirts and packed the remaining food away in the basket. She retrieved her book from where it lay in the grass. She knew that she would not be able to concentrate on it now. Her mind was still showing an obstinate tendency to dwell on Cory's appearance. She would do better to go back to the house and see how her mother progressed with the last of the unpacking.

She did not walk back through the wood for fear of meeting Cory again just as he was getting back into his clothes rather than out of them. Instead, she walked back along the edge of the Midwinter Royal burial ground, an ancient site that had drawn her parents to Suffolk in the first place. The sun was higher in the sky now and it bathed the excavation in its bright light. It was going to be another scorching hot day.

As Rachel entered the house, she heard her mother's voice raised in the hall as she gave the footman instructions on the morning's excavations.

'And make sure that you sift the soil from yesterday's trench, Tom, before you start digging the long barrow...'

Rachel smiled a little. Poor Tom Gough had had no idea when he had accepted the post that none of his duties would be of a conventional nature and all of them would relate to the excavation work that was going on in the field next door. For twenty-five years Sir Arthur and Lady Odell's entire life had revolved around the search for antiquities. This dig in Suffolk was just the latest in a long line of excavations. Sir Arthur fretted that the war against Napoleon kept them at home, and told tales of the time some six years previously when he had had to flee the advancing French army and leave behind all his discoveries in the Valley of the Kings.

By the time that Rachel had divested herself of her spencer and straw hat, and had taken the basket back to the kitchens, Lady Odell was in the library, removing some artefacts from a large packing case. Rachel wandered into the room. The bright morning light illuminated the cracks in the plaster ceiling and the threadbare patches on the carpet. Midwinter Royal was no worse than the other two dozen houses that Rachel had lived in and it was a lot less shabby than some. She had no expectation that she would stay there any longer than she had in the other places. Six months was a long time for Sir Arthur and Lady Odell to remain in one place.

Lavinia Odell was a stocky woman whose face habitually wore an expression of vague sweetness. Her eyes were a warm brown flecked with green and gold and were her finest feature, a feature that her daughter had inherited from her. Her hair was a faded mouse colour, lighter than Rachel's chestnut brown, and her skin had long since given up the struggle against harsh sun and abrasive sand, and was sunk in lines and wrinkles. One unkind *ton* dowager had likened Lady Odell's face to a leathery boot, crumpled and tough. Lady Odell, to whom a parasol was an alien notion, had laughed heartily when she heard this piece of spite.

'I met Cory down by the river just now, Mama,' Rachel said. 'You did not tell me that he was to visit.'

Lady Odell looked confused. 'Did I not? I had a letter from him only yesterday saying that he would be joining us on our excavation. Is that not simply splendid? And you say that he is here already?'

'Yes, Mama.' Rachel smiled. 'He was taking a morning swim. I believe that he will be joining you once he has got his clothes back on.'

'Good, good…' Lady Odell said vaguely. She held out what looked to be a statue of a small cat. The cat was brown and very shiny, its expression malevolent, its legs braced as though it were about to scratch. Rachel grimaced when she saw it.

'I thought that this could go on the drawing-room mantelpiece. It will bring us luck.'

Rachel shuddered. 'Mama, pray do not. The only thing that it will attract is the flies. I fear that it *smells*.'

Lady Odell looked affronted. She clutched the cat protectively to her large bosom. 'It does not smell! This is an antiquity, Rachel, from the third millennium before Christ—'

'Which is why it smells, Mama,' Rachel pointed out. 'The poor creature has been dead several thousand years and should be permitted to rest in peace now. It is no wonder that it looks so very bad-tempered.'

Lady Odell sighed and placed the cat reverently back in the bottom of a half-empty packing case next to a Greek vase. 'Well, perhaps you are correct. Embalming methods were not always completely successful.'

'No, Mama,' Rachel said. She knew all about the success or otherwise of ancient embalming methods for she had absorbed a great deal of knowledge simply through travelling with her parents. She had not learnt through inclination. Once, as a small child, her maternal aunt had found her sitting on the carpet, chewing a human bone that she held clutched in her small, fat fist. The aunt's scream had brought Lady Odell hurrying in, to coo with delight over her only child's precocious interest in antiquity.

It was the only sign of interest that Rachel was ever to show in her parents' work. At the age of six she had chosen to be addressed as Rachel rather than Cleopatra, her given name, and had refused to answer anyone who tried to call her otherwise. Shuffled from pillar to post as the Odells pursued their eccentric hobby around the world, Rachel had taken an utter dislike to her parents' passion. She would have given a great deal for a dining room full of Wedgwood, with not a barbaric death mask in sight.

'I do not believe that the ladies of the Midwinter villages are quite ready for your collection, Mama,' she said now. 'I doubt that anyone will call if they find themselves confronted by your set of Anglo-Saxon skulls.'

Lady Odell shrugged her plump shoulders under the cambric shirt that she always wore for working. 'I shall not have time to do the pretty with the visitors anyway, with all the work that is required on the excavation. I shall leave that to you, Rachel.'

'Of course, Mama,' Rachel murmured. She had done the pretty for their visitors in houses all over England. It was her role in life. Organising her parents, exhorting the servants, dealing with all the minutiae of daily life…Rachel had fulfilled such a role since she was about twelve years old.

She followed her mother out on to the front steps of Midwinter Royal. By now it was another hot June day. The grass along the carriage drive was already turning yellow from lack of rain and the sky was a hard steely blue without a cloud in sight. The weathercock on the top of the stables was motionless. In the fields to the south, Rachel could just make out the figures of her father and a couple of the servants measuring the length of one of the haphazard scatter of burial mounds that lay between the house and the river beyond.

Lady Odell sighed happily. 'What a perfect day for the digging. After all these years I still dislike excavating in the wet.'

'Pray be careful that the sides of your trenches do not crumble away into dust,' Rachel said, unable to help herself. 'It is very dry at present. Remember how you were buried under that landslide at the barrow in Wiltshire and Cory and I had to dig you out? Don't let that happen again. And Mrs Goodfellow and I shall have prepared a cold luncheon for you all at twelve. Please do not forget, Mama.'

Lady Odell patted her hand absent-mindedly. 'Of course not, my love. Now I must get back to work. Your father has already been out above an hour and a half.'

'I saw him down at the excavation,' Rachel said. 'Make sure that he is wearing a hat, Mama. The sun can be most fierce at this time of year.' She squinted along the line of dusty elm trees that shaded the drive, and was not surprised to pick out a figure riding towards them. 'I do believe Cory is here now.'

'Oh, how splendid!' Lady Odell positively ran down the steps, her necklace of Persian beads clicking excitedly.

Rachel followed more slowly. The advancing figure had now resolved itself into a gentleman on a grey horse. The horse was a prime bit of blood and Rachel could see that, whether his clothes were on or off, Cory Newlyn was what many ladies would also consider to be a prime specimen. He was considerably more formally dressed now, but he still looked extremely attractive.

Rachel watched, lips pursed in disapproval, as Cory galloped up to the steps of the house and dismounted in one fluid movement that sent the gravel flying from the horse's hooves. She instinctively stepped out of the way and grabbed the grey's bridle. Someone had to take charge and Cory was too busy greeting Lady Odell to notice that his highly bred steed was in danger of trampling them all to death.

Cory was smiling as he bent to embrace Lavinia Odell. His teeth were very white and his grey eyes were full of laughter and looked remarkably bright against his tanned skin. Cory always brought with him an air of warmth and laughing good humour. Rachel watched her mother respond to it as she had seen ladies respond to Cory's charm time and time again. It mattered not whether they were young or old, he bowled them over just the same. She, of course, was quite indifferent to him. Even so, a little prickle of awareness ran along her skin as she remembered her reaction to seeing him down by the river.

'How are you, Lavinia?' Cory asked, holding Lady Odell at arm's length and looking her over, a twinkle in his eye. 'You look in fine form!'

'Cory! Dear boy!' Lavinia Odell was clinging on to him and squeaking like an excited schoolgirl. 'We are so very pleased that you could join us!'

'Wouldn't miss it for the world,' Lord Newlyn said, releasing her gently and planting a smacking kiss on her cheek. 'The Midwinter burials are famous, you know. I've been wanting to get my trowel into those mounds for years, ever since I heard about the Midwinter Treasure!'

'If anyone can find the Treasure, it will be us,' Lavinia Odell said, eyes sparkling. 'I feel it in my waters!'

'Where is the stable lad, Mama?' Rachel interrupted, trying hard to hold the thoroughbred, which was currently exhibiting its quality by dancing skittishly on the gravel sweep. 'I suppose that he is down in the field with Father?'

'Of course, my love,' Lady Odell said, looking vaguely puzzled, as though it were natural for everyone to employ their servants as excavation assistants. 'I could send for him, I suppose, but your father needs someone to help him measure the barrows—'

'I'll put Castor away myself,' Cory said, the gravel

crunching under his boots as he came towards Rachel. He took the bridle from her hand and soothed the grey with a gentle stroke of the nose.

'Good morning again, Rachel,' Cory said. He gave her a smile that was slightly more quizzical than the one he had bestowed on Lady Odell. The smile deepened the creases at the corners of his eyes and for a moment it seemed that the morning sunlight was trapped in their silver depths. 'Are we to pretend that we have not yet met?'

He took her hand in his and Rachel was shocked and more than a little disconcerted to find her pulse racing at his touch. Two images flashed before her eyes: the real one of Cory standing before her now, fully dressed, and the other of him stark naked as he emerged from the river, the water rolling down his skin… She felt all hot and shaky again, as though she had sustained a sudden shock. Her knees actually trembled.

She swallowed hard, closed her eyes and by dint of sheer willpower banished the picture. This had to be an aberration. She was determined that her thoughts would not be haunted by the image of Cory's virile, unashamed nudity. She did not wish to think of her childhood friend in that manner.

But even so, she suddenly had the lowering feeling that it was going to be a far more complicated summer than she had ever imagined.

Chapter Two

It felt like a full minute later, but was possibly only a few seconds when Rachel became aware that Cory was still holding her hand and was waiting for her response with a faintly concerned expression on his face. She pulled her hand out of his grasp, pushed her feelings of self-consciousness back down where they belonged and looked him up and down. Cory might be fully clothed now, but he still looked completely disreputable. His boots were scuffed, his shirt neck open to reveal the strong, brown column of his neck, and on his tawny hair was a hat so disgusting that Rachel thought it fit for nothing but the bonfire. Concentrating on Cory's personal shortcomings served to steady her somewhat. He was a friend, and one of the privileges of friendship was that she could say whatever she chose to him.

'How do you do, Cory?' she said primly. 'I am very well, thank you, though I have to say that you scarcely look better with your clothes on than without. That jacket looks as though it has been slept in.'

'It is delightful to see you too, Rae.' A slight edge had come into Cory's voice now. He leaned forward and kissed her cheek lightly. 'I am glad that you have overcome your discomfiture and are back on astringent form.' He held out the tartan rug to her. 'I must thank you for the loan of your blanket. I can have it laundered for you before I return it, if you would prefer.'

'Thank you,' Rachel said, ignoring the sarcasm. 'I shall ask Mrs Goodfellow to arrange it.' She took the rug and folded it over her arm.

Cory gestured to Castor. 'Perhaps you could show me the way to the stables?'

'Of course,' Rachel said. She touched her mother's hand. 'I will see you later, Mama. Remember to make Papa wear a hat, and please do not forget that luncheon is at twelve sharp. Oh, and leave your bead necklace with me. You would not wish to get it caught on one of the buckets.'

'A good idea, my love,' Lady Odell said, beaming. She slipped the bead necklace over her head, put it into Rachel's outstretched hand and adjusted the battered hat that sat askew her faded brown hair. 'We shall see you shortly, Cory,' she said. 'Arthur will be so delighted that you are here!' And with that she strode off to the stile in the picket fence, threw a leg over and started across the fields towards the excavation.

Rachel sighed. She turned to see Cory watching her with amusement in his eyes. 'What is it?' she asked, a little ungraciously.

Cory shrugged lightly. 'You. You cannot resist managing them, can you? It is always the same.'

Rachel felt a sharp stab of irritation. She thought it rather impertinent that Cory, who should understand her situation, should be the one to criticise. He had known her parents for almost as long as she had, and knew perfectly well that, left to their own devices, they were incapable of managing anything practical at all.

'Someone needs to take charge of them,' she said, 'or they would both starve. That is if the sunstroke did not catch them first.'

Cory shrugged again. A hint of a smile still hovered at the corner of his mobile mouth. 'Then you must be pleased to be settled in Suffolk for a space, rather than the Nile Delta. It is considerably less dangerous.'

Rachel set off towards the five-barred gate that separated the drive from the stable yard. 'Settled? We are no more settled here at Midwinter Royal than we were in the twenty-five places that went before. Once the excavation is finished we shall be on the move again. Papa was speaking of Greece for the winter, hoping that it would be safe to travel on the continent again.'

'That seems like a particularly bad idea with Bonaparte running rampage abroad and the danger of invasion growing stronger each day,' Cory said. He unlatched the gate and stood back to allow her to precede him through. 'Can they not go to Cornwall instead? I have unearthed a very fine Iron Age fogou in the grounds of Newlyn.'

'Congratulations,' Rachel said politely.

'You are the only person I have met recently who does not need me to explain what a fogou is,' Cory said wryly, 'or is it that you are simply not interested, Rae?'

'Fogou—an underground passage or tunnel that is a feature of the Iron Age landscape, function unknown,' Rachel said economically. 'Please do not encourage Mama and Papa to go to Cornwall, Cory. The Midwinter villages are very pleasant and I wish them to stay here for a while.'

'Poor Rae,' Cory said. His tone had softened a little. 'You really hate it, don't you?'

Rachel turned slightly. Cory was a tall shadow against the sun and she could not see his expression. 'Hate what?' she said tightly.

'All the travel. They adore it and you detest it. You have been dragged all around the world, staying in—how many was it?—twenty-five different places and you hate it.'

Rachel relaxed a little. Cory's tone was gentle and she realised that he did not intend to make fun of her. Strangely, although his passions were the same as those of her parents, he actually understood how she felt. His own interests might be diametrically opposed to hers, but they did not blind him to the things that were important to her.

'Yes, I suppose I do,' she said.

'Antiquities are not to everybody's taste,' Cory continued gravely.

'Indeed not,' Rachel said. 'I wish that you would leave them where you find them!'

Cory looked vaguely offended. 'The amassing of a collection is a gentleman's pursuit, Rachel. There is nothing wrong in it.'

'I did not say that there was,' Rachel said. 'I speak only of my own opinion. I dislike antiquities and I detest the necessity of living out of a packing case and leasing residences the length and breadth of the country.'

'And to make matters worse, some of those residences are not even houses,' Cory said sympathetically. 'Some of them are only tents!'

Rachel looked at him, saw the smile in his eyes, and suddenly they were both laughing and the slightly prickly tension between them had evaporated like frost in the sun. Rachel pushed open one of the stable doors and led Cory inside.

'Oh dear, I suppose I do sound a misery,' she admitted. 'And it is lovely to see you again, Cory, even if I cannot approve of you. You know you are a bad influence.'

Cory removed the horse's tack, reached for the curry brush and started to rub the grey down. He shot her a smile. It was a smile that would make many a débutante tremble in her satin slippers. Rachel felt a slight quiver shake her and reminded herself that she was indifferent to Cory.

'I am a bad influence on whom, Rae?' Cory asked. 'Your parents were off digging for antiquities all over the world when you and I were mere children. If anything is true, it is that they influenced *me* into the sort of life I lead now, not vice versa.'

Rachel leaned against the doorjamb and watched him

work. She knew that what he said was true. The Newlyns were bankers, not explorers. It had been Cory's encounter with the Odell family, when he had been eleven and she had been five, which had sparked his fascination in travel and exploration. Arthur and Lavinia Odell, who had failed so singularly to excite in their own child an interest in antiquity, had had spectacular success with the young Lord Newlyn. He had joined their excavations in his school and university holidays and, as soon as he had reached his majority, had taken to travelling all over the globe.

Rachel watched Cory with an indulgent smile. He was engrossed in his task, speaking softly to the horse as he worked. As on many occasions in their lives, the silence between them was comfortable now. They had plenty of news to catch up on, but it felt as though there was all the time in the world to do it.

Rachel felt warm as she watched him. He was the closest thing to a brother that she had ever had, flashing across her life at various points, lighting it up and then disappearing off on another outrageous adventure. On one hugely memorable occasion he had arrived unexpectedly for her come-out ball, and all her débutante friends had almost expired with excitement. Rachel smiled now, remembering the stir Cory had caused when he strode into the ballroom, so handsome in his austere black and white evening dress. It was such a far cry from the filthy clothes he wore to work that she had had to look twice to make sure it was the right person. Cory had come straight up to her and had cut out the gentleman with whom she was supposed to be dancing. For a second, just a very small, split second, Rachel had thought Cory the most extraordinarily attractive man that she had ever met. Her whole world had trembled on its axis as she considered this new idea. And then he had smiled at her and started to talk to her in the same way he had always done, and the world had steadied and he was just Cory again.

'You make Mother over-excited,' she said now. 'That is why I disapprove of you.'

'I apologise.' Cory looked at her with an expressive lift of the brows. 'It is the effect that I generally have on women.'

Rachel made a noise of disgust and threw a brush at him. It skittered away across the cobbles and Cory put a foot out to stop it.

'You know what I mean!' Rachel said.

'Actually, I *do* know what you mean,' Cory said. He rubbed one lean brown cheek with the back of his hand. 'Your mother is superstitious and you think that I encourage her and that it is nonsense.'

'Precisely. You encourage her to believe in foolish stories like the Midwinter Treasure.'

'There may be more to the Treasure than a mere myth,' Cory pointed out. 'The very name Midwinter Royal suggests a connection to the burial of a king. And we know that the treasure existed once—and may one day be found again.'

'Rubbish!' Rachel said. 'Complete nonsense. If one gave credence to all the tales of buried treasure that we have come across, then the entire country would be like a gold mine.'

Cory shrugged. 'Your mother likes to believe it. And she thinks that I bring good luck to a dig.'

'She thinks that that smelly Egyptian cat brings good luck as well,' Rachel said crushingly, 'but I fear I have consigned it to the cellar.'

'Ah.' Cory straightened up and pushed his hat back from his forehead. 'Well, you need not concern yourself to find me house room, Rae. I am staying at Kestrel Court.'

Rachel paused. She had not expected this. Generally Cory lodged with them when he was working with the Odells. 'You are staying with the Duke of Kestrel?' she said. 'Is he come to Suffolk, then?'

She saw Cory's eyes narrow in amusement. Although the

interior of the stable was cool, she could feel her face getting hotter although she was not entirely sure why she felt embarrassed. Perhaps it was something to do with Cory's quizzical expression—and what it implied, as though she was one of those silly girls who occupied themselves in pursuing eligible gentlemen.

'Yes, Justin is in Midwinter,' Cory said, after a moment, 'although he does not intend to stay here for the entire summer. Are you particularly desirous of meeting him, Rae? I would not have thought him to be the type of gentleman who interested you.'

Rachel gave him a haughty look. 'I confess that I do not seek out the company of rakes,' she said. 'I told you that earlier. I was merely thinking that the Midwinter villages will be set by the ears to hear that the Duke is to be among us.'

'Not only Justin,' Cory said laconically, 'but several of his brothers as well.'

'How will all the young ladies contain their excitement?' Rachel said. 'Especially as you are visiting Midwinter as well, Cory!'

Cory's lips twitched. 'I have no doubt that Suffolk society will survive,' he said, straight-faced. 'We are not the only visitors this summer. I hear that the Northcotes are in Burgh and Sir John Norton is at Drybridge. Suffolk seems the fashionable place to be.'

Rachel frowned slightly, searching her memory. 'Norton… I have heard of him. Is he not the polar explorer?'

'That's right. He has just returned from an attempt to reach the North Pole.'

'How very pointless!'

Cory grinned. 'No doubt you cannot imagine why he should bother?'

'I can imagine why he would try,' Rachel said, with asperity, 'since no doubt he is as mad as the rest of you.' She shivered. 'I merely think it must have been prodigiously uncomfortable.'

'You may ask him yourself,' Cory said. 'I am sure that he will be happy to bore the ladies with tales of his exploits. The anecdote about his escape from an enraged polar bear is particularly good.'

Rachel tutted. She had heard enough tales of male bravado to last a lifetime. 'You are all the same! Will you not find it rather slow in Suffolk after hacking through the ice, or seducing women from Constantinople to China?'

Cory pulled a face. 'No doubt we shall manage. There is the sailing, after all, not to mention the races at Newmarket. And Justin has persuaded me to join the Suffolk Rifles.'

Rachel looked at him sharply. A bumblebee was trapped in the window, buzzing loudly as it beat against the cobwebby glass. She had just been thinking that it reminded her of all that was warm and safe and familiar about an English summer, but now Cory had cast a shadow across that.

'You have joined the Volunteers?' she said. 'Does that mean that you think these rumours of French invasion have some substance to them?'

Cory shrugged. 'Who knows? The Suffolk coast is but a day's sail from France in fine weather.'

Rachel stared. 'Yes, but surely with our fleet to protect against the threat...'

Cory shrugged again. 'It is true that we have command of the seas.' He straightened, resting one hand on Castor's broad back. 'I would not wish you to alarm yourself, Rae. I think that we are safe enough.'

Rachel was not so sure now. She had thought the Midwinter Villages a sleepy place, but they were only a few miles from the sea and even here she had been aware of the rumours of war and the threat of invasion. There was a garrison in Woodbridge, across the Deben, and the talk in the town had been full of the failure of the Peace of Amiens and the resumption of hostilities with France. Besides, she could suddenly see another and very different reason for the presence of Cory Newlyn and his friends in Midwinter, for along with the stories of Cory's exploits as an adventurer and explorer were tales of other, more shadowy, deeds. He had never spoken of these to her and she had never asked about the other errands his travelling could cover. Now she looked at him from under her lashes.

'You must be a prodigiously fine shot to have been invited to join the Suffolk Rifles, Cory,' she said, 'for they are very proud of their reputation. What did you do to deserve that?'

Cory gave her a look that said he knew exactly what she was about and that she would learn nothing. 'I have no notion,' he said evasively.

'And your friend the Duke of Kestrel,' Rachel pursued. 'Does he not have connections at the Foreign Office?'

Cory grinned. 'Lord Hawkesbury is a cousin of his, yes.'

'And one of the Duke's brothers is an Admiralty man,' Rachel said, 'and another is in the regular army...'

'You are very well informed, Rae.'

'And you are all here in Midwinter this year. How very interesting. There must be an extremely powerful reason that so many important men are gathered in this one place.'

A lazy smile curved Cory's lips. He put the curry brush down and came towards her. To her surprise, Rachel found herself feeling slightly out of breath as he backed her into a corner of the stable.

'You are too quick, Rachel Odell,' Cory said, with an expressive lift of the brows. 'I always said that education in a woman was a mistake.'

Rachel laughed. She tilted her head to look up at him. 'No, you did not, Cory. You are not the man to feel threatened by an intelligent woman.'

Cory's smile deepened. 'Maybe not. Nevertheless, I could wish you to see a little less clearly in this. Justin Kestrel is here for the summer merely for entertainment, as are his guests.'

'I see,' Rachel said. 'Well, you will not hear me contradicting that, Cory.' She sighed. 'Could you step back, please? This corner is very dusty and I do not wish my gown to be spoiled.'

'Of course,' Cory said. He held her gaze for a moment and then moved away, picking up the brush and resuming his work on the horse. 'So, is society here to *your* taste, Rae?'

'Oh, yes, I like it extremely,' Rachel said. She gave a sigh. 'It is so peaceful. So very staid and normal. Or at least I thought it so until you put me right.'

Cory gave her his brilliant smile. 'What do you do with your time?'

Moving over to the manger, Rachel pulled a handful of hay and proffered it to Castor, who gobbled it eagerly.

'I read and write letters, and take tea with the ladies of the villages, and go shopping. It is quite delightful. And then there are the balls and assemblies in Woodbridge…'

'The town plays host to the 21st Light Dragoons these days, I hear,' Cory said.

'Oh, they are prodigiously unpopular.' Rachel laughed. 'The soldiers get drunk and cause fights, and take over the theatre and all the amusements. One can scarcely move for red coats.'

'It sounds as though they find no more favour with you than my friends and I shall,' Cory observed.

'I do not suppose that you will repine,' Rachel said, smiling. 'Your arrival will cause a huge commotion amongst the wives and daughters of the military.'

Cory laughed. 'You imagine them to be ladies more susceptible than yourself, Rae?'

Rachel shrugged. 'I would think so. I confess I do not find adventurers attractive.'

'Most other ladies do not agree with you.'

Rachel gave him a speaking look. 'So I have heard. It is a pity you did not meet them by the river rather than myself.'

Cory was laughing at her, his grey eyes bright with amusement. 'Did I disturb you so much that you cannot put it from your mind, Rae?'

Rachel realised her mistake. 'Not at all,' she said with dignity. 'I was quite able to manage.'

'In your usual practical manner?' Cory put his head on one side. 'I do not believe I have ever seen you so ruffled before, Rachel. It was…interesting.'

There was something in his eyes that suggested that if Rachel had seen him in a different light, then so had he seen her. For a long instant they held each other's gaze whilst the warm, heavy excitement beat in Rachel's blood again. She broke the contact with deliberation and dusted the bits of loose hay from her skirts.

'I was certainly not expecting ever to see you in such a manner,' she said. 'It was like—' she struggled a little with her feelings '—like knowing too much about my own brother!'

Cory was watching her. It made her feel slightly uncomfortable.

'So your feelings for me are brotherly?' he asked.

Rachel fidgeted, pulling a sliver of wood from the doorframe. She felt rather hot and awkward, without really understanding the reason why. 'What else would they be, Cory?'

She saw Cory's expression change and had a sudden feeling of panic at the thought he might actually answer her—and that the answer might not be to her taste. She could hardly deny that their scandalous encounter by the river had had a wholly unexpected effect on her. Yes, she had been shocked, but she had also been captivated, tempted, excited… Her thoughts broke off in utter confusion as she saw that Cory was smiling at her with speculation in his eyes.

The clock on the tower chimed ten and Rachel felt almost faint with relief. 'Oh! I must go. I am promised to the reading group at Saltires at half past.'

Cory paused, brush in hand. 'At Saltires? Lady Sally Saltire hosts a reading group? Well, I'll be damned!'

Rachel paused. 'Do you know Lady Sally?'

'Everyone knows Sally Saltire,' Cory said. 'She is a most prominent London hostess. In fact, she is the only woman I know who has made being bookish a fashionable occupation. I believe that she was known as *La Belle Bas Bleue* when she was younger.'

'The beautiful bluestocking,' Rachel said, smiling. 'That is pretty.'

'It is a soubriquet that could equally be applied to you,' Cory said, his gaze warming.

Rachel blushed. 'Thank you, Cory, but you know that I look no more than well to a pass.'

Cory's eyes narrowed and once again Rachel felt a quiver of panic at what he might be about to say. For a moment he looked quite angry.

'What are you comparing yourself with, Rae? A classical Greek statue?'

'We were speaking of Lady Sally Saltire, not myself,' Rachel said hastily.

'So we were,' Cory said. 'I believe society was amazed that she chose to bury herself in the country this summer rather than visit the fashionable resorts.'

Rachel smiled a little. 'But surely everyone knows that Lady Sally seldom does the expected thing?'

'Those who know her well, perhaps.' Cory cocked his head. 'Had you met her before then, Rae?'

'We met in Egypt,' Rachel said, 'several years ago. Just before Napoleon's invasion.'

Cory nodded. 'Of course! I remember. Your father has a talent for choosing to excavate in precisely the place you would wish him not to be.'

Rachel smiled. 'Papa is so unworldly. He barely notices the great events unfolding around him. When we were forced to flee Egypt, he merely complained that Napoleon's army had forced him to lose a year's work.'

'You were lucky that you got away with your lives,' Cory said drily.

'I know. It was far too exciting for me. Which is why I prefer Midwinter Royal and Lady Sally's reading group.'

'What is the text that you are studying?' Cory asked.

'I have only been to one meeting of her reading group,' Rachel said, 'but we are currently discussing *The Enchantress* by Mrs Martin.'

She thought that she saw Cory's shoulders shake slightly. 'Why, what is the matter?'

Cory straightened and gave his horse a final pat. 'Your classical education has no doubt been magnificent, Rachel— I know of no other young lady who can read Hebrew and Chaldean—but your literary one is sadly lacking. I believe *The Enchantress* to be a Minerva Press publication.'

Rachel raised her chin. She did not care to have Cory make fun of her reading tastes. 'So? It is a charming book. I dare say that you have not read any Minervas, Cory, so you do not know what you are talking about.'

Cory inclined his head. 'There you have me. I do not. I beg your pardon. They are probably excellent publications.'

'You are suspiciously quick to retract your views. Either you are humouring me or else you are still secretly laughing at me!'

Cory raised a hand in mock surrender. 'Acquit me, Rae. I would not laugh at you. What is the plot of *The Enchantress?*'

Rachel shot him a mistrustful look, certain that he was still funning her. 'It is a most edifying tale,' she said. 'The hero, Sir Philip Desormeaux, has just put an advertisement in the newspaper in order to find himself a wife.'

'A most practical gentleman.' Cory quirked his brows.

'No doubt you approve of such a sensible approach to matrimony?'

'Naturally,' Rachel said. 'I have a lowering feeling, however, that he will succumb to romance in the end.'

Cory grinned. 'Is that what gentlemen generally do?'

'In fiction, certainly.' Rachel said. 'In real life, I doubt it.'

'Yet you advocate sense over sensibility yourself?'

'Of course.' Rachel said. 'Romance is like travel.'

'Exciting, daring, and dangerous?'

'Uncomfortable, inconvenient and hopefully of short duration,' Rachel said. 'Good day to you, Cory.'

His laughter followed her as she went out of the stable and into the bright sun of mid-morning. Already the heat was building and the white doves sought the shadow of the clock tower. Rachel, who intended to walk the couple of miles from Midwinter Royal House to Saltires, went to fetch her parasol. In the hallway her mother's packing boxes were still half-full and Rose, the only housemaid who had agreed to take the job, was laboriously polishing the banisters, wheezing as she worked.

Rachel went up the wide staircase, turned right where it branched, and entered the second door on her left. Midwinter Royal was only a small house and she had chosen for her own a bedroom on the west side with a view across Midwinter Common to the forest beyond. She had given her parents the biggest bedchamber on the south side of the house, for although Rachel knew that they would not have noticed if they had been sleeping in a trench, she wished them to be comfortable. They had a view across their beloved burial mounds to the river, the Winter Race, beyond.

Rachel's room was bright and full of sunshine. The curtains rippled in the breeze from the open window. She went across and extracted her parasol from the white-painted wardrobe in the corner. All of her belongings had been stacked away neatly upon arrival. Nothing spoiled the pristine neatness of her bed, for although she had to share a maid with Lady Odell, she would never have countenanced leaving her clothes draped about the room as her mother did.

It was as she was closing the wardrobe door that she turned and caught sight of Cory Newlyn strolling down the path that cut through the shrubberies towards the fields at the back. He had his hands in the pockets of his disreputable jacket and he was whistling under his breath. As Rachel watched, he took off his battered old hat and thrust his hand through his fair hair, pushing it back from his forehead. Then he looked up at her window, saw her watching and raised one hand in casual greeting. The sun was on his up-turned face as he smiled at her.

Rachel stepped back from the window suddenly. It was odd but she felt as though she had been caught in the act like a peeping Tom. Yet surely there was nothing wrong in looking out of her own bedroom window…

When she dared to look again, Cory had disappeared around the corner of the house. With a small sigh, Rachel tied the blue ribbons of her wide-brimmed straw hat under her chin, donned her light spencer and checked in the mirror that she looked neat and tidy. She did. Her russet-brown hair was braided ruthlessly to subdue the curl in it and there was not a thread out of place on her pale blue promenade dress.

She picked up her parasol and hurried down the stairs. Cory had disturbed her morning in more ways than one. Now she was going to be late, and in a strange way, it felt as though it was all Cory's fault.

Chapter Three

Rachel was halfway along the dusty road that led from Midwinter Royal to Saltires when she was overtaken by a gig containing two ladies. The pony was travelling at a lively trot and stirred up quite a cloud of dust in its wake, and the gig's passenger, turning and seeing Rachel struggling on the grass verge, put out a hand and urged the driver to stop. When Rachel caught them up, she recognised two of the other members of the Midwinter reading group, the Honourable Mrs Deborah Stratton and her sister, Olivia, Lady Marney. Deborah Stratton leaned over and addressed her in the friendliest of terms.

'Miss Odell! I am so sorry—we did not see you there! May we take you up with us? I assume that you are going to Saltires?'

Rachel looked at the gig's narrow seat rather dubiously. Lady Marney, who was driving, had not seconded her younger sister's invitation and Rachel felt a little awkward. She did not wish to force herself on their company.

'I am not certain that there is room—' Rachel began, but Deborah Stratton cheerfully overrode her.

'Of course there is! Move up and make room for Miss Odell, Liv,' she added, turning to her sister and suiting actions to words by huddling up on the gig's seat. 'It is only a mile or so further, at any rate. We shall all be as fine as ninepence up here.'

Rachel found her hand grasped in Mrs Stratton's own, surprisingly strong one, and without further ado joined her on the cushioned seat.

'Good morning, Lady Marney,' she said, nodding to Olivia. 'This is very kind of you.'

'A pleasure, Miss Odell,' Olivia said, although her voice lacked the warmth of her sister's. She turned her attention back to the pony and the gig lurched forward again.

Deborah Stratton gave Rachel an encouraging smile. When Rachel had first been introduced to the sisters at the reading group the previous week, she had been struck as much by the differences as by the similarities between them, and the same feeling was reinforced now. Both girls were slender with corn-coloured hair and blue eyes, but Olivia's face was grave in repose and held little animation. Deborah, in contrast, seemed almost to burst out of her skin with vitality. Rachel had liked her immediately and the two of them had fallen into conversation very easily and were now in the way to becoming firm friends. With Olivia, though, matters were different. Rachel thought that it might take some time to get to know Lady Marney.

'I hope that you are settled in at Midwinter Royal House, Miss Odell,' Deborah said now with a friendly smile. 'It is barely three weeks, is it not? I always find that it takes time to accustom oneself to a new place.'

Rachel agreed. 'I hope,' she added, 'that my parents will permit me to become settled in the Midwinter villages. We are forever on the move, you know.'

Deborah's face lit up. 'Of course! Your father is the prodigiously famous antiquary Sir Arthur Odell, is he not? We are most impressed to have such eminent neighbours.'

'Impressed and not a little excited to discover what he will dig up,' Lady Marney added unexpectedly. She gave Rachel a shy, sideways smile, taking her eyes off the road for a second. 'No doubt it is all old hat for you, Miss Odell, but we have never experienced an excavation in the Midwinter villages before, though everyone has been wondering what is in those mounds for time over mind.'

Rachel laughed. 'I cannot promise that it will be vastly exciting, Lady Marney, but I am sure that my parents will turn up something of interest. They usually do.'

'I expect that you have travelled with your parents to the most extraordinary places, Miss Odell,' Olivia Marney said encouragingly. 'Egypt, Greece, Italy…'

Rachel sighed. It was always the same. Everyone found her life tremendously exciting except she herself. 'Yes, I have been to all of those places and more, Lady Marney, although the recent hostilities have rather put an end to the more exotic assignments.'

The sisters laughed together. 'My dear Miss Odell,' Deborah said, 'you sound quite *jaded* by the whole experience!'

Catching Lady Marney's smile, Rachel realised that Olivia was not standoffish, but merely shy. She could not wonder at it. Having a sister as ebullient as Deborah Stratton would be enough to cast most siblings into the shade. Yet it was odd, for the widowed Mrs Stratton could only be the same age as Rachel herself, whilst Olivia was a good few years the elder, and married to a viscount into the bargain. Rachel would have expected her to have more address.

Deborah patted Rachel's hand consolingly. 'Never mind, Miss Odell. We are pleased to have you amongst us. I think that you might become quite a curiosity! There is not that much society in the Midwinter villages, you know, and even as far afield as Woodbridge…' She pulled an expressive face.

'My sister is more accustomed to the sophisticated delights of Bath, Miss Odell,' Lady Marney said drily. 'I fear she finds country life very tame.'

'I do not!' Deborah objected. 'I have lived in Midwinter

Mallow for fully three years without being in the slightest bit bored, Liv.'

'I hear that life in the Midwinter villages is likely to become much more exciting,' Olivia said. 'Ross, my husband, said that the Duke of Kestrel is paying one of his rare visits to Midwinter and has brought some of his family and friends with him.'

'Lud, a house full of rakes and adventurers,' Deborah said. 'That will cause a flutter in the country dovecotes!'

Rachel imagined that the lively Mrs Stratton would find a man like Cory Newlyn vastly entertaining. She could picture Cory regaling Deborah with tales of his outrageous expeditions, smiling into her eyes whilst he spun tall stories about buried treasure. She had always viewed Cory's conquests with an indulgent smile before, but now she felt slightly sick. She wondered whether it was the jolting of the gig that was responsible for her queasiness.

A moment later the carriage swept through the gates of Saltires and started its journey through the lush parkland that surrounded the house. Rachel looked about her with interest. Although she had visited Lady Sally a couple of times already, she had always walked from Midwinter Royal and the path along the river did not afford the same view of the beamed Jacobean hall as this long approach did. She gave a little sigh.

'Oh, it is pretty, is it not?'

'Vastly pretty,' Deborah said, smiling, 'and very old. It is the dower house for Kestrel Court, you know, Miss Odell. Lady Sally and her husband named it Saltires when the Duke leased it to them on their marriage. Justin Kestrel and Stephen Saltire were the greatest of friends, you know.'

Rachel had wondered how Lady Sally Saltire came to be living so close to Kestrel Court, for the tall, twisted chimneys of the larger house could just be seen beyond the trees of the deer park.

'One would have thought it unconscionably awkward,'

Deborah continued, 'for the Duke and Lord Stephen were both suitors for Lady Sally's hand in marriage. When she chose Lord Stephen it was rumoured that there would be a duel for her hand!' Deborah's eyes sparkled. 'How romantic is that?'

'Not very,' Olivia said crushingly. 'The whole story was only a hum—Justin Kestrel would scarce have offered his old friend a home afterwards if they had fallen out over a lady, would he?'

Deborah's face fell. 'I suppose not.'

'The Duke and Lady Sally have not rekindled their romance since her widowhood?' Rachel ventured, hoping that Olivia would not think her prying. 'If not, that might suggest there was no truth in the tale.'

'No, they have not,' Deborah said. She looked dissatisfied. 'I do not believe they see each other very often, for Justin Kestrel travels a great deal and Lady Sally is for the main part settled in London. Oh, it was such a romantic story and now the two of you have utterly deflated it—and me into the bargain!'

Olivia laughed. 'Romance, my dear Deborah, is a sadly overrated commodity,' she said, unconsciously echoing Rachel's comments to Cory earlier. 'Far better to aim for a comfortable match and a settled life.'

Rachel smiled. 'I had heard that Lady Sally was once a prodigiously famous beauty. Has she never wished to remarry?'

'No.' It was Olivia who answered. 'With wealth and position and good society, why should she need to marry?'

'Well,' Deborah began, 'she might need a man to—'

'Deb!'

Olivia shot her sister a warning look, which Rachel intercepted. She almost laughed. It seemed that Olivia had been worried that her sister would make some unguarded remark about a woman's need for male companionship. Such a comment was scarcely proper in front of a young unmarried lady, but Rachel wryly suspected that she would be unlikely to be shocked. It was Lady Marney and Mrs Stratton who would no doubt be horrified if only they knew the education that Rachel had been subject to from an early age. It did not matter that the frescoes and sculptures of bacchanalian pleasures and erotic excess had been unearthed by her parents and were supposedly classical; they were still explicit and shocking and had left the young Rachel Odell in open-mouthed wonder. She could remember clearly the day that Cory Newlyn had come across her almost standing on her head in an attempt to work out whether a certain position indulged in by two figures in a fresco was physically possible…

Still, it was better to allow Lady Marney her illusions, Rachel thought. She was enough of a curiosity as it was, without shocking the ladies further, and she knew her unorthodox upbringing would give some people a disgust. It was a great pity, when all she had ever wished for was to lead an ordinary life. She smiled gently and said nothing.

'I suppose it is too late for Lady Sally now,' Deborah said with a sigh, 'for she must be all of three and thirty if she is a day. Far too old to be contemplating remarriage!'

The gig drew up outside the main door and a liveried footman immediately appeared to help the ladies descend. Tucking her copy of *The Enchantress,* which she had borrowed from Lady Sally's extensive library, under her arm, Rachel followed Olivia and Deborah inside.

The reading group was a very select affair. Only six of them sat around the polished walnut table in Lady Sally Saltire's library. In addition to Deborah Stratton and Olivia Marney there was Lady Sally herself, Helena Lang, the vicar's daughter, and Lily Benedict, a dark beauty married to a gentleman who lived retired.

'Well, my dears,' Lady Sally said when they had all discussed the first couple of chapters of *The Enchantress,* 'we all suspect that Sir Philip Desormeaux will get more than he bargained for from his advertisement, but then any gentleman who *advertises* for a wife deserves to be put in his place…'

She smiled at them all conspiratorially and it felt to Rachel as though she was drawing them all into the warmth by the sheer force of her personality. From the top of her elegant head to the tips of her kid slippers, Lady Sally Saltire exuded the sort of style that left Rachel in open-mouthed envy. Lady Sally was sleek, elegant and effortlessly modish. Nor was it simply a matter of dress. Rachel reflected that Olivia Marney, for example, was fashionable but rather lifeless. Sally was vivacious, with all the style conferred through being a rich and supremely elegant society widow.

'I always think that a man who needs to advertise for a wife must have something seriously wrong with him,' Helena Lang said. Her tone suggested that she would never give such a poor-spirited fellow the time of day. 'After all, there are plenty of dreadful men who still manage to attach a wife without having to resort to the newspapers, so how bad would one need to be to advertise? It is quite shocking when one comes to think of it.'

There was general laughter at this.

'It is true that appalling men can marry quite easily if they are rich and titled,' Lily Benedict agreed. 'One sees it all the time.'

Lady Sally rang the bell for the servant. 'More refreshments, ladies? I have another project that I wish to discuss with you all before you leave.'

Two footmen brought in trays laden with cake, tea and lemonade. Rachel accepted a glass of the latter for the day was very warm and it was quite stuffy in Lady Sally's library. Though the casement windows were open to allow in a thread of breeze, the low, plaster ceilings seemed to trap the heat.

'Lady Sally is well known for her charitable projects,'

Deborah Stratton whispered in Rachel's ear. 'Last summer she sponsored a race on the river and all the fashionable crowd came down from London to attend. It was the most exciting occasion! We seldom see such society in Midwinter.'

'So, ladies…' Lady Sally said, when the footmen had retired, 'I wished to share the plans for my new project with you—and to ask for your help.'

Five pairs of eyes rounded with speculation.

'I would like,' Lady Sally continued, 'to raise some funds for one of my benevolent societies. I thought that a little project might distract everyone rather pleasantly from rumours of this annoying invasion, so…' she smiled with a hint of wickedness '…I thought that it might be rather fun to produce a watercolour book.'

A little sigh rippled around the group. A book sounded nowhere near as exciting as last year's regatta had been.

'Do you mean a book with watercolour drawings, Sally?' Lily Benedict enquired. 'That seems a little tame compared with your usual projects.'

'Local views would look attractive in watercolours,' Olivia Marney suggested. 'The river, the watermill…'

'I did indeed have local attractions in mind,' Lady Sally said, stretching out a languid hand to pour herself another cup of tea, 'but nothing so tame as the river, Olivia. I had in mind pictures of local *gentlemen.*'

Olivia almost choked on her tea and had to be patted on the back by her sister. Helena Lang, a buxom beauty given to vulgarity, gave vent to a thoroughly over-excited scream.

'Portraits of gentlemen in a book? Lady Sally, you are so *wicked!*'

'I know,' Lady Sally said calmly. 'Conceive of the potential profit to my charity, ladies. A few drawings of eligible gentlemen, with a little bit of text giving some essential information about them—'

'Such as whether they are married and the size of their

estate,' Deborah Stratton suggested. She laughed. 'It will be like a gazetteer!'

'Precisely.' Lady Sally nodded. 'I had it in mind to host a ball in town during the little season and hold an auction. The ladies would be queuing out of the door to place a bid on a book that gives details of the most eligible gentlemen on the marriage mart! I am persuaded it would be all the rage, particularly if the gentlemen in the drawings were to attend as well.'

Lily Benedict was laughing. 'It's an outrageous idea, Sally! No one but you could get away with it.'

'Which gentlemen will be featured?' Helena Lang enquired, putting the question that everyone else was too reticent to ask.

Lady Sally ticked them off on her fingers. 'Sir John Norton has already agreed to pose for me, as has Lord Northcote—'

'But he is married already,' Helena protested, pouting, 'and Sir John Norton is a dreadful bore. You must have some more attractive gentlemen, Lady Sally. Positively you must!'

'It would certainly make the watercolour book more popular,' Lady Sally agreed. 'Now that Justin Kestrel and his brothers are here for the summer, I intend to persuade them to take part...' she gave a little smile '...and then I do believe we shall be overwhelmed with eager purchasers!'

Rachel, who had been listening quietly, saw Deborah Stratton look quickly away and fidget slightly with the cover of her copy of *The Enchantress*. Her colour had risen at the mention of Justin Kestrel and his brothers and Rachel could not help wondering which Kestrel brother it was that could cause such a reaction. Fortunately Helena Lang distracted everyone's attention before Deborah's discomfiture became too evident.

'However will you convince the *Duke* to pose, Lady

Sally? I heard tell that he is very high in the instep, for all that he is a thorough-going rake!'

'I shall use my native charm, Miss Lang,' Lady Sally said. 'And if I fail, I shall ask one of you to approach him instead. Justin is very susceptible to a lady's persuasion, I assure you. In fact, that is where I need your help.'

The ladies looked enquiring.

'I need you to work your charms on all the gentlemen visiting Midwinter,' Lady Sally said, smiling. 'A little flirtation can work miracles, ladies! If you can persuade the Duke and his friends to take part in my book of watercolour drawings, then I shall be able to establish another school for the ragged children in Ipswich. No one can deny that it is for a good cause.'

'You are still a few gentlemen short,' Deborah observed. She appeared to have regained her composure. 'Did you have any others in mind?'

Lady Sally smiled at Olivia, who had remained quiet throughout most of the discussion, as she often did.

'I had thought that Lord Marney might be persuaded to take part,' Lady Sally said. 'I wondered if you might speak to him, dear Olivia.'

Olivia Marney's head jerked up and bright colour came into her cheeks.

'My husband pays no attention to my requests,' she said sharply. She brushed the biscuit crumbs from her skirt with sharp little movements. 'You would have better success were you to ask him yourself, Lady Sally!'

The atmosphere in the room was suddenly tense. Rachel had no notion why matters should be so awkward, but she could not miss the significant glance that Lady Sally shot Lady Benedict. The only person who appeared unaware of her sister's tension was Deborah Stratton.

'*I* will ask Ross if he will take part, Liv!' she said cheerfully. 'I am sure he will agree.'

'Oh, well, if *you* ask him, Deborah, I am sure that there

will be no difficulty at all!' Olivia Marney said, and the bitterness was suddenly clear in her voice, so marked that even Deborah fell silent.

There was another awkward pause.

Lady Sally threw herself into the breach. 'How splendid,' she said, quite as though there had been no undercurrent to Olivia's words. 'And if I might prevail upon you, Miss Odell, to speak to Lord Newlyn, then I think we might rightly be proud of the collection of truly distinguished gentlemen who will grace my watercolour book.'

Rachel jumped. She had just been reflecting that Cory would detest being part of a project such as this when she realised that Lady Sally was addressing her. Rachel felt the eyes of the group fixed on her. Helena Lang was looking rather envious all of a sudden.

'I doubt I have any influence with Lord Newlyn,' Rachel said. 'It is true that I have known him for years, but I would not say that he was a very persuadable gentleman.'

Lady Sally's eyes widened with amusement. 'Oh, do you think not?' she said. 'A great pity, for he is quite the most charismatic man of my acquaintance.' She smiled gently at Rachel. 'Would he not be susceptible to a little flirtation, Miss Odell?'

'Not if I was the one doing the flirting with him,' Rachel said, laughing at the very idea. 'I believe he would ask me if I had had too much sun!'

Everyone laughed, although Lady Sally looked pensive. 'It seems a pity,' she said. 'Lord Newlyn would look vastly attractive in watercolours.'

'He would look vastly attractive in anything,' Lily Benedict added drily, 'or nothing.'

Rachel bit her lip and concentrated very hard on not thinking about Cory wearing nothing at all. She had only just managed to banish the image and here it was back with a vengeance. She fanned herself surreptitiously with her book.

'Oh, please try to persuade him, Miss Odell,' Helena Lang interposed. 'Lord Newlyn would be the most perfect choice. He is so dashing.'

Rachel looked at the pleading faces. Her strongest impulse was to refuse. The thought of asking Cory to grace Lady Sally's watercolour book was an excruciating one.

'I really do not think—' she began.

Lady Sally put out a consoling hand. 'Please do not worry. I would not wish you to feel obliged to approach Lord Newlyn, Miss Odell, not if it would embarrass you. Perhaps one of the other ladies could exert a little charm to persuade him.'

'I am sure that we shall be drawing lots for the privilege,' Lily Benedict said.

Rachel frowned. The idea of another lady flirting with Cory made her feel rather possessive, although she knew this was entirely inappropriate. She looked at Lily Benedict's face, with the slanting dark eyes that held a flicker of malice, and decided that she did not like her very much nor would she give her the chance to flirt with Cory. The same went for that vulgar Miss Lang.

'I suppose I can at least talk to him,' she said. 'I should be happy to do that.'

'Oh, goody!' Helena Lang exclaimed. 'How exciting to have such a famous adventurer in our midst! Was it not Lord Newlyn who wrestled a crocodile in the Nile and survived the curse of Amenhopec? He is the most complete gentleman, is he not?'

'The crocodile incident was much exaggerated,' Rachel said coolly, wishing to depress Helena Lang's pretensions and reduce Cory's appeal at the same time. 'As for the curse, I do not believe that Lord Newlyn escaped so easily. He had a dreadful stomach upset for weeks after he excavated that tomb. They call it the Pharaoh's Revenge.'

There was a ripple of scandalised laughter from the group as the ladies took her meaning. 'My dear Miss Odell,' Lady

Sally said, wiping the tears from her eyes, 'I do believe that you have demolished Lord Newlyn's dashing reputation in one move. An upset stomach indeed! How very unromantic! I cannot wait to tease him about this.'

'You might sketch Lord Newlyn wrestling a crocodile, ma'am,' Helena Lang said hopefully to Lady Sally. 'Without his shirt, perhaps—'

'In the waters of the Winter Race?' Lady Sally said. 'What a fertile imagination you have, Miss Lang. Not that I totally discount the idea. So, ladies—' she looked around the group '—to work! I am relying on you.'

The meeting broke up on that note. Rachel declined Olivia Marney's offer of a ride back to Midwinter Royal in the gig, preferring instead to take the footpath that skirted the riverbank. The air was fresh here, straight off the water, and held a tang of salt. The Winter Race was a small tributary of the larger River Deben, originally feeding the watermill at Midwinter Bere, but these days the mill was derelict and the water flowed sluggishly between low banks in the summer and in the winter flooded the mud flats and marshes. On such a clear day she could see directly across to the Deben, where the yachts and wherries were moored on the quay at Woodbridge.

The sand track was soft beneath Rachel's shoes. A rabbit scuttered through the undergrowth, startling a pheasant out of the bracken. As she walked she thought about Lady Sally's reading group and the planned book of watercolour drawings. It was the most shocking matchmaker's charter and as such she was certain it would be a raging success.

Rachel paused to look out across the Winter Race. The breeze teased tendrils of hair from beneath her bonnet and she stopped to tuck it back in. Ahead of her the riverbank sloped up towards the Midwinter Royal burial ground. There was a knot of pine trees that gave a sheltered lookout across the river in one direction and over the fields to Midwinter Royal in the other. Last year's pine needles were a soft carpet beneath Rachel's feet and they gave off a sweet, resinous scent.

She paused on the top of the hill to watch the excavation. Sir Arthur and Lady Odell were working in the southernmost corner of the field, digging one of the long barrows and sorting the earth into a huge spoil pit. Rachel sighed. It all looked so messy and she detested untidiness.

Cory Newlyn was much closer to her, digging a trench into the side of a burial mound. Cory did not favour the accepted method of digging straight down from the top of a barrow; he maintained that this could damage the finds buried inside. Instead he would open a small, exploratory ditch and work inwards from there. Rachel could not see that it mattered one way or another. Soon her parents would be tramping the dirt through the house and she would have to spur Rose into action to clean it all up again. Then the scullery would be full of bits of pot to be washed and the dining room would have bones laid out on the breakfast table. It was always the same.

She watched as Cory paused in his digging and leaned on his spade, rubbing a hand across his forehead. His disgusting broad-brimmed hat tilted at a more rakish angle still. Rachel looked at him and tried to work out why Lady Sally had described him as one of the most charismatic men of her acquaintance. She had an appreciation of classical statuary and by those standards Cory was not particularly good looking. His face was too thin and his features slightly irregular. Nevertheless, the hard, clearcut planes of his face were somehow pleasing to the eye and it was difficult to tear one's gaze away. Then there was his thick, tawny hair and his cool grey gaze and his long, rangy body that looked so good in the saddle—or emerging from the river... Oh, yes, Rachel could appreciate Cory Newlyn in a completely objective manner. Even so, there was nothing objective about the strange pit-a-pat of excitement in her stomach as she watched Cory at work, and when he turned to look at her, she looked away and hurried off without speaking to him. She felt strangely embarrassed and certainly not brave enough to broach the subject of the watercolour book. That would have to wait for another day.

As Rachel hurried along the path towards the house she imagined that she could feel Cory's gaze on her retreating back. Impartial appreciation… Yes, she understood how attractive Cory might appear to another lady. For a brief moment, though, impartial was not how she felt at all, and she did not like it.

Chapter Four

Cory Newlyn straightened up, drove his trowel into the sand and reached for the earthenware pitcher of water. It was a hot day for an English summer, with a dry heat that reminded him more of archaeological excavations in Italy or Greece. He tilted the pitcher to his lips and took a long swallow. He felt the liquid spill from the pot and the refreshing coolness of the water run over his chin and down his neck under the linen shirt. After a moment he took off his hat and tipped the remains of the water over his head, slicking his fair hair back and shaking the droplets from the ends. The cold water raised the hairs on the back of his neck and he enjoyed the sensation of chill on such a hot day.

Despite the heat, the excavation site was a hive of activity. Sir Arthur Odell was directing operations in the far corner of the field, where the Odells' footman and gardener toiled over a wheelbarrow, moving piles of earth from the largest burial mound to the spoil heap some yards away. Lavinia Odell was sifting the earth through a huge sieve and picking out a few bits and pieces that caught her attention. So far the excavation of the Midwinter burials had been disappointing. Sir Arthur had turned up a few battered pieces of gold and some broken bits of pottery dating from Anglo-Saxon times, but most of the tombs that they had opened had been robbed out years before. This had happened to Cory time after time, and he was too old a hand to let it dismay him unduly. Since he had another reason for being in the Midwinter villages that summer, the Odells' excavation was a convenient and enjoyable excuse. Besides, Cory's instinct, which had never failed him before, told him that there *was* something there to find. Something big. Hidden treasure. It was just a matter of discovering where it lay.

Perhaps they might even find the Midwinter Treasure itself, although Cory was sceptical. The legend related that the gold cup had been discovered by an awestruck peasant in the fourteenth century, but when he had tried to take it from the tomb, a voice had stopped him in his tracks and he had run away, too frightened to carry out his intended looting. When he told his story later, a group of Midwinter villagers more hardy than he had gone to find the treasure, but had never returned. Neither they nor the cup were ever seen again, and there was a myth that if anyone tried to take the treasure they would come to an untimely end.

Cory stretched, then replaced the battered hat on his head. In the dining room of Midwinter Royal House there would be a delicious cold luncheon waiting and no doubt they would all be in trouble with Rachel for neglecting it. He could see her now, making her way up the path that ran alongside the burial ground towards the house. She had removed her bonnet and the sunlight gleamed on the rich chestnut of her hair, so ruthlessly plaited that not a single bright strand broke free of its constraints. Her pale blue dress was pin neat and she stepped over brambles and rabbit holes with precision. Cory smiled slightly. He remembered Rachel as a child of seven lining up her abacus with absolute accuracy. Ten years later, he could remember her picking a loose thread off his evening jacket when he had attended her come-out ball. She had always been the epitome of order and he had always nursed a subversive desire to shatter that composure. In the interests of friendship, he had resisted it.

The same desire to shake her self-possession had overcome him that morning when he had met her by the river and she had been so stunned to see him in the nude. He had known then that Rachel was not completely indifferent to him as a man. Some of her embarrassment had understandably sprung from the shock any well-bred girl would sustain when confronted by a naked man. But, more tellingly, he had seen the first long, intent stare that she had given him before she had realised who he was, and later the struggle she had had to resist the impulse simply to forget modesty and look on his nakedness. Cory smiled to himself. He was no gentleman to have prolonged the encounter as he had done, but he had been enjoying Rachel's consternation too much to put an end to it. It was fortunate that her flailing hands had touched his arm rather than any other more sensitive part of him. He would not have wished to make the situation any more difficult than it already was.

Cory deliberately dismissed the encounter from his mind and turned his attention instead to Rachel's situation within the Odell household. In some ways it seemed to him that Rachel had exchanged roles with her parents, worrying about what they wore and what they ate, making sure that their lives ran smoothly whilst they ran around collecting antiquities like irresponsible children gathering conkers. It infuriated Cory. He felt that someone ought to be looking after Rachel rather than the reverse.

Cory scraped the sand off his boots with irritable swipes of the trowel. The only time that he had expressed his views to Rachel, she had accused him of hypocrisy. And it was true, Cory thought fairly, that he also enjoyed the sort of life that the Odells pursued. But he was not married and nor did he have any children. His love of travel was the reason *why* he had never married. He valued his liberty too highly to compromise it.

His gaze returned to Rachel. She had caught the hem of the blue promenade dress on a trailing bramble and had bent to release her skirts. She was by necessity displaying her very attractive ankles, which she had kept demurely hidden from him since she was about ten years old. Cory grinned. Rachel had a figure as luscious as any of the Greek statues that adorned her parents' hall, but no one was ever likely to get a glimpse of it. Her necklines were always high and her hemlines low. She was as neatly tied up as a parcel packaged with string.

He felt a wayward male urge to unwrap that parcel.

Cory sighed and ran a hand over his hair. He was not sure when his feelings for Rachel had started to change. Certainly he did not feel remotely brotherly towards her. Cory had plenty of sisters and his feelings for Rachel were quite different. At some point he had started to notice her in an entirely masculine way, and having started, had been unable to stop. It was utterly pointless and he knew it. Rachel saw him as a reliable elder brother and he was honour bound not to step outside the part. Besides, even he was not so disreputable as to have dishonourable intentions towards the daughter of his mentor and friend.

'My lord?' Cory jumped, dragging his gaze from Rachel's figure and his thoughts from the fascinating subject of all the things that he could *not* do with her. He turned to find Bradshaw, his valet, at his elbow. The man was holding out what looked like a gold coin on his grimy palm. Cory picked it up.

'Very good, Bradshaw. That looks like a shield boss. We'll make an antiquarian of you yet!'

Bradshaw grinned. He had thick, dark hair and a muscular physique, and his arrival had caused a stir amongst the female servants. Before he had entered Cory's employ he had had a variety of jobs, but all of them had been on government business and none of them had been anything to do with valeting. That, however, was a fact known only to Cory and Bradshaw himself.

'Not whilst I have my strength you won't, my lord! I had no notion that these were the duties you had in mind for me.'

'Excavation work isn't to your taste?' Cory had taken a small brush and was flicking the soil off the disk so that more of the inscription was revealed.

'No, my lord. It is all too pernickety for me. I thought it would involve digging up big earthenware pots and shields of gold!'

'The Midwinter Treasure?' Cory murmured.

'Something of the sort, my lord,' Bradshaw said.

Cory laughed. 'Digging for antiquities is mainly tedious, Bradshaw, with rare moments of excitement.' Cory placed the shield boss carefully in the basket of finds. He lowered his voice discreetly. 'And this is useful intelligence work. We are getting the lie of the land, talking to people, picking up information… There is plenty going on here.'

He glanced towards the corner of the burial field where the ground sloped down to the river. 'There is some disturbance of the ground over in the eastern corner of the field, for instance. It's my belief that smuggled goods have been stored there. Steady…' he put a restraining hand on Bradshaw's arm '…we cannot simply go rushing in there drawing attention to ourselves! Remember that this is part of a bigger game. We will have our chance.'

Bradshaw nodded reluctantly. 'Aye, my lord.' He grinned. 'In the meantime, I shall concentrate on getting burned by the sun and developing muscles I was unaware I possessed!'

Cory clapped him on the back. 'That's the spirit! And I do believe—' he looked over his shoulder '—that we have you to thank for the additional help we are getting from Kitty the kitchen maid. Lady Odell was commenting that the maids had not shown any inclination towards excavation work until this morning.' He saw the valet's face flush. 'You are to be congratulated, Bradshaw. Kitty is surprisingly good at the job, as well as a fine source of gossip. If you could encourage her a little…'

Bradshaw nodded. He did not look as though he would find this particular task too onerous. 'I can try, my lord.'

'Splendid!' Cory gestured towards the finds basket. 'You could start by taking these over to Lady Odell for sorting. And whilst you are there, pray remind her ladyship that luncheon was ready an hour ago. Miss Odell will not forgive me if her parents fail to eat.'

He watched Bradshaw scramble over the trenches until he reached Lavinia Odell and the maid at her side and saw Kitty's face tilt up towards Bradshaw with a luscious smile. Cory sighed and turned away, his gaze searching out Rachel's figure on the footpath that skirted the site. She had passed by without a word and now she had reached the stile that led on to the drive. He saw her hesitate before taking the longer route round through the wicket gate. Cory smiled to himself. Of course. Climbing over a stile was not very ladylike and not even the neat Miss Odell could scale it with decorum. No doubt she thought it far better to preserve her dignity by walking round.

His smile became a frown as he realised that Rachel had passed him by without a backward glance. Not long ago she would have made a point of stopping at the dig and speaking to him, even detesting excavation work as she did. This new distance in her behaviour was puzzling and uncomfortable. He had felt it when they had greeted each other earlier that morning. There had been a prickle of tension between them that previously had not existed. And now Rachel had deliberately passed him by. Perhaps she had been more embarrassed by their encounter by the river than he had imagined. Whatever the reason, it seemed that she intended to keep her distance. He did not like the thought.

* * *

It was late that same evening, and the heat of the day had faded from the air, when Rachel came looking for Cory down on the excavation. It was not difficult to find him, for a small campfire burned in the southern corner of the field, sheltered by the stone wall that separated the burial site from the meadow beyond. The evening was still light, for it was almost midsummer, but the sun was down and the sky paling. Against its washed blue light the warmth of the fire looked bright and welcoming.

Cory was sitting on the edge of a trench, his long legs dangling over into the ditch beneath. Beside him, away from the fire, a cloth was spread out, and on it were the parts of a dismantled rifle set out ready for cleaning. As Rachel approached, Cory looked up from the piece that he was polishing and gave her his slow, heart-shaking smile.

'Good evening, Rae. What do you have there?'

'I have brought you something to eat and drink,' Rachel said. She put a packet of food beside him. 'It is nothing much, merely some bread and cheese and an apple. Oh, and some of Mrs Goodfellow's cider. I should warn you that it is strong stuff. I was drinking it this morning when I saw you come out of the river, and I thought I was having delusions.'

Cory flashed her a smile. 'How flattering that you thought me a figure of fantasy,' he said gravely.

'A delusion is generally a sign of madness rather than anything else,' Rachel pointed out crushingly, 'so I do not feel you should take it as a compliment.' She looked around. 'There is nowhere to sit here. How very uncomfortable!'

Cory sighed, slipped his jacket off and spread it on the ground with exaggerated care. 'There you are, Rae. I would not do that for everyone.'

'I imagine most people would not want you to,' Rachel said. 'It is scarce cleaner than the earth.'

Nevertheless she sat down on it, curling her legs neatly beneath her skirts, and for a few moments there was a silence between them. It felt warm and comfortable and familiar. A sliver of moon was rising in the eastern sky and the air was still faintly warm and scented with summer. The fire hissed and crackled and Rachel watched Cory's deft fingers as he thrust the bristle brush through the barrel of the gun.

She put a hand out and touched the shining rifle butt.

'Is this new?'

'Yes,' Cory said. 'A Baker rifle with a short barrel so that it can be fired whilst you are lying down. It is a new design—' He stopped and looked at her. 'You are not really interested, are you?'

'Not really,' Rachel said. 'I was only being polite. But it does look very clean.' She pulled a face. 'I hope that there will be no call to use it around here.'

Cory sighed. 'And I hope that your father still has his blunderbuss, Rae,' he said, by way of reply. 'At the very least, we know that there are smugglers operating in the area. There is digging around one of the tombs that suggests that they have been using it to store their booty, but I think the ground became too unstable for them.'

Rachel craned her neck and stared across the excavation. Away from the circle of firelight the fields looked dark, with the burial mounds standing like shadowy hillocks, black against the deeper darkness.

'It would make a splendid hiding place,' she said. 'Most people wouldn't dare set foot here with all those legends of treasure guarded by a curse.'

'Exactly,' Cory said. 'And whilst I am here I intend to make sure that the smugglers do not return and ruin all our work by digging out the trenches.'

He picked up a wad of cloth and started to polish the rifle hammer.

'What have you been doing this afternoon?' he asked. 'Your mother mentioned something about you tidying the books that used to belong to Jeffrey Maskelyne.'

Rachel nodded. The Maskelynes were the true owners of Midwinter Royal House and it was they who had let it to the Odells for the summer in order to conduct the excavation. Events that had fallen out so happily for Sir Arthur and Lady Odell had come about as a result of the Maskelynes' misfortune—their eldest son, Jeffrey, who had been in residence at Midwinter until some three months previously, had drowned in the Winter Race back in March.

'I am trying to solve the mystery of the Midwinter Treasure using books and maps instead of excavation work,' Rachel said.

She saw Cory smile. 'You want to beat us to the treasure?'

'Exactly,' Rachel said.

Cory laughed. 'I had no notion that you were moved by so competitive a spirit, Rae. How far have you got?'

'Not very far, I am afraid,' Rachel said. 'All the books and maps and plans seem to contradict each other. However, if I get stuck, Cory, you will be the last person I ask. I could not bear for you to solve the mystery and prove yourself cleverer than me!'

'You never could accept it,' Cory said.

'Just because you have the advantage of six years on me, and were therefore ahead in your lessons. And you went to university whilst I was obliged to study at home, like a girl!'

'You *are* a girl, Rachel.' Cory smiled at her in what Rachel considered to be a thoroughly annoying fashion. 'That is why you are treated as one.'

'I do not see why girls cannot study at university,' Rachel grumbled. 'I should have been happy to do that whilst you and Mama and Papa travelled the world.'

'I dare say. It is not the done thing, however.'

'Which does not make it *right*.' Rachel sighed irritably. She plucked a few blades of grass at random from the edge of the trench and shredded them between her fingers.

'You are so smug, Cory! You have no notion how fortunate you are. You can choose whether you study, or travel, or debauch yourself—'

Cory pointed the ramrod at her. 'Careful, Rae!'

'Well…' Rachel subsided, still feeling aggrieved but aware that they sounded like the squabbling youngsters they had once been.

'You have had the opportunity to travel,' Cory pointed out.

'Yes, but I did not choose it. That is the difference. More to the point, I did not want it.'

'And you are a bluestocking,' Cory continued. 'You did not suffer from being educated at home.'

His assumptions irritated Rachel.

'Thank you,' she said drily. 'You have no idea how it warms me to have your admiration.'

Cory grinned. 'Oh, you have that, Rae. More than you think.'

'Now you are funning me,' Rachel said.

'Not at all. You know I admire your fine mind.' Cory looked at her appraisingly. 'And more besides.'

Their eyes met. There was a moment when Rachel thought about taking him up on his comment, but decided it would be safer not to do so. She had no wish to act as a practice target for Cory's seduction until a more likely candidate came along, as they surely would.

She turned the subject. 'Speaking of fine minds, did you know Mr Maskelyne, Cory?'

'I knew him slightly,' Cory said, buffing the rifle butt until it gleamed in the firelight. 'What are you afraid of, Rae—that I might steal a march on your puzzle-solving through my superior knowledge?'

'No,' Rachel said. 'I merely wondered what you thought of him. He had a great collection of local maps and histories and yet the rest of his library comprised of false books! What use is that?'

Cory put the rifle down and stared at her. In the firelight his face was shadowed and still. 'False books?'

'Yes. Book frontages with blocks of wood behind.' Rachel looked disgusted. 'No one could be a true scholar who fills his shelves with wooden blocks. I found them all when I was clearing the library in order to put out Papa's journal collection.'

'And where are they now?' Cory asked.

'The journals?'

'No, Jeffrey Maskelyne's blocks of wood.' Cory picked up the rifle again and admired his work in the firelight. 'What did you do with them?'

Rachel looked at him. 'That is an odd question, Cory. I stacked them all in boxes and put them in the stables. Why do you ask?'

Cory shrugged. 'No reason.'

'Hmm. You do not generally ask pointless questions.'

'Humour me,' Cory said.

Rachel shrugged in her turn. 'Your behaviour is of the most suspicious,' she said. 'And you have not answered my question, if it comes to that. What manner of man was Jeffrey Maskelyne?'

Cory put his head on one side. 'Maskelyne was the sort of man that you would do well to avoid, Rae. He was a professional lover.'

Rachel gave a little crow of laughter. 'What a splendid description! You mean that he was a rake?'

'Of the worst kind. I believe that many cuckolded husbands and anxious fathers breathed a sigh of relief when he was drowned in the river.'

Rachel arched her brows. 'A rake of the worst kind? Is there any other sort?'

Cory gave her a wry glance. 'I suppose not. But Maskelyne was the worst of all for he had no scruples. And, no—he was not a scholar.'

'It makes one wonder why he went to the trouble of collecting all those maps and making notes on them,' Rachel said thoughtfully. 'I am surprised that he did not find it too taxing.'

'Oh, Jeffrey was not stupid,' Cory said. 'He merely chose to exercise his talents in other directions. All the same, Rae, I should be careful of deciphering Jeffrey's notes. Knowing his interests, I fear that you might find it far too shocking.'

Rachel laughed. 'Perhaps I should ask you to solve it after all. In all of our acquaintance I have yet to see you shocked.' She pushed the packet of food towards him. 'Are you not going to eat? Mrs Goodfellow prepared it especially for you, having heard how much you enjoyed my breakfast this morning!'

'I hope that you did not tell her the full tale of how we met,' Cory said feelingly.

'Of course not,' Rachel said. 'I would not do that to you, Cory. At present Mrs Goodfellow labours under the misapprehension that you are charming. If she heard of your penchant for strolling naked through the undergrowth, she would very likely attack you with her rolling pin and denounce you as a pernicious influence of the sort we do not want in Suffolk. She already believes that London folk are a byword for depravity!'

There was quiet whilst Cory ate some of the bread and cheese. A curlew called down on the mudflat and was answered by the breathy hoot of an owl.

'This is just like old times, is it not?' Cory said. 'Orkney, Egypt, Malta… A camp fire and a tent and the open skies…'

'You make it sound idyllic,' Rachel said. Her memories of the same events were far from rosy—cold, wet, dusty and dirty beyond toleration. She never wanted to see another tent as long as she lived.

'It was idyllic for me.' Cory looked up and gave her a faint smile. 'Why do you think I am out here now instead of enjoying the comforts of Kestrel Court?'

'I did wonder,' Rachel said, unpacking some more of the

food and helping herself to a piece of cheese. 'It is beyond my comprehension that someone who has the hospitality of the Duke of Kestrel at his disposal should choose to be out here cleaning his own rifle by a camp fire under the stars.'

'A good rifleman should always clean his own gun,' Cory said. 'Besides, I have volunteer drill tomorrow morning in Woodbridge and do not wish to disgrace myself.'

'And you had an invitation to a card party at the Langs' this evening,' Rachel said. 'Miss Lang told me herself when I saw her at the reading group today. She was looking forward to meeting you very much.'

Cory's lips twitched. 'I am desolated to disappoint her.'

'No, you are not!' Rachel looked accusing. 'You always do exactly as you please, Cory Newlyn. It is the greatest mystery to me why the ladies fawn on you so much when you treat them with such indifference.'

'There you have your answer,' Cory said, with a shrug of his shoulders.

Rachel looked at him, the indignation swelling within her. The firelight was sliding in slabs of orange and gold across him as he worked, flame and shade, darkness and light. His lean face was shadowed, the expression in his eyes one of concentration as he put the barrel of the gun aside and reached for the pot of oil to grease the mechanism. The tawny hair fell across his brow and tangled in the nape of his neck. Looking at him, Rachel felt a strange rush of pleasure that she could sit here talking to him like this when he would not tolerate other company. Then she felt annoyed at his arrogance.

'Your hair is too long,' she said abruptly.

'Thank you for that,' Cory said, without looking up. 'I shall not allow you to cut it for me. The last time you tried I ended with a fringe that would have graced a lady's shawl.'

'What did you expect? I was only fourteen at the time.'

'And I was twenty-one and a laughing stock. I only permitted you to touch my hair because I did not wish to hurt your feelings.'

'Handsome of you,' Rachel said. 'You would have done better to refuse since it evidently made such an impression on you that you remember it to this day.'

'Whereas you do not?'

'Of course not. I have far greater concerns than your sartorial disasters.' Rachel put her head on one side and studied him. 'On second thoughts, it is better that you do not attend any of the Midwinter social events. I would not wish the ladies to be disappointed in you.'

'Do you think that they would be?' Cory's tone was mild.

Rachel laughed. 'The temptation to give you a set-down is strong, Cory, but I cannot do it in all honesty. No, I do not think they would be disappointed. Your reputation precedes you. The combination of rake and adventurer is utterly lethal. They would expect you to look somewhat dishevelled and be dissatisfied if you did not.'

Cory threw back his head and laughed. 'That is what I like about you, Rachel. Your company is so bracing. You tell it just as it is.'

'Thank you.'

'But I do have to dispute the charge of being a rake,' Cory continued. 'I cannot lay claim to such a title.'

Rachel opened her eyes wide. 'Do you expect me to believe that?'

'On my honour.' Cory shifted. 'I simply do not have the time.'

Rachel stifled a snort of laughter. 'You are claiming that to be a rake requires an investment of *time?*'

'Of course.' Cory put the pot of oil aside and wiped his hands on his trousers. Rachel shuddered. 'Time, energy and strategy,' Cory said. 'Those are the prime requirements for life as a libertine and I am simply too busy.'

'You have evidently studied this in detail,' Rachel observed. 'Do you not have a cloth on which to wipe your hands? You will get oil on the food.'

'What? Oh...' Cory reached behind him for the greasy rag that lay in the grass. He rubbed his hands vigorously. 'That's better.'

'No, it isn't,' Rachel said. 'You have merely managed to spread the oil around more.'

Cory shrugged. 'We are not all of us so orderly as you, Rae.'

'I had noticed it,' Rachel said, wrinkling her nose up. She drew her knees up to her chin, making sure that her skirts were neatly deployed about her ankles. 'So if you did have the time and energy,' she said, 'would the life of a rake appeal to you?'

'No,' Cory said. 'It is far too boring. Compared to antiquities...' He sighed. 'Well, there is no comparison.'

'The charms of the female of the species cannot compare with the thrill of digging up ancient artefacts?' Rachel frowned. 'You are scarce flattering, Cory.'

'You cannot have it both ways,' Cory said, tilting the flask of cider to his lips and leaving dirty fingerprints on it that Rachel could see, even in the firelight. 'You take me to task for flirting and then criticise me for saying that I prefer antiquity hunting to the pursuit of love.' He delved into the packet of food. 'Antiquity hunting is a thrill,' he said, his mouth full. 'The thrill of the chase, the pleasure of discovery, the excitement of exploration...'

'Some people describe love in those terms,' Rachel pointed out.

'Would you?' Cory said.

Their gazes locked, suddenly heated. Rachel could see the flame of the fire reflected in Cory's eyes. The force of his gaze held her spellbound. It was intense and challenging and it asked questions that Rachel had never confronted in her life and stirred feelings in her that she had never experienced before. Her lips parted and she saw Cory's eyes narrow on them, and the jolt of feeling possessed her and made her weak.

'I cannot tell,' she whispered. 'I have no experience on which to judge.'

Cory nodded. He smiled a little. 'I am glad to hear that.'

The tension between them broke abruptly. Released from the strange power that had held her, Rachel felt shaken and cross. She did not really understand what had happened there other than that it had been akin to the odd compulsion that had captured her that morning when she had seen Cory by the river. She wished wholeheartedly to be free of such disturbing emotions.

She fidgeted with the paper wrapper that had covered the food. 'Why should it concern you anyway?' she said crossly. 'I suppose that as my honorary brother you feel obliged to defend my reputation?'

There was an odd note in Cory's voice when he answered. 'Something of the sort,' he said. He looked out across the darkened fields and then suddenly back at her face. 'You are too good for all that, Rachel, for the flirtation and the insincerity and the profligate waste of love. You are...' he hesitated '...too honest to play those games.'

Rachel's heart beat quickly and lightly. 'Dear me,' she said, trying to sound untroubled and only succeeding in sounding hard and unnatural, 'it sounds as though someone has broken your heart, Cory, to turn you so philosophical! Was it Lady Russell, last autumn? I heard that the two of you were inseparable for a while.'

'You heard wrongly,' Cory said. He looked moody. 'I have never had my heart broken, Rae.'

'Perhaps it would be good for you,' Rachel said. 'Sometimes I wish that someone would teach you a lesson.'

Cory looked up and met her eyes. He was unsmiling. 'That is a little unkind of you,' he said.

'Is it?' Rachel frowned. She had been trying to inject

some lightness into their banter and yet it seemed that Cory did not wish to respond. His expression was still sombre.

'I suppose it was a little cruel of me,' she said. 'I beg your pardon, Cory. I thought that we were only funning.'

There was a small silence. Rachel felt awkward. It seemed as though something had gone wrong between them that evening, and yet she could not see what it was. Cory had displayed that masculine high-handedness that always irritated her, insisting that she should be a pattern card of female virtue whilst he, of course, could do as he pleased. She looked at him under her lashes. He still looked morose, which was so unusual for him that she felt a pang.

'I did not mean to be unkind,' she said, anxious to mend the hurt.

Cory glanced up again and smiled at her. Rachel felt her heart ease a little. 'It is not important,' he said. 'It is only that I did not wish you to think that antiquities are the only thing that matter to me and that I cared for no one, Rae.'

Rachel stared, taken aback. 'Of course not! I never thought that. That is, I know that you care for your family, of course, and for my parents, and…' she stuttered, breaking off in unexpected confusion.

'And for you,' Cory said gently. 'I care for you, Rae.'

Rachel looked at him and then looked swiftly away. She felt hot and awkward. 'I… Yes, I know. I mean that I understand that, Cory.'

She heard Cory sigh. 'Here,' he said. 'Take some of the cider before I drink it all and give away all my most closely guarded secrets!'

He passed her the flask. Rachel took it gingerly between her fingers and drank from it, taking care that the oily smears touched neither her skin nor her clothes. Cory watched her, a faint smile on her lips.

'You will spill it if you don't hold it properly,' he said.

'I only want a little,' Rachel said. She felt the liquid trickle down her throat, heady and sweet. 'It is far too strong for me. Indeed, I think it carries on brewing in the bottle. Much more, and I shall be seeing apparitions down here amongst the graves!'

'No ghost would dare set foot out here whilst you are present, Rae,' Cory said wryly. 'Your stern common sense would soon scare them away.'

His words made Rachel feel a strange sadness. 'Is that how you see me?' she said, a little wistfully. 'Stern and practical, with a dislike of dirt?'

'Amongst other things.'

'What other things?'

Cory's head was bent and his expression hidden from her. She felt a sudden powerful desire to shake him until he looked at her. She felt a need to demand an honest answer from him. She was not sure why it was suddenly so important to her to know, only that it seemed the most urgent thing in the world.

Cory started to fit the rifle back together. It interlocked smoothly, with a little click each time a piece fitted into place.

'Sometimes,' he said, 'it is better not to persist.'

Rachel thought about that and then persisted. 'Why?' she asked. 'Do you hold an opinion of me that I would find unflattering?'

Cory sighed. 'Not in the least,' he said. He looked up and there was a smile at the back of his eyes and it made Rachel tingle with a most unforeseen pleasure. 'I do not wish you to get yourself into unexpectedly deep waters.'

They looked at one another. Rachel felt a *frisson* of anticipation.

'Are you about to pay me a compliment?' she asked, eyes wide.

'No,' Cory said. He locked the barrel of the rifle with a final snap.

'Oh.' The warm feeling inside Rachel fizzled out.

'I think I was about to kiss you.' Cory looked at her for a heartbeat. 'What would you have said then, Rae?'

Rachel crushed down the rogue flare of excitement that his words engendered. 'I would have said that you had taken too much of Mrs Goodfellow's inflammatory cider,' she said steadily.

'I do not think that it is the cider that is inflammatory,' Cory said, still holding her gaze, 'but no doubt you are correct, Rae. A kiss between friends is usually a mistake.'

'You sound very knowledgeable on the subject,' Rachel said, 'Do you kiss many of your friends?'

'No,' Cory said. He sighed again. 'When did I kiss you last, Rachel?'

'About fifteen years ago, I think,' Rachel said. 'I had lost my pet rabbit and I think you meant to comfort me. I remember it was a sticky and wet kiss and I wished you had not bothered. And anyway, I found the rabbit the next day.'

Cory laughed. 'A salutary tale! It is getting late. I will escort you back to the house.'

He put out a hand and pulled Rachel to her feet. His touch was warm and strong and she resisted the urge to hold on tightly and pull him closer. He let her go and bent to drag the charred branches from out of the fire, scattering the embers until they died away. Immediately the night seemed darker and less friendly. The crescent moon cast barely a glow. Rachel shivered.

'I wish I had thought to bring a lantern. It is strange how different it feels out here when it is full dark.'

'Take my hand and then if we fall over it will be together.' Cory's voice came out of the nearby shadows and sounded reassuring. Rachel gingerly put her hand out and touched the material of his sleeve. She jumped.

'Oh, I had forgot that I was sitting on your jacket.' She picked it up and started to brush the earth from it but Cory stopped her.

'Do not take the trouble. It will not make the slightest

difference. It is beyond saving, I fear.' He shrugged himself into it and bent down to pick up the rifle, holding his spare hand out to Rachel. 'Come on, Rae.'

Rachel took his hand. It felt odd to be holding hands like they had done when they were younger. The memories crowded in on her there in the dark. She was running along a white sand beach in Scotland, clasping Cory's hand and laughing when she was eight to his fourteen; she was grabbing hold of Cory and holding him tightly with grief when her pet lizard had died in Egypt the following year; she was taking his hand in a country dance at her first ball... She interlocked her fingers with his and held him close. It felt familiar—and subtly different.

They managed to reach the stable yard without falling into a barrow and when they were at the back door of the house Cory let go of her and turned to face her, resting the butt of the rifle on the ground.

'Goodnight, Rae,' he said. He smiled into her eyes. 'I enjoyed this evening.'

'Cleaning your rifle?' Rachel said lightly.

'It has its own peculiar charm,' Cory agreed gravely. He hesitated, then bent forward and kissed her. His cheek brushed hers, hard against her softness. Rachel's skin shivered.

'A kiss between friends,' she said lightly. 'One might even go so far as to say a brotherly kiss.'

For the second time that night she saw a flash in Cory's eyes that was wholly masculine but far from brotherly. It was a look that spoke of desire and conjured wanton images of tangled bed sheets and naked skin and all the things that Rachel had read about and never associated with her own life and in particular had never thought of in conjunction with Cory Newlyn, her childhood friend. She opened her mouth to speak, though she had no notion what she was about to say, and in the same instant Cory took a very purposeful step towards her.

The door of the house opened abruptly and Sir Arthur Odell appeared in the doorway, the *Antiquarian Review* trailing from one hand and his reading glasses clasped in the other.

'What the devil is going on here? Can a man have no peace in his own home? I am *trying* to concentrate on Crabbe's report on the Lincolnshire excavations!'

Rachel dragged her gaze from Cory's face, though the action seemed to take an inordinate amount of effort.

'There is no need to create a fuss, Papa,' she said. 'It is only Cory and I. We have been down at the excavation site.'

'Oh.' Sir Arthur looked nonplussed. 'I thought that some knavish creature was out to rob us.'

'Not at all, Papa,' Rachel said. 'And I do not believe that we can have been making a great deal of noise.' She took his arm. 'Come along inside now. Goodnight, Cory.'

Cory's gaze had not wavered from her during the entire exchange; though Rachel had not been looking at him she had felt him watching her. Now he bowed slightly. 'Goodnight, Rae,' he said. 'I will see you in the morning.'

He walked off in the direction of the stable and Rachel shook herself out of the strange, heated lethargy that seemed to possess her. For a second she leaned back against the door, feeling the handle cold against her hot palm. Perhaps she had imagined that flash of desire in Cory's eyes, but she did not think so. Nor could she dismiss the answering spark it had lit deep within her. From their very first meeting that morning, something had changed between them. She did not understand it and she was not sure that she liked it. She wanted their old friendship back, with all its comforting familiarity. She stood still for a moment, letting the cool breeze touch her face and calm her mind. Cory was her friend and her parents' colleague. He would never flirt with her or try to seduce her. Very likely he did not even wish to and she had imagined the whole thing. There was nothing to fear at all.

Yet still she wondered.

Chapter Five

'No,' Cory said. 'I won't do it, Rachel. I will not be an exhibit in Lady Sally's book of watercolours. The idea is absurd.' His set his jaw in a stubborn line. His silver gaze was hard. He shovelled another heap of earth out on to the pile to his right with unnecessary vigour.

He heard Rachel sigh. She was sitting on an upturned bucket at the side of the trench where Cory was digging. She had only been persuaded to sit down after the bucket had been thoroughly dusted—and after he had assured her that he was unlikely to dig up any bones, at least while she was there.

It was the day after the meeting of the reading group at Saltires and Cory acknowledged wryly to himself that he should have realised that Rachel would come back from it fired with Lady Sally's charitable zeal. In fact, he was a little surprised that she had not broached the subject immediately the previous night. Rachel was usually extremely direct with him; once she had an idea in her head, she could not be dissuaded.

Cory had already heard about Lady Sally's book of watercolour drawings from his host, the Duke of Kestrel, who had been petitioned to take part when he had met Lady Sally at the Langs' card party the previous night. Justin Kestrel had laughed at the idea, but had not been opposed to it. Cory was less enthusiastic.

Rachel tilted her parasol to shield her face from the sun. She looked composed and unruffled and it made Cory smile that she was the only person he knew who could sit in the middle of an excavation and look as though she was at a duchess's garden party.

Cory shoved his spade into the sand and rubbed the back of his hand across his forehead. Digging was a dirty business. He probably smelled of sweat already. No doubt Rachel would tell him if he needed to take a bath. She had been indelicate enough to speak of such things plenty of times in the past since they were friends and there was no artifice between them.

'Why did you not ask me about this when you came back from the reading group yesterday?' he asked. 'Why put it off?'

He thought that Rachel looked a little evasive.

'I knew that you would refuse,' she said morosely.

Cory laughed. 'Then why did you ask me at all?'

'I did not wish to make assumptions,' Rachel said, 'but I thought I knew you well enough to guess your answer.'

'You know me well enough to predict my reactions to most things,' Cory observed.

He saw a tiny frown dip between Rachel's brows as she pondered this. She looked a little uncomfortable with the thought but did not reply, and after a minute Cory returned to his digging. If Rachel knew him well, then he also knew her. She was stubborn. He had not heard the last of the watercolour book yet. In fact, he would lay money that she would return to the topic within the next five minutes. He dug out a few more feet of trench—and waited. It took two minutes, not five.

'Why will you not agree to pose for the book, Cory?' Rachel asked. 'It is one of Lady Sally's charitable ventures and all in a good cause.'

Cory looked up and adjusted the rim of his disgusting hat to shade his eyes from the sun. Rachel's brown gaze was steady and curious on him. Clearly she saw nothing wrong in a parade of eligible men being flaunted in order to sell Lady Sally's book. Cory set about disabusing her.

'Rachel, I dislike the idea of being exhibited like a piece of meat, to titillate the female appetite!' He stuck his spade into the earth in an impatient gesture. 'I can see the description now: Cory, Lord Newlyn, six foot one inch tall, possessed of an income of forty thousand a year and estates in Northamptonshire and Cornwall…' he made a noise of disgust '…and various other assets that an enterprising young lady might like to discover for herself!'

Rachel gave a peal of laughter. 'I had no notion that you were such a stuffed shirt, Cory. You have always been willing for the ladies to examine your assets up until now! Look at you down by the river!'

Cory did not reply. He felt irritable. He disliked the idea that he was a killjoy who was not prepared to help Lady Sally in her charitable venture. Damn it, he was always prepared to contribute to a good cause. What he was not prepared to do was to pose for the book. He was well aware that it was just an excuse for what was essentially a husband-hunter's handbook and he preferred to do the hunting himself rather than be a target for desperate females. He also preferred the whole business to be rather more subtle. This so-called book seemed to him to be a blatant excuse to parade a few eligible men before the young ladies of the *ton*.

'Why do you think that I *should* take part?' he asked abruptly.

Rachel had been idly watching her father, who was sifting a sieve full of soil on to the spoil heap further down the field. Now she looked up and focussed on him again. There was a faint smile still lingering about her mouth and the same hint of curiosity in her eyes. Cory knew that she was surprised by his reticence and that she did not really understand his reasons for refusing. She knew that he was neither naïve nor coy. After all, she had seen the proof of it herself.

'Why, because it is for charity—' she began.

Cory put up a hand. He held her gaze. 'Yes, I accept that. But why me?'

He saw puzzlement come into her eyes. Rachel had very beautiful eyes, speckled brown, gold and green. Taken all together, her features were pleasing, although Cory knew that she did not think so herself. But then, why should she, with no one to tell her? Lady Odell would be more likely to praise the attractive qualities of a Grecian urn than to extol her daughter's virtues. As for him, he had given up attempting to pay Rachel compliments for he was unhappily aware that she did not take them seriously. She gave his admiration the same weight that she attached to his casual affection for a pet kitten.

'Why you?' Rachel repeated. Her brow wrinkled slightly. 'I suppose…because you are an attractive man.'

Cory raised his brows. 'Do *you* think me attractive?'

Rachel looked slightly confused. 'Well, I…I mean that you would generally be considered attractive. By other ladies.'

Cory grinned. 'A fine distinction. You yourself do not believe it, then?'

Rachel's chin tilted up haughtily. 'I have never really thought about it.'

Cory found that this rankled. He kept his gaze on Rachel's face. A tinge of colour had come into her cheeks and though she held his eyes for a few seconds, she was the first to look away. Cory felt a rush of arrogant, masculine pleasure. So *that* was a lie. Rachel had looked at him and thought him attractive and the knowledge pleased him far more than it ought to have done. He sighed inwardly. Last night he had known that there was something between them when he had looked at her in the firelight and seen an echo of his own passion in her gaze. He had known then that he should not take matters further and he knew it now. There was a wariness between them at the moment and he suspected that it was largely down to the unease he had stirred in Rachel through his behaviour. He was slightly surprised that she had come to see him today. Cory looked around. There were plenty of other people on the excavation site and no doubt she felt quite safe. And at the moment he need not worry that he was arousing anything other than annoyance in her. She was looking at him with something approaching dislike.

'I always said that you were odiously conceited, Cory,' she said, crossly. 'Why do I have to join the list of females swooning at your feet? Can you not accept that there is at least one woman who isn't tempted?'

Cory laughed. Rachel always gave as good as she got and he enjoyed that. 'Oh, I can accept it, Rae,' he said easily. 'My self-respect is not damaged if you fail to acknowledge my attractions! I should like to know, however, what sort of man you do find irresistible.'

'I do not wish to find any man irresistible,' Rachel said. 'To my mind that argues a lack of self-control.'

Cory raised his brows. This was interesting. 'You mean that you would not wish to lose your head over a gentleman?'

'Certainly not.' Rachel picked up a shard of pottery apparently at random and turned it over between her fingers. Her head was bent and her cheeks a little flushed.

'You cannot envisage yourself being swept away by passion?' Cory pursued. He liked the fact that he could discompose her like this. It made the awareness between them much sharper.

Rachel was looking horrified. 'Good gracious, no! Swept away by passion? That would be very...'

'Untidy?'

Rachel flashed him a reproachful look. 'I know that you mean to make fun of me, Cory—'

'On my honour, no.' Cory smiled ruefully. He had to confess that he enjoyed teasing her and shaking her self-possession, but he found that he really did want to know the answer to his question. Both his questions. He was intrigued to know the sort of man who would appeal to Rachel. He was even more interested in finding out her attitude to passion.

Rachel spoke in a sudden rush. 'I do not seek romantic love as a basis for marriage. In fact—' she looked up suddenly and met Cory's eyes '—I have decided that I should start to look for a husband. A prudent man whom I can esteem would be my idea of a perfect match.'

Cory had not been expecting this. He felt as though someone had jabbed him hard in the ribs, temporarily depriving him of breath. Rachel was looking to *marry?* The thought made him feel physically sick. And yet, what could be more natural than that she should seek to wed? She had already told him that she was tired of the constant uprooting that came with her parents' mode of life. No doubt the idea of a worthy man and a settled home held immense appeal. The fact that the thought made him feel like doing some kind of injury to the as-yet-unidentified bridegroom was a problem that he would have to deal with himself.

'I am surprised that you have not had offers before now,' he said slowly. 'There was a fellow pursuing you during your London season, was there not?'

'Lord Sommersby.' Rachel nodded. 'He seemed quite ardent, but then Papa insisted on leaving London early in order to travel to Greece and I was not permitted to stay…'

'A good thing too,' Cory said with feeling. 'Sommersby is a dreadful loose fish, Rachel. He is in no way a prudent gentleman.'

Rachel gave him a small smile. 'Since I have been in

Midwinter I have been driving with Mr Caspar Lang. He seems quite pleasant—'

'Pleasant, yes. Prudent, no,' Cory said, laughing. 'The Langs do not have a feather to fly, Rachel, and Caspar gambles away what money he does have.'

Rachel frowned. 'But he is a vicar's son!'

Cory looked up. 'Which proves…what?'

Rachel's frown deepened. 'Are you implying that Mr Lang is only interested in my money?' she asked.

'Not at all,' Cory said. He eyed her angry pink face. 'Mr Lang would be a fool if that was all that interested him about you,' he said. 'However, I *am* implying that if he got his hands on your fortune he would run through it in one sitting at White's.'

Rachel scuffed the earth irritably. 'There is no need for you to sound so pious, Cory. I recall you telling me that you had spent a goodly portion of *your* inheritance on drink and gambling and women!'

'That was money well spent,' Cory said, grinning. 'The rest of my fortune I wasted.'

Rachel glared at him. 'Very witty, Cory. So do you have any other animadversions to cast on your fellow fortune-hunters before I throw myself away on an unworthy man?'

Cory reached for the flask of water and took a thoughtful swig. 'Of course.'

'On the principle that it takes a scoundrel to recognise a man cut from the same cloth?'

Cory winced. He was accustomed to sparring with Rachel but, because he cared for her, her barbs could draw blood. 'You are harsh, Rae,' he said. 'I could give you some advice if you wish.'

'Please do.'

'Then avoid Mr Lang since he is a wastrel. Sir John Norton is a rogue who would invite you out for a sail in his yacht and then seduce you, and all the Kestrel brothers…'

Cory shook his head. 'What can I say? They are excessively dangerous.'

'And Mr James Kestrel, their cousin?'

'Ah.' Cory laughed. 'Yes, the white sheep in a family of reprobates. The only danger you would be in from him, Rae, was of being bored to death!'

Rachel sighed sharply. 'I am beginning to think that I am unlikely to meet an eligible man in the Midwinter villages this summer. Either they are all gamblers or they are like your friends the Kestrels!'

Cory felt strangely relieved. 'Indeed, you are right. Give up the plan! Almost all the gentlemen here are rogues and scoundrels of the most unreliable sort.'

Rachel's eyes lit with laughter. 'Are you including yourself in that description, Cory?'

'If you like. But we have already established that I would not make the ideal husband, have we not, Rae?'

Rachel looked troubled and Cory felt a rather sweet tenderness for her swell inside him. It was the most damnable thing being Rachel's friend. It made him dreadfully vulnerable to her—in so many ways.

'I am sure that you would be ideal for someone,' she said.

Cory laughed. 'Now you are just being kind. And you have no need to soothe my ruffled feelings, I assure you.' He smiled at her. 'Besides, we were speaking of you, Rae, not of me. I assume from what you say that you do not look to marry for love at all.'

Rachel's troubled expression did not lighten. 'I would hope to have an affection for my husband.'

Cory's silver grey eyes sought hers. 'I am speaking of passion, Rae, of strong feelings. Are you sure that you have no wish to experience that within marriage?'

Rachel's eyelashes fluttered and she stole a look at him. 'No, I do not look for that. I fear I am not moved to strong passions.'

Cory was shocked at the sudden wave of desire that

slammed through him, echoed by a disturbing compassion. There was a shy, unawakened look in Rachel's eyes as she spoke of matters of which she had no knowledge. Cory knew it would be the most appalling waste for Rachel to commit herself to a loveless marriage. He knew her to be thoughtful and kind-hearted and loving. And he was willing to bet any money that beneath her composure was a passion strong enough to destroy all a man's defences and burn him down. But he would not be the man to find out if that was true.

Rachel was biting her lip now and Cory clamped down on the urge to kiss her. To step outside the role of elder brother would do neither of them any good. Instead he took a careful breath and gave her a gentle smile. 'I wish you good fortune, Rae. I hope that you find what you are looking for.'

Rachel gave him a smile of such dazzling brilliance that Cory's heart missed a beat.

'Thank you, Cory,' she said. She scrambled to her feet. 'I must go. There is still some unpacking to be done and dinner to be prepared.'

Cory put out a hand to her. He wanted to be with her even though it was, in some ways, a terrible temptation to him. 'Stay here with me for a while. We have barely had chance to talk yet—'

But Rachel was already halfway down the path to the stile. Cory watched her go, a slight frown on his face. It felt as though she was running away from him. Cory clenched his fists, then slowly relaxed. Perhaps he had frightened her, stirring everything up with his comments about passion and his refusal to stay neatly in the place marked out for him as her friend. He could tell that she was uncomfortable with the idea of their friendship changing into something else and yet it was not dislike of him that made her run away. He had seen the mix of desire and curiosity in her eyes the previous morning by the river, heard the breathless note in

her voice last night when she had made light of his suggestion that he might kiss her…

He picked up his trowel again and sighed as he started to
scrape away at a piece of pottery half-buried in the edge of
the trench. His trowel caught the lip of the vessel and it
shattered, several shards tumbling down into the ditch. Cory
swore. He bent to pick them up and stood cradling them in
his hand, looking in the direction that Rachel had gone. So
now she was coming between him and his work. He was
thinking about her when he should be concentrating.

Cory placed the pieces of pottery in a basket and shook
his head slowly. He knew that he was fortunate to have
Rachel Odell as a friend. He would be a fool to put that
friendship at risk when it was one of the most precious
things that he possessed. Nor could the friendship grow into
anything else, for they wanted different things. In fact, he
epitomised all the things that Rachel was rejecting, the
travel and the excitement and the restlessness of an unsettled
life.

Nevertheless, Cory watched her all the way back to the
house. Despite his best intentions and Rachel's wariness, he
had the conviction that something had to change.

In the cool of the hallway Rachel paused and pressed her
palms to her hot cheeks. She was not at all sure why she
was feeling so disturbed. It was not simply the heat of the
day that had made her feel so light-headed, for she had lived
in far hotter climates than Suffolk in June. The conversation
with Cory had made her feel self-conscious, and then she
had compounded her folly by rushing away from him. No
doubt he would think she had run mad. She was half-
persuaded that she had. Cory had never had that effect on
her before. At least not before their encounter by the river
the previous day. Since then something about his behaviour
towards her had unsettled her. He had disturbed her the
previous night and he had done so again now…

'*Do* you *think me attractive?*'
'*I have never really thought about it.*'

But she had thought about it. She had thought about it and she had looked at him and in that moment she had *felt*, not seen, what a very attractive man he was. The knowledge was so sudden and so shocking that she had been completely dumbfounded. It had been like the moment he had swept her into his arms at her début ball, only much more powerful. It felt exciting and it felt all wrong, because Cory was her friend and she simply did not think of him in such terms. And when he had fixed her with that clear grey gaze and asked her about passion, she had remembered his comment about kissing her and had felt a wrench of anticipation shiver along her nerve endings, and a most unaccustomed warmth in the pit of her stomach. She had *wanted* Cory to kiss her, but when he had smiled and gravely wished her luck, she had also felt a huge relief.

She looked at her reflection in the pier glass. Her eyes were bright, her cheeks flushed. She looked rather pretty. Rachel stared, arrested by the sight of her high colour and sparkling gaze. She looked…excited. She looked as though in some strange way her feelings were awake…

The opening of a door further down the hall distracted her. Sir Arthur Odell emerged, head bent, peering over his glasses at the papers in his hand. His dirty boots left a trail of sand across the stone floor. He narrowly missed colliding with a small rosewood table. Rachel moved it to one side and put her hand on her father's arm. Sir Arthur jumped.

'Oh! Didn't see you there, m'dear.'

'No,' Rachel said. 'What are you doing inside, Papa? I thought you were down at the dig.'

'Just came up to read this.' Sir Arthur said, eyes gleaming. 'Cook told me the post had arrived. The Royal Society Journal has an article by Cory on the Wiltshire barrows. Damned fine piece of writing. His conclusions are all wrong, of course, but can't dispute that he writes well. Must tell the boy. He's a damned fine antiquary, even if he draws the wrong inferences…' And he wandered out through the front door, the sand dropping from his boots and being trodden underfoot.

Rachel sighed and went through to the kitchen in search of a brush. Mrs Goodfellow, the cook, was standing at the table chopping carrots and grumbling under her breath in continuous monotone. Rachel smiled at her.

'Good morning, Mrs Goodfellow. Why are you doing the vegetables? What has happened to Kitty this morning?'

Mrs Goodfellow's grumpy face had melted into a reluctant smile at the sight of Rachel. She wiped her hands on a cloth and rested them on her broad hips. 'Good morning, my duck. Kitty's down at the excavations this morning.' She snorted. 'Your mama said they needed help with sorting the pots they've dug out, so the next thing I know, Kitty ups and offs down there. Any excuse. She's got her eye on that man of Lord Newlyn's, if you ask me.'

Rachel smiled slightly. Kitty, the kitchen maid, was no slouch when it came to spotting a likely young man, and Cory's valet, Bradshaw, was a very well set-up lad indeed.

'There's just me and Rose,' Mrs Goodfellow continued, nodding at the lumpy housemaid, 'and she's kept busy washing the pots your mama is digging out.' She gave a sudden bellow of laughter, her chins wobbling. 'Your mama asked if I'd like to help out today, Miss Rachel. Can you see me in a trench? I'd likely sink in the sand and need to be dug out myself!'

'I'm sure that you would do a splendid job, Mrs Goodfellow,' Rachel said, 'but we need you here. If my parents persist in borrowing all the servants to help run their excavation, we shall all starve.'

'Wouldn't catch me down there,' Mrs Goodfellow said, picking up her chopping knife again and attacking another carrot with gusto. 'I've seen those ghosts, so I have, Miss Rachel, and I'm keeping well away!'

Rachel frowned. She had come across superstitious servants often on her travels, but would not have placed Mrs Goodfellow as one of them. Her practical common sense had always seemed much like Rachel's own, leaving no room for fanciful ideas.

'Ghosts, Mrs Goodfellow?' she said. 'Surely you don't believe in such nonsense?'

'Seen them with my own eyes,' the cook said bluntly, 'flitting about down there on the mounds in the moonlight.'

'Ghosts flitting about in the moonlight? Have you been having a bedtime tipple, Mrs Goodfellow?'

Cory Newlyn had come into the kitchen, his hands full of pottery. Bradshaw was following him in with a bucket full of shards. Rachel jumped at the sight of him, then winced as more sandy soil was trampled into the house.

Mrs Goodfellow beamed at the newcomers. 'No need for your sauce, my lord! I haven't touched a drop since my John died. No, and I know what I've seen as well. Men with shields and helmets on, just like in the history books.'

Cory raised his brows. 'Men with shields? Really? We have just found some bits of Anglo-Saxon pottery, so who knows, you may be right, Mrs Goodfellow.'

He put the pot gently into the sink and gave the housemaid his heart-shaking smile. 'I do apologise for bringing you all this extra washing up, Rose…'

Rose looked as though she was about to melt under the warmth of Cory's smile. She bobbed a curtsy and mumbled something incoherent.

'It's no trouble,' Mrs Goodfellow said, changing her tune rather smartly. 'Anything for you, my lord.'

Rachel smothered an unladylike snort. She suspected that more than one woman had said that to Cory in his time.

'I could lend you Bradshaw later if you have any heavy jobs need doing,' Cory offered. 'By way of a thank you.'

Mrs Goodfellow eyed the valet. 'Thank you, my lord, but no. I don't want my girls' heads stuffed with any more silly ideas than are already there. You keep the lad with you and out of trouble.'

Rose giggled and blushed.

Rachel came forward to have a look at one of the pieces that Cory was washing gingerly in the sink. Clearly this was too delicate to be entrusted to Rose, and when she saw it Rachel could understand why. It was a drinking horn with a decorated metal rim and, though it was a little battered and had a piece missing, it was still very beautiful.

'How lovely! I wonder who this belonged to...'

Cory gave her his swift smile. He leaned closer, so close that his hair brushed her cheek and momentarily distracted her. His shirt sleeves were rolled up to the elbow and Rachel was taken by an insane desire to run her fingers over the smooth nut-brown skin of his arm. She put both her hands behind her back.

'I think it was for feasting and was modelled on an auroch horn,' Cory said. He held it out to her. 'The decoration on the rim is incredibly delicate.'

'It must have been kept for very special occasions,' Rachel said, touching the damp surface very gently. 'I can see Mrs Goodfellow's warriors all sitting around a fire in the great hall, passing the drinking horn and telling their battle stories...'

She looked up from the horn to see Cory smiling at her. She felt her knees go weak and caught hold of the edge of the sink to steady herself, pretending that she was checking the pieces waiting to be washed.

'It is nice to hear you so enthusiastic, Rae,' she heard Cory say. 'I thought you did not care for antiquities.'

'I like history,' Rachel said, trying to concentrate. 'It is all the digging I cannot abide.'

'Ah, then you will not wish to join us this afternoon.'

'No, thank you. I am visiting Mrs Stratton in Midwinter Mallow.' Rachel wiped her hands on a cloth. 'Papa was looking for you, Cory. He has read your article in the journal of the Royal Society.'

'I know,' Cory said. 'I saw him as we were coming in. He told me that my conclusions were all wrong.'

'He told *me* that you were a fine antiquary,' Rachel said. She saw how pleased Cory looked and felt warmed. 'So you had better get back out to the excavation and prove him right.'

Cory went, still smiling, and Rachel felt happy and relieved. Things were back to normal. She and Cory had achieved their old footing and the same easy friendship as before. No doubt everyone felt weak at the knees when Cory smiled at them. It was just his way.

'Yon's a fine gentleman,' Mrs Goodfellow said, pointing her knife in the direction that Cory had gone. 'Surprised you did not snap him up years ago, Miss Rachel.'

'Oh, Cory and I are just friends, Mrs Goodfellow,' Rachel said airily. 'Nothing more.'

She bent to sweep up the dirt on the floor and therefore completely missed the cook's look of transparent disbelief. Mrs Goodfellow even went so far as to roll her eyes and shake her head, setting Rose the maid off into a paroxysm of silent laughter.

'Friendship, eh?' Mrs Goodfellow murmured, as Rachel went outside to put the sand back where it belonged. 'The Quality can never see what's under their noses. They say that love is blind, Rose, but Miss Rachel gives a whole new meaning to the notion!'

And Rachel, pausing by the sand pit in the courtyard, was busy proving that very point for she found herself standing staring in the direction that Cory had gone, long after his tall figure had disappeared.

Chapter Six

A meeting of a very different nature from that of the reading group took place at Kestrel Court that night. Although the June dusk lingered, the curtains were drawn tightly and the candles were lit. Cory Newlyn joined the Duke of Kestrel and his two younger brothers, Richard and Lucas, in the drawing room, where Justin Kestrel dispensed glasses of brandy to the gentlemen and then put forward a certain proposal.

It was lucky that his companions had strong drink with which to fortify themselves, for the shock was extreme.

Cory was the first to regain his breath. 'I beg your pardon, Justin, but you wish us to do *what*, precisely?' he said incredulously. A look of complete disbelief spread across his face. 'Forgive me, but I thought that you said that, in order to trap the Midwinter spy, you wanted us to make love to the ladies of the Midwinter villages!'

Justin Kestrel sat back in his armchair and tilted his brandy glass to his lips. A smile lingered in his eyes as he surveyed the consternation on the faces of his guests. 'You heard me correctly, Cory,' he said. 'That is exactly what we would like you to do.'

Cory and Richard Kestrel exchanged a glance. 'You silence me, Justin,' Richard said, 'and that does not happen very often.' He threw himself down into the chair opposite his brother, completing the circle of three sitting before the fireplace. Lucas Kestrel preferred to stand, restlessly pacing the room whilst the others lounged at their ease.

In the flicker of the candlelight the expressions on the faces of the Duke's guests were varied. Richard Kestrel was a renowned poker player and his face, dark and saturnine, revealed nothing of his feelings. Lucas was looking frankly perplexed at his brother's words. And Cory, who had thought that a day of hard excavation work had made him unnaturally slow and possibly deaf, waited for Justin Kestrel to elucidate, with a half-smile still lingering on his lips.

Cory had come late to the group, for he had met with Justin Kestrel at his club only the week before coming to Suffolk. When Justin had heard that Cory planned to join the Odells at Midwinter Royal, he had immediately invited him to join him at Kestrel Court—and had co-opted Cory to his plan. The broad outline of this was that the Duke of Kestrel was commissioned to catch a French spy who was currently working on the Suffolk coast. The details of the plan to entrap the traitor were just becoming apparent. Cory, who had joined in any number of escapades orchestrated by the Kestrels since their days at Harrow, nevertheless thought that this time Justin might have over-reached himself. Make love to the ladies of the Midwinter villages… There was only one lady who tempted him in that respect and, since making love to Rachel Odell was out of the question, he was destined to a long, celibate summer.

'I had thought that gentlemen of your reputation would take such a suggestion in your stride,' Justin murmured, the calm tone of his voice belied by the twinkle in his eyes as he watched his brothers and his friend. 'Are you rejecting our commission?'

'I thought that we were working on behalf of the Foreign Office, not some Covent Garden bordello,' Cory observed.

'Good God, Justin, when I offered my services this was not quite what I had in mind!'

'One must do one's patriotic duty, I suppose,' Richard Kestrel murmured with a whimsical smile. He rested one broad shoulder against the back of the chair and crossed his legs at the ankle. 'I will accept your commission with pleasure, Justin.'

'Rein in your enthusiasm, Richard,' Lucas said drily, coming to lean against the arm of his brother's chair. 'I believe we should discover the true nature of the task before we get too excited!'

Cory took a deep swallow of the brandy and glanced appreciatively at the glass in his hand. There were many reprehensible things going on in the Midwinter villages, but the smuggling was the one thing that he would be loath to put at an end.

'Thank God you gave us a drink before you sprang that on us, Justin,' he said feelingly. 'I need it! Where do you find your brandy?'

'In a keg under the hedge, I'll wager,' Richard said drily. 'And I cannot blame you, Justin.'

The Duke grinned, but did not deny it. 'Let us be serious for a moment, gentlemen,' he said. He got to his feet and moved across to the table. A map of the county of Suffolk was folded there and Justin opened it, spreading it out on the green baize surface. Richard weighted one corner down with his brandy glass and Lucas took a book from the shelves and placed it on the corner diagonally opposite. The atmosphere in the room had changed from the good-natured banter of a moment previously. All of them knew that there was more to this than a convivial drink among friends and an outrageous commission.

'I realise that you are aware of why we are here,' Justin continued, 'but it might help to recapitulate.' He looked around at their intent faces. 'As you know, gentlemen, this is an invasion coast. It would take a French fleet no more than forty-eight hours to make the crossing from Dunkirk—less, in fair weather. It is generally accepted at the Admiralty that the bulk of the invasion army would be landed in Kent or Sussex, but that a diversionary force could land on the Suffolk coast and cause considerable difficulties.'

The others nodded.

'How many men?' Cory asked.

It was Richard, with his Navy background, who answered, 'Possibly twenty thousand.'

Cory gave a silent whistle. 'Hence the need for well-drilled volunteers to provide support for the regular troops.'

Lucas nodded. 'Exactly. It may not happen, of course, but one must be prepared. But our problem is closer to home. What is the latest intelligence, Justin?'

Justin took up the thread. 'Precious little. We know that French spies have been operating in the Midwinter villages, but we do not know who they are. They have been passing on information about troop movements, harbour defences, even, we suspect, the names of local men who might prove amenable to helping the French ships navigate the rivers—fishermen, smugglers and the like.' His mouth tightened to a grim line. 'Much of the information is in code and we do not know which cipher they are using, nor how the messages are being passed.'

Richard frowned. 'Had Jeffrey Maskelyne not found out any information before his death? I thought he had been working on the problem for some time.'

Justin was shaking his head. 'He had, but he left no record—' He broke off. 'What is it, Cory?'

'Maskelyne did leave something,' Cory said slowly. 'Miss Odell told me yesterday that she had found a collection of false books that Maskelyne left.'

'False books?' Richard frowned.

'Book frontages with nothing but blocks of wood behind,' Cory elaborated, much as Rachel had done. 'I wondered whether there might be a message of some sort hidden in one of them.'

'Any chance you could get a look?' Justin enquired.

Cory nodded. 'I can certainly try, though it would be difficult to explain if Miss Odell noticed what I was up to…'

'I am sure that you can think up a suitably plausible excuse,' Justin said. He shifted slightly. 'We are dealing with damnably clever spies here, gentlemen. These are people who do not make mistakes and do nothing to draw attention to themselves. They give us no clues at all. Hence the need to take a different approach and one that may seem a little…duplicitous at times.'

Lucas's eyes narrowed. 'So, speaking of duplicity… Your theory is that if we lay siege to the hearts of the Midwinter ladies, then we may learn something useful?'

Justin's grim expression lightened slightly. 'In part. Local gossip is often a fertile source of information. There is another reason, however.' He let go of the map and rolled it up with a sharp snap.

'All evidence suggests,' he said, 'that the Midwinter spy is a woman.'

This time the silence went on for a long time. Eventually Cory broke it with a rueful look round at his companions.

'I do not suppose that any of us disputes such a possibility, Justin,' he said, 'but what is the evidence?'

Justin sighed. 'There was a female spy working in Dorset last year. She was almost caught.' His mouth quirked ruefully. 'The reason she was not was because those seeking her found it so difficult to believe that the spy *was* a woman. They traced her to London in the winter, but then she disappeared.'

'And now you suspect that the same woman is here in Midwinter?' Richard questioned.

'That is correct.'

Lucas grimaced. 'Surely there cannot be many suspects who fit the bill? She should be easy to trace…'

Justin smiled. 'That is precisely the problem, Lucas. She is not. And this is a matter of life and death. A man has died and we are no further advanced. The activities of this person are putting thousands of lives at risk. If her information enables the French to mount a successful invasion, then put that at hundreds of thousands.'

'Treason,' Cory said. Put in such stark terms, it hardened his purpose. There could be no allowances made, nor chivalrous gestures. Cory's adventures, both covert and open, had taken him all over the globe and he had no illusions about the capabilities of women. Justin's next words echoed his thoughts precisely.

'There is no room for sentiment here, nor conventional views on the frailty of women, gentlemen. I assure you that our spy is not in the least frail.'

'Does she work alone?' Cory asked.

Justin shrugged. 'Probably not. But the organisation centres on her. Hers is the cool calculation behind all the planning—and hers is the execution.'

'Suspects?' Richard said succinctly.

'The obvious one,' Justin said, 'is Lady Sally Saltire. She is a rich widow, she has the freedom to travel a great deal, she was in London this winter past, and we know her to have the capability to plan such an operation. One has to question what she is doing in a backwater like Midwinter in the first place.'

'Planning a watercolour book to raise funds for charity, so I hear,' Cory said feelingly.

Justin Kestrel laughed. 'Indeed. Which gives us an ideal excuse for becoming involved in Lady Sally's circle. If we were all to volunteer to take part in the book—'

Cory groaned. 'Must we? All experience suggests that you will not need an excuse to become involved in local society, Justin. To the contrary, you will need protection from it! An unmarried Duke with a romantic reputation— you will be under siege!'

'Devil a bit!' Justin said cheerfully. 'I can handle it. I say we should all offer to take part.'

Richard raised his brows. 'I have no objection to the watercolour book, but one has to question your logic in suspecting Lady Sally of spying, Justin.' He hesitated. 'You know her better than anyone and I cannot believe that you would think her a traitor.'

Justin Kestrel's face was drawn. 'I used to know her a long time ago, Richard. I have no idea of her political sympathies now.'

Cory caught Richard's eye. They all knew that Justin had once carried a torch for Sally Saltire. Popular rumour said that he still did. He had never married.

Lucas was leaning over the map. 'Who are our other suspects and where are they situated?'

Justin reached for the brandy bottle and passed it around.

'The Marneys live in Midwinter Mallow,' he said, pointing to the west of the area. 'Ross Marney is a war hero who served in Egypt. He is married to Olivia, a lady of unimpeachable virtue whom I would swear could no more be a French spy than I could. But—one never knows.'

Lucas grimaced. 'And Lady Marney has a widowed sister, if my memory serves me correctly.'

Justin shot him a look. 'She does. Mrs Deborah Stratton. She was married to a soldier who died in action. That alone should give her no love for the French.'

Richard was smiling reminiscently. 'I have met Mrs Stratton before. She certainly has the capability and the intellect to organise an enterprise like this.'

'If you know her already,' Lucas suggested, 'why do you not renew the acquaintance?'

Richard laughed. 'Because she will not give me the time of day, dear brother. We fell out—rather badly—when I asked her to be my mistress last year.'

Cory smothered a laugh. 'Turned you down, Richard?'

Richard toyed with his brandy glass. 'I made the mistake

of not preparing my ground properly,' he said. 'I made some rash assumptions about her virtue—' He broke off and looked around at the circle of cynically smiling faces. 'Damned if I know why I'm explaining myself to all of you!' he said. 'A poor sort of help you can give anyway. Justin cannot douse an old flame, Cory is suffering from unrequited love and you, Lucas—I swear you do not have a heart to lose!'

'Thank you for that masterly summary of our romantic entanglements,' Justin said smoothly. 'Returning to the matter before us, do you wish to try your hand at seducing Mrs Stratton again?'

Cory did not miss the odd look in his friend's eyes as Richard answered his brother. 'No, I do not want to try to seduce Mrs Stratton again. But…I would not mind pursuing the acquaintance if I can persuade her to be civil to me.'

'Another mark up to unrequited love,' Lucas murmured irrepressibly.

'Thank you,' Justin said, his lips twitching. 'Now, I need one of you to devote yourself to Miss Lang, the vicar's daughter. Reverend Lang is an interesting case. He is a disappointed man, turned sour waiting for a preferment that never came. His allegiance may have turned sour as well, and may have infected his daughter.'

Cory nodded. He could see the logic in that. Disaffected clergymen could be the very devil to deal with.

'Is that all?' Lucas enquired.

'Not quite.' Justin pointed to the village of Midwinter Bere. 'There is also Lily, Lady Benedict. Her husband is a housebound invalid and she seems devoted to his interests.'

There was a pause. 'These ladies are all members of Lady Sally Saltire's reading group,' Cory said slowly.

'Reading group?' Richard Kestrel looked interested. 'Tell us more.'

Cory shrugged. 'I do not know much more to tell other than that they meet every week at Saltires.'

Justin and Lucas exchanged glances. 'What a marvellous way that would be to pass on information if one were so inclined,' Justin Kestrel said feelingly. 'This reading group—does it have any other members?'

'Only Miss Odell,' Cory said. 'I doubt that she could be involved, though. The Odells are but lately come to Midwinter.'

'It's not impossible, though,' Richard pointed out. 'Where was Miss Odell recently, Cory? Was it not London?'

Cory scowled. He knew where this was going. Richard was about as subtle as a runaway carthorse. 'I believe it was,' he said coldly.

'And she has travelled a great deal—'

'Not in Dorset,' Cory said, between shut teeth. He felt a rush of fury. It was absolutely ridiculous to imagine that Rachel could be a French spy. He did not dispute that she was intelligent and resourceful enough to do it, but to imagine that she was a traitor was absurd.

'I am merely suggesting that she should not be left out of the investigation,' Richard murmured. 'We must be sure—'

'Richard,' Cory said warningly, 'if you are thinking to get up a flirtation with Miss Odell on the strength of this, then I suggest that you think again!'

Richard raised both hands in a pacifying gesture. 'Wouldn't dare, old chap. You'd probably call me out. Besides, you are the one who knows Miss Odell the best. Perhaps you should take the matter on.'

Cory grimaced. 'My feelings notwithstanding, Miss Odell and I are like brother and sister. If I start making up to her after all these years she will think me run quite mad.' He sighed. 'There is no need. I give you my word that Rachel is no more a French spy than I am.'

Lucas and Richard exchanged a look of covert amusement that Cory fortunately missed. 'No exceptions,' Richard pointed out blandly.

Cory gave an irritable sigh and held on to his temper—just.

'If anyone is to flirt with Miss Odell then it should be me,' Lucas said, blander still. 'I'm not as dangerous as Richard and it will be my pleasure.'

Cory clenched his fists and slowly released them. He had never previously had any urge to inflict an injury on Lucas Kestrel, who was one of his best friends. There was always a first time, however. He took a deep breath and looked into the other man's amused hazel eyes as he tried to clamp down on his fury.

'I try to think of Miss Odell as a little sister, Lucas,' he said heavily, 'so I am hardly likely to encourage one of the greatest rakes in the whole country to flirt with her.' He looked at his friends. Justin was watching him quizzically, there was a laugh lurking in Richard's eyes and Lucas was grinning openly. Cory let his breath out in a long sigh. He was unhappily aware that his feelings for Rachel were as transparent as glass. He raised a warning hand.

'Not another word…'

Justin shook his head. 'We were not going to say anything at all, Cory,' he said innocently. 'Other than good luck, of course!'

Cory sighed. 'I am happy to keep a watching brief at Midwinter Royal House,' he said. 'If I might change the subject slightly, I have already observed that there are some odd things going on there.'

To his relief, his friends took the hint.

'Such as?' Lucas asked.

'Smugglers have been using the burial mounds to store their booty, for one thing,' Cory said. 'There is a lot of disturbance at the eastern end of one of the fields. It made a good hiding place, especially with the legends warning people to keep away from the treasure. I imagine they were not best pleased to hear we were to excavate there.'

'Smugglers,' Richard said thoughtfully. 'A good line of communication with the enemy.'

'Maybe.' Cory grimaced. It seemed that they were positively surrounded by treachery. So much for Rachel's view that the Midwinter villages were a haven of peace.

'Well, whatever you do, please do not interfere with my brandy supply,' Justin said with feeling. He topped up his glass. 'Would anyone care for more?'

The glasses were refilled.

'I suppose,' Lucas said, 'that we should be particularly careful in our dealings with the ladies. I cannot speak for the rest of you, of course, but I do not think we would wish our flirtation to be misconstrued as having a serious purpose. None of us wants to end up in parson's mousetrap.'

There was heartfelt agreement to this. 'How damnably ironic would that be?' Justin said, and they all laughed to think of it.

It was two nights later when Cory Newlyn made an unheralded visit to Midwinter Royal House and slipped through the gate into the stable yard. There was a half-moon, small, silver and bright, above the line of the stable roof. It was a perfect night for a spot of illicit activity, be that smuggling, piracy, spying, or perhaps a little tomb robbing, all of which Cory was certain might occur in the Midwinter villages at any time. The wind had dropped during the evening and barely a whisper stirred the tops of the tall pines down in the burial field. Cory prepared for his own covert activity.

He leaned back against the wall of the stables and waited silently to see if anyone else was moving in the quiet night. It was about two o'clock. Cory had spent a pleasant enough evening at a dinner at Midwinter Marney Hall. His head should have been full of plans for the night, but instead he had found his thoughts had been full of Rachel Odell. To his own disgust he could feel himself becoming as lovesick as a youth in his salad days.

Rachel had looked utterly charming in her pale pink evening gown. With her chestnut hair and brown eyes she had the rich cólouring to carry off a shade that looked so insipid on many of the blonde débutantes. The dress was demure and high-necked, but Cory could not help but admire the way that the material draped so gently over Rachel's curves, concealing but outlining her full breasts and the generous curve of her hips. He suspected that Rachel's dressmaker had cheated her. Without a doubt Rachel had told the woman to make her a gown of irreproachable modesty, but the modiste, with an eye to her professional pride, had created an outfit most flattering to Rachel's figure. Cory smiled to think of that figure now.

His smile vanished. Rachel had not paid him a great deal of attention that evening. During dinner she had been placed next to Caspar Lang and in the impromptu dancing that had followed she had given her hand more than once to Caspar and to various other admirers, including John Norton. It was galling when Cory had warned her away from both Lang and Norton. It was even more annoying that when Cory had approached her for a quadrille, Rachel had apologised and explained that she was spoken for. Lang had been hanging on the back of her rout chair and had smirked in a manner that had made Cory want to strangle him with his own neckcloth. John Norton had also overheard the remark and had laughed as he came to carry Rachel off into the dance. Cory had gone to cool his heels in the card room, but through the open door he could still see Rachel twirling from one end of the set to the other. Under the circumstances, he had swiftly lost the game.

It had been no hardship for Cory to leave Marney Hall early, return to Kestrel Court and prepare to venture out again, less formally dressed and certainly less inclined to draw attention to himself. He needed to sort through Maskelyne's books that Rachel had consigned to the stables, and he could not do it during the day when everyone was involved in the excavation and would notice his absence. There was only a slim chance that Maskelyne would have left any record of his activities in the house, but it was all they had to go on. Hence his presence in the Midwinter Royal stable yard at a time when Rachel was asleep in the room just above his head…

As if in response to this last thought there was a flicker of light above him and a pool of gold spilled from an upstairs window to mingle with the silver moonlight. Cory pressed back into the darkness. It would be disastrous for anyone to see him now, particularly Rachel, who was quite dauntless enough to come downstairs to see what was going on.

He looked up. The curtain at Rachel's window twitched. Cory kept absolutely still. He was sure that he had not made enough noise to attract attention, so what had disturbed Rachel sufficiently to wake her in the middle of the night? Had she not yet retired for the night, or could she not sleep after the excitement of the evening?

The curtain moved and he saw her. She was standing in the window, framed by the candlelight. She was peering out into the darkness. Her dark hair was a cloud that framed her face in a way that lent it an ethereal air.

Cory looked at her and discovered that he did not want to look away. The pale candlelight was behind her now and it shone through the insubstantial white nightdress that she was wearing, illuminating in glorious detail a view of Miss Rachel Odell that he had never been vouchsafed before. Cory smothered a grin. He was no gentleman to be standing here and staring, but since the opportunity had presented itself he was not going to turn it away. In the shadowy light he could see all Rachel's curves, previously only hinted at beneath her neat and tidy exterior. Cory's smile deepened. Her waist was small and nipped in, and her breasts were luscious. He could see the shadow of the cleft between them and the darker smudge of her nipples against the lawn of the nightdress. And lower, where the outline of her thighs pressed against the thin material, he could see…

Cory realised that he could not actually see anything, since the window sill cut Rachel off neatly at the waist, but his imagination filled in the gaps in intimate detail. His body hardened with desire and at the same time his mind intervened and slammed him up hard against a metaphorical wall. This was *Rachel* he was lusting after, Rachel whose soft body he wanted to tumble beneath his own, Rachel whom he wanted to kiss senseless and make love to until she cried out with a passion to match his own. Yet only the previous day, when they had talked of love and passion, he had sworn to himself that she could be no more than his honorary little sister. What the *hell* did he think that he was doing?

Cory pressed the palms of his hands against the rough brick of the stable wall and forced himself to look away. He was sweating with the effort of controlling his body and fighting off the images that plagued his mind. The night air touched his face and turned the sweat cold. He screwed his eyes up in agony.

When he glanced back at the window, the light had gone and the night was dark again. Cory let his breath ease out of him in a long sigh. It had to be a momentary aberration. He would never think about Rachel in that way again. Because if he did, it would turn a lot of his life's certainties upside down and nothing could be the same again.

Cory deliberately dismissed the episode from his mind and a moment later softly, carefully, edged his way around the side of the stable block. A cool little breeze scattered stray pieces of straw across the cobbles. It masked the lifting of the latch as he opened the stable door and stepped inside.

He stopped just inside the door and edged it closed, but left it unlatched. The thin sliver of moonlight cut out, and he was standing in the darkness, the tickly smell of hay in his nostrils and the dusty shadows pressing close. He did not move for at least a minute. Cory had been in some dangerous and unusual situations in his life and the one thing that he had learned from them all was never to make hasty decisions and always to be on his guard. His instinct was telling him now that something was amiss. Someone had been there before him.

He struck a light and looked about him in the flare of the flame. The stable was empty of everything but a mound of old hay, for the Odells did not keep a carriage. Cory trod softly across the cobbled floor and looked into the end stall. When he had collected Castor earlier in the day he had taken the opportunity to locate the pile of false books that Rachel had thrown out of the library. They were stacked neatly away in the corner of the final stall.

Or, at least, they had been. Now they were scattered across the cobbles, the covers ripped off, the wooden blocks splintered. Cory bent down slowly and picked one of them up. As Rachel had said, they were beautifully made. Each block of wood was cut to exactly the same size and each had an elegant printed leather cover stuck to the front. When they had been displayed on the library shelves it would have been impossible to tell from a distance that they were not real books. Now they were fit for nothing but the fire.

Cory gave a heavy sigh and straightened up. Evidently someone other than himself had heard about Jeffrey Maskelyne's collection of false books. Knowing Rachel, it was entirely possible that she had shared the information with Lady Sally's reading group, deploring the philistinism of a man who had to fill his bookshelves with fakes...

He felt a cool draught on his skin and a sudden shiver down his neck as all the hairs stood on end. He had not heard the stable door open, but now he realised that he had made a potentially fatal mistake. For one split second he had forgotten to be careful.

And in that second the blade of a dagger touched the skin of his throat and lingered there like a caress.

Chapter Seven

Rachel had been unable to sleep. She had tossed and turned, trying to find a comfortable position in the big four-poster bed. There had been a panel of bright moonlight that had crept through a gap in the curtains and illuminated the mantelpiece and a patch of the floor. It disturbed her. Rachel knew that sooner or later, she would have to get up and close the curtains properly. When she finally gave in and did so, she could not help but glance out of the window. The moon was high and the burial mounds were illuminated in black and silver, shadows flowing into darker shadows in a way that was as beautiful as it was mysterious. Nothing moved in the landscape, although Rachel could hear the soft rush of the river away to her right, and the breathy call of the tawny owl in the copse. With a sigh, she put out a hand to draw the curtains, pausing as a flicker of movement caught her eye. Someone was creeping around the edge of the stables.

Rachel almost drew the curtains and left them to it, for, in her opinion, anyone who wished to sneak around an An-glo-Saxon burial site in the dark was clearly quite unhinged. Then she thought of all the hard work that her parents had put into the site. They had not found the Midwinter Treasure yet, nor anything of any great value, but they had catalogued and preserved a great many artefacts that would be of interest to the Saxon scholars at the British Museum. It would be a shocking pity if their work should be sabotaged by an intruder.

Rachel was not afraid of confronting prowlers. She had single-handedly taken on an angry mob in Egypt when they had tried to wreck her parents' excavation and had vanquished a tomb robber in Derbyshire by hitting him over the head with a seventh-century pot. With an angry swish, she pulled the curtain back into place, then went over to her cupboard. She rummaged about inside, emerging with a thick cloak and a pair of stout outdoor boots. The ensemble was rather haphazard and would gain no plaudits from the fashionable, but Rachel did not care. Even though it was summer and had not rained for weeks, she was taking no chances on flimsy footwear. She did not stop to check her reflection in the mirror. Picking up her candle, she opened the bedroom door.

The moonlight spilled over the floor of the landing and lay in threads down the staircase. Rachel tip-toed down the stairs, holding the candle in one hand and the hem of her cloak up in the other. She paused at the bottom, toying with the idea of rousing her father to come and help, but then she dismissed the thought. Sir Arthur Odell would insist on bringing his blunderbuss and making an unconscionable amount of noise. It would be better to check out the situation and return for help if it was required. After all, it might be that she had simply spotted a poacher. Even so, Rachel paused to remove a medieval dagger from the wall. She had borrowed it before and found just the sight of it made most would-be villains think twice. It also made her feel much, much safer.

The sound of the bolt drawing back on the big front door was loud in the silence, and the crunch of the gravel under Rachel's boots even more so. At any moment she expected to hear an enraged shout from her father, demanding to know what was going on and putting all miscreants to flight. But there was silence. Nothing stirred under the moon.

Rachel had left the candle in the hall, thinking its light would be drowned out by the moonlight, but the loss of its warm flame made her feel slightly nervous and she wished that she had brought a lantern. She crept along the edge of the house until she reached the gate into the stable yard. In the daylight it did not seem very far. Now it felt like a mile. She slipped through into the cobbled yard. The gate swung open without a creak and Rachel blessed the fact that she had had the hinges oiled only the previous day.

She stood by the fence, scanning the yard. Her eyes must have been deceiving her. There was no one here.

Then she saw the movement. Once again it was no more than a flash on the edge of her vision, but it brought her head around sharply. Someone was in the stables and they had struck a light.

Rachel had no thought to challenge anyone unless they were actually stealing something, and the chances of that seemed remote, for the stable held none of the antiquity finds and precious little besides. Nevertheless she was curious as to the identity of the mystery intruder. She crept along the side of the stables until she could peer through the window.

The inside of the stables was dark, but for a corner where a small lantern was set on the cobbled floor. A man was crouched beside it, methodically sorting through the books that Rachel had stacked there only a few days previously. Except that now they were not neatly stacked. They were scattered across the stone floor in a haphazard muddle that made her furious. Covers were ripped from the wood; splinters lay in the grooves between the cobbles. It was the most unconscionable mess.

The lamplight fell on the man's tawny hair, but Rachel hardly needed it as a means of identification. She would have recognised Cory Newlyn anywhere, for she had seen him so many times in so many different stances that the images were familiar and unquestioned. With an exclamation of wrath she retraced her steps to the stable door and pushed it open.

She had been intending to declare her presence immediately, but when Cory did not look up from his position sorting the books, a new idea took her. She stole forward softly in her stout boots. The hilt of the dagger felt cold in the palm of her hand.

She crept forward until she was standing directly behind him. She put the dagger against his throat and bent forward until her lips brushed his ear. Apart from the first, sudden tensing she had sensed in him when he felt the blade touch his skin, he did not move.

'A rifleman caught off his guard,' she said in his ear. 'That will never do, Lord Newlyn.'

Cory put his hand up to the dagger and ran his finger along the edge, moving it away from his throat.

'You could kill someone with that,' he said conversationally.

'That,' Rachel said, 'was the idea.'

She reversed the dagger and stowed it away somewhere beneath the capacious black cloak. Cory's breath came slightly more easily. He knew that she had been taught how to use it. He had done the teaching himself.

'I knew it was you,' he said.

'I know you knew,' Rachel replied, without rancour. 'If you had not, you would have disarmed me.'

Cory laughed. She sounded as calm and collected as though they were in her parents' drawing room. He did not intend to tell her that she had had him at a genuine disadvantage. He had not seen or heard her approach, but he had felt her presence. And when she had crept closer to him, he had inhaled the familiar scent of her skin and for a moment it had so paralysed his senses that she would have had plenty of time to despatch him to his maker and he would not have moved a muscle.

'So you come armed with a dagger when you meet me now,' he said.

'It seemed a good idea,' Rachel said.

'Have you brought your pistol as well?'

'No, of course not.' Rachel looked askance. 'That is for real emergencies.' She looked at him critically. 'What are you doing here, Cory?'

Cory stood up. He felt less vulnerable that way for even without the dagger, Rachel had a way of getting under his guard.

'Well?' she said, a little sharply. She pushed one of the books with her foot. 'You have made a disgraceful mess.'

Cory smiled faintly. He might have known that that would be one of the aspects of the situation that occurred to her first.

'I beg your pardon,' he said. 'I will tidy it up.'

'It appears,' Rachel said, frowning slightly, 'that either you have been suffering acute insomnia and were desperately seeking some reading matter, or that you were searching for something.'

Cory hesitated. Now that the moment had come, he found that he was utterly incapable of lying to Rachel. This was inconvenient, since he had a secret purpose, but he had not lied to her in seventeen years and he did not intend to start now. He looked at her and she looked back, her brows raised slightly as she awaited his explanation. Cory took a deep breath.

Then she forestalled him.

'Oh! I know what you are doing!'

Cory's heart jumped. 'Do you?' he said weakly.

'Yes!' A wrathful gleam had come into Rachel's eyes. 'You are trying to steal a march over me in finding the treasure. You remembered that I said I had found some of

Mr Maskelyne's old books and you thought that they might contain a clue. It is plain as plain!'

'So it is,' Cory said. He felt a mixture of relief and guilt that Rachel had saved him the necessity of explaining.

'Well!' Rachel said. She put her hands on her hips and glared up at him. 'Of all the low tricks! To think that you crept out here in the middle of the night as well. That is taking our rivalry too far!'

'I know,' Cory said. 'It is shameful.' He picked up the lantern and took her arm, steering her out of the stall. 'I swear that I shall come and tidy them up tomorrow.'

'You had better do,' Rachel said, only half-mollified. 'I put them away in here to keep things neat.'

'I do not suppose,' Cory said, 'that you saw anyone else creeping about in the stables tonight?'

'No, only you,' Rachel said crossly. 'How many people were you expecting?'

'None,' Cory said truthfully. He wanted to ask her whether she had told anyone else about Jeffrey Maskelyne's books, but he knew that it was dangerous to do so. Rachel was no fool and would soon put the evidence together—and come up with a conclusion different from the one that she had just reached. For the time being he did not want her making any deductions of her own.

'I thought that no one had seen me coming in here,' he said.

Rachel brushed some stray pieces of straw off her cloak. 'I am sorry to disappoint you. You are not as surreptitious as you think.'

'Evidently not,' Cory said. He put the lantern down on the floor. 'Nor are you very sensible, Rae. Did you not think to rouse your father before coming out on your own in the dark, in pursuit of a scoundrel?'

Rachel was dusting the hem of her cloak, but now her hand stilled. She flashed him an irritable look. 'No, I did not. I had my dagger to protect me. Besides, you know how dangerous Papa can be with his blunderbuss. The last time that I called on him to secure a site, he almost shot a game-keeper.'

Cory allowed his gaze to travel over her. The hem of her nightgown peeped from beneath her thick dark cloak. Beneath the white lace edging, the heavy boots looked more incongruous still. Cory found himself dwelling on what lay under the nightgown and quickly re-focussed on Rachel's face. That did not help a great deal. Her hair was loose and it tumbled about her shoulders and down her back in thick, chestnut waves. It was so unusual for Rachel not to fasten her hair up that that in itself was a seduction to him. It put ideas into his head. Ideas that he knew he should dismiss. Ideas that he quite definitely wished to explore further...

He cleared his throat.

'So,' he said, 'you came out on your own in a state of undress to deal with whatever you might find lurking in the dark...'

Rachel blinked in the lamp flame. He could sense that some of his own feelings had communicated themselves to her, for she was looking at him a little uncertainly. Her eyes were wide and dark. Her tongue came out to touch her bottom lip. Cory felt his body jolt instinctively in response.

'I...' Rachel's voice sounded as husky as his '...I suppose that I did.'

'And how will you deal with it?'

Her gaze clung to his. 'I thought that I had already done so.'

Cory took a step closer. He allowed his eyes to linger boldly, thoughtfully, on her mouth. 'Oh, no, Rae. You have barely started to contend with the situation. Indeed, in some ways you have made it a deal worse.'

Rachel's back came up against the stable door. Cory followed her, stalking her until he was so close her cloak brushed his arm. He could feel the tension in her now. A pulse beat rapidly in the soft skin at the hollow of her throat.

He wanted to press his lips to it. She was holding herself together very tightly, but there was no trepidation in her eyes. They held his fearlessly. He moved in so close that he could feel the brush of her breasts against his chest. His body hardened into arousal.

Rachel tilted her chin up further so that her eyes met his. Their lips were about three inches apart now.

'So?' Cory said, with an expressive lift of his brows.

'So…' Rachel put her hand against his chest. 'Stand back, Cory.'

'Or?'

'Or I shall be obliged to demonstrate that I have not forgotten the manoeuvre you taught me to deal with libertines. It involves a sharp elbow in the stomach.'

Cory laughed and put one hand against the stable wall, trapping her with his body. 'You would not do that to me, Rae. You like me too much.'

'I can think of no one who deserves it more,' Rachel said steadily. 'You have behaved like the veriest rake towards me ever since you arrived in Midwinter.'

Cory drew in a sharp breath. This was upping the stakes indeed and he was happy to follow where she led. 'Behaving like a rake,' he said. 'Do you think so?' He paused for a heartbeat. 'I can do far better than this, I assure you.'

'I do not doubt it.' There were sparks of gold reflected in Rachel's hazel eyes, sparks of anger, amusement and challenge. 'You will not practise on me, however.'

Cory raised a hand and moved the tendrils of hair gently away from her neck. Her skin was smooth and warm. He felt the tiny shiver that she repressed at his touch.

'Shall I not?' he said. 'But then, perhaps I am not practising.'

He bent his head so that his lips took the place of his fingers at the curve of her neck. A sigh escaped her at the gentle abrasion of his stubble against the softness of her skin.

'You have not shaved,' she said. Her voice was very slightly unsteady.

'Do you like it?' Cory rubbed his chin experimentally against the line of her jaw and felt again the quiver that ran through her. Rachel's eyes were almost closed, the lashes a shadow against her cheek. Cory looked at her and felt the slow, sensual pleasure build in his blood. This was explosive. She looked abandoned and beautiful and it threatened the iron control that he was exercising. He could not quite believe that she was letting him do this.

'It...' She sounded dreamy. 'It is very pleasant. Like scouring...'

Cory laughed. 'I confess that I had not thought of it in those terms before, but if it pleases you...'

A smile curved Rachel's mouth. Cory could not resist. He touched his lips very lightly to hers in a shadow of a kiss that was as potent as it was brief. Heat ripped through him. He had to force himself not to pull her into his arms there and then and ravish her mouth as thoroughly as he wished to take her body.

Her eyelashes flickered. 'You do not play fair.'

'Did you expect me to?'

Her smile deepened. 'I had not thought of it before but, no, I suppose not.' Her eyes opened wide and at the same time she increased the pressure against his chest so that he had no doubt that she meant him to step back. 'And nor do I, Cory Newlyn. It is time to end the game.'

Shock and strong admiration hit Cory in equal measure. He stared into her eyes with dawning incredulity.

'You were *pretending?*'

'I was. Weren't you?'

Cory took her shoulders in a hard grip and stared into her eyes. She met his gaze defiantly but at the back of her eyes he could see the remains of sweet, drugging sensual pleasure. It gave him a grim satisfaction to know that she had

had to work hard to overcome it. She was not as indifferent to his touch as she liked to pretend.

'I do not believe you,' he said.

Emotion flickered behind her defiant mask. 'You had better believe me, Cory. Furthermore, I remembered one other precaution that you taught me.'

'Which was?'

Rachel put one hand behind her and pushed the stable door. It swung open silently on to the yard and she stepped back, out of his grasp.

'You taught me always to leave myself a means of escape,' she said sweetly. 'Goodnight, Cory.'

Cory waited until he heard the scrape of the front door closing, then waited again until he saw the flicker of candlelight behind the curtains of Rachel's bedroom. She was safe back in her bed, having avoided all the perils that the night had to offer. Cory smiled slightly. The most dangerous of those perils had undoubtedly been himself. Yet Rachel had acquitted herself magnificently, playing against him with a coolness that he was obliged to admire.

It was not often that his advances were so thoroughly rejected, but Cory could accept it. Rachel's undeniable response to him sweetened the bitter pill of her rebuff. For no matter that she denied it, he knew there had been a moment when her feelings had been as strong as his own. It roused all his predatory instincts and made him wish to pursue the game further. He had never imagined that crossing swords with someone who knew him so well could be so stimulating. Far from being predictable, it was incredibly exciting. They knew each other's minds, knew each other's reactions. It was like a game of chess where the stakes were high. He could make a mistake simply through assuming that he knew Rachel well enough to guess her response to him. Cory, who thrived on challenge, admitted wryly to himself that such a situation was extremely appealing to him.

He let himself out of the stable yard and set off down the

tree-lined drive to the road. The breeze on his face was pleasant and light and he welcomed its refreshing coolness. He found himself in something of a dilemma. He wanted Rachel Odell and had wanted her for some considerable time now. Tonight had only emphasised that. But this was no light flirtation to pass the summer and then be forgotten. He could not simply seduce the childhood friend that he loved, the daughter of a man who was his respected mentor. If he took the step of paying court to Rachel, then it would be irrevocable. He would have to persuade her to marry him. He would have to persuade her to put aside all the things that she wanted—a settled life, peace and tranquillity, a stable home—and convince her that they were as nothing compared to what he could offer her.

Cory was not at all sure that he had the right to even try. He was not in the least certain of success. On the other hand, failure was not an option. If he failed, not only would he lose Rachel, he would lose her friendship and would never regain it.

Cory was used to making decisions in seconds that would take other men days or even weeks. He was an adventurer, accustomed to risk. This felt like the biggest risk that he would ever take in his entire life.

He knew that his decision was already made, but he also knew that he had to be careful. He had to woo Miss Rachel Odell, his dearest and closest friend. And he had to do it in a manner that would not startle or scare her, a manner so subtle that she would not notice until it was too late and she felt as strongly for him as he did for her.

A sound from behind him interrupted his thoughts and caused him to pause and glance over his shoulder. The road stretched behind him like a silver ribbon on the moonlight. It was empty. Nevertheless, he thought he heard the patter of footsteps. He started walking again. The steps seemed to echo his. He paused again. There was silence. Cory reached very quietly for the pistol at his belt.

He started walking again, softly, carefully. The footsteps followed him. He could almost feel eyes on his back. Yet he knew that if he turned, there would be no one there.

The attack came with a silent uprush of shadows. There was the sound of running feet and then a bullet whistled past his ear, so close that Cory felt the breeze of its passing. He flung himself down into the ditch and drew his own pistol in one movement, firing by the same instinct that had prompted him to dive for cover and thus save his life. He heard a muffled cry. Hauling himself out of the ditch, he was just in time to see a shadowy figure leap over a farm gate and head towards a covert of trees some fifty yards distant. In the faint moonlight it looked insubstantial, a wraith of a creature yet one capable of murder.

The urge to pursue was a strong one, but a cool head and tactical thought overrode Cory's natural instinct. He was alone, he did not know the terrain and his assailant had a lead of twenty or so yards. He doubted very much that the attacker would return to take another shot.

Cory let his breath out in a long sigh. 'I am not so easy to dispose of as Jeffrey Maskelyne,' he muttered grimly as he stowed the pistol back in his belt. Doubtless his assassin would have been surprised to find that he was armed. He guessed that they had planned to bring him down with one shot and follow it up with a second from close quarters. And he had given them the perfect chance by electing to walk back on his own. They had come very close and only his instinct for danger had saved him. He could feel the cold sweat trickling from his brow now.

A carriage rounded the corner behind him, lamps blazing, and drew to a stop beside him on the road. The door swung open.

'Can I offer you a lift?' Richard Kestrel's voice said wryly.

Cory had never been so glad to see anyone in his life. He

swung up into the carriage and closed the door behind him
with a decisive click.

Once he was seated on the thick red cushions with the
Richard Kestrel looking at him with quizzical amusement,
he felt rather a fool.

'Everything all right, old fellow?' Richard asked. 'You
did not have any trouble at Midwinter Royal, did you?'

Cory shook his head. Rachel Odell was trouble, but of an
entirely different sort.

'Someone had been there before me,' he said. 'The books
had all been ripped apart. If Maskelyne had used them for
concealment, then the secret is lost.'

There was a silence. 'Someone else knew about them,'
Richard said slowly.

'It would appear that way, certainly.'

Richard eyed him closely. 'Was that all that happened? I
thought you were in better shape than to get in a sweat over
a walk home!'

Cory rubbed his sleeve across his forehead. 'Did you see
anyone on the road?' he asked.

Richard's eyes sharpened in interest. He shook his head
slowly. 'Not a soul,' he said. 'I've driven back from Midwinter Marney. Ross Marney and I went from dinner to
what passes for a club in this godforsaken spot—' He broke
off, eyeing Cory closely. 'But I do not believe you want to
hear my social engagements, old chap. What happened to
you?'

Cory grinned. 'Someone just took a pot shot at me,' he
said baldly.

Richard was too cool a hand to show a great deal of
surprise at this intelligence.

'Are you injured?' he enquired.

'Of course not,' Cory said.

'Did you injure your assailant?'

'Of course.' Cory's tone turned grim. 'Though not as

much as I would have wished. The bullet winged him—or her—in the arm, I think.'

'Her?' Richard questioned.

Cory shrugged. 'It could have been. I only caught a glimpse, and it was impossible to tell. It could not be Miss Odell, though,' he added on an afterthought.

Richard looked quizzical. 'Why not?'

Cory laughed. 'Because she would not have missed me,' he said. 'I taught her to shoot myself.'

Richard sat back on the seat and stretched his long legs out in front of him. In the light of the carriage lamps his expression had turned calculating. 'I will get Justin to ask around,' he said. 'He has the right contacts. Someone may know something. They always do if the price is right.'

'It could have been a poacher or a footpad,' Cory conceded, 'but I do not think it likely.'

'Neither do I,' Richard said. 'But how convenient that you injured your quarry, Cory.' His tone hardened. 'The reading group meets tomorrow afternoon. Lady Sally told me so herself at the dinner this evening. I think we might pay an impromptu call at Saltires.'

'It would be courteous,' Cory said, his lips twitching.

'And we shall see,' Richard added, 'which of the ladies is indisposed—or nursing some sort of injury. It should be most enlightening.'

Chapter Eight

The mood of the reading group had felt somewhat prickly that afternoon. Rachel's sleep had been broken by disturbing dreams after her meeting with Cory in the stables, and she was nursing a headache that not even Mrs Goodfellow's tincture of valerian had been able to banish. The other ladies all seemed a little out of temper and it was difficult to concentrate on *The Enchantress* under the circumstances. Helena Lang was absent with an indisposition that Lady Benedict unkindly referred to as over-indulgence at dinner the night before, Lady Benedict herself had her arm in a sling from a tumble down the stairs and Lady Sally Saltire had her hand bandaged and could barely turn the pages of the book. She explained that she had been tending her precious roses that morning when a thorn had driven into the palm of her hand. All in all, the ladies were subdued and a little sharp.

When Bentley, the butler, announced the arrival of visitors, they greeted the news with some relief. Lady Sally put her book aside and raised her brows enquiringly.

'Is it anyone to whom we wish to be at home, Bentley?'

'It is Lord Richard Kestrel and Lord Newlyn, ma'am,' Bentley said woodenly. 'Lord Richard said that he was certain that you *would* be at home, ma'am.'

A small smile twitched Lady Sally lips. 'Very well, then,' she said, rising from the sofa in an elegant flurry of silk. 'If Lord Richard is so certain that we are receiving guests, then who are we to disappoint him? Tea on the terrace, please, Bentley. I am sure that Lord Richard and Lord Newlyn are both most partial to a cup of tea.'

Rachel had dropped her book when Cory's name was mentioned and had to grope around on the floor to retrieve it. She felt her colour rise as everyone turned to look at her. Lady Benedict was staring at her in a speculative fashion, a malicious smile on her lips. Rachel, all fingers and thumbs, put the book on a side table and tried to breathe calmly.

By the time Cory was announced she was flushed and flustered and annoyed to find that her heart was beating a tattoo as she watched the door like a cat at a mouse hole. It was inexplicable; she had *seen* Cory many times before and his entry into a room had never caused this constriction in her throat before. She felt as though she wanted to turn and run, and it was all to do with the previous night…

As soon as Cory came in, he looked directly at her. Rachel's heart jumped. In that moment she knew that Cory wanted to come across to her straight away. He hesitated visibly, but after a moment walked over to Lily Benedict instead. Rachel saw him gesture to the sling, a look of concern on his face, and saw Lady Benedict tilt her face towards him, smiling like a flower reaching to the sun. Rachel felt cross and disappointed and obscurely angry with Cory. She was forced to remind herself rather strongly that she might be Cory's friend but it was of no consequence to her whom he chose to flirt with. Even so, she felt annoyed that last night his choice had fallen on her, but now he was happy to trifle with another lady's feelings. It branded him insincere and proved that he had only been entertaining himself at her expense in the stables. A tiny part of her, the part that had wanted it not to be a game, felt shrivelled at the thought.

Lord Richard Kestrel was chatting to Lady Sally, and Olivia and Deborah had wandered out on to the terrace to take tea, so Rachel took the opportunity to slip outside. She could feel her headache worsening and hoped that the fresher air might make it better.

The gardens at Saltires were small but beautifully tended, for Lady Sally, in company with her friend Olivia Marney, was a keen amateur gardener. Rachel wandered towards the small ornamental lake, but swiftly retraced her steps when she realised that Mr Caspar Lang was sitting by the gazebo, having his portrait painted for the watercolour book. Rachel had no wish to be caught watching. Mr Lang had quite a good enough opinion of himself as it was, without her adding to it.

It was as she was coming back through the rose arch that Cory stepped directly on to the path in front of her. Rachel had thought herself quite composed by now and was intending to take her place at the tea table in a cool and rational manner, but now such thoughts flew from her head. Perhaps it was the suddenness of Cory's appearance, or perhaps the fact that she had been thinking about him on and off—with rather more on than off—for the past fourteen hours. Whatever the reason, she gasped and coloured up like the most impressionable of débutantes. Cory eyed her blush with interest, which just seemed to make it worse.

'Whatever is the matter with you, Rae?' he remarked softly. 'You look rather guilty. What were you doing—running away?'

Rachel, unforgivably, vented her irritation by snapping one of Lady Sally's prize roses off the arch.

'Of course I was not running away! Why should I wish to do that?'

'I have no notion,' Cory said, driving his hands into his pockets. 'I merely thought that you had been acting strangely, dashing off before I could speak to you.'

'I was not aware that you had noticed,' Rachel said, before she could stop herself. 'You were far too occupied.'

She saw the humour deepen in Cory's eyes and was vexed with herself.

'I see,' he said.

'I doubt that you do,' Rachel said. 'If you choose to flirt with Lady Benedict, then it is no concern of mine.'

'Of course not,' Cory said soothingly.

'I don't care!' Rachel said childishly.

'I know that you don't,' Cory agreed.

Rachel stared at him, frowning. She was not quite sure why this unsatisfactory exchange made her feel worse, but it did. It reminded her strongly of childhood squabbles, but with an added element of adult friction that she could not quite explain.

'Why are you agreeing with me?' she demanded.

'Because I thought it would put you in a better temper,' Cory responded.

Rachel repressed the urge to stamp her foot. 'Well, don't!'

'You are very cross today,' Cory observed.

'Congratulations on your perspicacity. Of course I am cross.' Rachel pulled the head off the rosebud and tossed it aside, wincing as the thorn caught her thumb. 'I have the headache and you are deliberately setting out to provoke me, just as you did last night.'

There was a pause that suddenly seemed heavy with unspoken meaning. The whole tone of the encounter changed in an instant.

'I do not suppose,' Cory said, moving closer, 'that you slept very well last night, Rae.'

Rachel looked up and met the question in his eyes. Her heart skipped a beat. Last night they had been playing games, but she had no intention of doing so again. It had been far too disturbing. What had set out as a plan to teach

Cory a lesson had almost ended in her own downfall. She had nearly succumbed to his skilful seduction.

She deliberately moved away. 'Why should you think that?' she asked coolly.

Cory followed her. 'Because I did not,' he said.

'So?' Rachel raised her brows. 'I cannot see the connection.'

Cory gave her a keen glance. 'Then let me construe for you. I did not sleep well because I was thinking of you. And you, I suspect, did not sleep well because you were thinking of me.'

Rachel turned her shoulder. Her heart was beating with quick, light strokes. 'You are quite mistaken. And odiously arrogant! My inability to sleep last night had nothing to do with you. I was scarcely lying awake troubled by dreams of you!'

'Really?' Cory drawled. 'Then why mention it?'

'Mention what?'

Cory smiled infuriatingly. 'Those troublesome dreams, Rae.'

Rachel thinned her lips. 'Take a grip on yourself, Cory! We are not all of us fainting at your feet. As for your own insomnia, I cannot be held responsible for that either.'

'I hold you directly responsible,' Cory said, still smiling.

There was another loaded silence.

'You should take a cold dip in the river,' Rachel said. 'That would cure your difficulties—and your pretensions.'

'Thank you for the suggestion,' Cory said calmly. 'I cannot but remember what happened the last time that I went for a swim.'

Rachel could remember too, in vivid detail. She struggled against the memory. 'Then if cold water does not work, perhaps I could administer a knock on the head,' she said sweetly. 'It would be my pleasure. You will sleep like a baby after that.'

Cory started to laugh. 'You are fighting hard, Rae.'

'Against your conceit!' Rachel spun away through the arch. 'It is a difficult job, but someone has to undertake it.'

She could hear his footsteps following her along the gravel path. 'I do not believe that you were so indifferent to me last night in the stables,' Cory said, 'whatever you claimed.'

Rachel swung around to confront him. 'You were playing games last night, so I thought that I would do too,' she said coolly. 'But I am tired of that now. Go away and play with Lady Benedict instead. She appreciates these things far more than I do.'

There was a pause and then Cory laughed. 'Very well, I concede—for now,' he said. 'Friends?'

'Just that,' Rachel said. She held her hand out to shake on it. It was a mistake. The moment his hand touched hers, something akin to a shiver ran all the way along her nerves. She saw Cory's eyes narrow on her face, as though he were reading her mind. He rubbed his thumb over the palm of her hand, making the shivers worse.

'You have cut yourself,' he remarked, moving the lace edge of her cuff to one side and exposing the pale skin of her inner arm. 'How did that happen?'

'It is nothing.' Rachel pulled her hand away from his and tugged her sleeve down a little self-consciously. His gesture had made her feel naked. 'I cut myself on the jagged edge of a pot when I was helping Mama wash the artefacts this morning.'

Cory was looking thoughtfully at the scratch. 'You should be more careful.'

'I am not care*less*.' Rachel frowned. 'Though I thank you for your concern.' She glanced towards the terrace. 'We should go back before anyone comments on our absence. I do not want to give Lady Benedict the chance to make another of her cattish remarks. Do you join us for tea, Cory?'

'No, thank you,' Cory said, 'I cannot bear so insipid a beverage.'

'Then I will leave you to take your dip in the river,' Rachel said. 'Pray take care that no one sees you, though. Not everyone has as strong a constitution as I. The shock might be too much for them.'

'Will you be walking home that way?' Cory enquired with a grin.

'Certainly not,' Rachel said. 'I shall take the other footpath. I would not like to repeat that experience.'

Cory put his hand on her arm. 'Should you not?' he challenged.

'It seems to me,' Rachel said, 'that you are so entirely in love with yourself that you need no one else's admiration, Cory.'

Cory did not say anything but he let his gaze rest on her in a manner that contradicted her most effectively, and Rachel, who had sworn that she had put the matter to rest, found herself coming out with the one thing to which she required an answer.

'Last night,' she said in a rush, 'I asked you if you were pretending with me and you did not answer. You *were* pretending, weren't you, Cory?'

Cory smiled. 'You should ask yourself why that matters so much to you, Rachel,' he said. He sketched a bow and walked away.

Rachel watched him go, eyes narrowed. She was cross with herself for lowering her guard and asking a question that would have been better left unsaid. And yet... He had not answered her the previous night and now he had declined to do it again. He might merely be teasing her, but... She walked slowly towards the terrace, but in the back of her own mind the question still echoed: *'You were pretending, weren't you...?'*

And she knew that she should be asking herself the same thing.

* * *

'Who would have thought it?' Richard Kestrel said heavily. 'One might almost imagine that they are all in on it!'

'It is the most confounded piece of bad luck,' Cory agreed. 'I could scarce believe it.'

They were back in the drawing room at Kestrel Court and were capably demolishing the latest bottle of brandy that Justin had left behind on his return to London. They were also playing a desultory game of chess.

'Lady Marney claimed to be uninjured,' Richard said, with a smile. 'And Miss Lang was genuinely sick according to her brother. I sent Bradshaw to find out more from the Langs' housemaid. The girl said that Miss Lang had taken so much wine at Lady Marney's dinner that she had to be put to bed, and had not stirred since.'

'It could be an act,' Cory pointed out. He moved a pawn and sat back to watch Richard's strategy.

'True—' Richard sighed '—although I cannot see Miss Lang as a cool-headed traitor. Besides, we have more likely candidates. There was Lady Benedict and her apparent tumble down the stairs—'

'And Lady Sally and her gardening injury—'

'And Mrs Stratton, who was sporting a nasty slash on her hand that she claimed was from a bramble that caught her as she was out riding this morning,' Richard finished. He grinned. 'What about Miss Odell, Cory?'

'Cut herself cleaning a pot her mother had dug out this morning,' Cory confirmed gloomily. 'I do not think that she is the one we are looking for. Acquit me of partiality,' he added hastily, seeing the wry gleam in Richard's eye, 'and I shall do the same for you with Mrs Stratton!'

Richard laughed. 'I can make no special case for Mrs Stratton other than to say that I do not think she is the guilty party.'

'Instinct?' Cory asked drily.

Richard shrugged. 'My instincts towards Mrs Stratton are

best not discussed,' he said, with a sardonic smile. He sat forward and moved his castle to take the pawn.

'Lady Sally Saltire is certainly cool enough to pull it off,' Cory said.

'And Lady Benedict likewise,' Richard finished thoughtfully. 'She left the dinner early last night, but could have waited to ambush you on the road.' He frowned. ' You are more than usual preoccupied tonight, old chap. Swear you are throwing this game away.'

Cory shrugged. 'I'll admit to a certain distraction.'

'Miss Odell?'

Cory groaned. 'How does one make love to one's oldest friend, Richard?'

Richard looked amused. 'Thought I was your oldest friend, Cory. I'm not sure if I should be concerned or offended!'

Cory moved his knight directly into the path of Richard's queen. Richard scooped the piece from the board.

'You could try the direct approach,' he suggested. 'Tell her exactly how you feel about her—or show her!'

Cory grimaced. 'That is a little too direct, much as it might accord with my own feelings. Rachel thinks that I am playing games if I try to kiss her. She has yet to accept the idea that we could be more than friends. I do not wish to frighten her by declaring my feelings and risk losing her before I have even started to court her properly.'

'Then you need to be slow and subtle,' Richard said. He grinned. 'Think you can do that?'

Cory laughed. 'It is hardly my *modus operandi*,' he admitted. 'I suppose if one wants a thing enough…'

'Absolutely,' Richard said. 'Checkmate.'

Cory sighed. 'At least my chess might improve if I make some progress.'

'I doubt it,' Richard said. 'The greater the physical frustration, the poorer one's concentration and the more one's game is shot to pieces.' He passed the brandy bottle. 'Oh, and the greater amount of brandy one consumes. Trust me. I should know.'

Cory filled his glass. 'So where does that leave us?' he asked.

'No further on,' Richard said. He raised his glass in ironic toast. 'To the ladies of the Midwinter reading group! One way or another, they are running rings around us!'

Chapter Nine

'How delightful this is,' Deborah Stratton declared, sliding into a seat opposite to Rachel in the teashop in Angel Hill in Woodbridge, and placing a large quantity of brown paper parcels on the table. 'You have no idea, Rachel, how I have longed for different company. Oh, Olivia is the best sister imaginable,' she added hastily. 'No one could be more fortunate than I in their relatives, but sometimes it is pleasant to extend one's circle of friends.'

Rachel smiled. She moved Deborah's tottering pile of purchases carefully to one side, where they would not get splashed from the teapot or fall on the floor, and poured her a cup of tea.

They had spent an enjoyable morning in the town. First they had watched the volunteers being drilled on the green, although the Suffolk Rifles were not amongst the regiments drawn up for inspection. The riflemen practised out on the marshes where there was less danger of them injuring any innocent spectators. Deb had grumbled that this was a pity since the riflemen in their green uniforms looked the most handsome of all the volunteers. Rachel had pointed out that their appearance was immaterial if they could not shoot straight. There was a febrile air in the town, with gossip and rumour of French invasion rife. It felt a little odd to be shopping for ribbons and books and ordinary things when all about them there was the suppressed nervousness engendered by war. Rachel had found it a little inhibiting and her pile of purchases could not rival Deborah's, for Mrs Stratton seemed to spend money with the same profligate cheerfulness with which she dealt with the rest of her life. Rachel found her excellent company, even though they could not have been more dissimilar.

Deborah was watching the fashionable crowd milling on the street outside the teashop's bow windows.

'This is the place to come if you wish to witness the Woodbridge scandals,' she said cheerfully. 'Only look at that Captain of Dragoons parading in front of the ladies! That is George Brandon Smith, who is allegedly the most handsome man in the 21st Foot! He fought a duel with another officer over a lady recently and was almost cashiered as a result. Only his connection with the Devonshires saved him and caused the matter to be hushed up.'

'Do you know him?' Rachel enquired. 'He looks a rather haughty man.'

'Oh, he has a very inflated opinion of himself,' Deborah said, smiling. 'I know him a little, for he condescended to dance with me at the last Assembly. He told me that I was most fortunate, for he usually only deigns to dance with titled ladies!'

Rachel made a noise of disgust. 'Of all the pretentious nonsense! I am glad, then, that my father is a mere baronet.' She looked out of the teashop window. 'How busy it is! I confess that I had forgotten what it was like to live near a town. It is a long time since we were settled anywhere like this. I am more accustomed to the depths of Wiltshire, or the Shetland Islands or even Italy.'

'Your childhood must have been quite the opposite of mine,' Deborah said. 'What did you do with yourself whilst your parents excavated their antiquities?'

'I learned to distil whisky illegally in Scotland, to poach

pheasants in Wiltshire and to read Etruscan in Italy,' Rachel
said with a smile. 'None of them are the accomplishments
of a young lady.'

'Poaching and illegal whisky!' Deborah said, with the
greatest admiration. 'How marvellous, Rachel. But what
were your parents thinking?'

'I believe they were thinking about their artefacts,' Rachel
said composedly. She gripped her hands together about the
little blue-and-white china teacup. What she really wanted
to say was that she had always believed that her arrival had
been unexpected, a disruption to her parents' plans, and that
her subsequent existence had been a severe trial to them.
But it felt a little disloyal and she did not know Deborah
well enough yet to confide.

Mrs Stratton's animated face had softened slightly. She
put an impulsive hand out to Rachel. 'You poor girl! I do
believe that you would have given anything for a childhood
as ordinary as mine, whilst I would have given anything for
the excitement of yours!'

They laughed together.

'What was Lord Newlyn doing whilst you were learning
to poach?' Deb asked.

Rachel smiled a little. 'Oh, Cory would follow my parents
around like a faithful dog! He spent many of his holidays
with us, you know. At first I do not believe that his parents
approved, but his very determination won them over. He
was very kind to me,' she added, helping herself to a second
marshmallow. 'I did not appreciate it at the time, but I do
not suppose many boys would have been so tolerant of a
small girl. Most would probably have found me irritating.'

'Goodness!' Deborah said suddenly, sitting forward. 'I do
believe that it is Lord Richard Kestrel outside. And Lord
Newlyn! Are we to see a riot in Woodbridge, as all those
ladies try to attract their attention?'

Rachel looked. Cory Newlyn and Richard Kestrel were
strolling down Angel Hill in the sunshine with a casual

aplomb that was reminiscent of Bond Street rather than the decidedly more provincial surroundings of a country town. They were being followed at a somewhat indiscreet distance by a positive tidal wave of ladies fluttering and flouncing in their summer dresses.

Deb sighed. 'I wish that I could claim your acquaintance with Lord Newlyn, Rachel. He has taken me driving, you know, but although we talked on all manner of topics, I have the strangest feeling that he is not an easy man to get to know.' She wrinkled up her face. 'Oh, he is charm personified, but under the surface...' she gave a little shiver '...I suspect he is ruthless and rather dangerous—in a thoroughly fascinating way!'

Rachel fidgeted with her empty cup. She had not known that Cory had taken Deborah driving and was disconcerted to find that she did not like the idea. Seeing him now felt a little odd, as though she was looking at him from an entirely different perspective. They had not met for several days, for, in order to counteract the peculiar effect that Cory had had on her at Saltires that afternoon, Rachel had kept out of his way. She had assumed that he had been working on the excavation with her parents and she had been busy with... Well, busy with all sorts of matters that had kept her from his presence. It had been her choice to avoid him and yet she felt oddly dissatisfied with the results, which was in itself annoying and contrary.

'Under the surface, my dear Deb,' she said, as lightly as she could, 'Cory is as arrogant and self-opinionated as all other gentlemen of his type!'

Nevertheless, she could see why Cory was creating such a stir. With his long, lean frame and his careless grace, he compelled female attention wherever he went.

'I suppose that he is quite good looking,' she added, in a casual tone that sounded slightly false even to her own ears, 'but his looks are nothing compared to Lord Richard Kestrel. Glory, what a handsome man he is!'

Deb looked unimpressed. 'I'll allow that Lord Richard is nice enough to look at, but if you are speaking of arrogance, Rachel, there is a cast to his countenance that quite spoils his appearance in my opinion, and gives fair warning of his nature.'

Rachel bent over the teapot to hide her smile. Deborah had sounded quite indignant and Rachel suspected that her opinion was not entirely unbiased.

'Oh, no,' Deb whispered, 'they are looking this way! Pray make as though you have not noticed them, Rachel, for although I should be glad to give the time of day to Lord Newlyn, I do not wish to speak with Lord Richard at all.'

'It is a little difficult to ignore them when we are sitting in the window,' Rachel pointed out, as Deb shrank back against the wall in a vain attempt to disguise herself. 'I should not concern yourself. There is no danger of them joining us, for Lord Newlyn has never been known to drink tea. He considers it boring.'

She was foresworn almost immediately as Cory and Richard Kestrel entered the teashop and made directly for their corner. Suddenly the room seemed rather small and it became smaller still as an indiscreet rush of ladies poured through the door in hot pursuit and squabbled over who should take the remaining tables.

'Good afternoon, Rachel,' Cory said, smiling down at her. 'May we join you?'

Out of the corner of her eye, Rachel saw Deb's lips form a horrified 'no.' Deb was studiously avoiding looking at Lord Richard Kestrel who, rather to Rachel's amusement, had not taken his eyes off her since he came into the shop.

'Of course you may join us if you wish,' Rachel said, ignoring Deborah's scowl, 'but I fear that we were about to leave. It is very crowded in here.'

'We shall not keep you above a minute,' Cory said. 'Richard and I were both agreeing that there is nothing like a cup of tea for refreshment on a hot day.'

'Were you?' Rachel said disbelievingly, looking from Cory's innocent face to Richard Kestrel's saturnine one. 'How singular of you when you detest so insipid a beverage.'

Richard bowed to Rachel, a twinkle in his very dark eyes. 'How do you do, Miss Odell? I am delighted to see you again.'

'How do you do, Lord Richard,' Rachel said, smiling. 'I am well.'

'And Mrs Stratton,' Richard said, his smile deepening as he took in Deb's angry profile. 'How are you, ma'am?'

'I am very well, thank you.' Deb snapped. She did not meet his eyes, but turned ostentatiously to Cory and gestured him to the empty chair at her side. 'How do you do, Lord Newlyn? Please take a seat.'

Rachel saw Richard and Cory exchange one laughing, rueful glance, and then Cory did as he was bid and Richard shrugged lightly and took the seat beside Rachel.

Richard Kestrel was, as Rachel had noticed on several previous occasions, an exceptionally good-looking man. Tall, dark and with a commanding presence, he had the wicked, piratical looks that were characteristic of the Kestrel family. If there was any arrogance in his appearance, it was tempered by the humour Rachel could see in his eyes. She could not help but warm to him, although curiously, his riveting good looks did not attract her in the least.

They spent some time chatting and the gentlemen managed a cup of tea each and several Bath Oliver biscuits. Rachel found herself enjoying Richard Kestrel's company. He did not make the mistake of trying to flirt with her, but they engaged in an easy conversation about the town and the threat of invasion and the wider political situation. Even so, Rachel was conscious that she was watching Cory out of the corner of her eye for almost the entire time. She could not ignore his presence. She observed him talking to Deb and felt a distinct stirring of jealousy as she saw his head bent close to hers and watched the ready smile with which he responded to Deb's conversation. She had wanted to regain her comfortable friendship with Cory after the confusion she had felt over their previous encounters. This morning had seemed like a good opportunity. Yet now it was disconcerting to realise that friendship was not exactly what she felt towards him. Over the years she had taken both Cory's friendship and her own feelings for granted and it was profoundly disturbing to sense those feelings changing without any conscious reason. Several times Cory caught her looking at him and gave her a look of speculation. Rachel blushed and looked away. She did not wish him to think that it mattered to her, but it did.

Having been preoccupied with thoughts of Rachel all day, Cory Newlyn opened the door of the billiard room at Midwinter Royal later that evening and was greeted by a sight to deprive most red-blooded men of breath. It made him forget the message that he was supposed to be delivering, it made him forget the excavation he was supposed to be working on and for a second it practically made him forget his own name. For one long moment he simply stood and stared.

Rachel was leaning over the billiard table, her breasts straining against the thin cotton of her gown, her eyes narrowed in concentration as she sighted along her cue. A breath of wind from the open doorway must have distracted her attention, for she turned her head slightly a second before she played the shot—and missed. She straightened up and Cory's breathing returned slowly to normal. He closed the door and came forward into the room.

'You put me off my shot,' Rachel said. She seemed slightly put out, but Cory felt she did not have a great deal to complain about. That, he thought a little grimly, was nothing to the effect that *she* was having on *him* these days. He watched the sway of her gown as she moved around the table, sizing up the position of the balls. She paused, lining up a shot. Cory, realising that she was about to bend over the table right in front of him, pulled his thoughts away from what that would look like and tried to remember why he had come to see her in the first place.

'Ah…Rachel…'

'Yes, Cory?' Rachel straightened up again, her eyes wide and innocent as she turned to look at him.

'Your parents asked me to tell you that they have not quite finished work on the long barrow and will be in to supper in a short while—'

Rachel gave an exaggerated sigh. She checked the clock on the wall. 'It is past nine! Soon they will not be able to see their spades in front of their noses.'

'Have you taken supper yourself?' Cory asked.

'Yes, of course.' Rachel frowned. 'It is bad for the digestion to eat late at night.'

'And you had no engagements for this evening?'

'No.' Rachel turned back to the table and potted a ball with complete accuracy. 'Mama had indicated that she wished to attend the musicale at Lady Benedict's. I will send a message over that we shall not be present after all.'

'I will let them know on my way back to Kestrel Court, if you wish,' Cory offered.

Rachel smiled at him gratefully. 'Oh, would you?' She rested her cue on the wooden floor. 'That will save me trying to find Tom Gough when he is probably still out in the field with Papa.'

Cory nodded. 'You do not wish to go to the Benedicts on your own?'

'No, thank you.' Rachel turned away. 'I am no musician, as well you know, Cory. I fear that listening to music bores me. I shall go to the library and study Maskelyne's maps.'

'Have you had any success so far?' Cory asked.

'Not really.' Rachel sighed. 'I took the opportunity this morning of calling at the Priory and borrowing some of the parish records. There are some directions and measurements that I wish to check. It is all very slow.'

'Parish records,' Cory said, shaking his head. 'How your long evenings must fly past, Rachel!'

'I cannot see that it is any more tedious than unearthing long-dead bones,' Rachel said, with spirit. 'We each have our interests.'

'Very true.'

'And if it becomes too dry then I shall read *The Enchantress* instead.'

Cory leaned against the edge of the billiard table. If he could keep her talking on innocuous topics, then so much the better. It would distract his mind from other, far less innocent occupations—occupations such as kissing, which he had promised himself that he would not indulge in with Rachel—not yet.

'How does the story progress?' he asked.

'Oh, it is quite lively.' Rachel retrieved the balls from the pockets and placed them neatly in the triangle before lining up to break. 'Sir Philip is currently exhibiting the usual contrary male behaviour—he has met a charming girl, but refuses to fall in love with her. It is Lady Sally's contention that he will fall in love with quite the most unsuitable choice.'

Cory laughed. 'Lady Sally does not appear to have a high opinion of our sex.'

'No.' Rachel put her head on one side thoughtfully. 'She likes male company, but I do not believe she has a high regard for male intelligence!'

'And you, Rae,' Cory said, smiling, 'how do you rate the male of the species?'

He observed with interest the colour that this brought into Rachel's face.

'I have the highest regard for the intelligence of individuals,' she said sedately, 'but I fear that it is a masculine trait to have a rather inflated opinion of one's own worth.'

Cory gave a crack of laughter. 'You never did care for pomposity, did you, Rae?'

'No, I detest it.' Her gaze brushed his face and to Cory it felt like a physical touch. 'But I could never accuse you of it, Cory.'

Cory felt ridiculously as though she had given him some valuable prize. 'Thank you, Rae.'

'You have many other faults, of course,' Rachel said, deliberately spoiling the effect, 'but self-importance is not one of them.'

She put out a hand and touched the sleeve of his Volunteer uniform. 'This is very fine. Have you been at drill with the Suffolk rifles again?'

'I have.'

'Then you can give me a game,' Rachel said, gesturing towards the table. 'Your aim should be in.'

Cory picked one of the cues from the rack on the wall. Rachel potted two balls in quick succession and he watched her as she moved around the table. She sized up the state of play quickly and made swift decisions about which ball to pot. Cory, on the other hand, found it difficult to focus on the state of play, preferring to watch Rachel herself. He knew that his concentration was shot to pieces before he even started.

Rachel took on a risky pot and just missed the pocket.

Cory approached the table to take his shot. Rachel came and leaned on the edge of the table beside him. Cory gritted his teeth. He tried to block out her presence and ignore the scent of her perfume, a scent that seemed insidiously to wrap itself around his senses. She smelled clean and fresh and innocent. It was the scent of lavender and lily of the valley. When the *hell* had he started to find the smell of lavender attractive?

He missed his shot.

'Hmm.' Rachel's quizzical hazel gaze was on his face. 'It is to be hoped that the security of the nation does not rest entirely with you, Cory.' She potted two more balls with quick efficiency, brushing against him as she tried to get the optimum angle.

Cory watched the sway of her hips and tried to remember that his life depended on breathing at regular intervals. To distract himself as much as her, he said, 'So, did you enjoy your conversation with Richard Kestrel today, Rae? I seem to recall that you were quite taken with him.'

An unexpected dimple dented Rachel's cheek as she smiled. 'I think Lord Richard is absolutely charming.'

'Hmm,' Cory said, feeling a certain ironic amusement that the answer to his question was the opposite of the one he wanted. 'Do you think that he might be the sort of husband you are seeking?'

Rachel gave a peal of laughter. 'Certainly not! Lord Richard is almost the last person that I would wish to marry, even were he to be in the market for a wife. He is far too...' she paused, wrinkling her brow '...far too costly for me.'

'Costly?' Cory raised his brows.

'Yes.' Rachel straightened up and paused in her decimation of the billiard table. 'You remember the bit in Shakespeare—*Much Ado About Nothing,* I believe—when the Prince asks Beatrice if she would consider marrying him and she says that she would need two of him, one for best and one for everyday use? I feel like that about Lord Richard Kestrel. He is far too dangerous for me to tangle with in any romantic sense.'

Cory hesitated. 'Do you feel like that about me, Rae?'

Rachel looked at him for a moment. He allowed his gaze to travel over her, from her kid slippers to her neatly pinned Grecian knot, finishing at her face, which was now ever so slightly flushed. She dropped her gaze.

'The question does not arise,' she said, her voice slightly muffled as she turned back to the billiard table. 'I might feel like that if I was not such an old friend of yours. I know you too well to see you as other ladies do.'

She took the shot; Cory saw her hand tremble very slightly on the cue. Even so, she put the ball away.

He followed her round the table as she prepared for her next move. He could tell that she was ruffled now, for she did not have sufficient experience to hide it. The thought roused tenderness and ruthlessness in him in equal measure. What would it be like to exploit the attraction that he knew Rachel felt for him, an attraction that she would not admit, even to herself? The idea was such a potent one that he almost lost all his good intentions towards her and kissed her there and then.

Looking at her, he could tell that Rachel had read something of his thoughts; her troubled hazel gaze had flashed one look at his expression and then away.

'You seemed to appreciate the company of Mrs Stratton,' she said, a little breathlessly. 'You were enjoying yourself as much if not more than I was this morning.'

For a moment, Cory could not even remember who Mrs Stratton was.

'Indeed,' he said, when memory had returned. 'She was trying to persuade me to take part in Lady Sally's watercolour book.'

Rachel laughed. 'No doubt you were more receptive to her persuasions than you were to mine?'

'I was probably less outspoken with her,' Cory said, 'but the outcome was the same.'

Rachel leaned over to take her final shot. Cory moved until he was very close to her, their bodies just touching. Rachel shifted away. Cory moved imperceptibly after her. She looked up, her face red.

'Stop it! You are doing it on purpose!'

'Doing what?' Cory asked innocently.

'Trying to put me off,' Rachel said crossly.

Cory smiled. 'My proximity has never disturbed your game before,' he pointed out.

'Well, it does now!' Rachel bit her lip. 'Kindly stand further off.'

Cory moved away obediently, keeping his gaze on her face. There was a militant light in Rachel's eye, but beneath it he could see her uncertainty. His physical presence had not troubled her in the past. Probably she had not even been aware of it or aware of him. Yet since he had joined the excavation in Suffolk the awareness between them had been so sharp that it struck sparks. Cory intended to keep it that way. There would be no settling back into a comfortable friendship now.

Rachel hit the ball far too hard, jamming her cue into the top of the table. The ball leapt, jumping off the end of the table and bouncing on to the wooden floor. Cory heard Rachel swear, which in itself was a most unusual occurrence. He picked the ball up and held it out to her.

'Would you like another go?'

Rachel was struggling to control her temper. She looked like an infuriated child.

'No, thank you. And if you sabotage me again like that you will feel my cue between your ribs!'

Cory caught hold of her arm, pulling her close to him. He could sense the genuine distress beneath her childish anger and it was like a blow to the heart.

'Pax, Rachel,' he said. 'I am sorry.'

She looked up at him and he could see the conflict in her expression. She was aware that something had changed between them but she did not understand what was happening to them. Swiftly, briefly, unable to resist, Cory lowered his head and kissed her. It was not much different from the comforting caresses he had occasionally offered to Rachel when she had been younger and had bumped her knee. The images in his head were of consolation and reassurance, but such thoughts fled as his lips touched hers and the kiss transformed itself into something entirely different. Rachel's lips parted for him with a trusting innocence that incited a rush of desire and swept all memories away. Suddenly he was kissing her with a fierce heat that almost pushed all common sense beyond his reach. Rachel's lips were soft and helplessly accepting beneath his and he drove one hand into her hair to hold her still so that he could plunder the sweetness still further.

The billiards cue fell with a clatter beside them and they both jumped. Cory let Rachel go so suddenly that she almost fell and had to put out an instinctive hand to steady herself against the billiard table.

'Sorry,' Cory said. He caught Rachel's arm to help her regain her balance, flinching as he saw the way she pulled away from him.

'I'm sorry, Rachel,' he said again. He did not regret what he had done, but he was obliged to admit that he could have shown considerably more finesse.

Rachel's eyes were blank for a moment, then expression slowly returned to them. She put up a hand and touched her lips gently. 'What…what was that?'

Cory felt his stomach drop at the bewildered note in her voice. 'That,' he said, 'was a kiss between friends.'

Rachel nodded slowly. 'I remember you saying the other night that a kiss between friends was a mistake. Now that it has happened, do you think it is true?'

Cory did not think so, but equally he did not want to frighten her further. He could see how shocked she was at the way their comforting friendship had so abruptly shifted into something far more dangerous. Even though there had been intimations of such a change over the previous weeks, the suddenness of it had startled her as well as aroused her.

'What do *you* think?' he asked.

Rachel's hazel gaze focussed on his face. 'I think it was the inevitable consequence of getting too close to a rake,' she said.

Cory laughed ruefully. 'I cannot in all honesty deny that,'

he said, 'although I think there was probably more to it than that. Do you mind, Rae?'

Rachel gave him a brief glance. He sensed that she felt shy with him, which was an unusual state of affairs between them.

'No,' she said slowly. Her brow puckered. 'I suppose I ought to mind.'

Cory took her hand. He could feel her pulse racing beneath his fingers and the way she trembled beneath his touch. It lit a savage male urge within him. At its most primitive, it made him want to throw her down on the billiards table and make love to her there and then. He took several steps away from temptation, drawing her with him by the hand and forcing himself to be gentle.

'So you did not mind it.' Cory kept his tone soft. 'Could you even go so far as to say that you enjoyed it, Rae?'

Rachel pursed her lips. Cory wanted to kiss them again.

'It was quite pleasant,' she allowed, withdrawing her hand from his, 'but it was a mistake all the same.' She unconsciously pressed her fingers to her lips again. 'If we are to remain friends, Cory, I do not believe that we should kiss each other.'

Cory drove his hands into his pockets and tried to hold on to his self-control. 'Is that what you want, Rae—that we remain friends?'

Rachel nodded vigorously. 'I think that we should pretend that it never happened.'

Cory raised his brows. 'Do you think it will be as easy as that?'

Rachel hesitated. She looked a little bewildered. 'Is it not that simple?'

'I suppose so.'

But it was not. Cory knew it. Something had been transformed between them and time could never be turned back. More importantly, he did not want it to be, but he knew not to press the matter now. For all her retreat into friendship,

Rachel had admitted to enjoying the kiss. More than that, she had responded to him with a sweetness that had stirred his blood.

Rachel was still looking at him as though she expected him to say something else. Cory clamped down on all the things that he wanted to say to her and waited politely.

'Well,' Rachel said after a moment, I suppose that I shall see you tomorrow, Cory. Goodnight.'

Cory waited until he heard the soft patter of her footsteps die away along the corridor, then he took the billiard ball from his pocket, placed it on the table, took aim and hit it viciously and precisely into the corner pocket. It relieved some of his frustrations, but not all of them. Nothing short of taking Rachel to his bed would do that, and even then he had the suspicion that as soon as he touched her he would not want to let her go ever again. Given the difficulty he knew he would have persuading her into marriage, he almost groaned aloud. Never had a rake set himself such a daunting task. Never had he been more determined to succeed.

Chapter Ten

'Lady Sally is the most consummate hostess, is she not?' Deborah murmured to Rachel as they stood side by side in the long gallery at Saltires a week later. 'She promised us a ball and here we have one that would grace the *ton*. The Midwinter villages have not seen so many eligible gentlemen since Henry VIII came hunting here!'

'There seems to be plenty of hunting going on this evening,' Rachel said drily. 'The ladies seem determined to charm the gentlemen in order to get them to agree to take part in Lady Sally's watercolour book, and the gentlemen are not exactly resisting very hard!'

She leaned on the stone balustrade to scan the hall below. Saltires was too small to have a ballroom, so Lady Sally had cleared the Great Hall and had had a dais erected for the orchestra at one end, beneath the huge stained glass window. The iron sconces flared with candles and the stone walls were warmed with brightly coloured tapestries. The medieval atmosphere was further enhanced by a self-important little man who strutted through the guests dressed in doublet and hose, his chest thrust out like a ruffled pigeon.

'That is Lady Sally's tame artist, Mr Daubenay,' Deborah commented, following Rachel's gaze. 'He is the one who is commissioned to paint her watercolours. Does he not affect the oddest attire? I almost expect him to bring out a lute and start to serenade the ladies!'

The artist had in fact whipped out a sketching pad and was starting to draw one of Lady Sally's guests. As the crowd in the hall shifted, Rachel saw that it was Helena Lang. She seemed quite flattered by Daubenay's attentions, for she was preening a little under his attentions, tossing her curls and trilling with laughter. At her side lounged a tall man with very dark auburn hair and the classic good looks of the Kestrels. Rachel caught Deborah's sleeve.

'Deborah, you must tell me who Lady Sally's guests are, for I have not been introduced to them all. The gentleman with Miss Lang, for instance. He must be one of the Duke's brothers.'

Deborah laughed. 'That,' she said, 'is Lord Lucas Kestrel, the third of the unholy trinity! They say that he is even more unsafe to tangle with than his brothers because he *looks* a lot less dangerous!'

'He is the one who is an army man, is he not?' Rachel asked. She thought that Lucas looked extremely attractive. 'I had heard that he was recently returned from India.'

Deborah snorted. 'That poppycock! Lucas Kestrel is no more a soldier than Richard Kestrel can sail a ship. I heard the tale he was spinning you the other day about being invalided out of the Navy. I expect he trapped his hand in his desk drawer or some such injury!'

'Oh, Deb,' Rachel said reproachfully. She liked Richard Kestrel and thought her friend unduly harsh. 'You are unkind!'

'I know.' Deb caught Rachel's arm and turned her very firmly in the other direction. 'There is the Duke himself, chatting to Lady Sally. You have not met him yet, have you, Rachel? He is only in Midwinter Bere briefly, for I hear business calls him back to London. A pity he cannot take Lord Richard with him!'

Rachel sighed. There was a certain air of careless distinction about the Kestrel brothers, as though just their presence bestowed a dazzle upon the proceedings. And, indeed, it was a very fashionable crowd that Lady Sally had gathered that evening. Without realising what she was doing, Rachel's gaze instinctively sought out Cory Newlyn in the throng.

When she saw him, formal in his black and white evening clothes, her heart skipped a tiny beat as it had been doing every time she saw him since their kiss in the billiards room. It was pointless, it was annoying, but it was inescapable. Rachel had tried to cure herself of this strange affliction but to no avail. For someone who prided themselves on their common sense, it was particularly galling.

We should pretend that it never happened.

It had sounded quite easy at the time. Now she was not so certain. The following morning she had been possessed by a quite unexpected shyness where Cory was concerned. She had put off going down to the excavation for as long as possible and then conjured up some spurious excuse about asking Lady Odell if she wished for trout or salmon for supper. Naturally Lady Odell had no preference and was surprised to be asked, but at least it gave Rachel the chance to say a subdued good morning to Cory. He had given her a brief, smiling glance and had continued with his work, and after a moment Rachel had turned away and gone back to the house. She had seen Cory each day of the following week and he had seemed to be making a point of spending time with her. Normally Rachel would have enjoyed this, but now she felt a reserve in her manner towards him. She tried to behave as though nothing had happened between them but she knew that it had, and that seemed to make all the difference.

'There is Lord Newlyn,' Deborah said, suddenly. 'My goodness, Rachel, there is something about him…'

Rachel looked—and felt once again the tiny, telltale shiver along her skin.

'He looks most distinguished,' she said colourlessly.

'Well, yes…' Deborah put her head on one side thoughtfully '…in a thoroughly disreputable way!'

Rachel was obliged to laugh. Cory did indeed look supremely elegant tonight, but still rather dishevelled, in a manner that suggested that he had just got out of his own—or someone else's—bed. His tawny hair was tousled, his neckcloth tied with casual aplomb and Rachel was glad to see that he had at least done Lady Sally the honour of having his evening clothes pressed.

As she watched, Cory strolled over to Lucas Kestrel and Helena Lang, looked over the artist's shoulder and grinned. He made some comment to Helena that caused her to look at him archly through her lashes and Rachel felt another sharp twinge in her side, as though someone had stuck a pin in her.

'Are you quite well, Rachel?' Deborah enquired. 'Just for a moment, you looked a little sick.'

'I am very well, thank you,' Rachel said hastily. 'I do believe that your sister and her husband have arrived, Deborah.'

'Oh!' Deb beamed. 'Excuse me! I must ask Ross for a dance.' And she skipped away down the stairs to the hall.

Left alone, Rachel sighed and followed more slowly. Sir Arthur and Lady Odell were being fêted at one end of the hall, but Rachel had no wish to stand in her parents' shadow and hear them talk forever about their greatest excavations. Nor did she wish to hover about Cory Newlyn, listening to him flirt with Helena Lang and feeling like a spare part. Evidently Cory did not have the same difficulty that she did in forgetting. But then, Cory was a rake…

Rachel reached the bottom step and was almost immediately accosted by Lady Sally, the best of hostesses, who would not allow one of her guests to wilt in the shadows untended.

'Miss Odell, I have been looking for you everywhere. Pray come and meet my guests.'

She took Rachel's arm and drew her towards the baronial fireplace, where the Duke of Kestrel was standing. Justin Kestrel professed himself extremely pleased to meet her and Rachel had no reason to doubt his sincerity. His manner was entirely devoted to making her feel at ease, whilst also making her feel she was the most delightful creature in the room. Rachel appreciated this whilst recognising exactly what he was doing. They chatted happily for a few moments, but Rachel was amused to note that when the Duke thought that her attention was not upon him, his gaze was drawn back to Lady Sally like a compass to north.

'Justin, you have monopolised Miss Odell for quite long enough,' Lady Sally said reproachfully, returning after a minute with another gentleman in tow. 'I have brought your cousin James to make her acquaintance.'

Justin Kestrel bowed, a faint smile playing about his lips. Rachel had the strong impression that he was amused. 'Then I concede gracefully, of course, Lady Sally,' he said smoothly. 'Miss Odell… James…'

He bowed and strolled away, and Rachel looked at the newcomer with sharpened interest. This was the only remaining Kestrel that she had not met, and he stood out like a sparrow in a family of peacocks. He was neat where his cousins were flamboyant, quiet where they were gregarious. He seemed colourless beside them and Rachel felt her heart warming to him. She felt drawn to someone who did not quite fit into their surroundings.

The orchestra struck up for a country dance and suddenly the room was vivid with excitement. Justin Kestrel came across and solicited a dance from Lady Sally. Deborah Stratton strolled past on the arm of her brother-in-law, Ross Marney, whilst Cory Newlyn was prising Lily Benedict away from Sir John Norton with a skill that argued long practice. Rachel waited.

James Kestrel adjusted his cuffs and admired his reflection in the long mirror on the wall behind them. Finally he said, 'Would you care to dance, Miss Odell?'

'Thank you, sir,' Rachel said.

James offered a decorous arm.

'This is a very elegant occasion, is it not?' Rachel said, when they took their places in the set. 'Lady Sally entertains in great style.'

James looked around. His thin face wore a slightly disapproving expression as though there were an unpleasant smell beneath his nose.

'It is a little raffish,' he said, 'but that is what one expects when one invites a group of pirates and adventurers to visit.'

Rachel laughed. 'Pirates, sir?'

James primmed his lips. 'There are those here who are little better than pirates. John Norton, for instance…'

Rachel looked round. John Norton was close to them in the set. He saw her looking at him and gave her an exaggerated wink. Rachel blushed and looked quickly away.

'Sir John is bound to win the Deben Yacht race, then,' she said lightly, 'if he is a privateer. Do you sail, sir?'

'Good lord, no,' James Kestrel said. 'It is quite ruinous to the complexion, Miss Odell. Rather like polar exploration. Norton got the most shocking frostbite on his last trip. Almost ate through his nose.' James looked her over thoughtfully. 'I hear that you have been quite the traveller, Miss Odell,' he said. 'I am happy to see that the sun has not taken its toll on your skin. I suppose that you carry a parasol?'

'Always,' Rachel said. Her lips twitched. 'Even in a sandstorm.'

James nodded. 'Very wise. One cannot be too careful. Too much sun and one ends up looking a shocking fright.'

The dance progressed and they all changed partners. With

a flash of surprise, Rachel found herself taking Cory's hand for the next figure. His fingers closed strongly around hers and he gave her his heart-shaking smile.

'Good evening, Rachel. You look very pretty tonight. The golden gauze suits you.'

He was appraising her with a lazy familiarity that nevertheless held echoes of some other, more disturbing emotion. Rachel felt her heartbeat increase. There was something in his eyes that made her feel acutely vulnerable. But this was all wrong—Cory was not supposed to make her feel like this.

She fixed her gaze on a point beyond his right shoulder. It was a mistake, as it brought Helena Lang into her line of sight. Helena was dancing with Lord Northcote, but craning her neck to watch Cory. Rachel felt deeply irritated.

'Good evening, Cory,' she said. 'Are you enjoying yourself in such a…promising environment?'

She saw Cory's grey eyes widen at the sarcasm in her tone, then he flashed her a grin.

'I am having a splendid time, I thank you, Rae. Lady Sally's guests are charming.'

'They are indeed,' Rachel said, feeling cross. She was not sure why she wished to provoke him, but the need to do so seemed to go deep. 'And you seem to be enjoying them to full measure!'

Cory's hand tightened on hers and she looked up at him instinctively. There was a quizzical look in his eyes now. 'What is the matter, Rae?' he asked 'Did you eat a prune at supper?'

Rachel felt a little light-headed. She could sense herself drawing near to some precipice and felt strangely as though she was about to rush straight over the edge. It had something to do with the need to annoy Cory as much as he was angering her with his thoughtless attentions and careless kisses. She did not like to see him flirting with Helena Lang or Lily Benedict. She felt jealous and angry and confused.

Nor did she know what she wanted—Cory's friendship or his kisses.

'I am sure that you understand me,' she said tightly. 'You are…generous…in your attentions, are you not? One might almost say indiscriminate.'

Cory's gaze hardened into challenge. 'Can it be that you are jealous, Rachel?' he asked mockingly. 'I thought you professed to want no more than friendship from me?'

Rachel felt trapped. That was what she had told him. It seemed that it was increasingly untrue. And she did not know what to say.

They continued the dance in silence for a few seconds, but it was a quiet that was taut as a bowstring. After a moment Rachel shot an exasperated look at Cory's face.

'I believe we should have a little more conversation,' she said, 'just to pass the time. Unfortunately, this is a long figure.'

She heard Cory sigh. 'Very well. Since you claim to dislike rakes, then let us speak of men of another sort. Did you enjoy James Kestrel's company? I see that he was talking to you, whilst admiring his own reflection, of course.'

Rachel felt hot with annoyance. There was a strong note of sarcasm in Cory's tone and it infuriated her. Despite her own initial disappointment with James Kestrel, she was not prepared to allow Cory to disapprove of him.

'He seems a very sensible man,' she said.

'Ah. You admire good sense, of course.'

'I admire it more than I like recklessness, certainly. A sensible man is not so unreliable as an adventurer!'

She heard Cory draw a sharp breath. There was an undertone of anger in his voice now. 'You are quick to provoke me tonight, Rachel. I cannot but wonder why.'

Rachel glared at him. 'You are quick to criticise Mr Kestrel, if it comes to that, Cory! I also wonder why.'

Cory's mouth set in a hard line. 'Very well. It's true that I don't like James Kestrel. He is a worthless man. He cares for nothing but his place in society and the starch in his shirts.'

Rachel frowned. 'I had heard him described as a worthy man, not a worthless one. I think that he seems very sound.'

'You are mistaken.'

Their conversation had of necessity been conducted in low tones because the dance kept them in such close proximity to the other couples. Now, however, Rachel found her voice rising to match the frustrated fury inside her.

'You cannot forbear to meddle, can you, Cory? You always know best! This is the third time that you have warned me away from a gentleman who admires me. Well, you are *not* my brother and if I choose to recognise sober virtues where you do not, and value them above your own more dubious qualities, then that is my affair!'

With a shock, she realised that the music had stopped and the other dancers were regarding them with some curiosity. With a tight smile, Cory tucked her hand through his arm and steered her to the edge of the dance floor. Rachel could feel the tense anger that vibrated throughout his entire body. She was almost certain that he was about to drag her into a private room and continue the argument there. It would have been in character; on the rare occasions that they had quarrelled in their youth they had argued the matter out until it was finally settled. This felt different, however. Rachel did not know why, but this dispute felt sharp and painful and damaging. She knew that she had to act quickly in order to prevent any further hurt being done.

Unfortunately, she did not get the chance.

The dance had ended now and James Kestrel himself was approaching them with Lily Benedict on his arm.

Lady Benedict's eyes lit up when she saw the two of them.

'Miss Odell! What good fortune. Perhaps we might exchange partners?' She shot Cory a flirtatious look. 'I know that you will not mind if I importune Lord Newlyn to partner me in the quadrille, for as the two of you are such good friends I do not scruple to split you up!'

Rachel struggled to quell her fizzing temper. She wanted to have put things right with Cory and she also felt a strong aversion to surrendering him to Lily Benedict. Then, as she hesitated, Cory smiled at Lily and said unforgivably,

'Of course you may importune me with my very good will, Lady Benedict! Miss Odell and I are such old friends that we are quite run out of new things to say to each other. I shall hand her over to Mr Kestrel with pleasure. Perhaps he may entertain her more than I do.'

And, with a mocking bow to Rachel, he turned to Lily and drew her away.

Through a mist of outraged fury, Rachel watched them retreat. She and Cory might be very old friends, but he had never been anything but polite to her in public before. She stood frozen to the spot, trying to collect her thoughts whilst Cory walked away without a backward glance.

She thought that James Kestrel was also watching Cory and Lady Benedict as they took their places for the quadrille, but when she looked at him he was rearranging his cuffs and checking his neckcloth.

'I am surprised that you wish to claim acquaintance with Newlyn, Miss Odell,' he said censoriously. 'He can be a ramshackle fellow. Does as he pleases and has no manners at all.'

A hot denial sprang to Rachel's lips, but she beat it down. Her thoughts were in a turmoil. She had no notion why she would wish to defend Cory against criticism when she was so angry with him herself, but to hear James Kestrel condemn him just seemed to make her feel even more wretched.

'Lord Newlyn and I have known each other for years,' she said sharply. 'He is like a brother to me, and, as you saw, shows a brotherly lack of respect on occasion. I do not regard it.'

She knew that she lied. Cory's words had hurt her deeply

and a flame of anger was still burning hotly inside her as she watched him give Lily Benedict his undivided attention. She allowed James to take her arm and lead her over to one of the open windows, where the breeze did a little alleviate her heated feelings. Olivia Marney was sitting alone in the next alcove, drooping a little as she thought herself unobserved. Ross Marney was dancing with Lady Sally and Mr Daubenay, the artist, was standing a short distance away, sketching Lady Odell. A small, admiring group had gathered around them as Lady Sally's guests watched the portrait grow.

James Kestrel flicked a minute speck of dust from his sleeve.

'Would you care to meet tomorrow afternoon, Miss Odell?' he asked, sounding a little bored. 'If it is a pleasant day we could drive along the river.'

Rachel hesitated. She was disinclined to spend much time with James Kestrel, for she had quickly divined that his favourite subject was himself and nothing else could raise any enthusiasm in him. On the other hand she could not bear for Cory to think that she had turned Mr Kestrel away because of anything that he had said. It was a foolish and contrary reason to accept, and Rachel knew it. Nevertheless she nodded and forced a smile.

'Thank you, sir,' she said. 'That would be delightful.'

'It may rain, of course,' James Kestrel continued. 'If it rains, I think we should postpone our plans. It would never do to undertake anything so foolhardy as to go out in the rain.'

'No, indeed,' Rachel agreed, visions of weatherswept excavations in the Shetland Islands before her eyes. 'One could get most horribly wet.'

'One of my best jackets was once damaged by rain,' James said. 'One of Weston's finest creations. It never recovered from the experience.'

'It sounds as though you did not recover either, sir,' Rachel observed sweetly.

James's pale eyes gleamed. 'I did not, Miss Odell. Not only was the jacket ruined, but I took a shocking chill as well. I swear it took me a week to recover my spirits.'

Rachel found herself wishing that the chill had carried him off. She excused herself politely and made her way over to the group that encircled Lady Odell. Mr Daubenay was just finishing the drawing, with a flourish of his pencil and a triumphant exclamation. Rachel craned her neck to see. Daubenay really was very good indeed. He had made no concessions to the toll that time and weather had taken on Lady Odell's face, but the finished effort captured all her character and spirit. Rachel was impressed. She had never been a portraitist herself, but she had once sketched her parents' entire collection of Egyptian antiquities before they had lent them to display at the Egyptology exhibition at the British Museum.

'Devil take it, man,' Lady Odell exclaimed with great good humour, 'do I really possess four chins? How damnably unflattering!'

'I think that Mr Daubenay has captured you perfectly, Mama,' Rachel said tactfully. 'He sees through the outside and draws the soul.'

The artist beamed, clearly delighted. 'You flatter me, Miss Odell.'

'Not at all,' Cory Newlyn's voice said. Rachel jumped to see him looking over her shoulder. 'Miss Odell is in the right of it, Daubenay. Perhaps you could sketch her next. What would you see, I wonder? Youth, beauty and a sweet disposition?'

His tone was equable, but there was mockery in his eyes. Rachel felt herself flush with annoyance. Much more of Cory's provocation tonight and she would be demonstrating her sweet disposition by slapping his face. She drew a little bit away from the group and threw Cory a challenging look.

'Take my advice, sir, and do not attempt a sketch of Lord Newlyn,' she said to the artist. 'There are qualities there that are better left unseen.'

'One up to Miss Odell,' Sir John Norton murmured. His blue eyes were snapping with laughter. 'Come and dance with me, Miss Odell. I feel brave enough to take you on!'

Rachel allowed him to take her arm and lead her into the set. Sir John's admiration was balm after her quarrel with Cory. Something had to be done to cut him down to size, she decided. He was too arrogant, too sure of himself and too overbearing. She paused. If she was so good at drawing and Cory was so reticent at posing for Lady Sally's water-colour booklet, why could she not show him up neatly by sketching him without his knowledge? She could do a rough sketch for Mr Daubenay to work from.

The thought gripped her with sudden excitement. That would put Cory finely in his place and it would go a little way to paying him back for his unchivalrous conduct. She liked that idea. She watched Cory guide Lily Benedict towards the refreshment room, one hand in the small of her back. They were talking, Lady Benedict's dark curls brushing Cory's shoulder as she looked up at him confidingly. Rachel saw Lily give Cory a vivid smile and she felt quite out of proportion feverish with anger. It was not that she wanted Cory for herself. That was a ridiculous idea. It was simply that she was angry with him. Oh, yes, she would like to get even with Cory…

She became aware that Sir John was addressing her, inviting her to go driving with him the following afternoon. He was a decidedly more attractive prospect than James Kestrel, but she smiled sweetly and declined. 'I am sorry, sir, but I am already engaged. Some other time, perhaps?'

She saw the leap of interest in Sir John's eyes and reflected that men were strange creatures to be encouraged by a lady's lack of availability. Sir John was now looking positively determined.

'Friday, then,' he said promptly. 'I shall drive you into Woodbridge, Miss Odell, and I shall not take no for an answer.'

Rachel smiled back. 'Thank you, sir. That would be very pleasant. And now you must tell me about your encounter with the polar bear. I hear it is a truly terrifying tale.'

Sir John laughed and started to recount his story, utterly unaware that she had been teasing him. He was a man whose opinion of himself was evidently very good, Rachel thought, and that sense of importance was no doubt bolstered by the appreciation of the ladies who fawned on him. Just for a moment she longed for Cory's self-deprecating humour. Cory always knew when she was making fun of him and never took himself too seriously. Not that she felt comfortable teasing him any more.

The thought was depressing to her spirits. Nor did her marriage prospects in the Midwinter villages seem very great. There was James Kestrel, who was vain and lacking a sense of humour, and there was John Norton, who was full of his own importance and probably another rake to boot. Rachel sighed. She was not enjoying herself, despite Lady Sally's lavish entertainment, and the sight of Lily Benedict persuading Cory into yet another dance merely completed her bad humour.

After another hour, Rachel was tempted to change her mind about the ball. She had danced with Lucas and Richard Kestrel and with the Duke himself, and it was impossible not to enjoy oneself under the combined onslaught of Kestrel charm. There was a gravity about Justin Kestrel that was most appropriate to a Duke, but it was lightened by a pleasing good humour; Lucas Kestrel had a boyish insouciance that reminded Rachel heart-breakingly of Cory, and Richard Kestrel was simply the most dangerous rake she had ever met, with his outrageous flattery and his expressive dark eyes. Rachel danced and ate and drank and chatted, and on the edge of her vision Cory danced with Deborah Stratton and Helena Lang and Lily Benedict, and spared her not a single glance.

It was much later, when the carriages were being called and the guests were starting to leave, that Rachel went out onto the patio for some fresh air. The air was heavy with residual heat and the smell of night-scented stock and honeysuckle. She rested her hands on the stone parapet and looked out over the gardens of Saltires. All was in darkness, and yet she thought that she saw movement down on the lawn where the fountain splashed between the yew hedges. A faint, feminine giggle floated towards her on the still night air. Rachel raised her brows. So she was not alone in the gardens. Someone was indulging in amorous dalliance in the privacy of the yew walk and she did not wish to spy on their activities. She turned to go back into the ballroom, but as she did so another flicker of movement caught her eye. The door of the card room was also open, the candlelight spilling over the mossy stones of the terrace. Rachel saw the shadows shift as a couple of people moved through the doors and out into the night. A breath of cigar smoke reached her, mingling with the musky smell of the stocks. No amorous couple this, then, but a pair of gentlemen, deep in conversation. Rachel started to walk away, for she did not wish to eavesdrop, but then she realised that she could not retreat without being seen. She kept still.

'Damn it, Richard,' she heard Cory Newlyn say, 'when Justin said that this would involve a spirit of self-sacrifice I had no idea that it would be so bad! Just how much flirtation is one expected to undertake for the sake of the enterprise…'

Rachel heard Richard laugh, and then the voices faded away as they turned their backs and strolled down the terrace.

A tickle of pollen took Rachel unawares. She grabbed her handkerchief and raised it to her nose just in time to stifle the huge sneeze that erupted. Even so, it was not enough.

She heard one of the men give an exclamation and did not wait for more. She dived through the door to the ballroom, the handkerchief discarded on the terrace behind her.

No one appeared to have noticed her hasty entrance. She hid behind a pillar, breathing deeply and trying to calm her racing pulse. She was not quite sure why she was so shaken, but she felt as though she had been caught prying into something that did not concern her She watched the ballroom doors, but the only person who came in was Helena Lang, looking flushed and bright eyed. Helena did not see Rachel, for she was too busy scouring the ballroom for someone completely different. A moment later Rachel realised whom she sought. James Kestrel had entered the great hall from the direction of the refreshment room. He was dusting down his sleeves and adjusting the set of his jacket and looking rather pleased with himself. Rachel turned away.

She leaned one hand against the cool stone wall and pressed the other to her suddenly aching forehead. She could pretend ignorance of Miss Lang's flirtations, but she could not ignore what she had overheard and it disturbed her. Could Cory have had some sort of wager with the Kestrel brothers to flirt with the ladies of Midwinter for their own entertainment? She remembered the occasion on which Richard Kestrel and Cory had come into the teashop in Woodbridge. Cory had been most attentive to Deborah Stratton whilst Richard had made himself agreeable to her. And tonight Cory and Richard and Justin and Lucas had flirted with a great many ladies, damn them…

'I think you must have dropped something, Rachel.'

Cold dread clutched at Rachel's stomach, to be followed by a prickly heat running down her neck. She turned slowly. Cory was standing directly behind her, her handkerchief hanging limply in his hand. It had the letter 'R' embroidered on it, and the way Cory was holding it made this quite visible. Both of them knew that there was no point in her denying that it belonged to her.

Rachel licked her dry lips. Now was the moment to challenge him on what he and the Kestrels were up to. Now was the moment to speak, to be as open and honest as she had always been with him. She looked into his silver grey eyes and he looked back at her. His gaze was hard. Their earlier quarrel seemed to hang heavily between them.

'Thank you,' Rachel said. She took the handkerchief from his grip and tucked it into her reticule, hoping that her hands were not shaking too much. She had no idea why she felt so nervous. Perhaps it was guilt, or anger, or disappointment, or a mixture of all three.

'I must have dropped it when I went outside for some air,' she said.

There was a sceptical lift to Cory's brows. 'I did not see you when I was out there just now. Did you see me?'

Rachel hesitated. She had never told Cory a direct lie in her life. She took a deep breath.

'No,' she said, adding with deliberate flippancy, 'were you taking a young lady outside to look at the stars?'

Cory did not smile. 'No, I was not,' he said.

'Oh.' Rachel felt slightly at a loss. 'Well…thank you…' she gestured vaguely towards her bag '…and goodnight. I believe that Mama and Papa are ready to leave now.'

Cory bowed slightly, his handsome face as still as carved stone. Rachel was uncomfortably aware that he watched her progress across the room to Lady Odell's side. When she was almost there she could not help half-turning to look back at him, and saw that Richard Kestrel had come across to engage Cory in urgent conversation. She saw Cory shake his head once, decisively, then he looked across the room and met her eyes. His own expression was veiled.

The anger took Rachel again. She had liked the Kestrels and, whilst she had not deluded herself that they had any serious intentions, had at least thought them sincere in their compliments. The idea that they had made some odious wager made her feel quite furious.

She could scarcely exact revenge on the Duke or Richard Kestrel, but Cory at least was within her scope. She had thought earlier that he was too arrogant and needed to be cut down to size. Now she was doubly certain. She would surely take her revenge. And it would be sweet.

'What a delightful evening,' Lady Odell said, smothering a yawn as the carriage pulled away from the door of Saltires in the July dawn. 'I have not enjoyed myself so much since Lord Coate hosted the Egyptian Revue! Lady Sally's guests were remarkably cultivated and knowledgeable. Why, Lord Richard Kestrel knew all about Barrington's work in Oxfordshire and spent over a half-hour asking me about our progress on the dig.'

Rachel stifled a yawn of her own.

'Sound fellah,' Sir Arthur grunted. 'Told me he had come across some uncommonly interesting ruins on his travels in Asia. Thought I might look into it one day…'

Rachel felt her heart sink. There she had been trying to persuade Cory from inviting her parents to excavate in Cornwall so that they might be settled in Suffolk for a while, and instead her father was contemplating the deserts of Asia.

'Are you quite well, my love?' Lady Odell enquired, patting Rachel's hand. 'You seem quite done up and it is not at all like you.'

'I am a little tired,' Rachel conceded. 'I fear I did not enjoy the evening as much as you did, Mama.'

'Not surprising, quarrelling like that with Cory,' Sir Arthur said, displaying one of his rare but blinding flashes of perception. 'You are always miserable when you cut up rough with the boy, Rachel. Remember how matters were that time in Patagonia? You did not eat for three days.'

'I was only twelve then,' Rachel said, trying to quell her bad humour, 'and Cory deserved for me to wrangle with him. He was an odiously self-important young man! And he has not changed much either,' she added, with sudden bitterness.

'Best to make up with him,' Sir Arthur grunted, closing his eyes. 'You know you are always happier that way.'

Rachel looked out of the carriage window at the pale light streaking the eastern sky. The suggestion to make up with Cory sat ill with her intention of bringing him down a peg or two by sketching him for Lady Sally's watercolour book. She admitted to herself that such a revenge did seem a little childish. Yet Cory's discourtesy still rankled; as for the business of the wager, that was outrageous.

'I think I shall go straight out to the field when we get home,' Lady Odell said. 'It will be light enough in an hour or so to get an early start, and we wanted to open up the largest burial mound today, did we not, Arthur?'

'Good idea,' Sir Arthur concurred. 'Wake the servants, what, and get digging.'

Rachel wrinkled her brow. 'Is it really a good idea, papa?' she besought. 'You are likely to put a spade through your foot in the half-light.'

Sir Arthur chuckled. 'By goodness, do you remember when I did that at Jericho? What an outcry that caused! Had to send fifty miles to find a quack to treat me.'

'Precisely,' Rachel said. 'I am persuaded that you would not wish to cause such trouble again, Papa.'

Lady Odell leant forward to peer out of the window. 'I do not believe there will be any danger. There is a very good doctor in Woodbridge.'

Rachel sighed. 'At least take the time to change your gown before you go out, Mama. Yes—' she forestalled Lady Odell's next remark '—I am aware that you excavated the ruins of Delphi in a ball gown, but such eccentricity is not to be encouraged.'

There was a small silence in the coach. 'Am I truly eccentric?' Lady Odell sounded rather pleased.

'Yes, Mama,' Rachel said, thawing a little. 'You and Papa both.'

'Nonsense!' Sir Arthur rumbled. 'Just a little unconventional, Lavinia dear. And who would wish to be ordinary anyway?'

I would, Rachel thought, pressing her gloved fingers against the cool pane of the carriage window. That is exactly what I wish to be.

Cory Newlyn walked back to Kestrel Court in the midsummer dawn and this time he walked unmolested. He had dismissed Richard Kestrel's offer of company a little abruptly, but he wanted to think. Specifically, he wanted to think about Rachel Odell.

It was ridiculous to suspect Rachel of being the Midwinter spy. He had said as much to Richard on the night of the discussion at Kestrel Court and he still thought it. Every instinct that he possessed told him that Rachel would never commit such treachery. And yet there was no denying that she had been out on the terrace that night when he and Richard were talking. Worse—and quite inexplicably—she had denied that she had even seen him. Cory had known she was lying, but he had not known why she should do so. As far as he knew, Rachel had never lied to him before. It disturbed him that she should start now.

It was another clear, moonlit night. Cory pulled his neckcloth free with impatient fingers and screwed it up in his hand. He felt better without the constriction of tight evening dress. He felt better out in the open air, if it came to that. Dancing with the likes of Lily Benedict and Helena Lang had been a sore trial to him. Lily had been surprisingly discreet and whilst gossip had fallen from Helena's lips with no encouragement from him, he had learned nothing of interest. Instead he had been obliged to endure her prattle whilst watching Rachel being charming to that tailor's dummy James Kestrel.

He acknowledged to himself that the argument with Rachel had been foolish, but she could be a provocative creature when she chose. Her accusations of insincerity had got under his skin when he had tried so hard to court her gently. But Cory knew the reason for the unresolved tension between them even if Rachel did not. He knew that the kiss in the billiard room, mistake or not, could never be forgotten.

We should pretend that it never happened.

Rachel was trying very hard to make that pretence a reality, Cory thought, but she was not succeeding. Nor could she quite hide her anger when he paid attention to other women. She was jealous and he found that rather encouraging. He was obliged to admit that he was jealous too. Rachel could arouse such an emotion in him without difficulty. It was a new experience for him and one that he acknowledged with rueful recognition. Miss Rachel Odell was his nemesis. He would never escape.

Chapter Eleven

It was several days before Rachel saw Cory again. On the morning after the ball he failed to arrive at the excavation and though Sir Alfred and Lady Odell were inclined to dismiss this indulgently as the results of a late night, Rachel felt even more out of sorts. Secretly she had been hoping that Cory would arrive early and apologise for his ungentlemanly conduct towards her, after which they might be easy together again. It did not happen.

Instead, Rachel checked the contents of the stillroom with Mrs Goodfellow, who was making jam, and spent the rest of the morning reading about the Midwinter Treasure. She had borrowed some of the local records from the Reverend Lang and, though they were in Latin, found the reading very stimulating. It was interesting to see how the myths and legends had grown up around the story of the Treasure, and how deep was the belief that if anyone tampered with it, they did so at their peril. Jeffrey Maskelyne's maps and clues were making little sense to her, but they did seem to confirm that there was something hidden on the burial site. She did not intend to involve Cory in the search, however.

In the afternoon she went driving with James Kestrel, who was, of course, far too moderate in his habits to fail to get up the day after a ball. They had a pleasant hour's drive by the river and at the end of it Rachel knew him for a man with many opinions on a wide variety of subjects and no sense of humour whatsoever. As a marriage prospect he had initially seemed a promising choice, but that was before she had seen him dallying with Miss Lang in the gardens. She felt that this argued a sad unsteadiness of character.

James pressed her to drive with him again soon, but Rachel declined, softening her refusal by agreeing to accept his escort to the Deben Regatta in a few weeks. She wanted to see the spectacle of the Regatta and thought it unlikely that the rest of the family would attend. She felt slightly guilty over this, for she was aware of using James Kestrel almost as much as he appeared to be using Miss Lang.

It rained on the Thursday of that week, shrouding the excavation in a light grey drizzle that sent Sir Arthur grumbling indoors to read the annals of the Archaeological Society and Lady Odell to the library to write some letters. In the evening there was a musicale at Midwinter Marney Hall, but Cory did not appear and Rachel found herself missing him. Sir John Norton was present, pressing in his attentions and flatteringly pleased that he was driving her into town the following day. Rachel wished that she could summon a greater enthusiasm for the outing, but found she could not.

Saturday was bright and hot again and Rachel took her sketching pad and went down to the fields. She walked slowly up to the knot of pines above the river and settled down and was soon engrossed in her drawing. She had seldom drawn people before—all her efforts had been confined to pots and vases and ornaments, to illustrate her parents' extensive collection. For a little while she sketched her mother, trying to capture the movement of the trailing sleeves and flapping scarves, but Lady Odell's round figure looked like a butterball on the page, so with a sigh Rachel turned to her father instead. Sir Arthur was digging out a trench at the easternmost extent of the burial ground and his thin stooping figure looked like a stick man in Rachel's first attempt. She sketched him again, with concentration, only slightly distracted by the thought that his tweed jacket would be thick with dust by the end of the day and would require a good beating.

It was quite late in the afternoon when Cory Newlyn suddenly appeared, strolling down the path from the house, raising a hand to greet the Odells and walking across to the trench where Rachel had sat with him a few of weeks before. He moved with a casual grace. Rachel caught her breath as he approached. The passage of a few days had only hardened her intention to make him suffer for his cavalier behaviour at the ball, for she had been hurt and annoyed that their quarrel had meant so little to him that he had not hurried to apologise. Now that the moment of revenge had come, however, she felt strangely nervous.

She watched Cory as he exchanged a few words with Bradshaw, discarded his jacket and set to work. Not for Cory the formality of a tweed coat on a hot day. He was not wearing his disgusting hat today either and the breeze tousled his fair hair and tugged at his linen shirt, flattening it against his chest. His buff-coloured breeches hugged the taut lines of his thighs. Rachel blinked, decided that she had been staring for long enough, picked up her pencil again and set to work on the sketch.

Her first attempt was hopeless. She had got the proportions all wrong so that Cory ended up looking like a giant with a tiny head. It was ridiculous to think that such a picture could ever be the basis for one included in Lady Sally's watercolour book. Far from humiliating Cory, she would embarrass no one but herself. She was ashamed to even think of approaching Mr Daubenay with the draft of the sketch. Impatient, Rachel flicked over another sheet and tried again. When her second attempt also failed she stopped and bit the end of her pencil thoughtfully. Perhaps she had not given her subject the attention that was needed. Perhaps she needed to study him properly and analyse his physique.

Cory was about a hundred feet away from her, but he had his back half-turned to her so there was little likelihood that he would see her. Rachel rested the drawing pad on her lap and studied him for a good five minutes, watching the way that his body moved with such smooth precision. She examined him with the dispassionate gaze of the artist and felt quite undisturbed. Then she began again.

She started with his face, for she could see it in profile—the clear-cut line of his cheek and jaw, the dishevelled tawny hair that fell across his forehead. He had his loose linen shirt turned up to the elbows now, and the muscles in his arms corded as he worked, lifting and digging, moving with a fluid energy and elegance that was a pleasure to watch. Every so often the breeze would flatten the shirt against the hard, sculpted lines of his back. Rachel started to sketch his torso and this time she got the proportions perfect. She was extremely pleased with her progress.

And then Cory took off his shirt.

One minute he had been engrossed in shovelling a pile of soil out of the trench, the next he had put down the spade and with one movement pulled the linen shirt over his head. The late afternoon sun shone upon him, burnishing his skin to gold. Rachel's pencil fell from between her fingers and rolled away into the grass. She blinked, frowned and discovered that her mouth had fallen open. She closed it again quickly.

In a way, the experience down by the river should have prepared her for such an eventuality and yet it had not. In that moment it was as though a flame had been lit within her and it was utterly impossible for her to view Cory with the detached eye of the artist. Instead she was compelled to see him as clearly as she had seen him once before, strong, virile and devastatingly attractive. The knowledge was like a blow to the stomach, knocking all the breath out of her.

She looked down at her sketches and suddenly the idea of trying to humiliate Cory for his treatment of her seemed shabby and underhand and, above all, desperately sad. Rachel could see now that it had been a foolish idea from the very first, born of jealousy and frustration because she disliked the attentions that Cory was paying to other women. It was a mortifying thought and she understood neither why she should feel like that nor what she could do about it.

And whilst she sat there, frozen between shock and horror and desire, the breeze caught the edge of her sketch-pad, scattering the pages in all directions. She made an instinctive snatch for it and Cory glanced up from where he was working and looked directly at her. He grabbed his shirt in one hand and leapt out of the trench.

Rachel jumped to her feet, overcome by total panic. She did not know where to look or what to do first. The pages of the sketch-pad were dancing in the wind, evading her desperate attempts to gather them together. Out of the corner of her eye she saw Cory shrug himself back into his shirt and heard the crunch of the sand under his boots as he came up the slope towards her. It was bad enough that he should have caught her watching him, but if he realised that she had been drawing him as well... Rachel grabbed at the nearest pieces of paper with trembling fingers, feeling slightly sick as she saw Cory bend to pick up a couple of the sheets and glance at them with a casual interest.

He joined her in the lee of the pines and held the pages out to her politely.

'Hello, Rachel.' He did not sound in the least bit out of breath from the climb up the slope.

Rachel, in contrast, found herself gasping for air. 'Oh! Um...hello, Cory!' She snatched the paper from him and pressed it against her chest. 'Ah...thank you!'

'My pleasure,' Cory said. 'It is a windy day for sketching.'

Rachel risked a quick look at the sheets he had found. They were the pictures of her parents. Thank God. That must mean that she had already scooped up the incriminating drawings of him and he need never see them.

Cory was looking her over with cool appraisal. Rachel was horribly aware that her face was flushed and she was almost certain that she was sweating. She crumpled the drawings viciously in her hand. The idea of sketching him had been a terrible mistake from the first, in so many ways. Until now she had not quite realised just what a mistake. She was never, ever going to attempt to draw Cory again. Lady Sally's book of watercolours would simply have to do without him.

'I didn't realise that you were up here,' Cory continued, his silver gaze still on her face. 'Have you been here long?'

Rachel blushed harder. 'Yes…no! That is, just long enough to do a few sketches…' she gestured wildly '…of my parents, you know, and the scenery…'

'The scenery,' Cory repeated. A smile touched the corners of his mouth. 'I see.'

Rachel felt a sudden dread that he had, in fact, seen one of the drawings of himself. She fought down the urge to uncrumple the paper and check again.

'I apologise,' Cory said slowly, 'if you saw me without my shirt. I would not want to offend a lady. Not after the last time.'

Rachel's throat was dry. She stared at him, remembering in vivid detail the hard muscle and smooth brown skin beneath the linen. Her fingers itched to touch him. 'I…er…I was not offended,' she said.

Cory raised a brow. 'So you *did* see me?'

Rachel swallowed hard. 'I…I scarce noticed. I was busy drawing.'

Cory looked at her whilst the hot colour mounted into her face and her skin felt as though it was burning.

'Well,' he said, after a moment, 'I am glad that I have seen you, Rae, because I wanted to speak to you about the ball. I am sorry I could not do so sooner, but I was called away at short notice.'

Rachel turned away. She did not want to prolong their meeting. She wanted nothing more than to escape. And though she had wanted Cory to apologise, she now found that she did not wish to talk about the ball. She was too embarrassed at the situation he had almost caught her in.

'There is no need—' she began.

Cory put his hand on her arm. 'Please. There is a need. I was very discourteous to you, Rae, and I wish to apologise.'

Rachel paused on the edge of flight. 'It does not matter, Cory. As you said, we are such old friends that I dare say we need not stand on ceremony with one another.'

Cory was watching her face. Now she saw the swift frown that darkened his own. 'You sound very matter of fact, Rae,' he said. 'I had the impression that you were quite upset at the time.'

Rachel bit her lip. 'I was. But I feel a lot better now.' The edges of the papers bit into her palm, reminding her of the need to hurry away. 'Excuse me, please. I... There are things that I must do. The man will be here to mend the clock soon. Papa took it apart to prove some ridiculous law of physics and now there is sand in the mechanism.'

Cory smiled at her and it felt like the sun coming out on a dark day. Rachel felt the helpless, strong attraction catch her as it had done when she was sketching, and she sought to cover it by bending to retrieve her pencil from the springy grass.

'There is a card party at Mrs Stratton's this evening,' she said, a little at random. 'Do you attend, Cory?'

'Not tonight,' Cory said. 'Is James Kestrel escorting you?'

Rachel turned her head sharply. 'No, he is not. Why do you ask?'

'No particular reason.' Cory thrust his hands moodily into

the pockets of his trousers. 'I hear that you have been out driving together? I am surprised that Kestrel would risk an activity as dangerous as taking out a team of horses. He might damage himself.'

Rachel tried not to smile. James Kestrel had, in fact, been a competent whip, but there was no doubt that he had been more concerned for his own comfort on the drive than that of his passenger.

'Was this not how we started to quarrel last time, Cory?' she enquired lightly. 'There are certain topics that I feel we should avoid if we are to be comfortable together.'

Cory leant one hand against the trunk of the nearest pine tree and scrutinised her from top to toe. 'Such as our choice of dancing, driving and flirting partners?' he said softly.

'Precisely.' Rachel tilted up her chin with hauteur. 'I shall not comment on your flirtations if you do not pass judgement on mine.'

Cory gave her his slow, wicked smile. 'Why should we avoid discussing them, Rae,' he challenged, 'when we are good friends and claim to be able to talk about anything? Are we admitting that the nature of our friendship has changed?'

Rachel felt the colour creep into her cheeks. Her mind was split; half of it was concentrating fiercely on not letting go of the papers in her hand, and the other was wrestling with the difficulties of engaging with Cory on this particular topic. It was not that she felt she was about to quarrel with him again. Far from it. She felt in danger of an entirely different sort, disturbed, disquieted and disconcerted by her feelings for him. She stared at him, quite unable to formulate a suitable response.

The wind whipped the sheets of sketches out of her hand for a second time.

'Careful,' Cory said. He put his boot on one piece of paper and bent to pick it up, almost colliding with Rachel, who had pounced on it quickly. Her heart was beating as quick as a drum and she crumpled the pages into a tiny ball.

'Excuse me, Cory,' she said quickly. 'I really must go and get ready.'

'You are always rushing away from me,' Cory said gently. He smiled and Rachel felt even more heated. 'Some time soon, Rae, we must spend some time together.'

'I...' Rachel was not sure how she felt about that. Spending time with Cory now felt like inviting danger. She could not look at him. She felt edgy and nervous, and assured herself that it was entirely to do with the incriminating piece of paper screwed up in her hand rather than anything to do with Cory himself.

'That would be pleasant,' she said rapidly. 'Excuse me, please...' It came out like a plea.

Cory nodded slowly. He touched her cheek, his fingers cool against her hot skin, then turned on his heel and strolled back down towards the excavation. When he had gone five paces, he stopped and turned back.

'Oh, by the way, Rachel,' he said, 'I have been giving some thought to what you said about Lady Sally's book of watercolours and I think that you are right. I have been a little...ungenerous...in refusing to take part. I think that I might sit for my portrait after all.'

Rachel gave a little gasp. It was all that she could do to avoid looking guiltily at the paper she was clutching so tightly. She attempted a nonchalant tone, but it came out rather high and breathless. 'Oh, do you think so, Cory? That would be nice.'

'I am glad that you approve.' Cory was smiling at her gently. 'That is, of course, unless you would prefer to sketch me yourself? As you are taking a renewed interest in your drawing...'

Rachel clutched convulsively at her sketchpad and her pencil snapped, the two ends shooting off into the undergrowth. 'I fear that my skill could not equal the subject,' she said tightly.

'No?' Cory said. 'If you are sure.' He sauntered off down the path to the excavation and Rachel could hear him whistling under his breath as he went. She was sure that he knew exactly what she had been doing.

Chapter Twelve

'Ladies, please!' Lady Sally Saltire clapped her hands together like a schoolmistress reproaching her recalcitrant flock. 'How are we to discuss *The Enchantress* when you are none of you paying attention?'

The members of the reading group were seated on the lawn at Saltires, under a large white marquee. It was another scorching day and it was a pleasure to be out of doors where the faint breeze from the river brought at least a little relief from the blistering heat. The air was warm and full of the heady scents of an English summer: the sharp sweetness of cut grass, the dry, nose-tickling smell of lavender and the faint pale perfume of the pink roses that tumbled over the arbour to their left. It made Rachel feel very somnolent.

Lady Sally had arranged for iced lemonade and almond biscuits to be served to her guests and the ladies had settled into their chairs and opened their books at chapter twelve, beginning an animated discussion of whether Sir Philip Desormeaux was genuinely in love now, or whether he was merely infatuated. Lady Sally contended that their hero, like many a man, was fickle and afraid to commit himself. Lady Benedict chided her for her cynicism and Miss Lang said that, for her part, she found the book slow and wished the author would simply get on with the story.

It was at this point that a counter-attraction occurred and the attention of all the ladies was, to a greater or lesser extent, distracted. Rachel was the first to notice it. Around the side of the house had come Cory Newlyn, accompanied by Mr Daubenay. The artist set his easel up on the lawn facing the rose arbour and instructed his subject to stand on the step under the archway and adopt the attitude of a man scanning distant horizons.

Rachel smothered a giggle. Evidently the idea was to create the impression of a fearless adventurer striding out across the desert, but since Cory was standing in Lady Sally's rose garden and one of her prized Austrian Copper roses appeared to be growing out of his head, the effect was decidedly more prosaic. Furthermore, she could tell that even at this distance Cory thought the whole thing ridiculous. There was something stiff in the way that he held himself, an impatience that was barely concealed. And when he saw the ladies watching him, he positively scowled.

They soldiered on for a while longer but when Cory, on the instructions of Mr Daubenay, took his jacket off and slung it casually over one shoulder, all concentration was lost. Helena Lang's mouth was open and even Deborah Stratton had to be recalled to the discussion twice. Rachel was annoyed to find herself as culpable as anyone else. She tried to concentrate on Sir Philip's infatuation with Miss Milward and only succeeded in finding her thoughts suspended as she considered Cory's lithe figure. She looked up to find Lady Sally's amused gaze resting on her.

'I cannot tell you, Miss Odell,' Lady Sally said, 'how grateful I am to you for persuading Lord Newlyn to pose for my watercolour book. I do believe the credit must all be yours.' She closed her book with a snap. 'And the blame for disturbing my reading group must rest entirely with him. Johnson!' She called one of the footmen over. 'Pray ask Mr Daubenay to take his sketching elsewhere. His subject is distracting my ladies!'

It seemed, however, that the mood of the group was broken. Even after Cory and Mr Daubenay had walked away to take up another position in the walled garden—locked in and out of sight, Lady Sally said—the ladies could not settle back to their discussions. In exasperation, Lady Sally sent them all home to read the next few chapters on their own.

'Pray be prepared to make more of a contribution next week,' she said severely, on parting from her guests, but there was a twinkle in her eye.

Rather than take the path by the river, Rachel accepted a ride from Olivia and Deborah as far as Midwinter Mallow village. The movement of the gig at least set up a small, refreshing breeze, which was very welcome on so hot a day. As they drove the ladies quizzed her about her matrimonial affairs, in which they had taken a proprietary interest. Deb maintained that James Kestrel was Rachel's most ardent admirer and, since Rachel had promised herself not to share the information of James's flirtation with Helena, she could do nothing more than laughingly disagree.

'Indeed, Rachel,' Olivia commented, 'you have quite a proliferation of admirers, do you not, just like Sir Philip Desormeaux in *The Enchantress!*'

'And as is the case with Sir Philip,' Rachel said, 'I am not content with any of them. Mr Lang is a wastrel, Mr Kestrel is a bore and Sir John is an out-and-out rake. He tells me that he wishes to marry, and indeed he may do so, but I doubt that would encourage him to give up his other amorous pursuits.'

Olivia sighed and encouraged the fat pony to a faster trot. The gig gathered speed down the hill towards Midwinter Mallow.

'That would certainly appear to put him out of the picture,' she agreed. 'Some women do not regard it, but I confess that it would not be to my taste for my husband to be unfaithful.'

Rachel shook her head despondently. 'I do not understand

why it is so difficult to find a respectable man in the Mid-winter villages,' she said. 'All the gentlemen are completely unacceptable!'

'Now if you were looking for a rogue and a scoundrel you would be positively overwhelmed with candidates,' Deb said, laughing.

They rounded the bend at the bottom of the hill.

'You may find,' Olivia said shrewdly, 'that these so-called rogues of yours are sound men underneath the surface.'

'Oh, pooh!' Deborah said. 'Lord Richard Kestrel of steady disposition?'

Olivia gave her sister a speaking look and Deborah flushed under her scrutiny.

'I am sure,' Rachel said hastily, 'that I understand what Deborah means, Lady Marney. I do not know Lord Richard well, but I can state with certainty that Lord Newlyn, for example, could never be described as of steady disposition.'

Olivia was smiling faintly. 'Maybe not, but does he possess a sense of humour, Miss Odell?'

Rachel laughed. 'Oh, indeed he does.'

'And does he also possess sufficient humility?'

'Not at all. He is quite arrogant at times.'

Now it was Olivia's turn to laugh. 'Yet that can be quite an attractive trait in a gentleman. Surely you would not deny that in comparison with Sir John Norton, for example, Lord Newlyn is charmingly self-deprecating?'

Rachel thought about it and she was obliged to admit that there was some truth in what Olivia was saying.

'Well…' she said cautiously, 'it is true that Cory—Lord Newlyn—is not self-important in the same way as Sir John.'

'And you think him attractive?'

Rachel blushed. 'I suppose I can see that he is.'

'That does not signify,' Deborah objected. 'One would have to be dead not to find Lord Newlyn attractive!'

'Very well.' Olivia conceded the point. 'But you like him, Rachel? You esteem him as a man?'

Rachel frowned. She realised that her feelings for Cory Newlyn were becoming very complicated. She felt for him an emotion far stronger than mere esteem. She liked Cory tremendously. She always had done. The reason she had regretted their quarrel so much was because she valued Cory's friendship highly and could not bear to lose it. In fact, she did not merely *like* Cory. She loved him... The colour flooded her face.

'Yes,' she said quietly. 'I hold him in the highest esteem.'

'So,' Olivia said inexorably, 'in point of fact, Lord New-lyn possesses almost all the qualities you would look for in a gentleman. Whereas Sir John and Mr Lang and Mr Kestrel are sadly lacking.'

Rachel was saved from replying, for the gig was pulling to a halt at the crossroads in Midwinter Mallow.

'We should all go on a trip to the seaside,' Deborah said, fanning herself lazily, 'if the weather holds. Would you like that, Rachel?'

'I would enjoy it extremely,' Rachel said. She waved goodbye to them and watched as the gig turned down the track that forked right towards Midwinter Marney and the sea, then she prepared to walk the remaining mile to Mid-winter Royal House.

The sun seemed even more intense out in the open. It dazzled the eyes and squeezed the head with lassitude until Rachel wanted nothing more than to lie down in the shade and sleep. By the time that she reached the square in Mid-winter Mallow, she was already too hot and wished that she had taken advantage of Olivia's offer of a ride in the gig all the way home. The village was quiet—even the birds were silent, weighed down by the heat. On impulse, Rachel crossed the dusty square and went under the lych gate into the churchyard. Here the slabs of the path burned the soles of her shoes, but the yew trees cast their shade on the uneven gravestones. She sat down in the shadow of the lych gate. That was better. Now she could draw breath and cool down, for she was unpleasantly aware of the sweat running between her shoulder blades and the flushed heat of her face. She did so hate to sweat; not only was it unladylike, it also caused more laundry.

Perhaps it was the intensity of the heat or perhaps it was something else—Olivia's comments, maybe—that made Rachel's thoughts turn back to Cory Newlyn and the conversation that had gone before. Olivia had put her finger on matters with uncanny accuracy. Cory possessed many of the qualities that Rachel admired. He was the sort of man that she wanted.

Rachel stared hard at an avocet picking its way delicately across the distant mudflats in its search for food, but the outline of the bird blurred before her eyes. She was staring intently, but her gaze was turned inward, not outward. For the first time she was confronting her feelings without artifice.

She wanted a husband like Cory Newlyn. Rachel wriggled her shoulders under the thin material of her spencer. No. It was more than that. The truth was that *Cory* was the man she wanted.

A cold sliver of fear and doubt touched Rachel's spine as soon as the thought came into her head. That had to be wrong. Cory was an adventurer, reckless, rash and unpredictable. She disapproved wholeheartedly of his lifestyle. And yet she also cared for him. She knew she could trust him utterly. She never doubted him.

Rachel blinked sharply, as though trying to clear her head. She felt that she was on very dangerous ground and should begin a retreat here and now, before she got herself into a hopeless position. There was no harm in admitting that she cared for Cory as she would for an elder brother. Furthermore, she was willing to allow that he possessed qualities that she liked and admired. She would even permit herself to go so far as to admit she wanted a man who embodied those characteristics. But Cory himself… She pushed away the insidious thought. It was quite impossible that she should be drawn to Cory in that manner. They wanted different things from their lives. And she was sure that he would never, ever, see her as more than a friend.

She paused. Had Cory seen her as a friend when he had kissed her in the billiards room? Was it friendship that she had felt for him when she had sat watching him in the lee of the pine trees and felt that deep and disturbing sensual awareness? She could not lie to herself. What she had felt was something far more troubling than mere friendship. What she had felt was attraction. And she was going to have to cure herself. Fast.

When she reached home she found Cory in the hallway, talking to her father. Sir Arthur greeted her absent-mindedly and wandered off to the excavation and Cory turned to Rachel with a smile. The late afternoon sun was making warm puddles on the marble floor and burnishing Cory's hair to a rich bronze. Rachel swallowed hard. She was disturbed to realise that she was fast becoming fixated on looking at him. She must be suffering from too much sun. What was needed was a good thunderstorm to clear the air and return them all to the right minds.

'Are you quite well, Rachel?' Cory asked, touching her arm. His tone was gently mocking. 'You seem very flustered.'

'I…yes, thank you!' Rachel pulled away from him. 'I believe I am feeling the heat a little today.'

'Ah, the heat,' Cory murmured. 'Such a useful explanation for all sorts of maladies!'

Rachel narrowed her eyes at him. 'Was there something that you wanted, Cory?'

'Plenty of things,' Cory said. His gaze wandered over her face and lingered on her mouth. Rachel fidgeted.

'Yes?' Her voice was husky.

'I wondered whether you could find me your father's October 1802 copy of the *Ipswich Journal*?' Cory said. 'It seems that there is an interesting reference to the Midwinter Treasure in it.'

Rachel felt an absurd pang of disappointment and was angry with herself for it. She shook the feeling off and managed to match his casual air.

'The paper? Oh, yes, of course. I will have a look through Papa's files and have it ready for you later.'

'Thank you.' Cory smiled at her. 'I suppose I had better be going. Did you enjoy your meeting of the reading group today?'

Rachel furled her parasol. 'Yes, thank you. We all saw you in the gardens. I am surprised that you escaped Mr Daubenay so soon, though. Surely he cannot have achieved his sketch for the watercolour book so quickly?'

Cory pulled a face. 'I fear that I became bored and told him that I had pressing business to attend to. Standing around doing nothing whilst my likeness is taken is not my idea of a good use of time.'

Rachel shook her head. 'You achieved plenty. You managed to distract our attention from *The Enchantress* for a start! Lady Sally was most dismayed to have the book upstaged.'

She thought that Cory looked rather pleased with himself. 'Did I distract you?' he said.

Rachel hesitated. It seemed that lying to Cory was coming a little too easily these days.

'You did not distract me personally,' she said, 'but Mrs Stratton and Miss Lang were both quite overwhelmed and even Lady Sally herself had an appreciative gleam in her eyes.'

'Whereas you, having grown up indifferent to me, were wondering why everyone was stuck on page forty-five?'

Rachel smiled. 'Not precisely. I could see why you would be an asset to Lady Sally's book of watercolours.'

Cory looked surprised. 'Could you, indeed? That is quite an admission, Rachel. Not long ago you were telling me that you were sure there were other ladies who might be impressed by my charms, but that you were not amongst them.'

Rachel realised that she had made a tactical error.

'Well,' she said, blushing, 'I feel it my duty to prevent you from developing too good an opinion of yourself.'

'Someone has to take on the job, I suppose,' Cory said, 'though God knows, I wish it was not you, Rachel. You are the person whose good opinion I most value. The only reason I agreed to Lady Sally's drawing was to please you.'

Rachel looked at him. 'Truly? But surely my opinion cannot matter that much to you?'

'You would be surprised,' Cory said drily. 'Surely you know by now that I only wish to make you happy?'

His tone was mocking, but underneath it was a note of sincerity. Rachel searched his face. The hall was cool and shadowed and hid Cory's expression, and she was not certain if he was smiling. It seemed remarkably difficult to tear her gaze away from him.

'I had not realised…' Rachel pulled herself together. 'That is, I am glad that you decided to pose for the watercolour book…'

Her throat dried up and her words with it as she took in the expression in his eyes.

'And what do you think about the other things I said?' Cory asked gently. 'Rachel, you know that yours is the opinion I most value.'

'I…' Rachel could not reply. All afternoon she had been trying to erect barriers against Cory in her mind and now he was intent on demolishing them as soon as they were made. He raised a hand and brushed a strand of hair away from her cheek. There was a look of deep concentration in his eyes. He leaned closer.

He was going to kiss her. Rachel's heart was racing. Her lips parted instinctively. She saw Cory's gaze drop to them. They were very close now. Cory's touch made her feel quite dizzy. In a moment she would be in his arms and she would not fight it, would not resist for a second, for she did not want to do so. The idea filled her with shock and excitement and a sweet longing.

The door to the servants' quarters opened and Mrs Good-fellow bustled out, stopping abruptly as she saw the couple in the hall.

'There you are, my lord! Lady Odell wondered if you wished to join the family for dinner tomorrow night? She mentioned something about a picnic down by the river. Isn't that right, Miss Rachel?'

Wrenched from her sensual dream, Rachel blushed bright red and backed several steps away.

'I… Oh yes, yes, it is.' She risked a look at Cory's face, saw the humour there and blushed harder. Damn him for being able to do this to her. She took a deep breath.

'By all means join us,' she said, trying to sound gracious rather than merely breathless. 'In the interests of friendship, of course.'

She saw Cory tense slightly. 'Friendship. Of course.' He smiled again. 'I should be delighted.'

'Good.' Rachel felt relieved. This should put an end once and for all to the strange nuances between them. They could recapture their old footing and be at ease. The company of Sir Arthur and Lady Odell would make it appear just like old times.

She gave Cory a faint smile. 'Goodbye then, Cory.'

Cory waved and went out, and Rachel went slowly up the stairs to her room and threw herself down on the bed, staring up at the canopy. This attraction to Cory had to be a fleeting thing, a matter of proximity only. Their friendship had endured for seventeen years, but it would not last another five minutes if she were to give in to the temptation of his kisses. For how could they go back after that? Cory was not the marrying kind, and even if he was, he was not the man for her. They wanted such different things from their lives that their hopes and aspirations could never match.

Rachel rolled over and pressed her cheek against her cool pillow. She knew that she was being sensible. She knew that she was being logical. She knew that she was drawn to Cory with an inexplicable but undeniable attraction and that she was still no closer to discovering a cure.

Chapter Thirteen

At eight o'clock the following evening, Rachel made her way down through the gardens to the knot of pines overlooking the river. The air was warm and heavy and the river flowed slowly. The sun had not yet set and her parents and the servants were still busy about the excavations. Cory, however, had finished work in the afternoon and sent her a message that he was returning to Kestrel Court to change his clothes and that he would see her for dinner later.

Rachel had been touched. She would not have expected him to be so thoughtful or to attach so much importance to their meal. There had been times in the past when Cory had finished digging for the day, rolled his sleeves down and come to join her for a casual supper—having washed his hands first, of course. Apparently tonight was to be different.

She realised the extent to which she had underestimated Cory when he appeared, for he was dressed in tight buckskins, gleaming Hessians and a coat of green superfine that fitted his broad shoulders like a second skin. He came down the slope to join her, took her hand and kissed her on the cheek. Rachel, breathing in the scent of lime cologne, felt very slightly dizzy. She took a deep breath of the fresh evening air and reminded herself that this evening was the one that was meant to set everything back in its former place. She wanted the familiar and the comforting claims of friendship, not the disturbing demands of attraction.

'Good evening, Rachel,' Cory said.

'I am sorry that I am not as smart as you,' Rachel said, suddenly feeling self-conscious in her old green cotton dress that was sprinkled with embroidered daisies. 'You show me up, Cory, in all that finery.'

Cory smiled. 'Indeed, Rachel—' his eyes skimmed her in a thoroughly disconcerting way '—you look charming. I have no complaints over the company.'

They sat down on the blanket and Rachel passed him a glass of lemonade.

'Would you care to eat? Mama and Papa are still at work, but I have reminded them that the picnic is ready and they have sworn to join us shortly.'

Cory propped himself up on one elbow and reached for the bread and cheese. 'They are very dedicated,' he said.

'They are certainly dedicated to their antiquities and devoted to each other,' Rachel agreed, with an edge to her voice. 'I cannot dispute that.'

There was a pause. 'They love you too, you know, Rae,' Cory said. He was holding a chicken leg in his strong, brown fingers. 'They may appear to be obsessed with their work, but they do care about you.'

Rachel sighed. It felt comfortable to have Cory here with her now, rather like the old days when they had sat together and chatted about all manner of subjects at any hour of the day or night. For once there was none of the edgy wrangling that had so beset their encounters over the last few weeks. She had never felt a strong attraction to a man before in her entire life, and it felt odd that it should be Cory, for beneath the disturbing awareness, there was the closeness and familiarity that seventeen years of friendship had built. Which was why it was so utterly important that she should cling on to that friendship and not put it at risk.

'I know that my parents love me,' she said now. 'It is

simply that I come third on the list.' She cut herself a piece of cheddar cheese and broke off a piece of the bread. 'I remember hearing Mama tell Lady Cardew it was the greatest nuisance when I was born, for she had just uncovered a Roman temple in Gloucestershire and could not get out to the site for an entire week!'

Cory laughed. 'That sounds like your mother.' He tossed the chicken bone aside. 'Nevertheless, she cares for you, Rae. She must do. She did not send you to boarding school when she travelled abroad, but took you everywhere with her.'

Rachel nodded. 'I know. I am an ungrateful wretch. I begged and begged to be sent to school, you know. I wanted to be like all the other girls. I have seen half the world when all I really wanted was to have a settled life.'

Cory smiled at her. 'That is a reasonable enough aim too.'

'Not for you. You have no desire to settle in one place.'

'True. I want very different things in my life.'

Rachel looked at the slow drift of the river and from there to Cory's shadowed face. 'What do you want, Cory?'

She thought that he hesitated before answering, but when he spoke his tone was easy. 'All the things that I have now. The excitement of travel and exploration, the freedom, the uncertainty…' He flashed her a smile. 'All the things that you dislike, Rae.'

Rachel reached for an apple from the basket and took a small bite. 'Why do you like it so much?'

Again Cory hesitated. 'Because it is so unpredictable. I never know where I might go, or what I might find.'

'What about the ordinary things? A home and a family?'

Cory tilted his glass of lemonade to his lips. 'I have a home. Newlyn Park will always be there for me.'

'Like a perpetual bride in waiting,' Rachel said. 'What about a family, Cory?'

'One day, maybe,' Cory said. He smiled at her.

'You need someone who shares your dreams,' Rachel

said. Her heart felt a little achy at the thought. For so many years she had been there with Cory, not through her own choice, perhaps, but because fate had thrown them together. To relinquish that closeness to someone Cory loved, someone who shared his hopes and plans… Her throat closed and she made a little fuss of sorting through the contents of the picnic basket.

'I do not suppose,' she said, after a moment, 'that marriage is a particularly appealing option for a rake.' She shot him a look. 'Not when there are so many ladies who are willing to give you what you want without the benefit of clergy. I'll wager that you have had many and many an offer, Cory, and not necessarily of matrimony.'

'I do not believe that we should be speaking of such things,' Cory said, with a wicked smile. 'But if you wish to discuss matrimony, Rae, perhaps you should talk of your own plans. Have you met a man with whom you could settle down? Someone to give you your heart's desire?'

Rachel shot him a sidelong glance. He was lounging beside her, his long, lean frame relaxed, his grey gaze on the river, where a heron was picking its way through the shallows. Behind them the sun was dropping in the sky and a full moon was climbing to take its place. The air was becoming chill. Rachel reached for her shawl.

'Here, let me help you.'

Cory's touch was light and impersonal as he arranged the shawl about her shoulders, but still she shivered beneath his touch—and told herself that it was only the effect of the breeze.

'I have no marriage plans at present,' she said, holding the shawl to her almost as much for comfort as for warmth. 'As you have no doubt observed, I cannot find a man who pleases me.'

Cory's hands stilled, then fell away. 'Indeed? Why not? I thought there were a score of men queuing up to pay their addresses to you, Rae.'

Rachel sighed. 'There may be a score of them willing to pay court to my fifty thousand pounds, but they are sadly indifferent to me personally. Besides, as you so presciently observed a few weeks ago, they are rakes and scoundrels to a man.'

'James Kestrel seemed more than a little interested,' Cory said, 'and surely he cannot be a rake. What is the stumbling block?'

Rachel looked at him through her lashes. 'Do you require that I reply to that question or do you already know the answer?'

Cory gave her a quizzical look back. 'I hesitate to get my head bitten off again by criticising one of your admirers, Rae.'

'*Touché,*' Rachel said, with a small smile. 'I give you full permission to make an educated guess.'

Cory relaxed. 'Then I should say that he has no sense of humour and you could not bear to be tied to a man so pompous.'

'Precisely,' Rachel said. 'You know me so well.' There was an odd silence. Cory was watching her, a faint smile on his lips. She hurried on to cover the pause.

'There is another reason,' she said, 'but if I tell you, you must promise not to laugh.'

Cory raised his brows. 'I cannot guarantee it. Not if what you tell me is amusing enough.'

Rachel dug him in the ribs. 'It is not in the least amusing!' She took a deep breath. 'You must promise not to tell anyone as well. You remember Lady Sally's ball? Miss Lang was…flirting with a gentleman in the gardens and I think it was James Kestrel.'

Cory looked thunderstruck. 'James Kestrel indulging in amorous dalliance? Good God! He is more like his cousins that I thought.'

'It is not funny,' Rachel said crossly. 'I was a little shocked.'

'So am I! I would have thought that Kestrel would avoid kissing in case it interfered with the set of his coat!'

'Cory…' Rachel said disapprovingly.

'Sorry.' Cory grinned. 'Were you very disappointed, Rae? After all, he was dancing attendance on you all evening.'

'Oh, I did not repine,' Rachel said honestly. 'At least, not for myself, for I had known almost from the first that Mr Kestrel would make the most tedious husband. I was simply disappointed to discover yet another gentleman whose conduct did not live up to the title.'

Cory pulled a face. 'I can see that you might be. Did James Kestrel ever try to kiss *you*, Rae?'

'Certainly not.' Rachel smiled. 'But then I was not as ardent for his embrace as Miss Lang must be.'

'Ouch,' Cory said appreciatively. 'You are not so sweet-natured yourself, sometimes, Rae! So if Kestrel is out of the frame, what about John Norton?'

'What about him?'

'Did you have any hopes of marrying him?'

Rachel gave him a frown. 'Oh, Sir John has no thought of marrying. You told me that yourself.'

'I hope you did not take my word for it.'

'Well, of course I did!' Rachel smiled at him. 'If you tell me such a thing, then I do not doubt you, Cory. I trust you.'

'You silence me,' Cory said after a moment. 'Thank you, Rae.'

'Anyway, I think you are quite right that Sir John is a rake who will say anything to trick a lady,' Rachel said thoughtfully. 'On the day that he escorted me into Woodbridge, he told me the most affecting tale about how he was out at sea in a storm and almost drowned. All he could think of as he drifted half-unconscious to shore was of his home, and the fact that if he had his time over again, he would marry and settle down there instead of going back to the sea.' She laughed. 'And *then* he tried to kiss me.'

She felt Cory stiffen beside her. 'The blackguard!'

'Oh, do not worry,' Rachel said airily. 'I sidestepped him in time, so it ended up as a sort of kiss rather than a real kiss.'

Cory laughed. 'It seems to me,' he said, 'that a kiss is a kiss is a kiss, Rachel. How can one have a sort of kiss?'

'A sort of kiss is when you miss,' Rachel said. She looked up to see Cory watching her with interest and felt a faint stirring of the disturbing emotions that had captured her before. Talking about kissing was not a good idea. She hurried on.

'I did think it was rather clever of Sir John to try to gain my sympathy with his tale of gallantry and near death,' she said. 'It might well have worked on some other, more susceptible lady.'

'I imagine it has worked a score of times,' Cory said drily. 'You are hard-hearted, Rachel.'

Rachel started to pack the remains of the picnic back into the basket for her parents.

'The Midwinter villages are full of rakes at present,' she said. 'A young lady must protect her reputation as best she may.'

Cory shifted. 'And do you consider me to be one of those dangerous rakes in question?'

Rachel looked at him through her lashes. 'I cannot believe that you are dangerous to me, Cory. We are such old friends that I do not imagine you would either wish to seduce me or be successful if you tried. Such things do not happen between friends.'

There was another pause that felt curiously alive with all kinds of emotions. Rachel drew a short breath to retract her remark, but Cory forestalled her.

'You are mistaken,' he said smoothly, and the tone of his voice sent a shiver squirming down Rachel's spine. 'I cannot guarantee the outcome, of course, but I can assure you that it would be a positive pleasure to seduce you...'

He put a hand about her wrist and tugged, so that Rachel,

taken by surprise, tumbled beneath him on the picnic rug. Cory's grey eyes were dark with some emotion she did not understand, and she lay still, looking up at him. And suddenly it felt as though she had been waiting for this moment for all her life without really knowing what it was she was waiting for. Cory's mouth came down on hers and Rachel's lips parted beneath his and the sensation tore through her like wildfire in the blood, and Rachel was lost.

Chapter Fourteen

Cory had never intended to kiss Rachel. He had been struggling for days to subdue his most predatory of instincts and treat her gently. Then she had looked at him and he had seen the mixture of passion and shyness shimmer in her eyes when she had spoken of kissing. He had known then that she was feeling the same disturbing awareness that he was and he had been totally unprepared for the effect that this knowledge had had on him. Desire had ripped through his body and when Rachel had smiled and said innocently that no doubt he would never wish to seduce her anyway, Cory had known that he had to show her the error of her ways. He had succumbed to his deepest impulses and taken her in his arms.

He had never expected to fall in love with Rachel Odell. He had thought that he had known her too long and too well. Yet as soon as he had seen her again that day by the river his attraction to her had known no bounds. It had lain below the surface of their friendship the whole time, leaving him permanently half-aroused and wholly frustrated. He had been tormented by Rachel's involvement with James Kestrel and John Norton and Caspar Lang. It mattered not one whit that she had engaged in nothing more than a few harmless carriage rides with her admirers and a few hands of cards.

All that was primitive in Cory had wanted to stop her and claim her for his own and now he had her where she was meant to be.

She lay in his arms, her lips open beneath his, her mouth soft, ripe and very inviting, and already Cory had taken this far, far further than he had ever intended. He could not help himself. When she parted her lips so readily for him he felt an astonishing mix of protectiveness and sheer, dazzling male triumph, and he touched his tongue to hers, revelling in the ripple of delighted shock that he felt echo through her entire body. His arms tightened about her and when he felt Rachel's fingertips tentatively brush the back of his neck and delve into his hair, his body reacted with a tense and surging need. He deepened the kiss, his tongue invading her mouth, his senses ablaze. He could feel the roundness of her breasts pressing against him and he let his hands skim the curves of her body, down to the flare of her hips and back up to the swell of those full breasts. Rachel moved against him, making a tiny incoherent sound against his mouth that did nothing to dampen Cory's ardour or help him gain a grip on his self-control. He was dimly aware that he wanted Rachel more than any woman he had ever known, and that he was about to do something utterly irrevocable.

There was a sudden clatter above them, followed by the intrusive sound of voices and a flare of light that was as shocking as it was abrupt. Cory reacted completely on instinct, rolling over, sitting up and pulling Rachel into the curve of his arm so that they were both sitting looking out over the river, her head on his shoulder. She felt boneless against him, soft and sweet and completely spellbound. He knew that she had not had time to recover herself properly, had no idea where she was. A swift tenderness took him and he pressed a kiss against her hair.

'Are you all right, sweetheart?'

He felt her nod very slightly, but she did not speak. Then

Arthur and Lavinia Odell were coming down the bank and greeting them with satisfaction.

'Cory! And Rachel! Are we too late? Is there any food left for us?'

There was a pause. In the flare of the torches, Cory could see that Rachel's face was blank and bemused. He felt a little worried, but he could not deny that he also felt a certain arrogant pleasure to have had that effect on her. It made him want to kiss her again.

The expression came back into Rachel's face and she focussed on her mother. 'There is some food, Mama, but I think it better if we retire to the house. It is getting a little chilly here by the river.'

Sir Arthur consulted his watch. 'I say, it is close on nine thirty! Thought I felt a little peckish. Could not tear myself away—discovered a fifth-century pot in a particularly good state of repair.'

Cory heard Rachel sigh. She got to her feet, stumbling only slightly. Cory leapt up and put out a hand to steady her, but she was already turning away. She was being very careful not to look at him.

'I will come back with you, Papa,' she said. 'I would not wish you to lose your way between here and the dining room.'

Cory thought that she did not intend to say goodbye to him, but at the last moment, she turned and flashed him the briefest of looks.

'Goodnight, Cory. Th…thank you for…' She hesitated and Cory had a ridiculous thought that she was about to thank him for kissing her. 'Thank you for your company,' Rachel finished.

Cory bowed formally. 'Thank *you,* Rachel. I enjoyed our evening. I will bring the hamper back for you.'

That brought him another glance from troubled hazel eyes. He could tell that she wanted to escape his company. Rachel's lips were swollen from his kisses and now she ran her tongue along them uncertainly. Cory subdued an instinctive movement towards her.

'Pray do not worry about the hamper,' she said. 'I will send one of the servants down to collect it.'

Cory smiled a challenge. 'I insist.'

Rachel frowned. 'No—'

'It is no trouble.'

He saw a flicker of displeasure in her eyes. Evidently she wished to be free of his company as soon as she could and to forget what had happened.

'Very well, then. If you must,' she said.

She set off up the path to the house at so brisk a pace that her parents and Cory were left floundering in her wake. By the time that Cory reached the hall, she was nowhere to be seen. He fancied that he just spotted a flash of daisy-spotted muslin whisking around the newel post at the top of the stair. He smiled to himself. If Rachel's strategy was to pretend that their kiss had never occurred, his would be to make sure that it recurred within as short a time as possible.

'Please say goodnight to Rachel for me, sir,' he said politely to Sir Arthur Odell as he propelled the baronet and his lady into the dining room and placed the hamper on the table. 'I shall see you tomorrow.'

On the hall table he found the copy of the *Ipswich Chronicle* that he had requested earlier in the day. Tucking it inside his jacket, Cory went back out into the night. He did not turn his footsteps towards Kestrel Court, however, but retraced his steps to the river, where he divested himself of his neckcloth, jacket and boots—without the aid of a valet—and jumped in the river. It was cool and refreshing. And it was getting to be rather a habit with him.

Rachel sat on her bed in her nightdress. In her hand she held her hairbrush, but the strokes she had started to brush vigorously through her long chestnut hair had stilled some time ago. Now the candle was burning down and she had forgotten the brush and she was only in her room in body rather than in mind or spirit.

She was not quite sure what had happened to her. One moment all had been comfortable and familiar. She had been talking to Cory in the way in which she had done year on year for as long ago as she could remember, sharing confidences. Then she had made her foolish remark about seduction, and then there was a moment when everything had been poised, waiting, before Cory had kissed her with a desire and an intensity that she had thought would steal her very soul.

Rachel's lips parted and she gave a tiny sigh. There was no point in pretending any more. It was impossible now to profess that Cory was her friend and that she was utterly indifferent to him as a man. She had thought that passion was for other people and was overrated at that, and Cory had proved the folly of her belief with one kiss. She corrected herself. Two kisses. The embrace in the billiards room should have alerted her to what to expect and given her fair warning of what would happen if she mentioned the words seduction and rake within a few sentences.

Rachel realised that her feet were chilled. She slid into bed and pulled her knees up to her chin, hugging them close. She remembered the feeling of absolute rightness that had taken her in the moment before Cory had lowered his lips to hers. It was as though he had always been there for her and that moment held the promise that he always would be. But those were foolish thoughts. She did not deceive herself that Cory had kissed a great many women in his time and that it had probably not meant a great deal to him. After all, she had brought everything upon herself with her ridiculously naïve comment about him not wishing to seduce her. No doubt a rake would take that as a challenge, and a most provocative one at that. And so Cory had kissed her to disprove her theory.

Rachel pulled the brush through her hair with brief, distracted strokes, then put it down on the nightstand, lay down, and pulled the blankets up about her shoulders. It seemed a little unfair to Cory to think that he would view the matter as nothing more than a flirtation. She was sure that he cared for her. She had heard the tender note in his voice when he had asked her if she was all right. Yet loving and being in love were two very different matters. She knew that she loved Cory and for a moment she trembled on the edge of wondering whether she was falling in love with him. Then she turned her thoughts from that troubling idea. Such a way would lie nothing but disappointment and unhappiness, for they were utterly incompatible.

Rachel lay with her eyes wide open, staring into the dark. Briefly she wondered what might have happened if her parents had not burst upon them at that point. She could not answer the question with any certitude. Presumably Cory would have stopped kissing her at some point—she did not pretend that she had had either the inclination or the will to stop it herself. Or perhaps, being a rake, Cory would have taken matters to their natural conclusion and proved once and for all that if he had set out to seduce her completely he would not fail in his aim.

Rachel turned over on her side and curled up tightly. She could not let it happen again. One kiss was a mistake, two was carelessness, but three… Three would prove that she wanted Cory to be more than a friend to her. And even if she did, she could not have him.

She fell asleep on the thought and was most disconcerted in the morning to discover that she had left her clothes strewn all over the room and had had no thought at all to put them away.

The following morning was a Sunday, a fact for which Rachel was profoundly grateful. It meant that there was no work on the excavation site and that her mind was fully occupied with the task of marshalling Sir Arthur and Lady Odell and the servants for the trip to church in Midwinter Mallow. This was no small matter. Sir Arthur was completely oblivious of which day of the week it was and when he discovered that it was Sunday, grumbled that Mr Lang was as windy a parson as he had ever met, and his preaching was a dead bore. Lady Odell fussed vaguely over the fact that Rachel would not let her wear her Inuit tribal dress to church, and Mrs Goodfellow threatened that they would be obliged to have a cold collation for dinner if she had to walk all the way to and from Midwinter Mallow with her bunions in the state they were. Eventually the party was packed into the carriage that Olivia and Ross Marney had sent to convey them to church, and Rachel, feeling exhausted, clambered in as well.

Despite the length of the Reverend Lang's sermons, there was an excellent turn out at St Martin's that morning. The Duke of Kestrel was in the front pew and had graciously invited Lady Sally Saltire to join him. Rachel sat one row behind and admired the elegant curl of the jaunty feather in Lady Sally's hat. Concentrating on the feather also prevented her gaze from sliding sideways to where Cory Newlyn sat. Cory had come in very late, just when Rachel's nerves had settled with the thought that he would not be present. He had taken a seat directly in her line of sight, and studying his clear-cut profile distracted Rachel completely from the message that Reverend Lang took a good forty minutes to deliver from the pulpit. As his voice droned on Rachel fixed her gaze on Lady Sally's hat, but her mind kept returning to Cory with increasing repetition. She wondered if he would approach her and, if he did, how she would feel and what she would say. She wondered if he would make reference to the previous night and, if so, how she could respond. Then she wondered why everyone was looking at her and realised that they had all moved on to the prayers whilst she was still standing up.

Once the service was over, they all stood about the church door and on the path to the lych gate, chatting in the sunshine. Mr Lang had buttonholed Sir Arthur and was trying to persuade him to agree to take a party around the excavations. Sir Arthur, who hated groups of what he referred to as antiquity tourists, was being decidedly awkward about it. Rachel fretted. She could see Cory moving towards her, pausing for a word with the Marneys, exchanging a greeting with Lady Sally Saltire, working his way unobtrusively in her direction. She repressed a childish desire to dive for cover behind the nearest gravestone.

'Papa...' she said beseechingly, 'I am sure there can be no difficulty in showing some of our neighbours the work that is progressing on the excavation.'

'Splendid idea,' Cory said. He was standing beside her. 'Lady Sally has just been asking if she might join a party to view our work.'

'Sightseers, tourists,' Sir Arthur grumbled, under his breath.

'I think that was an agreement,' Rachel said, smiling sweetly at Mr Lang. 'I will make the necessary arrangements.'

Cory took her arm and drew her to one side. Rachel went, a little unwillingly. She was very conscious of the milling crowds and curious glances.

'I would like to talk to you, Rae,' Cory said. 'About last night. Please.'

Rachel looked around again. It seemed a rather public place to be choosing for such a discussion.

'I cannot,' she whispered. 'Mama and Papa—'

'Will be perfectly safe if you leave them for a few moments,' Cory said smoothly.

He took her arm and drew her towards the relative privacy of the lych gate. Rachel went with him, scarcely aware of where she was going. Now that Cory was here with her again she felt almost paralysed with embarrassment and awareness. It felt as though she was obliged to discuss a peculiarly intimate topic with someone who should be no more than a friend. Something felt out of kilter. A wave of heat washed up from her toes to envelop her whole body.

'I am not certain that this is a good idea, Cory,' she said. 'May we not pretend that it simply did not happen?'

'Not this time,' Cory said, a little grimly.

'I thought,' Rachel said a little desperately, 'that it was a mistake.' She looked at him, willing him to agree with her.

'A mistake,' Cory said thoughtfully. A smile curled the corners of his mouth and Rachel's pulse jumped in response to the expression she saw in his eyes. 'Was it a mistake that you responded to my kiss like that?'

A burning blush swept over Rachel again. She clutched at another idea. 'Perhaps that is not the correct word. Shall we say that it was just an accident?'

'It was an accident waiting to happen,' Cory said. 'You must see, Rachel, that it was bound to occur sooner or later.'

That stopped Rachel in her tracks. She looked at him. 'Was it? How do you know?'

Cory smiled at her. 'Now I think about it, I think that I have always known it. One day you and I were going to kiss each other. It was inevitable.'

They looked at each other. Rachel thought that Cory looked rather pleased with himself and she felt her temper rise, rather as it had done when they were younger and Cory had been so brash and conceited and she had wanted to take him down several pegs.

'Well, I wish you had told me,' she said crossly.

Cory cocked an eyebrow. 'Do you? What would you have liked me to say to you? Something along the lines of ''Rachel, you and I are strongly attracted to each other and it is to be expected that at some point we shall kiss each other?'''

Rachel frowned harder. 'It would have helped.'

'Helped you do what—run away from me?' Cory spread his hands wide. 'I think you have done quite enough of that already, Rae. The very fact that you are always running leads me to believe that you feel exactly as I do.'

Rachel bit her lip. She could not contradict him. 'I do not deny that I have been somewhat…taken by surprise by my feelings for you,' she said.

Cory made a move towards her and she took an instinctive step away.

'No! Wait! That does not mean that I think what we did should be repeated.' She looked around. 'Certainly not here!'

The tense lines about Cory's mouth softened slightly. 'Might you be prepared to consider it elsewhere?'

Rachel repressed a smile. He was very persuasive. 'I think not,' she said reluctantly. She sighed and looked at him appealingly. 'This is very awkward. What are we to do now?'

She saw the answer in his eyes. He wanted to kiss her again and she felt an answering tug of desire deep within her. It was terribly tempting.

'I do not think so,' she said softly, again, in answer to the unspoken thought. 'One kiss is not so terrible, but any more is quite out of the question.'

Cory looked quizzical. 'So it was not so terrible?'

Rachel blushed. 'Not really. Indeed, not at all, but that is not the point.' She pulled herself together. 'The point is that it is over now. We have done it and I dare say that we should not think of it again.'

Cory took her arm and drew her deeper into the shadow of the gate. 'I confess I had not viewed it in quite that way, Rachel,' he said. He stepped in close, until she could feel his body just brushing against hers. 'I spent most of last night thinking about it, not to mention the best part of the service this morning. My mind was on matters of which the Reverend Mr Lang could not approve.'

Rachel blushed. She had had the same difficulty.

'I do not think that this is something so easily dismissed,' Cory continued, 'and this time I cannot permit you to dismiss it either.'

Rachel looked at him with troubled eyes. 'But I do not understand why this has happened to us! We are *friends,* Cory, and friends do not kiss each other like that.' She scuffed at the soft sandy earth beneath her feet. 'You must promise me that you will not kiss me again.'

She saw the slight, negative shake of his head even as she spoke. He took her hand.

'I cannot give you that assurance,' Cory said, and though he spoke quietly his words had an undertone of steel now. 'If you wish to take refuge in thoughts of friendship, that is your choice, Rae.' His fingers tightened and she looked up and met the blazing light in his eyes. 'It will, however, be my ardent endeavour to prove to you how much more than friends we have become.'

And he gave her a curt bow and walked away.

Chapter Fifteen

The Deben Regatta fell on the following day, which was a public holiday. It was another bright blue summer's day. Rachel viewed the arrival of James Kestrel to escort her with something less than enthusiasm. As she tied the ribbons of her straw bonnet beneath her chin, she wished that she had not accepted James's invitation. Unfortunately the arrangement had been of such long standing that Rachel had thought it discourteous to snub him at so late a stage. Even so, her thoughts were full of another man entirely as she went downstairs and allowed James to help her up into his curricle.

She was to regret her choice even more when James stationed his curricle at the very back of the crowd and she had to crane her neck to see anything at all. The river was some hundred yards distant and Rachel wished she had brought her opera glasses.

'I hope that we shall be quite safe here,' James said, viewing the shining water with disfavour. 'I should not wish to be splashed.'

'I do not believe there is any possibility of that,' Rachel said, trying not to sound snappish.

The entire town seemed to have turned out for the regatta. Across the river at Woodbridge, Rachel could see that the quay was colourful with the uniforms of the soldiers and the bright summer dresses of the ladies. The residents of the Midwinter villages had elected to line the opposite river-bank, however, and were all assembled on the sloping grassy incline that led down to the water's edge, where there was also a refreshment tent and a musical quartet playing. A light wind came off the river, ruffling the ladies' bonnets and setting the spinnakers of the yachts ringing.

Up ahead of them, Rachel could see a barouche containing the Marneys and Deborah Stratton. Justin Kestrel and Cory Newlyn were both lounging by the side of it, deep in conversation with the occupants. There was much laughter and chatter, particularly when Lady Sally Saltire and Lily Benedict came up to join the party. Rachel could not help feeling a little like the plain girl stuck on a rout chair at the ball, especially as James Kestrel was not paying her a great deal of attention, but appeared to be looking around for someone else entirely. Nor did Cory seem interested in making good the promise he had delivered in the churchyard only the previous day. He had glanced across at Rachel when she and James had arrived; he had smiled and sketched a bow, but he had not approached her yet. Rachel, whose errant heart had been racing at the thought of seeing him again, felt extremely disappointed.

The ringing of the church bells was the signal for the races to begin and a cheer went up from the other bank. First were the various rowing competitions for prizes of a few guineas, and the townspeople of Woodbridge threw themselves wholeheartedly into these. Rachel could not see the races very well, since Mr Kestrel's curricle was too far back and the boats were low on the water, but when the yacht race began she had a fine view. Five yachts had entered, and the contest was keenly fought. In the end Sir John Norton was the winner with his elegant craft, *Breath of Scandal,* just beating the yacht *Ariel,* by a head. He carried off the silver trophy and beautifully engraved glass bowl in triumph.

'Excuse me, Miss Odell,' James Kestrel said suddenly. 'I shall be back directly.'

He swung himself down from the curricle and disappeared past the refreshment tent.

For a while, Rachel sat alone and watched the Duck Hunt, which was the culmination of the regatta. There was much merriment as one of the local fishermen in a wildfowling punt took the part of the 'duck' and was chased by four other oarsmen. The punt was quick, but the rowers were quicker and the duck ended up jumping over the side and being chased over the mudflats and into the crowd on the Midwinter bank, where the ladies screamed and twitched their skirts aside from the mud and the water he sent flying.

After that the crowd began to disperse, for some of the gentlemen had been invited to dine at the Anchor Inn and the ladies were to prepare for the ball in the evening. Rachel waited for James Kestrel and started to feel a little irritable. He had been gone a good half-hour and she was marooned in the curricle with no way of getting home. People were starting to stare at her now. Rachel tilted her parasol to shade her face from the curious glances, whilst inside she fizzed with irritation. She sat getting hotter and hotter and more and more annoyed, until finally she scrambled down from the curricle and went in search of James Kestrel. He was not in the refreshment tent, nor could she find him among the rapidly dwindling crowd on the shore. Rachel was accustomed to walking and decided that James Kestrel's discourtesy deserved that she should leave him there and walk home. Hot, bothered and with the wrong footwear for a two-mile walk, she set off up the path towards Midwinter Royal.

She had not gone more than fifty yards when she saw James. He was standing in the shelter of a copse of oak that stood back from the path, and he had certainly not seen

Rachel. He was too busy, for Miss Helena Lang was locked in his arms and he was kissing her passionately.

Rachel stopped. Her first thought, absurdly, was that she would never have expected Mr Kestrel to do anything so rash as to embrace a lady in public in full daylight. Her second thought was a not unreasonable anger at being left sitting like a lemon in James's curricle whilst he paid court to Miss Lang. It was not that she was jealous, precisely, for she had never wished his amorous attentions to be turned in her direction. It was more that she felt cross-grained and a fool when she had known what was going on between James Kestrel and Miss Lang and yet she had still accepted his attentions. Perhaps, Rachel thought wretchedly, James had been using her to deflect interest from his courtship of Miss Lang. Perhaps under his sober exterior he was as much of a rake as the rest of the family and fully intended to court Rachel's fifty thousand pounds—whilst making love to another woman. And perhaps *she* was almost as culpable, for had there not been an element of immaturity in her behaviour in wanting to make Cory jealous by accepting James's escort?

Rachel set her jaw, turned her back and retraced her steps to the shore, where she decided that it would be fitting punishment for James Kestrel if she were to requisition his curricle and drive home, leaving him behind.

It was unfortunate for Rachel that Sir John Norton, flushed from his victory in *Breath of Scandal,* had just come ashore, waving the silver cup above his head. The engraved glass bowl that was his other prize gleamed on the stern of the yacht as Sir John splashed through the shallows and clambered on to the bank. Seeing Rachel walking alone towards the others, he slid an arm about her waist with odious familiarity and gave her a smacking kiss. 'Congratulate me, Miss Odell! Was that not the most tremendous victory?'

Rachel just managed to restrain herself from slapping his smug face. His wet arm was still about her waist and it was causing an unpleasant dampness to seep through her muslin dress. She flushed bright red at the curious and amused looks on the faces of those watching, and slipped from his grasp. 'Excuse me, Sir John. I shall leave you to celebrate with your friends.'

Sir John made another grab for her. It was clear now to Rachel that he had been drinking, a course of action that seemed rather foolhardy when in control of a sea-going yacht.

'Not so fast, sweetheart! What are you doing all alone, anyway? I'll take care of you. Come aboard with me...'

'No, thank you,' Rachel said, feeling the panic rising. The Marneys' barouche had gone and she did not recognise any of the stragglers on the shore. She was almost tempted to run to James Kestrel's curricle, where the groom still stood, wooden-faced, at the heads of the patient horses. It was ridiculous to be stuck here and at the mercy of a drunken and oafish Sir John.

'Miss Odell!' Rachel turned with relief to see Lord Richard Kestrel at her elbow. 'May I be of service to you? Escort you back to your party, perhaps? You seem in some distress here.'

Rachel turned to him with gratitude. 'Thank you, Lord Richard. I fear that my companion has rather left me at the mercy of all and sundry.'

Richard cast John Norton a disdainful glance. 'Go and sleep it off, Norton,' he drawled, 'and confine your attentions to your yacht in future.'

Sir John mumbled something that might have been an apology and sloped off, and Richard offered Rachel his arm.

'What can my cousin be doing, leaving you on your own like that?' he queried with a smile. 'Surely James has lost what little sense he had in the first place—and all his manners.'

'I do believe your cousin became distracted by something else,' Rachel said with a hint of asperity. She caught the edge of Richard's look and saw amusement and a certain degree of admiration in its depths.

'Then more fool him,' he said easily, 'for his loss is my gain.'

Rachel smiled inwardly. It was curious that she was strolling along the water's edge with a gentleman generally accepted to be the most dangerous rake in the kingdom, and yet she felt not the slightest degree of apprehension and certainly no *frisson* of attraction. She *liked* Richard Kestrel, and surely mere liking was the kiss of death for a rake. Yet she could not seem to help herself. Even knowing that the Kestrels had some odious wager going on amongst themselves could not dampen her enjoyment of his company.

'Since we are such good friends these days, Miss Odell,' Richard said, 'I do not scruple to ask a personal question. My cousin's bad manners notwithstanding, how do your romantic affairs progress?'

Rachel arched her brows at his familiarity and decided to repay him in kind. 'About as well as your own, my lord,' she said.

Richard pulled a face. 'That badly? You are in dire straits indeed!'

They were still laughing together when they walked slap into Cory Newlyn. Rachel had not even noticed his approach, so engrossed was she in Richard's company. Now, however, her throat tightened with apprehension and she felt her breathing constrict. There was such a look on Cory's face as he watched them together that she genuinely wondered what he was about to say.

Richard, too, had noticed the tension in the air. He raised his brows imperceptibly. 'Ah, there you are, old fellow,' he drawled. 'I was hoping to see you. Do you object if I take the curricle to escort Miss Odell back home? She finds herself benighted here—'

'All evidence to the contrary,' Cory said. His voice was smooth, but there was an odd expression in his eyes. 'No young lady who has been befriended by you could consider themselves benighted, Richard.'

The lines of amusement deepened about Richard Kestrel's mouth. 'You flatter me, Cory. I am, of course, honoured to have Miss Odell's company.'

'And fortunately I may now take your place,' Cory continued, 'for I recall that you have an engagement in Woodbridge, do you not?'

Their eyes met and Rachel, watching, saw some kind of message pass between them. It did not seem entirely friendly. Then Richard laughed and raised both hands in a gesture of amused resignation.

'Of course I do, Cory. I am indebted to you for reminding me. And I am more than happy to surrender Miss Odell to your protection.'

Rachel reddened with a mixture of ire and embarrassment. For Cory to revert to behaving like an over-zealous elder brother was too much, particularly when she had warned him against it before. She glared at him.

'I have no need of your escort, thank you, Cory,' she snapped. 'I can quite easily walk back to Midwinter Royal from here.' She turned pointedly to Richard Kestrel. 'Thank you for coming to my rescue, my lord. It is much appreciated.'

Richard bowed elegantly. There was a spark of humour in his eyes. 'Yours to command, Miss Odell.'

'Richard—' Cory said, and now the threat in his voice was quite clear.

Richard laughed. 'How entertaining that I have at last found a means to irritate you so profoundly, old fellow. It is the first time in twenty years you have given me the advantage!' He raised a hand in farewell and strolled away, leaving the two of them together.

Cory's hand closed around Rachel's elbow and he practically dragged her away. After they had gone twenty-five yards, Rachel shook herself out of his grip.

'I do not believe that you have a carriage in Suffolk, do you, Cory?' she said sweetly. All her bad temper seemed to be building up into a positive tidal wave. 'Are you intending for me to ride before you on poor Castor until he founders, or had you thought to drag me all the way home on foot?'

Cory shot her a hard, unsmiling look. 'Just because you have made a fool of yourself in front of everyone with Sir John Norton, Rachel, I do not see why you should vent your displeasure on me.'

Rachel knew that this was what she was doing and the knowledge just made matters worse. She had been expecting something quite different from Cory and she now discovered that she did not want him to revert to acting as her friend. This was foolish, for she was the one who had demanded only the previous day that he should never kiss her again. Standing there on the shore of the Deben, with Cory looking at her as though she were a slightly tiresome little sister, she found that this was not in the least what she really wanted. It seemed to be all that was on offer, however.

Her voice rose with indignation. 'I did not make a fool of myself. Sir John was drunk and importunate, but I could quite easily have taken care of myself—'

'Indeed?' Cory said silkily. He gave her a comprehensive look that brought even more angry colour into her face. 'It did not look like that to me.'

'You were not there!'

'No, but I saw what happened.'

'Then,' Rachel said, with childish contrariness, 'why did you not come to my rescue yourself? Fortunate that Lord Richard was on hand to do what you were reluctant to do yourself!'

She heard Cory draw a sharp breath. 'Lord Richard…yes…' he said slowly. 'You are playing a dangerous game there, Rachel.'

Rachel shot him another furious look. She had a stitch in her side from the speed with which Cory had hurried her away from Richard Kestrel, and now she stopped and pressed her hand to it.

'Lord Richard and I are friends,' she said haughtily. 'There is no more to it than that.'

Cory's expression was frankly disbelieving. 'Friends? Good God! Having seen how you treat your friends, Rae, he must be honoured to receive such a mark of distinction.'

Rachel pressed her lips together. 'I think,' she said, 'that you can be the most loathsome man of my acquaintance sometimes, Cory.'

'And that is up against some pretty stiff competition,' Cory observed. 'Sir John Norton, James Kestrel…'

Rachel bit her lip hard to prevent herself from exploding.

Cory put his arm around her waist and tossed her up on to the seat of a phaeton painted in green and gold with the ducal crest of Kestrel on the side. Tom Bradshaw had been standing beside it with the patient expression of a man who has been trained to wait—and to pretend that he is deaf under all circumstances. Cory took the reins from him.

'Thank you, Bradshaw. You may walk back.'

'Thank you, my lord,' the valet said resignedly.

'How ungenerous of you,' Rachel exclaimed, looking back as Cory turned the phaeton on to the road and the luckless Bradshaw started to trudge towards Midwinter Royal. 'Besides, this is not your phaeton, Cory. Have you stolen it?'

'Do not be ridiculous,' Cory snapped. 'I borrowed it from Justin Kestrel.'

Rachel gave an angry sigh. 'You need not put yourself to the trouble of taking me home, you know.'

Cory gave her an unpleasant smile. 'Believe me, Rae, at the moment the prospect of setting you down by the wayside is an appealing one. Did you get out of bed the wrong side this morning?'

Rachel's temper snapped. 'No, but I wish I had not got out at all! I have had the most intolerably tiresome time of it. Besides, I do not see why you felt the need to offer in the first place. Lord Richard would have been quite happy to escort me.'

'Richard is dining at the Anchor,' Cory said, 'whereas I am returning to Midwinter and so may take you up with me instead. I am sorry if you do not like it.'

Rachel let out an angry sigh. All her accumulated resentment about the wager burst out like a cork exploding from a bottle.

'I do not suppose that it matters whether it is you, or Richard Kestrel, or his brother the Duke who escorts me home! The ladies of the Midwinter villages are interchangeable to you, it seems. Perhaps Sir John Norton is in on your little wager as well, hence the scene by the river?' Another thought suddenly struck her so forcibly it hurt. 'Perhaps when you kissed me that night it was part of the same game that you are all playing! I will say this for you all, Cory— you are a bunch of scoundrels who certainly know how to enliven a dull stay in the country!'

There was a silence so sharp that Rachel could hear her own angry words echoing in her head. She saw Cory's hands clench on the reins.

'Just what the devil are you talking about, Rachel?' he said, with deadly calm. 'What wager is this?'

'Oh, do not pretend not to know,' Rachel exclaimed. 'I heard you speaking to Lord Richard at the ball, asking how much flirtation you were expected to undertake as part of Justin Kestrel's plan—' She broke off as Cory took one hand off the reins and closed it hard about her wrist. He did not hurt her, but the shock was sufficient to silence her momentarily. She gasped. 'Ouch! What are you doing?'

Cory did not reply for a moment. He let her go and Rachel sat rubbing her wrist with her other hand, though it was not in the least bit damaged. Something had changed the tone of their discussion, however. Rachel was forced to admit that in a strange way she had been almost enjoying the slightly childish, irritable squabbling with Cory. But now his face was hard and set and she felt a tremor of apprehension run right through her.

'I am asking you to keep quiet for the time being whilst we are on this road,' Cory said pleasantly. He shot her a look. 'I am begging you, in fact.'

The road was slow and busy with pedestrians and traffic returning from the regatta, but Cory turned the phaeton down a narrow lane where the hedges pressed in and the branches arched overhead to create a green tunnel. Once they were out of sight of the main thoroughfare, he drew to a halt on a sweep of grass in front of a hay barn. He turned to her, his expression stern.

'What did you overhear that night, Rachel?'

Rachel's puzzled gaze searched his face. He looked severe and unyielding, and she frowned, all childish squabbles forgotten. 'What are we doing here? This is not the way to Midwinter Royal—'

'Just answer the question,' Cory said.

Rachel jumped at his tone, she knew Cory would insist on a reply. 'Oh, very well. It is merely as I said. It was near the end of the ball and I had gone out on to the terrace for some fresh air when you and Lord Richard came out of the card room. I heard you saying that when you had agreed to Justin Kestrel's plan you had had no notion that it would involve such a spirit of self-sacrifice.' She screwed her face up as she tried to remember his exact words. 'You made some remark about the amount of flirtation you were obliged to undertake. That was all. What—?'

Cory was frowning. 'What were you doing out there, Rae?'

'I told you! I required some fresh air.'

'But when you dropped your handkerchief and I brought it in to you, you denied that you had even seen me, let alone overheard my conversation,' Cory pointed out.

Rachel felt her heart lurch. She had forgotten about the handkerchief. 'So I did,' she said slowly.

To her surprise, Cory did not pursue that immediately, but asked a completely different question. 'Was anybody else with you, Rae?'

Rachel's frown deepened. 'No.'

'Are you certain?'

'Yes, of course! I was quite alone.'

Cory's eyes were narrowed on her face. 'And have you told anyone else about what you heard?'

'No!' Rachel could feel herself blushing. She looked away, fiddling with the seam of her gloves. 'I have told no one.'

'Look at me,' Cory said inexorably. Then, when she raised her head and met his eyes, 'Are you sure you have not mentioned this to anyone?'

Rachel gave him a level look. She found that it was important that he believed her, but, given that she had already lied to him, she could understand why he might not trust her.

'No, I told no one. I promise you.'

'Then why are you looking so guilty?'

Rachel pressed her hands together. 'Am I? I suppose it is because I lied to you about seeing you on the terrace, and because I did think about telling someone…' She gave him a defiant look. 'I wanted to tell Deborah—Mrs Stratton— because she is my friend and I wished to confide.'

Cory was frowning now. 'Why did you not?'

Rachel fidgeted again and settled on a half-truth. She did not wish to admit that it was some residual loyalty to him that had held her silent. She had been disappointed that Cory might be involved in such a low trick and she had not wanted to tell anyone else.

'I do not know,' she said. 'I suppose it was because I thought I might have misunderstood what I had heard.'

'And why did you not simply ask me?' Cory asked, going

to the heart of her difficulty. 'Why did you lie to me and why did you not challenge me over what you had heard? If we are such good friends as you think, why could you not do that?'

This question was even harder than the first. Rachel knew that not so long ago she would have confronted Cory without hesitation, but those days were gone.

'We always seem to be in dispute these days,' she said, her voice a little bleak. 'I did not wish to make it worse.'

It was not the whole truth, but she did not want to tell Cory how angry she had been with him, nor how she had planned the foolish revenge of the drawings. She watched his face, and felt relief flood her when his expression eased slightly.

'I see,' he said slowly. 'Well, I may put your mind at rest on one issue at least, Rae. You did misunderstand what you heard.' A hint of a smile touched his mouth. 'There is no wager.'

Rachel stared. 'No wager? Then what were you talking about with Lord Richard?'

Cory sighed. 'I will tell you if you swear not to say a word.'

Rachel made a little gesture. 'I promise.'

'You already know that Justin Kestrel and the rest of us are at Midwinter for more than one purpose,' Cory said. 'You guessed as much on the very first day that I arrived.'

Rachel's eyes widened. 'You mean—the threat of invasion and you joining the Volunteers, and Lord Richard being an Admiralty man—'

'Precisely,' Cory said. 'There is a French spy and their criminal associates at work in the Midwinter villages, Rae. Richard and I—and one or two others—are attempting to unmask them and discover how they operate.'

Rachel's eyes opened even wider. This seemed too fanciful to be true. 'Surely not! Not in sleepy old Midwinter!'

'It is precisely because Midwinter *is* sleepy that it makes such a wonderful hiding place,' Cory said, an edge to his voice. 'And believe me, Rachel, it is not such a quiet place as you think. One man has already died—Jeffrey Maskelyne. That is why this is so serious. The fate of all of us could rest on smoking this person out. And that is why you must keep silent.'

Rachel's mind was spinning. 'But what has that to do with what you said to Richard Kestrel?'

There was a pause. 'There are many different ways of gathering intelligence,' Cory said mildly.

Rachel's eyes rounded in astonishment. 'No! I cannot believe it.' Her surprise warmed into anger. 'I cannot believe that you and the Kestrel brothers are making love to the ladies of Midwinter just to get them to tell you all their secrets. That is outrageous. And so underhand! Oh, how dare you?'

Cory's smile had deepened. 'It is a matter of life and death, Rae—'

Rachel snorted. 'What absolute rubbish! That is a very poor excuse.'

'Not so,' Cory said. 'Besides, there is one thing that you do not know, Rae. The Midwinter spy is a woman.'

Rachel was so shocked that she fell silent, her outrage forgotten. It seemed scandalous enough that the gentlemen would use such underhand tactics in getting to know the ladies of the Midwinter villages, but that one of those ladies themselves should be a French spy seemed unbelievable. Rachel mentally considered the members of Lady Sally's reading group and immediately discounted the possibility that any one of them could be a traitor. It was simply not possible. Then a thought came into her head and she became very still. When she looked up at Cory she saw that he was watching her with the ghost of a smile. She knew he had read her thoughts. She caught her breath.

'You suspected *me,* didn't you, Cory Newlyn!' she whispered. 'You thought that I might be your spy.'

Cory shook his head. He took her hand in his. 'Rachel, I can honestly say that I never believed you guilty of such a thing.'

Rachel stared at him, trying to divine whether or not he was telling the truth. Suddenly she felt cold and afraid; not afraid of Cory's suspicions, but deeply scared that he might not hold the good opinion of her that she had always taken for granted.

Cory's fingers tightened on hers and an urgent note came into his voice.

'Rachel, I promise you...I never thought that.'

Rachel swallowed an unexpected lump in her throat. She felt a ridiculous urge to burst into tears. 'Are you sure?' Her voice sounded very small.

'I swear it.' There was tenderness in Cory's voice now. 'Good God, Rachel, how could you think such a thing? We have known each other this age. Why do you think that I am trusting you now? It is only because I know I *can* trust you and that you would never betray the secret.'

'Thank you,' Rachel said. She felt a little better. 'I am glad that I still hold your good opinion, Cory, for sometimes I think that I do not know you very well at all.'

She heard Cory sigh. 'I confess that you did give me a bad moment when you lied about being out on the terrace.'

Rachel stifled a small giggle. 'I am sorry. I did not realise it would make you suspect me, or I should have spoken up at once.'

'I still do not understand why you did it,' Cory said.

'I am sorry,' Rachel said again. 'I was confused by what I had heard and...' she hesitated '...rather angry with you as well.'

It seemed as though Cory was waiting for her to say more, but when she did not speak, he sighed and let go of her hand. 'I suppose that I can understand that,' he said. 'God knows, I have been doing enough covert things to arouse anybody's suspicions—'

Rachel froze. 'The books!' she said, her voice warming into anger again, 'You said that Maskelyne was the man who died. That must mean that he was part of the Duke of Kestrel's counter-spying plan.' She turned her angry gaze on Cory again. 'I suppose that when I found you in the stables that time you were checking that Maskelyne's books did not contain a clue. Yet you told me you were looking for clues to the Midwinter Treasure! You lied to me!'

'No, I did not,' Cory said mildly.

'But you said—'

'I said nothing. You were the one who made the assumption that I was in the stables to try and steal a march on you in the hunt for the treasure.'

Rachel felt as though she was about to burst with indignation. 'But you let me carry on believing it!'

'Of course. I did not wish you to become suspicious and possibly put yourself in danger.'

Rachel frowned. 'You did not correct my false assumption. There is some deceit in that.'

'Rachel,' Cory said, 'we have just been discussing you telling me a direct lie about your presence on the terrace at the ball. I do not think that you are in a position to haul *me* over the coals for deceit.'

Rachel had the grace to feel slightly ashamed. 'I suppose not. This whole matter smacks of deception, if the truth be told.'

'Spying usually does,' Cory pointed out. 'It is an ugly business.'

Rachel was still sorting the information in her head, assessing and re-assessing all the things that had happened, thinking of Cory's behaviour. 'When you and Richard Kestrel came to Saltires that afternoon,' she said, 'what was your purpose there? For surely you had one…'

'You require us to have more of a purpose than simply to flirt with the ladies of the reading group?' Cory asked mockingly.

Rachel studied his face. 'Yes, I do.' She waved a hand about in agitation. 'You are doing it again—trying to encourage me to make assumptions so that you do not have to answer my questions!'

Cory possessed himself of her hand again and gave her a smile that made her feel quite weak. 'I assure you that I had no intention of deliberately misleading you again,' he said. 'The truth is that someone took a shot at me on my way home from Midwinter Royal that night, Rachel. When we came to the reading group the following day, it was with the intention of discovering who it had been.'

Chapter Sixteen

Rachel stared at Cory in utter disbelief. There was a singing in her ears and she could almost feel the colour draining from her face. Cory was watching her with a mixture of concern and speculation as he took in her distress. He looked exactly the same to her and yet somehow her perspective had shifted one final time, the pieces clicking into place with the neat precision of a wooden puzzle. Rachel knew then that if she ever lost him she would feel wrenched in two, as though a most fundamental part of her was missing. She felt shocked and dazed and terrified. Then she felt angry.

'Someone shot at you?' she whispered. She freed her hand from Cory's grasp and thumped him ineffectually on the chest. 'Someone *shot* at you, Cory Newlyn, and you sit there telling me about it weeks later, as though you are relating an incident at a garden party? Good God, I knew that you had a reputation for coolness, but this is beyond anything!'

She was startled to see that she was shaking. She put her hands up to her face briefly, then sat back, blinking. Someone had shot at Cory. Someone had tried to kill him. Nothing that he had told her up to this point had made anything like the impact on her that that simple sentence had done. She felt shaken to the core.

She saw something change in Cory's face then and he pulled her into his arms and held her close. With a muttered imprecation he loosened the ribbons of her bonnet, pushing it back so that he could rest his cheek against hers. One hand stroked her hair. He was murmuring soothing words and the combination of his voice and the gentling of his hands steadied her. It felt very right to be in his arms and safety and comfort flooded through her. The tears that threatened her receded a little.

'I cannot believe it,' she said unsteadily.

Cory's arms tightened about her. 'There is nothing to be afraid of, Rachel. I am quite safe.'

'That is not the point.' Rachel's gloved fingers tangled with his lapels and she gave him a little shake. 'You could have been killed.'

Cory pressed his lips to her hair. 'But I was not. Rachel, I swear that I did not mean to frighten you. The only reason that I did not tell you this before was because the whole of this business has been secret and I had no wish to put you in danger.'

Rachel relaxed slightly. Gradually the fear melted away and another awareness crept in. She could feel Cory's heart beating steadily under her ear. With her nose buried in his shirt, she could inhale the dry, pleasant smell of the material and beneath it the muskier, sensual smell of his skin. Her nerves prickled. It felt warm and familiar to be in his arms, but there was another feeling there, an excitement underneath that was very different.

With deliberation, Rachel drew away a little and looked at him. 'So you came to the reading group the following day to see if you could work out who it was who attacked you?'

'I had injured them,' Cory said gently.

Rachel shook her head slightly. 'I cannot believe it could be one of us. It simply is not possible…'

Cory did not say anything and after a moment she sighed.

'What are you thinking?' Cory asked.

'I am wondering what would happen if they tried again,' Rachel said honestly. 'Until the culprit is caught it cannot be safe for you, Cory.'

Cory gave her his brilliant smile. 'Do not be concerned, Rachel. My attacker took a chance because I was alone that night. These days I make sure that I am in company all the time.'

Rachel rubbed her fingers absentmindedly over the material of his sleeve. 'Do not jest, Cory. Whoever it is knows that you suspect them and as a result you are in danger.'

'I can look after myself,' Cory said, with what Rachel felt was a deplorably casual air. 'Besides, we *will* catch them, Rae. It is only a matter of time.'

Rachel held his gaze. 'There is something that I must know, Cory.' She sighed again. 'I suppose that when Justin Kestrel and his brothers were doing the pretty by all of us it was merely in the interests of finding out the identity of the spy? Not that I thought them sincere, of course, but I had no idea they were quite so shallow.'

She felt hurt. She had known the Kestrels were not interested in matrimony, but it felt like a betrayal to think that their charming manners were completely false.

Cory laughed. 'Oh, you do not need to fear that it was all pretence,' he said drily. 'Richard Kestrel likes you immensely. Why do you think I was so damnably jealous just now?'

Rachel's gaze flew to his face. 'Jealous? But—' She struggled, grasped at a straw, anything to keep the conversation away from the two of them. 'But Lord Richard is in love with Mrs Stratton…'

'I know,' Cory said. 'In fact, Richard is so in love he can barely keep his mind on what he is trying to achieve. The more time he spends in her company, the less sense one gets from him.'

Rachel gave a little gesture. 'Then I do not see—' She stopped. She knew that she was wandering into dangerous ground, but it was too late now. All half-truths and half-measures between them had to be at an end.

'You do not see why I was jealous?' Cory asked ruefully. 'I dare say I have no cause, but that has nothing to do with emotion, Rae. I do not wish to share your attention with anyone.'

Rachel felt a rush of powerful feeling. 'You speak most convincingly,' she said sharply, 'but how am I to know that your protestations are true when this whole business has been a charade from start to finish—?'

She broke off at the expression in Cory's eyes. 'Rae,' he said, 'there was no pretence. Never between me and you. Shall I prove it to you?'

Cory took her hand in his again and it was all that Rachel could do not to wrench it away from him, so sharp was her awareness of him. She wanted to tell him that he was being foolish, to beg him to say no more, to retreat to the comfortable grounds of friendship. But it was far too late for that. She had already betrayed herself with her accusations of disloyalty. She knew she had given away the fact that she cared for him. And she knew what Cory's next question would be. She waited, her breath coming quickly, lightly.

'Why were you so upset when I told you about what had happened to me?' Cory asked softly.

Rachel did not meet his eyes. Her answer stumbled a little. 'Cory, you are my dearest and my oldest friend,' she said. 'How could I possibly greet with equanimity the thought that someone had taken a shot at you? You may have that hardihood, but I do not.'

Cory smiled. He was stroking her hand softly, sending little quivers of feeling along her nerves. 'Are you certain that that was all it was?' he pursued.

Rachel's gaze clung to his. Her senses felt cloudy, confused. 'That is all it can be,' she whispered.

There was a moment of stillness, then Cory pulled her to him, his arms hard about her again. This time there was no attempt at comfort. This time his mouth took hers hungrily, almost angrily, as though he were trying to prove a point. The kiss was rough and demanding, overpowering with pent-up need. Rachel's mind spun. The minute he had touched her she had been lost, aware of nothing but the hard muscles of his arms beneath her fingers, the heated, insistent claim of his mouth, the scent of him, the pressure of his body against hers.

She forgot that they were in the phaeton, forgot that it was standing in full view of the track, forgot her scruples and doubts. Her heart was hammering and she could think of nothing but the absolute bliss and perfection of being in Cory's arms, the overwhelming sensation of yielding to him, of coming home.

Cory tossed her hat on to the seat beside them and with one swift movement pulled half the pins from her hair so that it slithered down her back in heavy chestnut waves. Rachel gave a little cry. It felt extraordinary, intimate, as though he had stripped her naked. She opened her mouth to protest at the disorder to her appearance, but before she could say a word Cory had tangled one gloved hand in the shining tresses and covered her mouth with his again, kissing her deeply. Rachel forgot all about neatness and gave him back kiss for kiss, adrift with an uncontrollable need for him, clutching at his shoulders to draw him closer, to taste and to tease and to demand from him a reaction as powerful as the one he aroused in her.

She got it.

Cory's lips left hers and he took the lobe of her ear between his teeth, tugging gently. His breath feathered across the tender skin of her neck and sent shivers right through her body. Rachel's senses spun. She felt his fingers on the

buttons that closed her spencer. The coolness of the air
about her shoulders told her that it had been shed. And then,
without warning, he stunned her, made her senses reel.
Quickly, gently, he scooped one of her breasts from the
rounded neckline of her gown and bent his head to tug at
the nipple, lick it back and forth, with expert skill. A short,
high cry escaped her. She arched against his hands and his
mouth and tumbled back against the seat, her body abandoned to his. His hands were hard on her waist, his mouth
at her breast and she wanted to die from sheer, inexorable
desire.

The curricle jolted suddenly and Rachel almost tumbled
from the seat. A flock of birds rose from the sheltering trees
with cries of alarm. From the fields behind the hay barn
came the sound of voices and the scrape of iron on wood.
Sanity returned to both Rachel and Cory instantly. He let
her go. His eyes were blazing and his mouth was a hard
line.

'So, are we friends now?' he asked.

Consternation shook Rachel. She knew that she had responded to him in full measure, wanting nothing more than
to lose herself forever in his arms. She kept her head bent
and adjusted her dress and reached for her spencer with
short, jerky movements. After a moment Cory helped her.
His own hands were shaking. Rachel noted the fact and felt
an aftershock of love and helpless need. She folded her arms
tightly. She felt chilled.

'Rachel…' Cory said, and there was a note in his voice
that brought her gaze up to meet his. She twisted her fingers
together in her lap.

'I do not think that we should have done that,' she said.

She heard Cory laugh a little unsteadily.

'Certainly not here and now,' he agreed. His hand came
down hard on her clasped ones, compelling her to look at
him. 'But that was not what I asked,' he added. 'I asked if
your feelings for me were those of mere friendship.'

The rose colour flooded Rachel's face as she realised that she needed to meet his demands with her own brand of courage. She tilted her face up so that she met his gaze very straight. 'No,' she said. 'I do not think that we are friends now. I do not feel particularly kindly disposed to you at the moment.'

Cory's expression eased. He almost smiled. 'So what do you feel for me, Rachel?'

Rachel pulled at the seam of her glove, almost splitting it in her agitation. 'I must admit...I have to confess to a shocking attraction to you,' she said. 'It worries me and I do not like it.'

She saw the shadow of a smile deepen on Cory's face. 'You do not like it or you do not like me?' he enquired. 'Please be specific.'

Rachel bit her lip. 'Oh, I like you, Cory. That must be demonstrably obvious to you! I was not fighting you off—' She stopped and her voice fell. 'But I do not like feeling like this about you.'

'Friendship can change,' Cory said. 'It can grow and develop into something different...'

Rachel felt her throat close with nervousness. Such sentiments did not reassure her, for where could her friendship with Cory go now? To explore a mutual attraction might be exciting beyond belief and just the thought of it made her heart leap, but it would leave a true companionship in tatters, for at the end of it all there was nowhere for them to go. They wanted different things. They always had and they always would.

She looked up and met Cory's silver gaze. 'I do not know what to think,' she said.

Cory turned her face up to his, his gloved fingers spread against her cheek. 'Yes, you do,' he said. 'You do know what to think. Tell me now,' he invited softly, as his eyes held hers. 'Tell me *exactly* what you think.'

Rachel was thinking that she ached for him and wanted

no more than to be back in his arms. She did not need to speak. He read the truth quite easily in her face. She saw his gaze go to her parted lips and his eyes darken, and she turned her face full up to his under the caress of his hand. Her invitation was unmistakable to both of them. His head swooped down and she closed her eyes. She felt his lips against her throat and the line of her jaw, pressing little kisses on her skin that felt as though they burned her very soul. When he finally guided her mouth to his, Rachel gave a gasp of pleasure and opened for him in wanton delight. Her mouth moved beneath his, responsive to the onslaught of his relentless tongue, eager to satisfy the clamour of her senses. She had no idea of how long they clung together, but then she felt Cory ease away from her and she almost cried out in frustration.

He was looking at her with a mixture of desire and disbelief and the old amusement.

'And after all that you want us to be friends?' he said. His voice was husky and he shook his head slightly as though he was finding it as difficult as she to believe what had happened. He picked up the reins. 'All the same, I must take you back, sweetheart, or I will pick you up and carry you into that barn and make love to you here and now.'

Rachel pressed her fingers to her lips to repress the gasp that his words provoked. The image burned in her mind, excluding all other thoughts. She struggled with herself and after a few moments was able to regain a little composure. Cory was deliberately avoiding looking at her now and she understood why. The air was so tense between them that it would take a minute spark to set off the entire conflagration. Instead he concentrated on turning the carriage with inch-perfect precision and set off back up the track to the Wood-bridge road. For Rachel the scenery passed in a complete blur. The only thought in her mind was that she had enjoyed Cory's caresses beyond reason. She felt shocked and vulnerable and passionately excited. It was an utterly new experience for her and it held her silent all the way home.

Chapter Seventeen

'I have to ask you your intentions, old fellow,' Richard Kestrel said to Cory Newlyn that night at the Regatta Ball.

'My intentions?' Cory dragged his gaze from the sight of Rachel dancing with Caspar Lang and fixed his old friend with a look of enquiry. 'My intentions about what?'

'Don't be dense, old chap,' Richard said. 'Your intentions towards Miss Odell, of course. I would not like to think that you were cherishing any dishonourable aspirations in that direction.'

Cory gave him a hard stare. 'I fear I do not quite understand you, Richard. Are *you* quizzing *me?* You have heard the phrase concerning the pot and the kettle, I take it?'

Richard drove his hands into the pockets of his evening suit, thereby spoiling the elegant line. 'You may be as indignant as you wish, Cory, but my concerns are with Miss Odell. With no brother to protect her—'

'*I* have acted the role of Miss Odell's brother for the past seventeen years—' Cory began, only to break off as Richard laughed.

'Yes, and forgive me, but recently you have exchanged that role for the one of Miss Odell's protector,' Richard said, 'in a completely unfraternal sense.'

Cory stiffened and then, seeing there was no mockery in

Richard's face, relaxed slightly. 'Devil take it, Richard,' he said, 'has everyone noticed?'

'Pretty much everyone,' Richard confirmed gently. 'Which is why I have to ask the question. You are in danger of damaging Miss Odell's reputation if you continue.'

'Surely you cannot believe that I would have dishonourable intentions towards a lady I hold in such high esteem, the daughter of a colleague I respect?' Cory said incredulously.

Richard shrugged. '*I* do not doubt you, old chap. But then I am not a gossiping old tabby who likes to make trouble for others. Nor,' he added thoughtfully, 'am I as bored and spiteful as, say, Lady Benedict, and looking for a target for my malice.'

'Damnation!' Cory expelled his breath sharply. He had not foreseen this. He knew that he could not, with honour, allow Rachel's reputation to be questioned. He could not even bear the thought of it. He rubbed a hand across his forehead.

'I am trying to give Miss Odell a little time to become accustomed to my suit,' he said.

'Time?' Richard placed his empty wine glass gently on the table. 'You have had seventeen years, old fellow. Thought you generally worked quicker than that.'

Cory smiled faintly. 'I suppose I asked for that. Once again I suggest that you look to your own situation before you criticise mine.'

Richard laughed. '*Touché,* Cory.' He drew a step closer. 'Did Justin tell you that he had found a witness to the attack on you, by the way? A poacher, name of Simm, saw a figure running away from the scene that night. Naturally he did not reveal himself since he had a brace of Justin's pheasant under his arm at the time.'

Cory laughed. 'So I could have perished for all he cared! Did he get a good look at my assailant?'

Richard shook his head. 'Did not even know if it was a

man or a woman. But he saw two people—and saw them take the road towards Benton Hall.'

Cory's lips pursed in a soundless whistle. 'Benton? Then it *does* centre around Lady Benedict?'

'It would appear so.' Richard shook his head ruefully. 'But what we need—and have not got—is hard evidence in place of supposition. And until we have it—' he clapped Cory on the shoulder '—you should watch your step, old chap.' He laughed. 'Enough business for one night. Since you are not yet betrothed to the lovely Miss Odell, I shall take this opportunity to dance with her…'

He pressed a full glass of wine into Cory's hand and strolled away. Cory watched him approach Rachel, saw the tilt of her head as she smiled up at him, felt the now-familiar physical wrench of jealousy, and smiled wryly to himself. He had never thought of himself as a possessive man. He had never *been* possessive until there had been something as precious as Rachel that he wanted to possess. All the other things that he had ever pursued in his entire life were as nothing in comparison.

Cory watched Rachel take Richard's hand and they walked over to the set of country-dances that was forming. He admired the gentle sway of her pale blue gown. Tonight Rachel was pin neat again, and he was willing to bet any money that it was in part a reaction to the violent disorder in which she had found herself that afternoon. Her hair was arranged in a complicated series of knots and curls, her gown was demure and fastened up to the neck with a row of tiny pearl buttons. But this afternoon he had loosened that hair and felt it wrapped around his hand in all its provocative glory, he had seen beneath the layers with which Rachel so tidily covered herself. He had touched that soft skin that no one else had ever touched. He *knew*… His body tightened unbearably at the memory.

Cory turned away and concentrated on Rachel's predicament rather than his own. He loved her. He would not expose her to scandal. He would give himself a week more to woo her, but then he would have to make his declaration before the entire world, whether she was ready or not.

He drained the glass of wine. He felt as green and uncertain as a youth in the throes of his first love affair and it was completely disconcerting. He had no certainty that she would accept him.

It was the strangest thing to find herself courted by the man she had been accustomed to think of as her dearest friend; stranger still to feel her resistance dissolving into something warm and exciting and intimate, that melted her heart and set her concerns at naught. Rachel was under siege and the seduction was so subtle, so gentle, that she was already halfway lost before she even noticed it.

Cory brought her flowers, wild roses snatched from the bushes that ran rampant beside the Winter Race, and sprigs of yellow gorse that she grumbled pierced her fingers. He took her driving and persuaded her to go boating on the river. He escorted her to the Woodbridge assembly and danced with her three times. He made her laugh. He sat talking with her whilst the sun went down and the ducks whistled and called on the river and the shadows merged into dark.

He did not kiss her once.

Rachel knew that he wanted to. It was implicit in the way that he held her when they danced or when he helped her down from the curricle. Once, she had been talking about her reading of the texts about the Midwinter Treasure and had looked at his face, seen that his gaze was devouring her and had stopped abruptly. They had stared at one another and Rachel had seen the heated desire in his eyes and her smile had faltered as she felt the now-familiar weakness invade her senses.

'You are not listening to me!' she had said.

'I am sorry,' Cory had said charmingly. 'You are quite

right. I confess that I did not hear a word that you were saying.'

Rachel had blushed and Cory had laughed and kissed her fingers, and she had known that he had wanted to do a great deal more than that.

Friendship was special, Rachel realised, but love and friendship together was proving a deeper and more perfect experience than she had ever imagined. It threatened to steal her very soul. Yet at the back of her mind was one last thought. It whispered across her happiness when she least expected it, and cast a long shadow. For Cory Newlyn was the man everyone swore was wedded to his pursuit of antiquities, the adventurer, the traveller, always on the move, possessed of a restless spirit. And she...she wanted nothing more than the calm and peace of home, and these two opposites would never be compatible, not in a thousand years.

Oddly, it was one small incident that happened at a dinner at Saltires that finally brought the whole matter to a head. The meal was over and the ladies had retired to the drawing room to take tea and play a few desultory rounds of cards whilst they waited for the gentlemen to join them. Rachel had been sitting out that hand of whist and had lost interest in following the progress of play. She got up to inspect Lady Sally's bookcases instead, and was soon quite engrossed in a copy of *The Faery Queen.* Only the sound of Cory's voice, as he re-entered the drawing room with Richard Kestrel and Sir Arthur, roused her attention.

'I should be delighted to go up to London to discuss organising an exhibition of our finds at the British Museum, sir,' Rachel heard him say. 'It would be a great honour. Whilst I am up in town I need to make some arrangements for my forthcoming expedition to Scandinavia.'

'Some marvellous finds at Uppsala,' Sir Arthur enthused. 'You must write to me and report on them.'

Cory bowed. 'I should be pleased to, sir. I hear that they

have a boat burial of the type we hoped to find here at Midwinter. I shall be most interested to view it...'

Rachel's blood ran cold. For a moment it seemed that Lady Sally's drawing room, the most warm and pleasant place imaginable, was as cold and barren as the Arctic wastes. Cory's words repeated in her brain with the emphasis of hammer on metal: *I need to make arrangements for my forthcoming expedition...*

Rachel pressed her hands together and stared blindly out of the diamond-paned windows into the dark gardens beyond. Cory had not mentioned this trip to her at all. In all their conversations over the past week he had not intimated that he would be going up to London, let alone embarking for more distant shores. Which meant that either he was intending to go alone or...

Rachel paused. Over the past week she had become increasingly convinced of Cory's honourable intentions towards her. He had assured her that his feelings were sincere and she did not doubt him. But the inevitable corollary of that was that he would expect her to travel with him. He would expect her to marry him and then to go with him wherever he chose. Through mountain and desert and flood and desolation, without home and security and respite... Cory's lifetime's pursuit was antiquities—what would be more natural than that he would expect her to accompany him in his work? It was, after all, the role of a wife. It was what she would be expected to do.

She watched Cory as he took a seat beside Lady Odell. He had given Rachel one look across the room as he had come in, a look of tenderness that had promised that he would join her soon. Suddenly Rachel did not wish him to do so.

She went across to her parents. 'I am sorry, Mama,' she said, 'but I fear I have the headache. It is nothing,' she said hastily, as Cory got up, an expression of concern on his face, 'but I feel I require to go to my bed.' She turned to Lady Sally, carefully avoiding looking at Cory again.

'Please excuse me, ma'am,' she said, and there was no need to manufacture the wobble in her voice. 'I apologise for leaving the party so early…'

Lady Sally was all that was gracious and soon the Odells were travelling down the drive away from Saltires on their way back to Midwinter Royal. Rachel sat in the corner of the coach and rested her now genuinely aching head on her hand. She tried not to think too much about what she had heard that evening, but in the privacy of her room she lay awake for hours, staring at the canopy on her bed and weighing all the things that mattered in her life. By the morning, though, she had come to no conclusion.

'I think that it will rain soon,' Olivia Marney said, gazing at a horizon that was the same dull silver as a used sixpence. 'Maybe not today, nor even tomorrow, but a storm will come some time within the week. I can feel it brewing.'

Rachel and Olivia were sitting on a picnic blanket beneath the pine trees at the edge of Kestrel Beach. It was the day that Deborah had arranged for them all to go to the seaside, and because life had been so full of late, Rachel had completely forgotten about the trip until the Marneys' barouche had rolled up the drive to collect her.

She had almost been tempted to cry off.

During the morning they had explored the ruined castle that overlooked the beach, Rachel making sure that she was in company with either Deborah or Olivia or a combination of the others. She had even tolerated Helena Lang's girlish squeals and high-pitched enthusiasm as a defence against being alone with Cory. Yet it had not enabled her to ignore him. She was conscious of his presence the whole time, and whenever she glanced in his direction—which was frequently—it was to see him watching her with a quizzical look that made her heart skip a beat. She knew that look. It told her that she might be able to avoid him for the present, but that he was biding his time and she would not be able to escape for long.

After a picnic luncheon, Olivia had decided that she would like to rest in the shade and Rachel had elected to join her whilst the others strolled down to the water's edge. She could see them now. Helena Lang was pouncing on seashells, exclaiming in glee over each new find, careless of the fact that her skirts were wet from the incoming tide. Deborah and Ross were walking arm in arm, chatting animatedly. Behind them, Richard Kestrel and Cory Newlyn were walking, deep in conversation. As Rachel watched, Cory glanced up and looked directly at her. Rachel blushed and looked away, drawing circles in the hot sand with her fingers.

The heat was becoming oppressive now, trapping them all under a sky like a furnace.

Beyond the shelter of the trees the sun beat down on Kestrel Beach. The shore was wide and sandy, with wind-blown dunes at one end where the beach turned to pebble. It shimmered in a heat haze.

'I think that a thunderstorm is just what we need to clear the air,' Rachel said. 'This constant heat gives me the head-ache.'

'The storms here are tremendous,' Olivia said. 'They roll in off the sea and the air is ripped by the lightning and the whole landscape shudders. *Then* I find it very easy to believe in the ghosts of dead warriors walking!' She looked around and shuddered slightly. 'At night, when the owls are calling and the moon is up, I could quite easily believe in six sorts of nonsense before supper!'

Rachel laughed. 'Would you prefer to live in town?' she asked.

Olivia shook her head slowly. She was watching the shore, where Deborah was clutching Ross's arm and shriek-ing with laughter as she ran back to avoid the waves.

'No. I love the country.' Olivia said. She turned her head suddenly and Rachel was shocked to see the tears in her eyes. 'What I would like,' she added fiercely, 'is to be married to a man who wants to be married to me!'

Rachel put out an impulsive hand and touched Olivia's own. 'Olivia, I am so sorry.'

'Do not be,' Olivia said, giving her hand a brief, hard squeeze. 'Forgive me, I should not have said such a thing.' She scrubbed her eyes with a scrap of cambric handkerchief and gave Rachel an embarrassed smile. 'I am the one who should be sorry, Rachel.'

Rachel shook her head slightly. She watched Deborah and Ross strolling along Kestrel Beach, a little ahead of the others in the group. Rachel sighed. She wondered that Deborah, so kind in other ways, could be so blind to her sister's misery.

Olivia picked up her copy of *The Enchantress,* which she had discarded in the sandy grass beside them. She flicked a few pages over, then sighed. 'I think I shall ask Lady Sally if we may read something a little more astringent next time,' she said. 'I find that romance accords ill with my mood at present!'

Rachel laughed. 'I believe I shall add my voice to yours,' she said ruefully.

'Lord Newlyn?' Olivia asked, with an expressive glance. 'I have seen the way that you are studiously avoiding him. Has something happened?'

Rachel blushed. 'I had not thought it was so evident to everyone.'

Olivia smiled at her. 'I am sorry to put you to the blush. I had not intended it. It was simply that I had noticed you did not wish to be left alone—and that Lord Newlyn is waiting for the exact moment when you are.'

Rachel felt a flare of alarm. She knew that sooner or later she would have to speak to Cory and ask him about his plans but she felt a certain reluctance to do so. In fact, she was afraid. 'Do you think that he will approach me?' she asked.

Olivia laughed. 'I believe that is what Ross would call a racing certainty, Rachel. Lord Newlyn is a most determined gentleman, by my guess. If you do not give him an opportunity, he will engineer one for himself. He has been watching you all day.'

Olivia stood up and shook the sand from her skirts. 'In fact, I see that Lord Newlyn has lost his patience and is coming to find you. I think I shall go to join the others down by the water. Miss Lang had some scheme to go sea bathing, but I cannot say that it appeals to me.'

Rachel craned her neck. Cory was taking his leave of Richard Kestrel with a brief word and an upraised hand, and was coming towards them across the sand. She scrambled to her feet. 'I will come with you.'

'I should be delighted, of course,' Olivia said, smiling, 'but I do not think that Lord Newlyn would be.'

Cory's shadow fell across them. He bowed politely to Olivia, but there was a hint of a smile at the corner of his mouth. 'Good afternoon, Lady Marney. Your sister wondered whether you would care to join her?'

Olivia smiled broadly. 'I sensed that Deb was asking for me,' she said. 'I will join her directly.' She put up her parasol and walked slowly away.

Rachel and Cory looked at each other.

'I thought that you would never give me a chance,' he said.

Rachel's heart beat a little faster. 'I was not aware that I had,' she said wryly.

Cory laughed. 'No,' he said. 'I am indebted to Lady Marney for her perception. I would like to talk to you, Rae.'

He took her arm and drew her deeper into the relative privacy of the trees. When they were sheltered beneath the dense cover of the forest he turned to her and allowed his gaze to travel over her slowly, consideringly.

Rachel trembled slightly. 'What is it, Cory?'

'I want to know why you are avoiding me,' Cory said bluntly. He rested one hand against the sturdy trunk of the nearest pine. 'Last night, and again today, you have been very careful to make sure that we are never alone together. I would like to know why.' He took her hand. 'What has changed between us, Rae?'

Rachel evaded his gaze. It was so difficult when they knew each other so well. She felt as though she had nowhere to hide, no place to keep secrets. He knew her thoughts and he knew her mind. Every reaction was exposed to him and there could be no concealment.

She paid him the compliment of being as blunt as he.

'I hear that you are to go away,' she said.

She saw his face ease, as though he had expected some far more difficult problem. 'I see,' he said. 'It is true that I shall be leaving for London shortly, but I do not plan to go for a week or so yet. I am sorry that you had to hear it by a roundabout route.'

There was a hollow feeling growing within Rachel. 'And your trip to Scandinavia?' she said. 'Is that also something that you wish to tell me about?'

This time the silence was longer.

'This was not how I wished to do this,' Cory said, at length. His gaze held hers. Rachel could feel the tension in him tight as a coiled spring.

'I want you to marry me, Rae,' he said. 'When…if I go away, I wish you to come with me. You cannot have misunderstood my feelings or my intentions, I hope. It is my most ardent desire that you will accept my proposal.'

Rachel stared at him. She felt breathless, as though she was on the edge of something too huge to be contemplated. Cory looked quite calm, but then she saw the faintest hint of uncertainty in his face, the way that he squared his shoulders as though expecting a rejection. The moment of vulnerability from such a strong man sent a wave of love through her that was so acute that she trembled.

'I do not know…' The words were wrenched from her. 'There is much to consider, Cory. I need time.'

'Time,' Cory said, with a ghost of a smile. 'Yes, I understand that, Rae.'

Rachel felt her fears and doubts press in on her. 'It sounds foolish when I have known you so long,' she said, 'but I have not yet become accustomed to our situation.'

Cory nodded. 'I am not a patient man, Rae…' he pulled her close to him '…but if you can give me hope then I can give you at least a little time.'

His mouth brushed hers in a tantalising shadow of a kiss that set Rachel's pulse racing. It was the lightest, most teasing of contacts, and yet it sent flickers of desire burning through her. Barely aware of her own reactions, she leaned into the kiss, feeling the rough material of Cory's shirt under her fingers and the hard muscle beneath that. In his arms it was all too easy to forget her misgivings, her fears of the future. The kiss changed, became heated and fierce, and Rachel felt herself turn hot all over, her skin prickling with desire and awareness. She knew that she had no defences against Cory's undeniable expertise. He kissed her with a concentrated passion that made her shiver down to her toes.

'Damn it, Rae,' he said, against her mouth, 'do not keep me waiting too long.' He let her go and she could see the conflict in his face before he smoothed the expression away. 'I must take you back,' he said reluctantly. 'Until I can claim you as my future wife I must not do anything further to endanger your reputation.'

He drew her hand through his arm and led her out of the shade and on to the beach. No one seemed to have noticed their disappearance. Deb and Olivia, Ross and Richard Kestrel were still wandering along the water's edge. Helena Lang and James Kestrel were nowhere to be seen.

Rachel tilted her hat to shield her face from the sun and from Cory's perceptive gaze. Her mind was in a turmoil.

Until I can claim you as my future wife... There seemed no doubt in Cory's mind that she would accept. Rachel wished that she had his confidence. For although the physical attraction between them threatened to sweep all sanity away, she knew that it required more than that to make a life together.

They rejoined the rest of the party and soon Helena Lang and James Kestrel appeared along the beach and it was generally agreed to return home. The others seemed to be in good spirits and Rachel smiled until her face ached. It was only later that she sat on the edge of her bed and thought about Cory and about what he wanted from life.

She knew now that Cory's intentions were honourable, but she was also aware that there was a very great problem indeed in marrying him. She knew that she loved him—he was the man that she wanted as her husband, just as Olivia had suggested to her all those weeks ago.

But she did not love his way of life.

Just thinking about it made her come out in a cold sweat of fear and depression. When she had come to Midwinter, she had allowed herself to think that her travelling days might be over for good. For years she had traipsed around the world in her parents' wake like a small rowing boat bobbing helplessly behind two purposeful galleons. She had craved a settled home and a stable life—the chance to carve out something of her own—and from that point of view, Cory Newlyn was the worst possible choice for a husband.

She thought of Cory then; of his fervour for life, and his enthusiasms and the spark of excitement about him that she had always condemned as recklessness, but now saw was the essence of the man himself. She had a dreadful feeling that that spark would be extinguished if he were to marry a woman who did not share his passions in life, or, worse still, a woman who followed him reluctantly and could not disguise her unwillingness. It made her feel quite sick to think of it.

She turned her face against her pillow and felt the hot tears sink silently into its cool surface. For the kissing had to stop now and so did any idea of marriage, and she was rather afraid that the friendship would be lost too.

In fact, she stood to lose everything.

Chapter Eighteen

When Cory found her the following morning, Rachel was standing on one of the library chairs, plying a feather duster to remove the cobwebs from the candelabra. It was not the position that she would have wished to be in when she met him, for it set her at a distinct disadvantage. She had endured a miserable night, tossing and turning as she thought over what she had to say to him. She knew that she had to talk to him at the first opportunity. Early in the morning she had gone down to the excavation to see if he was there, only to discover that he had not yet arrived and no one knew where he was. In desperation, Rachel had sought refuge in cleaning. It had always worked in the past when she felt unsettled, but now she was so unhappy than not even a brisk sprucing up of the library could make any impression on her blue-devilled mood.

The library chandelier was an ugly object. It was suspended from a hook on the ceiling that looked uncannily like a butcher's rack for hanging game, and there were long trails of candle wax hardened on to the branches in a dreadfully dirty fashion. Just seeing it there offended Rachel's sense of cleanliness. Although Sir Arthur Odell was the only one who used the library in the evening, she knew that she simply could not countenance leaving such a dirty object hanging there. The difficulty was that the hook was just out of her reach and even if she stood on tiptoe she could not quite ease the heavy iron candelabra from its catch.

She put the feather duster down on the table, moved the chair to precisely the correct position beneath the candelabra, and climbed up again. If she stretched up as far as she could…

The chair lurched beneath her with sickening suddenness. Rachel made a grab for the back of it and her hand raked thin air. She felt her balance going and then strong hands grabbed her about the waist and she was swung through the air and placed gently on her feet.

Cory's voice said, 'Trying to break your neck, Rachel?'

Rachel felt flustered. Cory still had his hands about her waist and she could feel them warm through the thin muslin of her dress. His expression was quizzical as it rested on her flushed face.

'I was trying to dislodge the candelabra,' Rachel said.

'And instead you almost dislodged yourself,' Cory observed. 'Why did you not call one of us to help you?'

'You were all busy,' Rachel excused. She tried to step out of his grasp, but Cory did not let go. He was watching her expression, amusement in his own face.

'What are you doing inside, Cory?' she asked. 'I thought that you were working.'

'I came to see you,' Cory said, 'and there is no need to make me sound like the kitchen cat. I swear I took my boots off before I came inside.'

Rachel looked him up and down. He was indeed in his stockinged feet and the sight gave her a rather odd feeling, as though he were in a state of intimate undress.

'I am glad that you are here, for I wished to talk to you about something important,' she said, averting her gaze to the table and glaring rather hard at a smear of dust on the shining surface.

'I wished to see you too,' Cory said, smiling, 'although not necessarily to talk.'

Something twisted inside Rachel at the happiness she saw in his face. It made it all the more difficult for her to reject him. Already she felt sick with apprehension and misery at what she was going to do.

'Cory,' she said desperately.

'Yes?' Cory asked.

Rachel looked at him. Her heart gave a painful leap into her throat. She swallowed hard, but found that the words of dismissal that she had practised for the best part of the night simply did not come. Cory moved closer to her, his gaze disturbingly intent on her face.

'You have cobwebs in your hair, Rae,' he said softly.

'Oh…' Rachel put a self-conscious hand up to her head. She felt a little confused. 'I knew that I should have worn a cap,' she said.

'Thank the lord you did not,' Cory said feelingly, 'for I should have had to take it off you. They are as unbecoming as a frumpish gown, and you are only two and twenty, Rae, far too young to be donning a spinster's cap.'

His fingers tangled with hers in her thick, brown hair. 'Hold still. I will get the cobwebs out for you.'

'You will loosen all the pins!' Rachel wailed. She felt his fingertips brush her scalp and felt acutely self-conscious. This felt dangerous, reminding her of the experience in the phaeton when she had been completely abandoned in her response to him. At such close quarters her senses were full of him; his touch and the scent of his skin made her head spin. She felt slightly dizzy, put out a hand to steady herself and found herself clutching his arm. The linen shirt was smooth beneath her fingers and Cory's arm hard and strong beneath that. Thinking about it, she felt even more shaky.

'You are making me forget what I wanted to say,' she said faintly.

Cory smiled into her eyes. His voice was soft. 'I am only

removing the cobwebs from your hair, Rae.' His fingers tangled once again in her curls. 'There. I have finished.'

'Thank you.' Rachel realised that her voice sounded a little husky. She cleared her throat. 'Thank you, Cory.'

'You look charmingly dishevelled now,' Cory said, his gaze appraising her. There was a disturbing light in his eyes. 'I think I have made matters worse rather than better.'

He picked up the feather duster, turned it over in his hands and laughed. 'In fact, you look like a tousled Cinderella.' He touched her cheek lightly with the feathers. 'This is rather nice…'

'Don't…' Rachel began. Her voice almost failed her again. The touch of the feathers was soft, sensuous, disturbingly arousing. Her skin prickled. Goose pimples teased their way down her back. Cory was watching her face and she knew he could read her feelings. Slowly, so slowly, he let the feathers drift across her throat and down one of her arms. Even through the material of her gown, it felt like a lover's touch. Rachel could feel her eyes starting to close as shivers of sensation coursed through her body. The expression in Cory's eyes made the heat burn in her blood as she saw the echo of her own desire, hot and hard, in his eyes. The feathers brushed her bodice and her nipples hardened in shameless response. She knew the outline of them must show clearly through the thin material, knew that Cory could see it too. The knowledge heated her senses past bearing.

'Cory…' she said, on an anguished whisper.

She grabbed the feather duster from his hands and almost snapped the handle in the attempt. In a second it would be too late and she would be helplessly caught in her desire for him. No, it was already too late. Cory pulled her roughly to him and the feather duster fell unnoticed to the floor. He kissed her hard and long and very thoroughly until Rachel was breathless and her knees were in danger of buckling beneath her.

They were both so engrossed that they did not hear the tramp of footsteps in the hall nor even hear the upraised voices until the door burst open and Sir Arthur Odell burst in, blunderbuss in hand. His boots were still on and he was scattering sand all over the neatly swept floor.

'What the devil is going on here?' Sir Arthur demanded. 'Kissing and hugging in full view of the window!' The blunderbuss wavered alarmingly in Cory's direction. 'When I invited you to join us in our work, sirrah, I didn't throw my daughter in as well! What do you think you are at?'

Rachel had seldom seen Cory look so taken aback. He took a step forward—and one back again, when the blunderbuss menaced him.

'My apologies, sir. I realise that this looks bad—'

'Damned right it does!'

'But it is not as it seems.'

Sir Arthur glared. 'In what way is it not as it seems? Seems pretty clear to me!'

'Papa,' Rachel interposed, placing herself between them, 'there is no need for such a scene. Cory was just leaving—'

'Not before time,' Sir Arthur growled.

'Sir,' Cory interposed, with increasing desperation, 'please! It is not as it seems because I wish to marry Miss Odell. I was intending to ask your permission shortly—'

'Seems to me you are accustomed to doing everything the wrong way round,' Sir Arthur barked. 'Young people today—'

There was a flutter in the doorway as Lavinia Odell hurried in. 'Arthur? Mrs Goodfellow said that you had brought your blunderbuss into the library—' She stopped as she took in Cory's desperate expression and Rachel's agonised one.

'Whatever is going on here?' she enquired mildly.

Rachel looked at Cory. Cory turned back to Sir Arthur and ploughed on.

'Indeed, sir, if you would give me permission to call on you we may sort this matter out—'

'Just a moment,' Rachel interposed. She was trembling. 'I need to talk to you about this, Cory.'

Cory gave her a smile that made her whole body tremble. 'My dearest Rachel—' he began.

'Please don't,' Rachel said wretchedly. 'Oh, Cory, there is no need for all this simply because we have shared a few kisses.'

There was a sharp intake of breath from Lady Odell and an angry bellow from Sir Arthur.

'A few kisses! Damn it, Newlyn, seems you have been playing fast and loose! Heard you were a scoundrel—never believed it until now!'

Cory made a gesture of desperation. 'Sir! My intentions are of the most honourable. Rachel—' he turned to her '—please tell them that this is no flirtation.'

Rachel took pity on him. 'Cory's intentions *are* honourable, Papa.' She frowned. 'It is simply that I have not said that I will marry him.'

'Modern girls,' Sir Arthur said disagreeably, turning his displeasure on her. 'Never seem to know what they want.'

Cory was looking as chagrined as a man might under the circumstances. He came across to Rachel and entangled his fingers with hers. His touch undermined all her defences.

'You have not said that you will marry me,' he said musingly. 'Can I really not persuade you, Rachel?'

'Yes…no!' Rachel said wildly. 'We cannot talk about this now, Cory. Please be sensible and leave. I can manage Papa. He will have forgotten the whole matter by tomorrow and be engrossed in *The Antiquarian*.'

'Damned if I will,' Sir Arthur said. 'Dashed poor show!'

'I fear that you are outvoted, my sweet,' Cory said. 'I shall not have forgotten, your parents will not have forgotten and I would swear that you will not have forgotten either.' He turned to Sir Arthur. 'I shall call on you tomorrow, if I may, sir.'

Lady Odell pushed aside the blunderbuss and stepped forward. 'Do put that thing down, Arthur,' she said. 'You will shoot yourself in the foot if you are not careful. Cory, dear boy, we should be delighted to see you.'

'Thank you, ma'am,' Cory said, bowing formally. He turned to Rachel. 'I know this is a little abrupt, my love, but I do hope that you will accept my suit.'

Rachel rubbed her forehead. This was not turning out as she had planned and every moment made matters more difficult.

'I had barely become accustomed to the idea that we were courting, Cory,' she said.

'Hah!' Sir Arthur bridled. 'Seems to me that you have been engaging in a great deal of dalliance for a young lady who barely considers herself to be courting!'

'Really, Arthur,' Lady Odell said, 'it is a little late to wake up to ideas of conventional propriety now, in your fifty-fourth year. I seem to recall,' she added with a little, blissful smile, 'that we had our own unconventional courtship.'

Sir Arthur's moustache quivered.

'And,' Lady Odell continued, 'since dear Cory wishes to marry our daughter and we esteem him so highly, there can be no barrier.'

To Rachel's surprise she herded Sir Arthur out of the room with the efficiency of a well-trained sheepdog.

'We must get back to work now, my love,' she said, pausing to kiss Rachel's cheek on the way out. 'Congratulations!'

Rachel waited until the door had closed behind them and then sat down rather heavily on the library chair. Cory came across to her, but before he could touch her she put out a hand to stop him. She saw the arrested look that came into his eyes as he took in the anguish in hers.

'What is it, Rae?' he said softly.

'I am sorry, Cory,' Rachel said. 'I am very honoured, but I fear that I cannot accept your proposal.'

The words came out in a rush and once she had said them, she felt greatly relieved. Then she saw the hurt in Cory's face and felt absolutely dreadful.

'That sounds remarkably well rehearsed, Rae,' Cory said. 'Have you been practising it all night? Was that what you were trying to tell me before?'

Rachel evaded his gaze. That was the trouble with having a suitor who knew her so well. There could be no concealment or pretence. They knew each other too well for falsehood. Some things had changed between them, and some had not.

She was remembering her doubts of the previous night and now she was trembling with the effort of trying to explain herself whilst holding on to the thing that was most precious to her: Cory's friendship.

'This does not feel right,' she said. 'I do not think we should announce our betrothal simply because Papa has got some mad idea of impropriety in his head and seeks to enforce it with his blunderbuss.'

Cory gave her a little, gentle shake. 'Sweetheart, you know it is not like that. I asked you to marry me yesterday because I wanted to and if we have to tell everyone sooner rather than later, then what is the difference?'

'Our betrothal seems to be a little hasty,' Rachel said miserably.

'I agree that we may not have had much of a courtship,' Cory said with a grin, 'but we have had an acquaintanceship of seventeen years. I hope that you will consider that sufficient preparation?'

He looked closely at her woebegone face. There was a grim line to his mouth now and it did not ease. 'You are not telling me the whole truth, are you, Rae?' he said. 'There is something else that troubles you.'

'I am sorry,' Rachel said.

There was an edge to Cory's voice now. 'What is it that is making you unhappy, Rachel?' He took both her hands in his and looked directly into her eyes. 'Why do you not wish to marry me?'

There was a pain lodged somewhere in Rachel's breast. It mirrored the pain that she could see in Cory's eyes.

'It is not as simple as wishing to or not wishing,' she said with difficulty.

She saw Cory's eyes darken. Without warning he pressed his mouth to the palm of her hand.

'How difficult does it need to be?' he asked. 'Rachel, I love you! I have not been able to stop thinking of you. I want you to marry me and travel with me.'

Rachel's hands were trembling but she wrenched them away. She was staring into Cory's eyes, where she saw the vestiges of their old friendship fading away. There was nothing of the childhood companion there and everything of the ardent lover. She could see the concentrated desire and the control that he was exercising over it. It frightened her even as she felt the answering tug of desire.

'I...' The word came out as a whisper. 'Oh, Cory, do not ask it of me. I cannot.' She was on her feet, turning her back on him for she could not bear to see the hurt in his face. This was terrible, far worse than she had imagined. 'Cory, do not,' she repeated. 'I do not want this.'

Cory stood up too. 'Please tell me,' he said, with constraint, 'that I am not forcing my attentions on an unwilling lady. Please tell me, Rachel, that you are as attracted to me as I am to you.'

Rachel spun round. 'Yes, it is true!' she said. She put her hands up and covered her face briefly. 'I could never lie to you, Cory. I feel the same desire that you do, but—' her gaze challenged him to keep his distance '—that is not enough.'

Cory shook his head slowly. 'Why not?'

'Because we do not want the same things!' Rachel burst out. 'I have been thinking and thinking about this. To travel and explore is your life and to stay at home is mine! We would do better to try to salvage our old friendship before it is too late. That is more valuable that a transient attraction.'

Cory's eyes narrowed. He spoke very softly. 'Is that what you want, Rachel?'

Rachel screwed up her face to repress the tears. 'Yes! I want us to be friends again. I want that friendship back the in the same manner it was before!'

'You wish matters to be undemanding and easy between us?' Cory shook his head. 'It can never be that, Rachel. Never again.'

'But why not?' Rachel wailed.

'Because I do not want that any more. And neither do you in your heart.' With a swift move Cory caught her arm and pulled her close to him. 'How can we ever be friends when I cannot forget the feel of you in my arms?' he said. 'Tell me you do not want the same thing that I do, Rae.'

This was new to Rachel, this intensity in him. Cory had always seemed the most easy and relaxed of men. Yet she remembered the persuasive insistence of his kisses with a shiver. There was a different side to Cory that she was beginning to discover, a side that was forceful and passionate and intriguing. She wanted it as much as she wanted to let him go.

'I cannot deny that I am attracted to you,' she said desperately. 'I *have* admitted it! But I still maintain that it is not enough.'

'It is a good beginning,' Cory said. 'I understand what you are saying, Rae, but we already have more than most other people. Surely we can at least try.'

Rachel shook her head. 'No.' Her voice went flat. 'You wish to travel, Cory, and I wish for nothing more than a settled home. You cannot give me that and I cannot ask it of you. And that is an end to it.'

She felt Cory go still and his hand fall from her arm, and when she dared to open her eyes she realised with a mixture of relief and intense disappointment that he looked the same as he usually did—cool, assured, slightly quizzical.

'Then there is no more to be said,' he said.

For Rachel there was. 'Please—' the hot tears stung her eyes again '—if you withdraw your friendship from me, Cory, then all will be lost.'

She saw the pity in his face then and felt her heart miss a beat that it could be for her. But his expression was softening and he almost smiled.

'Poor Rae,' he said. 'Of course I shall not withdraw my friendship from you, but I cannot promise that it will ever be the same again.'

He bowed and walked away and Rachel felt that, despite his words, it was too late. She had lost something irretrievable.

Chapter Nineteen

The thunderstorm struck the following day. Rachel had given the servants the afternoon off and Sir Arthur and Lady Odell had gone to a *fête champêtre* at Saltires. Rachel had felt far too miserable to be in company and had sent her apologies. She had retired to the library to read, as she had done so often in the past when she was unhappy, but this time neither the romantic overtones of *The Enchantress* nor the beautiful language of Shakespeare nor the philosophical common sense of Marcus Aurelius could soothe her. Instead she stared blindly out of the window and thought about her quarrel with Cory, her mind going round and round over the same ground until she was utterly exhausted. It was some time before she realised that the glass panes through which she was staring were liberally streaked with rain.

When she finally went over to the window, a shocking sight met her gaze. The sky overhead was a strange pale brown colour with puffy rain clouds building angrily over-head. Away to the east, where the black horizon met the sea, lightning flickered and there was the distant sullen growl of thunder.

Rachel went to the door. A sheet of rain hit her full in the face as soon as she opened it and the rising wind sent her stumbling back into the hall. There was a roaring in the air, the sound of the wind in the high trees combining with the rushing of the Winter Race as it lived up to its name and pounded the bank that ran alongside the burial ground.

'Oh, no! The excavations!'

Rachel's anguished exclamation echoed through the empty house. There was no one here to help her secure the site and no one to save the trenches from being swamped with water or the precious artefacts from being washed away. Rachel knew that there was nothing she could do. Even so, she grabbed one of Sir Arthur's old cloaks from the hall cupboard and dashed outside.

Out in the rain, the storm was even more frightening. Rachel struggled through the wicket gate into the field, her body bent almost double against the power of the wind. The black outrider clouds were already overhead and the thunder rumbled much closer now. Rachel half-stumbled, half-ran along the footpath that bordered the field. She was blinded by the flapping material of the wet cloak as it whirled about her in the wind. The rain came down in torrents. The ground underfoot was already running like a stream, for so much water on the dry ground could not be absorbed all at once. And it was hopeless to imagine that she could ever save the excavation. Rachel could see that at once. The trenches were filling with water and the sandy soil was crumbling, turning to mud and flood, drowning all that was in it.

As she came to the corner of the long barrow near the knot of pines that overlooked the river, Rachel saw that she was not the only person who had thought to save the excavation. Cory Newlyn was standing on the riverbank, looking across the flooded trenches. There was no time for embarrassment or surprise. Rachel merely found that she was very pleased to see him.

'Cory!' she said. 'What are you doing here? I thought that you were at Saltires?'

'I came to check on the site,' Cory said. His tawny hair was plastered against his head with the rain and he wiped the water droplets from his eyes. 'I promised your parents that I would do what I could. They cannot get through, Rae. The road is already flooded.'

He pushed the soaking hair back from his forehead. 'This is worse than I had thought, for soon the river will burst its banks. Come away, Rae. There is nothing that we can do here.'

'But the dig!' Rachel said hopelessly. 'All your work! Mama and Papa will be utterly bereft if it is all swept away.'

'There is nothing that you can do,' Cory said again. 'It is dangerous to stay out here, Rachel. Come along.'

He took her arm and they retraced their steps along the edge of the bank. The soil felt strange and unsteady, both clinging and shifting at the same time.

'Mind the edge!' Cory said sharply. 'The sand is unstable here—'

But even as he spoke, Rachel felt a strange sucking sensation beneath her feet, like the tide pulling at her heels. There was a rumble and the grating of shingle on stone, and the sensation of falling down and down into darkness. She heard Cory shout, but her eyes were blinded by rain and sand, and though she put out a desperate hand, her fingers slid helplessly through his grasp. And then she hit something hard and flat, and lay winded and still, staring into the dark.

Rachel was not sure how long she lay there, her thoughts tumbling in shock, her eyes wide and staring through the darkness for a glimmer of light or a clue as to what had happened. The sliding sound of sand and pebbles had ceased and beneath her the rock felt smooth, hard and dry, but she could see nothing at all. She was lying on her back, but now rolled cautiously on to her knees and from there tried to stand. It was fortunate that she did so slowly, for she hit the back of her head on stone and stifled a groan.

She sat down again, drawing her knees up to her chin and curling up as much for comfort as warmth. Her clothes were unpleasantly damp and encrusted with sand, and she could neither see nor hear anything but the rapid breath of her own panic. The air smelled stale. It seemed that the ground above her—the very river bank itself—had collapsed in upon itself and plunged her into a burial chamber that they had not even realised was there.

Rachel tried to breathe more slowly and calm herself, remembering at last all the things that she had learned over the years.

'If you are trapped underground, do not panic,' Sir Arthur Odell had once told her when as a child she had become locked in the cellar of a house and had roused the entire neighbourhood with her screams, *'for you will only use up all the air and achieve absolutely nothing at all.'*

Keeping calm was more easily said than done, however, for Rachel had always had a sneaking fear of the dark. She bit her lip and thought of Cory trying to catch her before she fell, and reassured herself that he would dig her out soon, just as together they had dug out Sir Arthur and Lady Odell when a trench had collapsed on them in Wiltshire. The memory made Rachel feel a tiny bit better, until she thought that perhaps Cory had also been injured in the landslide and was even now lying unconscious, or buried like she, or washed away by the Winter Race as it burst its banks…

Rachel gave a little sob and stifled it furiously. Action, not thought, was the key to helping herself now. Cautiously, she started to feel about her, running her hands over the rocks beneath and to the side of her in order to ascertain the dimensions of her trap. That she was in some sort of cave seemed certain, and also that it had opened up as a result of the torrential rains, only to be sealed like all the tombs about it when the fall of mud and sand had swept away the bank. She started to crawl forwards gingerly, feeling her way, each inch seeming a mile, each fresh brush of sand against rock making her heart beat faster in case it presaged another landslide. The air was heavy and warm and Rachel felt light-headed, with panic only a heartbeat away.

She had no notion how far she had crawled before her hands came up against a lip of rock that seemed to stretch upwards, and then another beyond it, rising up in the darkness. Rachel's fingers clutched at the steps and her heart clutched at the hope, for steps led upwards, towards the light and the fresh air. Towards escape.

She stood up. The roof was high enough to stand here and slowly, following the line of the wall, she slowly followed the line of shallow steps upward. Was it her imagination, or did the stifling air become a little fresher here? And was that not a faint sliver of light that she could see ahead of her, as though down the end of a long, dark passage?

When she finally reached it, it was disappointing enough. She was in another, larger chamber and the light came fitfully through what looked like tiny cracks in the earthen walls. Rachel tried to visualise where she could be, but she had lost her sense of direction almost immediately and could not guess which of the many barrows she had come up into. It was one that Sir Arthur and Lady Odell had not yet started to work upon, for there was no evidence of digging or disturbance here. Nor, to Rachel's immense relief, could she see any bones or burials, nor smell the unmistakable scent of decay. In the dim light the chamber seemed completely bare.

Rachel went over to the earthen wall and put her face up to the nearest chink of light. She could see nothing, but she felt the chill of the fresh air against her skin and the stray coldness of rain against her lips. She scrabbled at the wall with her fingers, but it was more sturdy that it looked. It would take her hours to dig herself out.

There was a sudden rush of air and a rumbling sound as the whole of the tomb shifted behind her and another wall of mud and sand pressed down, closing the steps up which she had so recently come. Rachel caught her breath and pressed more closely to the wall. And as she opened her mouth to shout for help, she heard the scrape of movement and felt the shift of the walls, and drew back in fear again in case the whole edifice was about to collapse.

A moment later, when she heard the scrape of a shovel on stone, she realised that it was not another landslide that had caused the noise, but human hand. Cory had come for her, as she had known he would. Suddenly Rachel felt as though all the stuffing had been knocked out of her. She sat down heavily on the earthen floor and tried to quell the trembling in her limbs.

'Rachel?' Cory's voice echoed about the tomb, bouncing off the roof. 'Are you there?'

'Cory!' It came out as a rather pitiful squeak. Rachel tried again. This time it was a high-pitched shriek. 'Cory! Help! The chamber is filling with sand.'

The movement stilled.

'Rachel? Thank God! I'll get you out of there soon. Stand back.'

Just to hear his voice was reassuring. She could see him now, a darker shadow against the slim sliver of light. The spade bit into the earth, sending a shower of soil tumbling into the tomb.

'Rachel?' She scrambled across to the widening gap. 'Are you hurt?'

'No,' Rachel said. 'Just a little bruised and shaken. Please be quick, Cory.' Her voice shook a little. 'I think the whole tomb is going to collapse!'

'The entire riverbank is washing away,' Cory said. 'I am doing what I can, Rae, but I cannot work too quickly for fear the roof will come down on you.'

Rachel stifled a sob. 'I understand. Just be as quick as you can…'

It was another couple of minutes before the gap was large enough to pass the lantern through.

'Take the light,' Cory said, pushing it through the space.

The brightness made Rachel feel much better in some ways and worse in others. She could see her prison now, with its two sturdy walls to the south and west, where Cory was digging. On the northern side, where the river ran, the sand had completely blocked the steps down to the lower chamber and the roof sagged perilously low. The rest of the tomb was as bare as she had initially thought, but for what looked like a small, empty ledge on the eastern wall that looked as though it was intended as a shelf for a vase or chalice. There were no bones or offerings, or artefacts of long-dead kings, for which Rachel thanked God. She pressed herself to the western wall and prayed for Cory to be quick.

The gap widened and Cory's face appeared, lit from beneath by the lantern. It was dirty, creased with worry, his hair tumbled across his brow.

'Rae—another few moments only...'

There was an ominous rumble of sound from below, then a swirl of water swept across Rachel's feet. The steady thud of the spade filled the tomb above.

'Cory! The water is coming through!'

'Hold on, Rae.' Cory's voice was a little out of breath but remarkably calm. 'I am nearly there. Pass me the lantern—'

What happened next was quick and confusing. As Rachel held the lantern up there was a grating roar and the back wall gave way. In the lantern light, Rachel saw the little shelf appear to slip and slide sideways, revealing a large cavity beyond. It was full of wooden brandy casks. In the lamplight they appeared ghostly white with cobwebs clinging like glue. They were tumbled on the floor and stacked against the wall. A few were broken and the jagged wooden edges showed in the light.

Rachel stared, transfixed. Then icy water swept up to her waist and clinging mud dragged on her skirts. Cory was pulling her through the gap, but the whole roof was coming down and it threatened to take him with it. Rachel scrambled to safety and turned desperately to see Cory fighting for his footing as the ground gave way beneath him. With a super-human effort she caught his flailing arm and pulled so hard she was afraid she would dislocate his shoulder. They rolled over, Cory dragging Rachel beneath him, his body arched over hers for protection and her cheek against his chest. They fell over and over in a tumble of limbs and brackish water, finally to lie still.

Rachel uncurled herself slowly. Her hands were spread against Cory's chest and she could feel the beat of his heart, slowing now to its normal pace. Her mouth and nose were buried against the wet material of his jacket. She could feel the rain still falling in sheets, running down her face, but she lay still, clinging to Cory as though she never wanted to let him go.

'Rachel?' Cory shifted, his mouth pressing against her temple.

'I am all right,' Rachel said. She reluctantly moved a little away. 'You?'

Cory nodded.

'Thank you,' Rachel said, her voice breaking a little. 'Thank you for rescuing me.'

Cory smiled. 'Any time, Rae. And thank you. I rather think I would have been washed away by now without you.'

Rachel raised a hand and rubbed it against his lean cheek. 'You have mud on your face…'

They stared at each other for a second and then Cory's arms went around her again. Their lips met in a tingle of rainswept cold, and it was heaven, and then Cory had crushed her close and Rachel gasped in pleasure against his mouth. They could have been standing at the gates of hell itself and neither of them would have paid the slightest notice.

Eventually Rachel freed herself from Cory's embrace slightly, grabbing his arm again as her knees threatened to give way. 'Come inside the house,' she said. 'Quickly, before we are both drowned.'

Clasping the lantern, and staggering like a pair of drunken sailors, they wended their way towards the house. Though it was barely four o'clock the sky was completely dark and heavy with unshed rain and the house had a shuttered, quiet air that felt very different from the atmosphere of suppressed tension between them. It seemed to Cory that Rachel was burning up like a torch with the relief and the release of tension. There was high colour along her cheekbones and a hectic sparkle in her eyes. All the passion and excitement that he had known was latent within her was awake and burning and it was demanding a response from him.

'You should get out of your wet clothes and take a hot bath,' he said, trying to control the most inappropriate images of lust and desire that tormented him. 'I will heat you some water and fetch you a drink—'

He got no further. Rachel put a hand around the back of his head and pulled it down, touching her lips to his. Cory gasped. He felt her tongue slide along his lower lip, a little hesitant, seductively innocent. He grabbed her and kissed her back with no half-measures.

Five minutes later they were both panting, but Cory still held on to his self-control. His body was burning up with need but there were a thousand and one reasons why to take Rachel to bed now was the worst idea in the whole world.

'Rachel,' he said, 'we must stop this. You will only regret it later.'

Rachel placed her hand against his chest. 'I think not. I love you, Cory. You saved my life today.'

Cory closed his eyes in an agony of denial. 'Please,

Rae—there is no need for you to express your gratitude in this particular way.'

'Don't joke,' Rachel whispered. 'Not now.'

Once again she placed her arms about his neck and drew his head down to hers, pressing the whole length of her body against his. Cory shook with suppressed passion. He knew that this was in part a natural reaction to the release from death and the need to celebrate that escape by celebrating life. The same force that drove Rachel possessed him too. When he thought that he might lose her his entire being had cried out against it. Rachel had been a part of his life for so long that he could not bear to lose her now. Not now, not ever.

She was kissing him again, teasing his lips with hers, driving him to wildness. The scent of her hair and her skin sent sanity spinning from his mind.

'Rae,' he said, 'if we do not stop this now, then you will end in my bed—or rather, I shall end in yours.'

Rachel eased back and looked into his face. 'It is the second door on the left upstairs,' she whispered.

Cory looked down at her, his eyes blazing. Then he picked her up and carried her up the stairs, sending the bedroom door crashing open and kicking it shut behind them.

Their clothes were sodden but quickly shed. Cory ripped off his jacket and shirt whilst Rachel knelt behind him on the bed, nipping his collarbone, nibbling his earlobe and pressing her lips to the soft skin of his neck. He could scarce believe that this was Rachel, the prim young lady who had spoken of passion as though it were an unwanted encumbrance in life. And when he turned to her, maddened by her caresses, she giggled and pulled him down with her into the billows of the big four-poster bed. She made a soft sound and rubbed against him, their bodies separated now by nothing other than her soaked chemise and his pantaloons. She ran her hands over his bare chest and back, arching against him and exulting in the contact.

Cory freed himself sufficiently to find the fastenings of her chemise, but the saturated material failed to co-operate.

'Tear it,' Rachel said. Then, when he stared, she set her hands to the material and simply pulled it apart. It separated with a ripping sound and Rachel wriggled out of it. Her shoulders were pink and stung with cold. Before Cory's fascinated gaze she dropped the scrap of material over the side of the bed to lie discarded on the floor. If he had not seen the shaking of her fingers, Cory would have thought her completely composed as she half-sat, half-lay before him in her nakedness.

It was just like his most fevered imaginings, only more so. Her breasts were big, but they were high and round with small, pink nipples already tight from cold. Her stomach was flat and her legs long and lissom. Cory's body felt so rigid that he thought he must explode there and then. He reached instinctively for her, saw the tiniest hint of anxiety in her face, and remembered in a rush that she was a virgin.

He forced himself to patience, wrapping his arms about her and holding her close. He ran his fingers very lightly over the skin of her back and upper arms, feeling her shiver under his touch. He brushed his hands over the rounded softness of her buttocks and the sweet curve of her breasts, sucking her nipples and licking the pulse at the base of her throat. He heard her make a small mewing sound of pleasure. Rachel's eyes were closed now, her head thrown back, her eyelashes dark against the pink-staining of her cheeks, and her breath coming in little gasps. Cory lowered his head to her breast, and slid his hand gently up the silken softness of Rachel's inner thigh. She moaned and her legs parted for him, and he touched her tentatively, feeling her body tense against his fingers. She opened her eyes. They were drowned with passion and they smiled at him.

'Are you not going to take off your trousers?' she asked.

It was agony to leave her even for a moment, but Cory followed her example, ripping the pantaloons and casting them aside on the floor before pressing the full, hard length of his naked body against hers.

She shifted her body to accommodate his, soft and willing, and Cory brought his lips back to hers, kissing her deeply, possessively.

'I love you, Rachel…' It was true. He felt a huge exultation sweep through him. Rachel was here in his arms, just as she was always meant to be, and she was his, only his, now and always.

Rachel made a little sound of pure pleasure and pulled him to her, and Cory grasped her hips, easing himself gently inside her. She was hot and tight, and within a few seconds he had forgotten all about gentleness, and had caught her fiercely to him thrusting powerfully, until he was swiftly overcome. Through the explosion of rapture he felt like groaning. This was not what he had intended for Rachel, this callow selfishness. He had been overwhelmed by his need for her and the frustration of abstinence. And now Rachel would be severely disappointed.

He could see by the small frown on her face that she was dissatisfied. He rolled away from her and propped himself on an elbow, kissing her brow, stroking the soft skin of her shoulder.

'Sweetheart, I am so sorry…I could not help myself…'

Rachel smiled uncertainly. 'Was it my fault?'

Cory's heart swelled with tenderness. 'Of course not. Only for being so utterly desirable. In fact, it was my fault. I have wanted you for so long. You see now what I have been trying to tell you all along—my rake's reputation is completely unjustified.'

He rained tiny kisses along the curve of her shoulder and down over her breast. Rachel wriggled.

'I do not believe you can be so bad,' she said, 'for I was

starting to enjoy myself. I think it might have been rather pleasant had it gone on longer.'

Cory smiled. 'I am glad that you think so, for we have not finished, Rae. In fact, we have only just begun.'

He saw Rachel's eyes widen with shy curiosity. In the slumberous depths Cory could see a passion that had barely diminished. He slid both hands possessively over her breasts and heard her gasp.

'Cory…'

He bent his head to one rosy crest, nipping it between his teeth. Rachel squeaked. She opened her mouth to speak, but before she could, Cory kissed her, thrusting his tongue deep whilst his fingers moved back to the secret place between her legs. She was slick and wet and he felt her tremble helplessly, her thighs falling apart to allow his fingers entry. And then she was writhing with pleasure beneath his hands and he was filled with the most triumphant tenderness as he eased her shuddering body to ecstasy.

He held her possessively close, feeling the echoes of pleasure subside through her body. After a moment she gave a tiny yawn.

'I was right. That was very nice.'

Cory smiled against her hair. 'I am so glad you think so,' he said.

Rachel turned her head and kissed him sleepily.

'Is that the end, then?'

'No,' Cory said. 'Now we sleep. And later…' he smiled '…later there's more.'

Chapter Twenty

When Rachel awoke it was full dark outside and she was alone. The sound of rain drummed on the roof and the curtains were not drawn, leaving the window a pale grey square of dark. The wind shrieked and thunder echoed away on the horizon.

She put out a hand. The bed was still warm and there was an indentation where Cory's body had lain. She rolled over and pressed her face to the pillow. It smelled of him and her heart filled with love and a curious kind of pride. Her body ached faintly but felt replete and her mind drowsy. She knew that soon she would have to start thinking again, but for now she was content to drift.

She wondered where Cory had gone. The answer came almost immediately. There was a sound from below and Rachel tensed, reality flooding back. Had the servants returned? Or her parents? She squinted at the clock. Eight o'clock! They should all have returned long since.

Then she heard whistling and realised that Cory was down in the kitchen. She relaxed back against the covers. He was fetching food. He really was a hero.

Rachel got up and went across the window. She paused for a moment, staring out into the dark in amazement. The landscape was awash, the whole of Midwinter Royal land cut off like an island. The river had flooded the burial ground and only the tops of the barrows were visible. It would take a boat to reach them now.

There was a step in the doorway behind her.

'Very nice,' Cory said, and Rachel realised with a sudden surprise that she was still naked. She did not appear to have been paying a great deal of attention to her clothes recently, for they were scattered across the floor. She whisked into bed and pulled the covers up to her chin.

'Please do not do that on my account,' Cory said pleasantly. 'You looked quite delightful as you were.'

He was wearing Rachel's dressing robe and was carrying a tray laden with food, which he placed on the end of the bed. He took the candle from it and put it on the night stand. Suddenly the room seemed smaller and more intimate, a haven against the outside world once again.

'I see that we are cut off,' Rachel said.

Cory nodded. 'The river has burst its banks and surrounded the house.'

'So no one can get in?'

Cory's silver gaze was quizzical on her. 'No.'

'And you cannot get out?'

'I suppose not.'

'Good,' Rachel said.

Cory's gaze turned thoughtful. 'Rachel…' he began.

Rachel's heart gave a lurch. She held up a hand.

'Cory, please do not say anything. Not yet. I do not want to spoil anything.'

Cory sighed. 'Rachel, we shall have to talk soon…'

'Soon, yes,' Rachel said. 'But not now. This is *too* soon.' She hesitated. 'This is so special. It is time out of time. And just at the moment I do not want to have to think too much.'

She reached for the food and sank her teeth into the bread. It tasted good. Cory sighed again. 'I do not like the sound of that,' he said.

Rachel reached for the cheese. The sheet slipped a little.

She watched Cory's gaze go to her breasts and felt a little shiver go through her. Her mouth dried and suddenly she did not feel so hungry any more. Cory was visibly holding himself in check and the sight of his struggle for control was immensely exciting. She brushed the crumbs off the sheet, aware that he was watching her every move.

'Perhaps I should put some clothes on,' she said.

'That would be pointless,' Cory said, 'since I would only have to remove them again.'

He lifted the heavy fall of her hair off her shoulder and started to kiss the back of her neck. Rachel almost choked on the bread as shivers of delightful pleasure ran along her skin. His hands came round to cup her breasts and the sheet fell to her waist. Rachel sighed, a long, wavering sigh of surrender. There was no escaping the feeling that this was where she belonged, here in the circle of his arms, safe, protected and true. She watched as Cory carefully moved the tray off the bed before discarding his robe and coming back to settle his naked body against hers. In the candlelight he was as glorious as she remembered from the time by the river. His skin was a lucent gold, firm, hard and well muscled. She rubbed her lips exploratively against the paler soft skin by his collarbone and felt the ripple of his stomach muscles against her spread fingers. He turned his head and claimed her lips in a deep and demanding kiss.

'Don't move,' he ordered.

Rachel lay with her eyes wide open and her nerves tightened to fever pitch as he slid down her trembling body and began kissing her all over, the arch of her foot, the soft fold behind her knee, the outer curve of her thigh. Her breathing came more rapidly still as he shifted his body to trail kisses along the soft skin of her inner thigh. She arched in frustration as he pressed his mouth in sweet, hot kisses against her belly, moving up to caress her swelling breasts.

Rachel turned her head languorously on the pillow. A huge flash of lightning illuminated the room, dimming the candles. By its fierce light she could see Cory poised over her, his face dark with emotion. He cupped her breast and flicked the nipple lightly with his tongue. The thunder made the house shudder. Rachel's senses reeled. She was coming quite undone. All her inhibitions and reserve and restraints were being swept away, destroyed, shattered under the onslaught of Cory's love for her.

Cory smiled down into her eyes and bent to kiss her passionately, sliding inside her with exquisite gentleness. Rachel reached blindly for him, squirming restlessly and begging for release from the delicious friction of his body against hers. As the sensations grew she felt herself arch like a bow and fall quickly, violently into utter bliss, her eyes opening wide in ecstasy and disbelief, her fingers clutching at his shoulders. The white lightning burned behind her eyes and the thunder crashed in her ears and the pleasure consumed them both, sweeping them up and binding them one to the other, merging past and present, the shadow of their childhood selves and the people they had become.

Later, much later, they lay in each other's arms in the dark and Rachel raised a subject that had been at the back of her mind.

'Did you see them?' she asked.

'The casks of brandy?' Cory said with a smile. 'Yes, I saw.' He turned her slightly so that her body fitted even more snugly into the curve of his shoulder.

'That was what Maskelyne was trying to tell us with his maps and his plans,' Rachel said with a muffled laugh. 'It was nothing to do with the treasure or even to do with the spy. It was about a lost cache of smuggled brandy!'

'Jeffrey always did like a drink,' Cory said, smoothing the hair away from her face so that he could trace the line of her cheek. 'And some people would consider a lost cache of brandy treasure indeed.'

Rachel burrowed closer to Cory's warmth.

'So now that you know that it is there,' she said, 'will you go to dig for it?'

She felt Cory move slightly and settle more comfortably, his body wrapped around hers.

'I doubt it. The entire burial site is flooded and when the waters subside the damage will be tremendous.'

'And what about the real treasure?' Rachel asked.

In the dark she felt Cory's cheek rub against hers as he smiled. 'You know I am superstitious. The Midwinter Treasure does not wish to be found. If—and when—it comes to light, it will find its own way.'

Rachel turned her head and kissed his bare shoulder. 'I admire you for that,' she said softly. 'So many are blinded by greed and will take all they can.'

'I have all that I want here in my arms,' Cory said. He kissed her. 'Go to sleep, Rachel, for in the morning we must talk.'

In the morning, everything was different. This time Rachel woke to grey skies and rain that had lost its fierceness but still fell in miserable lines from the dark sky. Cory had gone to find some of Sir Arthur's clothes for there was no possible way that his own could ever be made respectable again. Rachel felt in much the same case. She dressed and tidied her room with mechanical movements, part of her shocked at what had happened the night before, part of her accepting. What had happened with Cory had been the most exquisite, the most deep and blissful experience of her life and she would never forget it. She loved him so much. Yet fundamentally she was very afraid that nothing had changed.

'And now we talk,' Cory said, when he joined her in the drawing room. He gestured to the sofa beside her. 'May I?'

'Of course.' Rachel shifted slightly to give him space to sit down. It felt odd, almost familiar and somehow radically different. It was still Cory sitting beside her, but a different Cory—someone she knew inside out in some ways and in others was only beginning to know. But what she *did* know was that he was not going to like what she had to say to him.

'I asked you to marry me a few days ago,' Cory said, 'and you refused. *Now* will you marry me, Rachel?'

Rachel looked at him—at the expectation in his face and the tension she could see just below the surface. It was so similar to his previous proposal and yet so different. Now she knew that she loved him with every fibre of her being and would always love him. Now he had told her he loved her too. He had made love to her with passion and tenderness and taken her heart and soul for his own. And now she had to let him go.

'I am sorry,' she said. 'I fear I must refuse you again.'

She felt Cory go very still and held her breath, waiting for the explosion of temper. Instead he took her hand in his.

'Must you, Rae?' His tone was very quiet. 'Please tell me why.'

His gentleness brought a lump to Rachel's throat. His voice had been even, but one quick glance at his face told her that she was hurting him and that in the course of the conversation she would inevitably hurt him more. It felt wretched. She knew him so well and cared for him so much that the pain was her own and yet she knew her resolve could not waver. Not if they were to avoid a lifetime of misery.

'I cannot allow what has happened between us to weigh with me,' she said miserably. 'When I refused you before, Cory, it was because we did not want the same things from our lives.' She put a quick hand out to stifle his protests. 'I know now that I love you and you love me. But the things that we want are utterly incompatible. That has not changed.'

There was a silence.

'You say that you love me,' Cory said dully.

The lump in Rachel's throat intensified. 'Yes, of course

I do. You know it. I love you with my whole heart. But that does not alter our situation.' She hurried on. 'From the first you have known that I wanted nothing more than a settled home. That has not changed.' Her gaze searched his face desperately. 'But you… Travelling and exploration are your very life. And a wife must adapt to her husband's style of living. I understand that. I would not ask you to give it up! Which is why I must give *you* up.'

'You could travel with me,' Cory said. 'I would like nothing more—'

The first tear rolled down Rachel's cheek and splashed on to her skirts. 'Cory, I cannot! How soon would it be before you came to resent me, knowing that I travelled with you under duress? I hate the very thing that you love! I need a home of my own!'

'You would have Newlyn.' Cory had gone a little white now, as though he could see the futility of his arguments, but did not want to accept it. 'I understand how important it is to you to have a home, Rachel, and I know that we could make matters work.'

A second tear splashed beside the first. 'I could not bear it,' Rachel said, her voice cracking. 'To sit at home in that great barn of a place with a brood of children, waiting for you to come back or not knowing where you were or when I would see you again.' She shook her head. 'Better to suffer the pain of separation now, than to suffer it constantly throughout our life together.'

Cory ran an agitated hand over his hair. 'Rachel, I understand what you are saying, but I cannot give up my travels or my excavations! It is my life's work! Not even for you—' He broke off and gathered her into his arms, pressing his lips against her hair. 'I love you so much. I want you with me…'

Rachel wriggled free of his embrace. 'Please do not make this any more difficult. Cory. You know it cannot be.'

Cory was shaking his head. His mouth had set in obstinate

lines. 'You cannot simply dismiss what has happened between us and pretend that nothing has changed.'

'I do not,' Rachel said. 'But we may carry on as before. No one need know.'

Cory got to his feet. 'No one need know? *I* know! And you know! Do you think you will ever forget?'

'I doubt it,' Rachel said, with a watery smile that wobbled a little. 'But I can school myself not to think of you all the time.'

'Not if I am always there before you, reminding you of what could have been!' For a moment Cory looked furious. 'You cannot deny the passion between us, Rachel. You cannot simply put it away and pretend that it does not exist—that it has never existed!' He made a noise of disgust. 'I suppose that you have not relinquished your dream of finding a prudent man with whom to settle down? What kind of a pale, cold existence would that be compared with what we could have together?'

Rachel was shaking now. 'I do not plan to marry, Cory. Even I can see that that would probably be a mistake now.'

Cory's eyes blazed into hers. 'Why? Because of what happened between us? There is nothing shameful in that, Rachel. Do not, I beg you, force yourself into the box society dictates for you just because of your wish for an ordinary life.' His voice was savage as he caught her to him. 'It would crush your spirit. Do you really wish to become the perpetual spinster who suffered a disappointment in love in her youth or the wife to a worthy man who discovers that you were indiscreet enough to have a love affair and makes you pay for it every day in petty little ways? Have the courage to marry *me* instead! I love you so much!'

Rachel clenched her fists with fury and grief. 'Very well, Cory! You have thrown down a challenge to me and now I offer one to you! Give it all up. Give it all up for me to prove how much you do love me! Take the risk that it will not be as bad as you think!'

They stared at each other for a very long moment, then Cory let Rachel go and she fell back in her chair. 'You cannot,' she said. 'I knew it.'

Cory's grey eyes were full of pain. 'How odd it is,' he said, almost conversationally, 'that I cannot give up all the things that I hold dear for you, Rae, and you cannot risk all for me. Even in that we are well matched.'

He got up, but stopped when he reached the door, pausing with his hand on the panels. 'You once wished that someone would break my heart,' he said. He smiled at her. 'I know you well enough, my love, to realise that it will give you no satisfaction to have been the one to do it.'

Rachel heard the front door bang and the sound of his footsteps on the gravel, and then there was nothing but silence.

Chapter Twenty-One

Time crept by with astonishing slowness for Rachel. Sir Arthur and Lady Odell returned from Saltires later that day full of concern for her, but strangely less worried at the watery fate of their excavations. They exclaimed over Rachel's wan appearance, sympathised over her hopeless attempts to save the site from flooding and asked no awkward questions at all about the whereabouts of Cory Newlyn. It was the first time that Rachel had ever blessed their absentmindedness. She concluded that they had forgotten that they had despatched Cory to Midwinter Royal to find her and she prayed devoutly that they would not raise the subject again. She went to bed early and cried and cried with a mixture of exhaustion and emotion as soon as her bedroom door was closed.

The following morning, Deborah Stratton called, and in the course of the conversation Rachel heard that Cory had left for London. It was not known when or if he would be back. Sir Arthur, when applied to, was equally vague. He had commissioned Cory to take some pieces of pottery and other artefacts to the British Museum and the work might take some time. Rachel had felt both sick and relieved at the news. She wanted to see Cory desperately; she missed him with an aching longing that seemed to worsen as the days went by. Occasionally she would see his writing on some of her father's documents and her heart would jump and the misery intensify into a sharp pain in her chest. Her parents spoke of him constantly, careless references to events and memories that could not help but torment Rachel further. And yet she knew that this was something she would have to live through and accept for the rest of her life. She had made her choice and could only hope that the pain of loss would diminish in time.

The flood waters receded slowly. Sir Arthur sat in the library and wrote articles for the *Antiquarian Review* and Lady Odell cleaned and packaged the finds ready for exhibition. Rachel worked her fingers to the bone to help. She went shopping with Mrs Stratton and Lady Marney in Woodbridge, went driving with Lord Richard Kestrel and refused an offer of marriage from Caspar Lang. She dragged herself through the meetings of the reading group where Sir Philip Desormeaux's romantic difficulties in *The Enchantress* seemed a pale parody of her own. As she had predicted some months before, Sir Philip succumbed to romance in the end and rode through the night to claim his bride.

She lay in her bed in her neat and tidy bedroom and thought about Cory Newlyn. She remembered the touch of his hands on her body with a shiver of pleasure she knew she would never forget, no matter how long she lived or how hard she tried. She remembered the deep, deep friendship that had turned to love and then to ashes. She wondered if she had been a fool, but then she thought with fear and misery of all the times she had uprooted herself and started again in a new place, and she turned her face into her pillow and lay still.

Oddly, it was Richard Kestrel whose company she could best tolerate. He took her driving several times a week, and though people gossiped, Rachel did not care. She found she did not care for much these days. Often she and Richard would not even talk, but it did not matter. It mattered slightly more that the situation caused Deb Stratton to be uneasy in her company, but Rachel was too weary to try to explain to Deb that she had no designs on Richard and never would.

One day, when they had driven down to the sea and were sitting on an outcrop overlooking Kestrel Beach, Richard did speak. 'I want to talk to you about Cory Newlyn,' he said.

Rachel turned her face away and looked out to sea. The weather was fresher these days with the approach of autumn and the wind was cold on her face.

'Please do not,' she said.

Richard sighed. 'Very well then. If I cannot talk about Cory, then I will tell you about myself, Rachel. About the one chance that I had, and the way I threw it away.'

Rachel turned her head sharply and looked at him. 'Richard,' she said, 'you are not being in the least subtle.'

Richard shrugged. His handsome face was moody and dark. 'I do not believe that subtlety can reach you, Rachel, and I am a great believer in brute force where subtlety has failed.' He took a deep breath. 'No one will have said this to you, so I am going to take it on myself.' He squared his shoulders. 'You are being the greatest fool in Christendom to spurn true love where it is offered. Not only are you making yourself unhappy, but you have almost destroyed a good man, and that I find very hard to forgive. It is only because I like you so much that I am still speaking to you at all.' He stood up. 'I am no gentleman to say this to you, but someone had to have the courage.'

Rachel stared at him. A tiny corner of her heart was starting to unfreeze. She could feel the warmth spreading. 'You are right,' she said slowly. 'It was most uncivil of you.'

Richard started to smile. 'Well?' he said.

Rachel got up and shook the sand out her skirts. She did not look at him. She felt suddenly nervous, as though she was on the edge of a momentous decision. Richard's words had echoed what she had been trying to say to herself for weeks; words she had been too afraid to hear. Who could tell what happiness she might find with Cory if only she was prepared to compromise on those wishes to which she had obstinately clung for years? She had been so blind, so determined that a settled home was the only thing that she wanted, so afraid to take a risk. Yet she had been more unhappy without Cory than she could ever imagine being with him by her side, even if she had to travel for the whole of the rest of her life. She loved him too much to lose him forever.

'Do you ever hear news of Cory?' she asked, without looking at him.

'I keep in correspondence with him,' Richard said drily.

Rachel glanced sideways at him. 'And do you know if he might be returning to Midwinter?'

Richard gave her a very straight look. 'It…could be arranged,' he said.

Rachel felt a huge smile starting and bit her lip to repress it. 'Then if it might be arranged I…I suppose it would be good to see him again.' Her smile faded. 'Although he may not wish to see me, of course.'

'That,' Richard said, 'is up to you.'

Rachel took his arm as they started to walk down the stony path back to the curricle. The groom was walking the horses and looking slightly bored.

'What was it that you were going to tell me about yourself?' she asked suddenly.

Richard glanced down at her and then shook his head. 'No matter,' he said. 'That must wait for another occasion, I think. Let us resolve your romantic difficulties first before we even attempt a start on mine.'

The hope and excitement and expectation bubbled up in Rachel again. Suddenly she flung her arms about Richard and hugged him hard.

'I do not care what they say about you, Richard Kestrel,' she said breathlessly, 'I think you are a very kind man!'

'Good lord,' Richard said, 'keep that to yourself, if you please, Rachel. If that is not death to a rake's reputation then I do not know what is,' and he hugged her back in full view of the astonished groom.

It was a week later and Rachel had scarcely finished breakfast when Mrs Goodfellow informed her that her parents would like to speak with her in the drawing room. Curious but unsuspecting, Rachel put down her napkin and wandered in. Both her parents were sitting on the sofa in the window. Her mother was holding Sir Arthur's hand extremely tightly. Rachel could see that her knuckles were white and that Sir Arthur was wincing, though he made no protest. Indeed, he had the slightly dazed look of a man who had made a miraculous discovery. And Lady Odell's eyes were glowing with a mixture of excitement and apprehension. Rachel's heart leapt.

'We have something to tell you, Rachel,' Lady Odell said. 'Something very exciting.'

'You have found it!' Rachel exclaimed. 'Oh, Mama, you have found the Midwinter Treasure!'

Lady Odell frowned. For a moment she looked as though she had no idea what Rachel was talking about, then her brow cleared. 'The Treasure? Oh, no, indeed not, my love.'

Now it was Rachel's turn to look puzzled. She sat down slowly. 'No? But I thought… You seemed so excited…'

'Oh, I am!' Lady Odell smiled again. There was something softer about her face, a luminous quality in her eyes that Rachel had never seen before. 'You see, darling—' she shot a quick look at Sir Arthur's face '—I…we…we are having a baby.'

'Your mother's *enceinte,*' Sir Arthur said, his gruffness belied by the sweet smile he gave his wife. 'Pregnant, in an interesting condition…'

'Thank you, Papa,' Rachel said, 'I understand.' She put a hand to her head, feeling a little dazed herself. 'This is a great surprise, Mama. I am pleased for you, of course, but…I assume that it was not what you intended.'

Lady Odell had been watching her daughter's face anxiously, but now her own brow cleared. 'Good gracious, I would not wish you to think that it was an *accident,* Rachel! I have been wanting another child these twenty-three years past, ever since you were born. It was the greatest grief of my life that you were destined to be an only child, for your father and I wanted a large family, but as the years passed and no playmate arrived for you, we began to think that it was not to be. So we took you everywhere with us so that you were not too lonely, and we were not lonely too…' Lady Odell sniffed. 'We tried to make up for your lack of siblings by involving you in everything that we did, but…' she sighed '…you never did care for antiquities, did you? Still, I hope that you have been happy travelling with us and seeing the world.'

Rachel opened her mouth and closed it again. This was not the moment to shatter her mother's illusions about her happy childhood and love of travelling. Indeed, it seemed that such confidences would never be exchanged now, for Rachel saw very clearly that she had made some wrong assumptions. Sir Arthur and Lady Odell had kept her with them at all times because they were desperate for a family and she was all they had. And also because they were afraid that she would be lonely, the only child with no siblings. They had always wanted children. They had always wanted *her.*

Rachel swallowed the huge lump in her throat. 'I am so *happy* for you, Mama! Papa—' she turned to Sir Arthur, who was beaming benignly '—oh, Papa, this is wonderful news!'

Lady Odell stood up to embrace her and Rachel rushed

around the table so that her mother should not be obliged to come to her.

'Pray sit down and put your feet up on the stool, Mama. You must take matters very carefully now! No more excavating for the time being, and no shifting heavy objects…'

Lady Odell hugged her tearfully. 'We are giving up the excavating and the travelling, Rachel. We feel that it is time to retire. With a new family, you know, there will be much else to do. We thought that we should like to stay at Midwinter Royal, at least for a while, and then if your father decides that he needs to do some more work he will have the burial ground on hand.'

'Young man's game,' Sir Arthur grunted. 'I leave all that to Cory.'

Rachel looked at him sharply. 'Is Cory returning to Midwinter Royal, Papa?'

Sir Arthur looked shifty. 'Coming to consult with me on my paper for the *Antiquarian Review*,' he said. 'Did I not tell you?'

Rachel felt a mixture of exasperation and sheer nervousness. 'No, Papa. No, you did not tell me. You never remember to tell me anything!'

Sir Arthur looked a little taken aback at her vehemence. He checked the clock. 'Should be here soon,' he offered. 'Thought I should let you know. I need some coffee first though. All this emotion, you know. You'll find me in the library if you want me.'

The door closed behind him. Rachel stared wildly at Lady Odell.

'Cory is coming here…now? This morning?'

'Yes, my love,' Lady Odell said. She sat back and closed her eyes wearily. 'I believe he is to call at Kestrel Court first. I feel a little tired. I think I will take a rest.'

Rachel was already halfway to the door, but she paused with her hand on the knob and looked back at her mother sitting peaceably by the fireside.

'Mama,' she said suddenly, 'I wondered about names. If it is a girl…'

'We shall call her Aethelflaed,' Lady Odell said contentedly, without opening her eyes. 'We thought it appropriate to honour the Anglo-Saxons.'

'Hmm,' Rachel said. Perhaps, like her, Aethelflaed would have a sensible second name that she could use.

'And if it is a boy?' she said. 'Tostig, perhaps?'

'That's good!' Lady Odell said, opening her eyes and looking at her daughter thoughtfully. 'Very good, Rachel. But we had already decided upon Edgar. What do you think?'

'It could be much worse,' Rachel said, smiling. 'I should like to have a little brother called Edgar.'

'Edgar Ptolemy,' Lady Odell said. 'It will be perfect.'

'Can I offer you some coffee, old fellow?' Richard Kestrel said to Cory Newlyn, steering him solicitously into the study at Kestrel Court. 'You look as though you have been riding hard. Don't want to send you off to see Sir Arthur in such a state of disarray.'

Cory took the proffered cup and drank half of it down without really noticing. He felt exhausted. He had spent a poor night at the Star and Garter near Colchester where he had tossed and turned in a flea-ridden bed. Prior to that he seemed to have spent endless sleepless nights for weeks and weeks, lying in his bed listening to the sounds of London by night and thinking incessantly about Rachel Odell. During the day he had dragged himself to the British Museum and spoken of relics and antiquities and hieroglyphics, and dry-as-dust matters that suddenly seemed dead and empty to him. Life had had no spark without the promise of Rachel's presence. It seemed there was no joy any more. Not even the prospect of travelling could light the enthusiasm that once he had possessed.

And now he was to see her again. A part of him did not

want to and another part was determined to put his fate to the touch one more time. One more chance to persuade Rachel to his point of view. With one major difference...

Richard was offering to refill his cup. Cory took the coffee and tried to concentrate on the matter in hand.

'Sir Arthur...' he said abstractedly. 'Yes...' He frowned. 'I must confess that I was somewhat surprised to get your letter, Richard. Sir Arthur has never required my help previously in putting together an article for publication. Indeed, he is the acknowledged expert in the field.'

He thought that Richard looked innocent, which was in itself suspicious, but when his friend spoke he sounded completely sincere. 'Is that so?' Richard said. 'I would not know, of course. I merely agreed to pass on his request to you.'

'Mmm...' Cory frowned at him. His abstracted look was lifting and a more familiar look of acute intelligence taking its place. 'And then there was this curious errand for Justin,' he continued. 'Told me that he had some urgent intelligence to pass on to you that he could not possibly commit to the postal service and could I possibly deliver it whilst I was here.'

'The latest intelligence from Whitehall on the dangers of invasion in the locality,' Richard said, crossing his legs at the ankle. 'It was too sensitive to send any other way.'

Cory produced a package and set it down on the table beside him. 'Here it is. I slept with it under my pillow last night. No one can have tampered with it.'

'Thank you,' Richard murmured. He gestured his friend to take a chair. 'Won't you sit down for a minute? No point in rushing over to Midwinter Royal whilst the family is still at breakfast.'

Cory sat. He drank his coffee. He fidgeted. He was aware of Richard watching him with amusement.

'Richard,' he said suddenly, 'how much would you be prepared to give up for a woman?'

Richard was silent for quite a while. 'Any woman or the *right* woman?' he queried lightly. 'The answers are very different. For the first I'd venture very little. For the second, I'd give everything I have.'

Cory got up again. He went over to the window and stared out sightlessly. 'You would give up everything?' he repeated.

Richard shrugged. 'Sometimes you have to lose all to gain all, Cory. And very often the thing that you fear is nowhere near as bad as you imagine. Sometimes—' he smiled wryly '—you gain everything in the world.'

Cory closed his eyes for a second. 'I thought that I enjoyed taking risks,' he said, 'but this is an entirely different matter.'

'I am told,' Richard said, smiling, 'that it is not as dangerous as it sounds. My sister Bella calls it the art of compromise.'

'Compromise.' Cory tried the word out. 'I own that is not a familiar concept.'

'Not for any of us, old fellow,' Richard said drily. 'We are for the most part selfish beings and we have always had the means to indulge our desires. Until we come up against something that is so valuable that it requires us to reconsider what is truly important, we do not even need to think about it.'

Cory was silent for a moment, then he turned and looked at his old friend. The worn look had lifted slightly from his face. 'How the hell did you get to be so wise anyway?' he asked.

'Native perception,' Richard said airily. 'Is there anything else I may do for you, or would you like to be on your way?'

Cory moved decisively to the door. 'I think I may as well go,' he said.

After he had gone out, Richard sat back in the chair and unwrapped the parcel from his brother. There was a brief covering note from Justin that he perused with a grin. Then he unfolded the contents of the package. There were several copies of *The Times* and the *Gentlemen's Magazine* and nothing else at all. Richard opened the paper at the racing page and settled back in his chair.

'Splendid,' he said.

After Rachel had sat in the window for fifteen minutes staring down the lime avenue for a glimpse of Cory's arrival, she found that she could sit still no longer. Her stomach was knotted with nervousness and she felt quite ill with anticipation. Despite the fact that she had absolutely no idea what she was going to do or even to say to Cory when she saw him, she decided to confront the dilemma head on. She slipped on her spencer, took up her parasol and went outside. In her preoccupation she totally forgot to change her shoes.

She hurried along the drive and through the stone gates that led on to the road. Here a little stream, an offshoot of the Winter Race, ran beside the road amongst the brambles and the nettles. The river level had subsided now, but the stream still ran higher than usual, splashing over stones and sparkling in the sun. The day was quiet, the sun out again, but less hot than it had been before the storm.

For a hundred yards Rachel kept up a punishing pace, but after a while she was obliged to slow down and moderate her speed a little. Her hair was starting to come down and her skirts were already stiff with dust. At this rate she would arrive at Kestrel Court looking like a vagabond.

She stopped in the shade and took several deep breaths, putting her hands on her knees and bending over in an unladylike but effective manner, to regain her breath. How foolish she had been to rush off like this to Kestrel Court on foot. It was several miles and she so ill prepared. Already she needed a drink.

Rachel clambered carefully down the bank to the brook

and cupped her hands in the refreshingly cool water. She raised it to her lips and it ran down over her chin, splashing on her dress. She looked at the stain and shook her head. No matter. She was already too untidy to care. And she was wasting time.

She straightened up and a dazzlingly bright light struck across her eyes from the surface of the stream. Something was reflecting the sun directly at her. She put a hand up to shade her gaze and almost tumbled into the water. The Midwinter chalice, perfect replica of all the pictures that she had ever seen, was sitting amidst the brambles much as she imagined King Richard III's crown might have sat on the thorn bush after the Battle of Bosworth.

Rachel stared. The beautiful golden cup rolled slightly in the water, catching the light. Rachel set her lips. She took several steps away. The cup tumbled over in the current and floated a few yards downstream before stopping again. It was almost as though it was waiting for her.

With a little, irritable sigh, Rachel scrambled down the bank again and reached into the water. The Midwinter Treasure rolled closer, coming neatly into her hand. Rachel smiled ruefully and pulled it from the water. It felt cold and clean and precious. It felt as though it was meant for her.

'Well,' she said aloud, 'since you are here now, you had better come with me.'

Almost at the same time, she heard the sound of hooves on the road and looked up, startled. Cory was riding along the track towards her. Rachel watched him approach. He looked heart-breakingly the same and yet somehow different. Thinner, older, more worn, perhaps… Rachel felt an overwhelming love that closed her throat and left her trembling. Her heart was beating like a drum.

It was about three seconds before Cory realised that she was there and then he reined in and slowed the horse to a walk. He did not take his eyes off her as he came closer.

Rachel found that she could not speak and she could not

move. She waited. She had even forgotten the gold chalice,
although she was clutching it so tightly that the sand scored
her fingers.

Cory reached her side and swung down from the horse
and stood before her. At last she found her tongue.

'How are you, Cory?' she said, and it amazed her that
her voice sounded so steady when inside she was in turmoil.
'I heard that you had returned to Midwinter. I was coming
to see you.'

'Rachel.' Cory's gaze did not waver from her face. He
had not even glanced at the cup in her hand.

'I…' Rachel looked down. She felt utterly tongue-tied, so
instead of speaking she held out the Midwinter Treasure. 'I
found this just now…along the river bank. It must have
washed up there after the floods. I thought that you should
have it.'

Cory glanced briefly at the chalice, but did not take it.
'The Midwinter Treasure,' he said. 'I see. Is that why you
were coming to find me?'

'No,' Rachel said. She put the cup down gently on the
ground. 'I came to find you because I wanted to talk to you.'

Cory's face did not change. He looked expressionless,
remote. Rachel felt her heart shrivel a little. She realised
now that she had hoped there would be no need for expla-
nations. She had wanted to run into his arms, to love and
be loved without reservation. Instead there was a coldness
and a distance that had to be bridged between them. And
there was no guarantee of success.

'What did you wish to say to me?' Cory asked.

Now that the moment had come, it was even more difficult than Rachel had imagined. She felt that she was relin-
quishing something of her dreams and yet a tiny, excited
hope pushed her onwards in the faith that she would gain
something infinitely more precious.

'I have been thinking about your proposal,' she said, with

difficulty. 'If you have not withdrawn your offer of marriage, then I would like to reconsider.'

She thought that she saw a brief flash of humour in Cory's eyes but he still looked grave. 'Did you come all this way in your slippers to tell me that, Rachel?' he asked. 'I thought that you could not bear to abandon your dreams of a settled life.'

'I have changed my mind,' Rachel said, her voice wavering slightly. She glanced down at her ruined shoes. 'I can do it for you. I *will* do it for you. If you still want me.'

There was a moment of silence that seemed to stretch into infinity and Rachel was utterly terrified of what Cory was about to say. Then he dropped the horse's reins and reached for her. His arms went about her, gently, sweetly, drawing her home. He held her and Rachel closed her eyes and rested her head against his chest and inhaled the scent of him and felt such an overpowering relief that her legs trembled and her hot tears scalded his shirt.

'I love you,' she said, muffled. 'I love you, Cory Newlyn, with all my heart.'

'I know,' Cory said. 'Brace up, Rachel. Do not turn sentimental on me now or I may change my mind.'

'Beast,' Rachel said, with a little sparkle of spirit.

She felt Cory smile and rub his cheek against her hair. 'We never were conventionally polite to each other, were we?' he said. 'I suppose that there is no need to start now.' All the same, his arms tightened about her.

'I thought about you every minute we were apart,' he said, and the raw emotion in his voice cut straight to Rachel's heart. 'I thought that I would never touch you again, Rae, and I could not bear it.'

Rachel tilted her head to look up at him and snuggled closer against his chest. 'I rather enjoyed you touching me,' she said dreamily. 'May we be married soon?'

Cory laughed. 'That is a good plan.' His voice changed. 'Rae?'

'Mmm?' Rachel did not want to move.

'I have something to tell you too.' He loosened his grip and Rachel reluctantly fell back a step so that she could see his face.

'What is it?' she asked.

'I too had been thinking that life would be no life without you,' Cory said. 'There are plenty of things that I can do without the need to travel. There is my hieroglyph work for the British Museum and there is the fogou to excavate at Newlyn and should you wish to stay here in Midwinter...' he smiled '...then there is still plenty of work to be done on the Midwinter burials. Now that you have found the cup—' he looked down at it '—it may be that the rest of the Treasure is willing to be found. So you see, we need not stray far from home at all.'

Rachel flung herself back into his arms and hugged him tightly. She knew without words the sacrifice that he was prepared to make for her, just as he knew what she was prepared to give up for him. The old friendship was still there, warm, comforting, familiar, strong enough to build on. Cory drew her closer to him and the shadows of the past faded and they faced the future together.

'I expect that you might still want to travel sometimes,' she said, putting a hand up to his face to trace lovingly those familiar lines she thought she might never see again.

'I might,' Cory said, turning his lips against her palm. His silver eyes were bright as he looked down at her. 'Do you think that you would be able to come with me?'

'I might,' Rachel said, smiling rosily, 'if you would be able to stay at home with me the rest of the time.'

Cory was laughing as he bent his head to kiss her. 'We neither of us bend easily, do we, Rachel Odell? I fear that we are both obstinate people. We might quarrel...'

'It will be worth it,' Rachel said, kissing him back, 'if we can make up like this.'

There was a very long pause whilst they kissed each other

with passion and love and commitment, then Cory took her hand in his and bent to pick up the Midwinter Treasure, holding it up to the sun.

'It looks a little battered,' he said, 'but it is treasure right enough.'

Rachel smiled up at him and nestled into the curve of his arm.

'Treasure indeed,' she said.

Epilogue

Rachel and Cory were married two weeks later at the church of St Martin's. Mrs Deborah Stratton was the bride's attendant and Lord Richard Kestrel was the groomsman and they spent a large part of their time studiously ignoring each other. The Reverend Lang officiated, but when his daughter Helena rushed to be the first to catch the bride's bouquet, it sailed over her head and landed in the arms of Richard Kestrel instead.

'I do think,' Lady Sally Saltire said to the Duke of Kestrel, adjusting the brim of her outrageously fashionable bonnet against the autumn sunshine, 'that there might be quite a *spate* of weddings in the Midwinter villages this year. It seems that there is something in the air.' She watched in amusement as Lord Richard tried to present the spray of delicate pink roses to Deborah Stratton, only for Mrs Stratton to turn her shoulder and bid him pay his addresses to a more receptive lady.

Justin Kestrel was also watching his brother, who looked rather forlorn with an unwanted bouquet wilting in his hand. 'Poor Richard,' he said. 'It will take more than pink roses to make Mrs Stratton view him more kindly. Will he succeed, do you think, Sally?'

'Oh, yes,' Lady Sally said comfortably. She gave the

Duke a sparkling look. 'They will be married within three months, mark my words. Mrs Stratton, for all her coldness, is not indifferent to Lord Richard.'

Justin looked vaguely startled. 'Indeed?' he said. 'And Lucas? Will he be caught as well?'

They both turned to look at Lord Lucas Kestrel, who was flirting outrageously with Lady Burgh of Northcote.

'Ah.' Lady Sally smiled indulgently. 'There is a man who swears he will never enter parson's mousetrap, but—' she shrugged charmingly '—pride comes before a fall!'

'All bachelors married…' the Duke murmured.

'Save one, Justin,' Lady Sally pointed out.

'Oh, I feel I am almost too set in my ways for matrimony now,' Justin Kestrel said. 'Let Richard or Lucas and their future brides provide the Kestrel heirs!'

He offered Lady Sally his arm and they started to walk slowly up the path towards the church door, where Cory was kissing the new Lady Newlyn with considerable fervour amidst a swirl of rose petals thrown by the appreciative congregation. 'What of you, Sally?' Justin added, with a sly glance at his companion. 'Have you ever considered entering the state of matrimony again?'

'Marriage is a noble undertaking,' Lady Sally said, dimpling, 'but I have had my fill of it. I do not seek to wed again.'

'That is your final word?' the Duke questioned gently.

'It is, dear Justin.' Lady Sally smiled at him. 'You and I, my dear, will wear the willow and dance at other people's weddings.'

'A melancholy prospect.'

'The dancing?'

'Wearing the willow. I confess that I look forward to the dancing, however, if you will grant me your hand for the first.'

'Of course,' Lady Sally said. They fell into step behind

the wedding party as it started the short walk back to Midwinter Royal.

'The toast at the wedding breakfast should be to old friends,' Justin said thoughtfully, eyeing the entwined figures of Rachel and Cory. 'A most fitting end to a long and deep friendship.'

'Old friends and new lovers,' Lady Sally agreed, her observant gaze noting that Deborah Stratton would glance up every so often from her conversation with her sister and fix upon the tall figure of Lord Richard Kestrel.

'Three months, eh?' Justin said, following the direction of her look. 'I cannot believe it. Would you care to bet on that, Sally?'

'I will take that wager,' Lady Sally said. 'Your brother and Mrs Stratton will be married within three months. My hand on it!'

'Done!' the Duke said. 'I look forward to collecting on my debt.'

Lady Sally looked at him, the expression in her eyes suddenly arrested. 'Almost, Justin, I regret making that wager with you,' she said.

'So you should,' the Duke said softly, 'when I come to demand payment.'

Lady Sally's green eyes were suddenly wary. 'I forgot to ask the stake,' she said.

'So you did,' Justin Kestrel agreed. He smiled, kissed her hand and walked away. Lady Sally watched his tall figure for a few moments and then sighed softly.

'This time I shall be safe,' she said, half to herself, 'for I am *certain* that Deborah and Richard will be next.' She shook her head slightly. 'The next time Justin challenges me to a wager, though, I shall have to think twice. Decidedly I shall.'

And following the direction the Duke had gone, she went to raise a glass to the bride and groom.

* * * * *

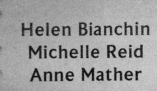

FREE

2 BOOKS AND A SURPRISE GIFT!

We would like to take this opportunity to thank you for reading this Mills & Boon® book by offering you the chance to take TWO more specially selected titles from the Historical Romance™ series absolutely FREE! We're also making this offer to introduce you to the benefits of the Reader Service™—

- ★ **FREE home delivery**
- ★ **FREE gifts and competitions**
- ★ **FREE monthly Newsletter**
- ★ **Books available before they're in the shops**
- ★ **Exclusive Reader Service offers**

Accepting these FREE books and gift places you under no obligation to buy; you may cancel at any time, even after receiving your free shipment. Simply complete your details below and return the entire page to the address below. You don't even need a stamp!

YES! Please send me 2 free Historical Romance books and a surprise gift. I understand that unless you hear from me, I will receive 4 superb new titles every month for just £3.59 each, postage and packing free. I am under no obligation to purchase any books and may cancel my subscription at any time. The free books and gift will be mine to keep in any case.

H4ZEE

Ms/Mrs/Miss/Mr...Initials ....
BLOCK CAPITALS PLEASE

Surname ....

Address ....

....

....Postcode ....

Send this whole page to:

The Reader Service, FREEPOST CN81, Croydon, CR9 3WZ

Offer valid in UK only and is not available to current Reader Service™ subscribers to this series. Overseas and Eire please write for details. We reserve the right to refuse an application and applicants must be aged 18 years or over. Only one application per household. Terms and prices subject to change without notice. Offer expires 28th November 2004. As a result of this application, you may receive offers from Harlequin Mills & Boon and other carefully selected companies. If you would prefer not to share in this opportunity please write to The Data Manager at PO Box 676, Richmond, TW9 1WU.

Mills & Boon® is a registered trademark owned by Harlequin Mills & Boon Limited.
Historical Romance™ is being used as a trademark. The Reader Service™ is being used as a trademark.